Sir David Lindsay

The Poetical Works of Sir David Lyndsay

of the Mount, Lion King at arms - Vol. 1

Sir David Lindsay

The Poetical Works of Sir David Lyndsay
of the Mount, Lion King at arms - Vol. 1

ISBN/EAN: 9783337287788

Printed in Europe, USA, Canada, Australia, Japan

Cover: Foto ©Andreas Hilbeck / pixelio.de

More available books at **www.hansebooks.com**

EARLY SCOTTISH POETS.

LYNDSAY.

Edinburgh : Printed by Turnbull and Spears,

FOR

WILLIAM PATERSON, 74 PRINCES STREET

LONDON,	. . . .	J. RUSSELL SMITH.
GLASGOW,	. . .	SMITH & SON.
BOSTON,	. . . .	LITTLE, BROWN, & Co.

THE
POETICAL WORKS
OF
SIR DAVID LYNDSAY
OF THE MOUNT,
LYON KING OF ARMS.

A NEW EDITION CAREFULLY REVISED.

IN TWO VOLUMES.—VOL. I.

EDINBURGH: WILLIAM PATERSON.
MDCCCLXXI.

TABLE OF CONTENTS.

EARLY SCOTTISH POETS.

THE Publisher has the satisfaction to intimate that the next volumes of this Series, Edited by Mr LAING, he expects will be a new and revised edition of

THE POEMS OF WILLIAM DUNBAR,

as first published in 1834, including the SUPPLEMENT of 1866.

Some Copies of the above Supplement, to complete the columes issued in 1834, may still be had. Price 5s.

PREFACE.

SIR DAVID LYNDSAY has the distinction of being reckoned by general consent the most popular of the early Scottish Poets. Some of his works were undoubtedly circulated during his life in a printed form, but of the existing early impressions, it cannot positively be asserted that any one of them had the advantage of his own superintendence. Henry Charteris, the bookseller in Edinburgh, who at a later period also joined the business of a printer, published the first collected edition of "The Warkis" in 1568. On the title it professes to have been "Newlie correctit, and vindicate from the former errouris quhairwith thay war befoir corruptit: and augmentit with sindrie warkis quhilk was not befoir Imprentit." Yet Charteris added merely a few pieces to the minor poems included in the two editions printed in France with the name of Jascuy in 1558, nad in the rival publication in this country from the press of John Scot that immediately followed, without either place, name, or date of printing. Charteris, however, in that edition not only furnished a recognised text, but prefixed an interesting preface containing some important information regarding the Author, and apparently the latest representation of his Play, at Edinburgh in 1554.

Charteris, who survived till August 1599, republished Lyndsay's Works in 1571, 1582, 1592, and in 1597, retaining on the titles of each the same words, *Newly corrected, and augmented,* while the contents were precisely the same, and simple reprints of that of 1568.

Similar words, with a like want of propriety, or truth, continued to be repeated by subsequent printers for upwards of two centuries, each one proving, by increasing mistakes and alterations in orthography, to be of less intrinsic value than its predecessor. The want of a critical edition therefore was long felt, and this was at length undertaken by Mr GEORGE CHALMERS, best known by his great work CALEDONIA, who, in his usual energetic manner, set himself resolutely to his task, by extensive correspondence, and diligent search of the public records, to collect information regarding the Author's life and writings. His own words may be quoted :

"The attention of this intelligent and polished kingdom has been drawn very much, during late times, to the simple, and rude, but natural lays of its ancient Poets. Meantime, *the Critics* of Edinburgh called for a more accurate edition of the Poems of Sir David Lyndsay than the public enjoys, after the corruptions of two centuries and a-half. . . .

"I obeyed this call, with the more alacrity as I had recently traced, with a different view, the history of the Scoto-Saxon language, and had cast a curious eye on the life and labours of Lyndsay, the Langelande of Scotland. The notions of Lyndsay, indeed, are very different from mine, both as a politician and a poet: but, I perceived, that the republication of his poetry might be made the commodious vehicle of my own sentiments, with regard to the origin, the nature, and the introduction of the Teutonic tongue into Gaelic Scotland. In performing the task, which I had thus imposed on myself, I now lay before the reader a new edition of the Poetical Works of Sir David Lyndsay, corrected and enlarged, with the *Historie of Squyer Meldrum*, and the *Satyre of the Three Estaitis*. By troubling several friends, and making many searches, I have been enabled to give some new notices of our satirist, who, to use Dryden's phrase, may be said to have *lashed vice into reformation*. I have endeavoured to adjust the chronology of Lyndsay's several poems, which had never been before essayed. I have given an historical view of the Scottish speech, previous to his age, with observations on his language. I have settled the text of our vernacular poet, from a diligent collation of the oldest editions of his poems. And I have subjoined an appropriate *Glossary* which incidentally demonstrates that the common source of Scottish speech is the Anglo-Saxon dialect of the Northumbrian kingdom."

The Poetical Works of Sir David Lyndsay, appeared in due time as "A new edition, corrected and enlarged; with a life of the author; prefatory dissertations; and an appropriate glossary. By George Chalmers, F.R.S., S.A. In three volumes." London, 1806, post 8vo. This elaborate publication had only a limited and slow success. In later years, owing in part to the increasing attention bestowed on the remains of our early Poetical Literature, the book became scarce, and at sales it has fetched double its original price. A new edition seemed to be required, not as in Chalmers's time by " Edinburgh critics," but by Edinburgh and other publishers. When urged to act as editor, I more than once declined the task, chiefly on the ground, as no mutilated text would be acceptable, of the extreme coarseness which disfigures some portions of his writings.

Having at length consented, without deciding on the precise mode of editing, it was at first intended to be little more than a republication of the edition by my old friend Mr Chalmers, but not having any theories to support, I purposed to curtail his dissertations, notes, and glossary. His volumes accordingly were taken for the ground work of the present edition, as I could see no good reason to make any great change in the chronological order he was the first to adopt. I soon found that a careful revision of his text with the earlier editions was indispensable, and that it would require much more time and labour than I anticipated. Nor did it seem likely to serve any good purpose had I persisted in giving the public an expurgated text. I will not vindicate Lyndsay in his use of vulgar indelicate words and expressions. His works are now chiefly designed for antiquarian readers, and his utter disregard of decency is not such as tends to corrupt the mind, while they are considered valuable in presenting a true and vivid reflex of the manners of his age; and still more so in their having contributed to the great cause of Ecclesiastical Reform in Scotland.

After the text and notes of the new edition of the Poems in three volumes had nearly been completed, some unexpected delays intervened, and the appearance of the volumes was postponed. Having long had a desire to commence a series of the early Scottish Poets, in the style of the English Aldine series, in a convenient form, and at a moderate price, the Publisher himself was the first to suggest that such a series might commence with Lyndsay in Two volumes, to satisfy any immediate demand for books of this class of our vernacular Poetry; and allow me more time, as leisure permitted, to make further inquiries for the Memoir to be prefixed to what may be called the Three volume Library edition.

In carrying this suggestion into effect, it is proper to state, that the Author's text as given in that edition remains unaltered, while the Memoir of his life may be afterwards enlarged or illustrated. The Notes have been greatly curtailed, and the Various Readings omitted, that the work might be comprised in two volumes. The Bibliographical descriptions of the various Editions are likewise withheld as of comparatively little interest for ordinary readers. The Glossary in

this edition is, for the most part, an abridgment of
Chalmers. I must also add that, not unwillingly, I
availed myself of such an opportunity (being rather
ashamed of the Author in this respect) to withdraw
from an edition intended for general readers several
coarse and very offensive passages in the Satyre of
the Thrie Estates, as their omission in no way affects
either the spirit or progress of this remarkable specimen of the Early Drama.

DAVID LAING.

Edinburgh.

The Armes of St David windesor of the more Aurcht. Also hath bene of armes anno of this psnt bibbe. Anno dni 1642.

Caritas · Fides · Caritas · Spes ·

LYME

MEMOIR

OF

SIR DAVID LYNDSAY

OF THE MOUNT.

T cannot be said that the name of Lynd-
say has been overlooked in Biographical
Dictionaries and other similar works,
although they consist chiefly of information derived from his own writings.
Later writers have adopted the statement of Chalmers,[1] that he was the eldest son and heir of David
Lyndsay of the Mount, in Fife, and that he was born
there about the year 1490. The paternal estate with
which his name has always been associated, was a
small property in the parish of Monimail, situated

---

[1] The later authors chiefly worthy of notice, are the following : —

CHALMERS (George), Life, prefixed to the Poetical Works of
Sir David Lyndsay. 3 vols. London, 1806.

IRVING (David,) LL.D., History of Scotish Poetry, Edinburgh,
1861. (A Posthumous Work prepared in 1828).

Also Article by Dr. IRVING in Encyclopædia Britannica.
Seventh Edition.

three miles north from Cupar-Fife. Notwithstanding
this general consent, another property in East Lothian,
to which the Poet himself succeeded in early life, and
which he retained in his own possession, might as
likely have had the honour of being the place of his
birth. I mean Garmylton, two miles north of the
town of Haddington, where there still exists, in ruins,
a considerable portion of a large castellated manor
house of the fifteenth century. How the title of
The Mount was preferred is quite unknown.

The lands of Garmylton-Alexander, in the con-
stabulary of Haddington, formed part of the adjoin-
ing barony of Byres, when possessed by Sir William
Lyndsay, who conveyed them to his natural son
Andrew and his heirs legitimate, towards the end
of the fourteenth century (about the year 1390).
In 1724, the property of Byres and Garmylton (now
called Garleton) was purchased by the Earl of Wemyss
from Seton of Garleton. In the Inventory of title-
deeds then prepared, Mr Chalmers having found the
notice of the above charter, he took occasion to
correct his statement regarding the proprietors of
Garmylton, concluding that William Lyndsay, who
survived till 1478, was the son of Andrew. For this

TYTLER (Patrick Fraser), Lives of Scottish Worthies. Vol.
    III. London, 1833.
LINDSAY (Lord), Lives of the Lindsays. Vol. I. Wigan,
    1840. 4 vols. royal 8vo (privately printed).
        The same: republished in a revised form. London,
        1846, 3 vols. 8vo.
BRUCE (James), Lives of Eminent Men of Fife. Edin., 1846.

I see no evidence.[1] It is quite as likely that Andrew died without issue, and that William might have been a legitimate grandson of Sir William Lyndsay of Byris. However this may be, sasine of these lands was given to David Lindsay de Mountht on the death of *quondam Willelmi Lindesay Patris sui, ultimi possessoris ejusdem*, at *Biris*, 22d November 1478. Chalmers, from an erroneous description in the Inventory, makes this David to have been the Poet's father, and to have died in the year 1507, and in so doing he has misled later writers on this point. Having been kindly favoured by Thomas Graham Murray, Esq., with a sight of the MS. Inventories, and also with the use of some of the original deeds specially connected with Garmylton, I find among these the Charter of 1507.[2] It was granted upon the death of the Poet's grandfather, thus making three Davids in succession; and, for ought we know to the contrary, the Poet's father survived for many years, and had a younger son, also named David, probably by a second marriage.

It obviously would in some measure depend upon

---

[1] Caledonia, Vol. II., p. 435, foot note.

[2] The Charter in question was granted by Patrick, Lord Lindesay de Biris, as Superior of the lands of Garmylton-Alexander, confirming the same *dilecto nostro consanguineo David Lindesay filio et heredi apparenti David Lindesay de Montht* nostri eciam consanguinei . . . quas terras de Garmiltoun cum pertinen. quondam David Lindesay consanguineus noster AVUS DICTI DAVID habuit hereditarie et de nobis tenuit, &c. It is dated 19th October 1507; and the Sasine on the 6th April following.

this question, whether the Poet was born in the Kingdom of Fife, or on the fertile plains of East Lothian, as
to the place where he was educated. In the one case,
would be the neighbouring town of Cupar-Fife; in
the other, the town of Haddington. There were
Grammar Schools established in both, and in either
of them he would receive the groundwork of a liberal
education, preparatory to his being sent to the University of St Andrews. The College Registers of that
period do not throw much light on this part of his
history. We only find the name, DA. LINDESAY,
among the incorporated students in St Salvator's
College for the year 1508 or 1509. This name was by
no means uncommon, but the date corresponds closely
enough to the only period when he could have pursued
his academical studies. The students, after three
years' attendance, were styled *Incorporati*, and had, in
consequence, a right of voting, and this would fix
his matriculation to the year 1505. It is a singular
enough coincidence that the name which immediately
follows in the Register is DA. BETONE, the future
Archbishop and Cardinal, with a [ ] in the margin,
as if to call special attention to one who became so
distinguished by the rank he attained. Beaton is said
to have been born in the year 1494, and it is not probable that any marked difference of age existed
between the fellow-students. We have no evidence
that the Poet remained another session, which
would have entitled him to take the degree of Master
of Arts; nor, like his more opulent associate, (who
had the certain prospect of high preferment in the
Church), that he was sent abroad to complete his

studies in Civil and Canon Law at Paris, or other foreign university.

Mr Tytler,[1] in referring to the Poet's early life, justly says—"The truth is, that of the youth of Lyndsay nothing is known." Yet an older writer, without the slightest scruple, asserts "he had his education at the University of St Andrews, where, after he had finished the course of his studies in philosophy, for his further improvement, his Parents sent him Abroad ; and having travelled, (as he himself tells us,) through England, France, Italy, and Germany, he returned to his native country about the year 1514."[2] All this, however, is nothing but bold assertion, without the least evidence adduced to support it. Lyndsay himself in no place speaks either of his parents sending him abroad to any foreign university, or of his travels in these countries at that early period.

Later writers, from an allusion to the dress of the Italian ladies,[3] and founding upon a passage in his Dialog on the Monarchies, have concluded that Lyndsay not only had visited Italy, but had served a campaign there in the year 1510. The lines referred to are as follows, in which, in the person of the Courtier, he is made to say,

> I saw Pape Julius manfullye
> Passe to the feild triumphantlye,
> With ane rycht awfull ordinance,
> Contrar Lowis the King of France.[4]

[1] Scottish Worthies, vol. iii., p. 192.

[2] Lives of Scots Writers, by George Mackenzie, M.D., vol. iii., p. 35, Edinb. 1723, folio.

[3] Vol. i., p. 73.   [4] Vol. ii., line 5417.

No doubt Lyndsay speaks of the Italian women as an eye-witness, but only in verses assigned to the year 1538 ; and the occasion on which the Pope appeared in the character of a military commander was the Siege of Mirandola, in January 1511. There is some reason to believe that at that time Lyndsay was in Scotland ; or if he actually had been in Italy in 1510, it was not as a soldier of fortune—this was not his vocation—but it might have been in the train of an Ambassador to the Papal Court or one of the Italian Courts.

The loss of the Treasurer's accounts between August 1508 and September 1511, has deprived us of any information respecting the exact time and circumstances of Lyndsay's first employment at the Court of James the Fourth. The King, while liberally promoting all public works and other means of advancing the prosperity of the country, and encouraging literature and the arts, inherited a jovial disposition, and attracted persons of all sorts—tale-tellers, minstrels, stage-players, singers, fools, or privileged buffoons and jesters, who might contribute to the amusement of the court. Our youthful poet was here in his element, and the earliest entry in the Treasurers' accounts that mentions his name is very characteristic. It occurs on the 12th October 1511, when the sum of £3, 4s. was paid for blue and yellow taffeties, " to be a play coat to David Lyndsay for the play, playit in the king and queen's presence in the Abbey of Holyrood." At this time, he must have held some appointment in the Royal Household, being one of

eight or ten persons who each received £40 from the
Treasurer (in the Accounts 1511-1512) as the quarterly
payments of £10 for the terms of "Alhallowmes, Can-
dilmes, Rudmes, and Lammes, in his pensione and fee,"
these terms falling upon the 1st November 1511, 2d
February, 2d May, and 2d August, 1512.

On the birth of Prince James, Lyndsay obtained a
special appointment as usher or chief page to the
infant Prince, having, as he reminds the King in
his "Complaynt," written in 1529, that he had been
his servitor or personal attendant from the day of
his nativity, the 12th of April 1512. His residence
at Court led to his witnessing a remarkable scene
in the Church of St Michael, Linlithgow. The
date is not specified, but it must have been in the
year following, when James the Fourth was placed
in a peculiarly difficult position from his marriage
to the sister of Henry the Eighth, and his political
alliance with France, upon the hostile invasion of that
kingdom by the English monarch. But in a sketch like
this of Lyndsay's life, it is not necessary to enter upon
any minute details of public affairs. At this period,
Scotland was rapidly advancing in wealth, civiliza-
tion, and importance in the affairs of Europe, by the
energetic and liberal policy of the King ; but, by his
rash and impetuous conduct, partly proceeding from
a high sense of chivalric honour, he resolved to enter,
with a formidable army, the North of England, at the
urgent solicitation of his French ally.

The passage in Pitscottie's History, which so strik-
ingly narrates the incident alluded to, has often been

quoted. It cannot, however, be passed over in this place, as it rests solely on Lyndsay's authority. The apparition has been explained as a scheme devised, it has been thought, by the Queen, for the purpose of working upon the superstitious feelings of James, by a solemn or supernatural warning against his proposed invasion of England.

"The King," says Pitscottie, "came to Lithgow, where he happened to be for the time at the Counsell, verie sad and dolorous, makeand his devotion to God to send him good chance and fortune in his voyage. In this mean time, there came ane man, clad in ane blew gowns in at the kirk doores, and belted about him in ane roll of linning cloth, ane pair of brotikins on his feet, to the great of his legs, with all other hose and clothis conforme therto ; but he had nothing on his head, but syde red yellow haire behind, and on his halffets, which went down to his shoulders: but his forehead was beld and bair. He seemed to be a man of two-and-fiftie yeeres, with ane great pyke-staffe in his hand, and came first forward among the Lords, cryand and spearand for the King, sayand 'he desired to speak with him :' While at the last, he came where the King was sitting in the dask at his prayers : but when he saw the King, he made him little reverence or salutation, but leaned downe grovellings on the dask before him, and said to him in this manner, as after followes :—'Sir King, my Mother hath sent me to you desiring you not to passe, at this time, where thou art purposed ; for if thou does, thou wilt not fair well in thy journey, nor none that passeth with thee.

Further, she bade ye melle with no woman, nor use
their counsell, nor let them touch thy body, nor thou
theirs ; for, and thou do it, thou wilt be confounded
and brought to shame.'

"Be this man had spoken thir words unto the King's
Grace, the Even-song was neere done, and the King
paused on thir words, studying to give him an answer ;
but, in the meane time, before the King's eyes, and in
presence of all the Lords that were about him for the
time, this man vanished away, and could no wayes be
seene nor comprehended, but vanished away as he had
bene ane blink of the sunne, or ane whiss of the whirle-
wind, and could no more be seene. I heard say, Sir
David Lindsay (Lion Herald), and John English (the
Marshall), who were at that time young men, and
speciall servants to the King's Grace, were standand
presentlie besyd the King, who thought to have layd
hands on this man, that they might have speared
further tydings at him : but all for nought ; they could
not touch him, for he vanished away betwixt them
and was no more seene."

Buchanan has also, much to the same effect, given
a concise account of this apparition, with this additional remark in regard to Lyndsay himself :—

"Among those who stood next the King, was
David Lindesay, of the Mount, a man of unsuspected
probity and veracity, attached to literature, and during life, invariably opposed to falschood ; from whom,
unless I had received the story as narrated vouched
for truth, I had omitted to notice it, as one of the
commonly reported fables."

It is scarcely necessary to add, that this singular

incident furnished Sir Walter Scott with "Sir David
Lindsay's Tale," in Canto iv. of "Marmion."

The daily attendance on the infant Prince may have
prevented Lyndsay being one of the Royal household who accompanied the King in this fatal expedition, which terminated on the Field of Floddon, in
that disastrous national calamity, when the gallant
James, surrounded by the best and noblest of his
realm, perished in the carnage on "that most
dolent day." The Treasurer's Accounts from August
1513 to June 1522 (with the exception of 1515-
1518) are unfortunately not preserved; but it
is quite certain that during the whole of that
period, Lyndsay's charge of his young master continued uninterrupted, sometimes styled "the Kingis
maister usher," or ischear, and "the Kingis master of
houshald," with the yearly salary of £40. He had
associated with him "as chaplain," a congenial spirit
in the person of Sir James Inglis, a priest, who
was also Secretary to the Queen Dowager, and for a
time, Chancellor of the King's Chapel Royal, Stirling,
and Master of Works. In the prologue of the
Papyngo, Lyndsay thus mentions him first among
the living Poets :—

> And in the Courte, bene present, in thir dayis,
> That ballattis brevis lustellie, and layis,
>   Quhilkis tyll our Prince daylie thay do present:
> Quho can say mair than SCHIR JAMES INGLIS sayis,
> In ballattis, farses, and in plesand playis?
>   Bot Culrose hes his pen maid impotent.

That is, by his promotion to the Abbacy of Culrose.
But within a few months after the date of Lynd-

say's poem, the Abbot was basely murdered by John
Blackader of Tulyallane and his servants.

Another ecclesiastic, who became, in 1516, "the
King's Master" or chief instructor, was Gawin Dunbar,
of the family of Cumnock, and nephew of the Bishop
of Aberdeen. He was Dean of Murray and Prior of
Whithorn, afterwards (in 1524) receiving higher promotion as Archbishop of Glasgow, to which (in 1528)
was joined that of Lord Chancellor of Scotland. Lyndsay, in a more humble capacity watching the Prince in
the tender years of his infancy, so endeared himself
that he tells us the first words the child could mute or
articulate was to call him, "Pa (Papa), Da, Lyn."
This need excite no surprise when we consider that
his chief occupation consisted in devising scenes of
merriment, playing on the lute popular airs or tunes,
reciting tales, assuming various disguises and fantastic
characters most likely to interest a youthful fancy.
All this, Lyndsay has described in his first poem,
THE DREME, addressed to the King when, in order
to strengthen claims for expecting a suitable reward,
he recalls to the King's remembrance the various
amusements with which he had entertained his infancy :—

> Quhen Thow wes young, I bure thee in myne arme
>> Full tenderlie, tyll thow begouth to gang ;
> And in thy bed oft happit thee full warme,
>> With lute in hand, syne, sweitlie to thee sang :
>> Sumtyme, in dansing, feiralie I flang ;
> And sumtyme, playand farsis on the flure ;
> And sumtyme, on myne office takkand cure :
> And sumtyme, lyke ane fiend transfigurate ;
>> And sumtyme, lyke the grislie gaist of Gy ;

      In divers formis, oftymes disfigurate :
       And sumtyme, disagysit full plesandlie.

     Ten or twelve years were thus passing quietly and pleasantly away ; and led, about the year 1522, to an important event in Lyndsay's life by his marriage with Janet Douglas. It has not been ascertained whether she was related to any family of distinction, and the date is erroneously placed ten years later by Chalmers and subsequent writers. But one or two extracts from the Treasurer's Accounts (1522-1524) leave no doubt on the matter. They also show that the lady held the appointment of Semstress to the King, during the rest of his reign, with an annual fee or pension of £10.—

Compotum etc. redditum apud Edinburg 15to *mensis Aprilis* 1524, *a* 5to *die Junii* 1522, *usque in diem hujus Compoti.*

     " Item, to Jonet Douglass spous to Dauid Lindesay, Maister Ischeare to the King, for sewing of the Kyngis lynnyng claithis, *de mandato Domini Gubernatoris,*   xxiiij lib.

     (The Governor, John, Duke of Albany, was then in Scotland : he returned to France in April 1524.)

     " *Compotum, etc.,* 15to Octobris 1526,—29to *die Augusti* 1527.

     " Item, gevin to Dauid Lindesayes wife to sew the Kingis sarkis, v. double hankis gold, price hank x s.

     " Item, v. vncis and quarter vnce sewing silk, price vnce v s.

     " *Pensiounis and Feallis.*—Item, to Jonet Douglas takand for hir fe   x li.

     " Item, (December 1530) for xiij double hankis of

gold, quhilkis war deliuerit to Dauid Lindesayis wyf
to sew the Kingis sarkis, the price of ilk hank x s.

"Item, (March 24, 1537) to Jonet Douglas the
spouse of David Lindesay of the Month, at the Kingis
grace command, as the precept beris,   .   xi. li.

This mode of a married woman retaining her
maiden name was quite customary.   After his knighthood she was or might have been styled Lady of
the Mount, or Lady of Garmylton, but neither Lady
Lioness nor Lady Lindsay.

After the Governor's return to France, 20th May
1524, various political changes occurred during the
King's minority, partly through the intrigues of the
Queen Dowager, who had obtained a divorce from
her husband, the Earl of Angus.   Notwithstanding
this, in August 1524 he assumed and exercised the
supreme power, putting nominally the sceptre in
the King's hand.   James at this time was twelve
years of age, naturally of a quick, intelligent disposition, and a few more years of sound and careful
instruction might have had the most beneficial influence on his after life.   On this head, Lyndsay, in his
Complaynt, says :

> The Kyng was bot twelf yeris of age
> Quhen new rewlaris come, in thair rage . . .
> Imprudentlie, lyk witless fuilis
> Thay tuke that young Prince frome the scuilis,
> Quhare he, under obedience,
> Was learnand vertew, and science,
> And haistelie platt in his hand,
> The governance of all Scotland.

By turning to this passage (p. 51.) the reader will

see how strongly he inveighs against the folly of such a proceeding, and adds,

I pray God, lat me never see ryng
In to this Realme, so young ane Kyng.

Lyndsay no doubt felt aggrieved, as one of his early tutors or guardians, that the hopeful young Prince was left exposed to the baneful influence of worthless persons about the Court, who to ingratiate themselves, encouraged him in all idle frivolous amusements, in gaming, horse-racing, and, even by flattery and priestly licence, in pursuing a vicious course of life, while public affairs were sadly mismanaged or neglected.

When the persons who had been entrusted with the charge of the young Prince were dismissed, Lyndsay acknowledges that his pension or salary was duly paid, until he was otherwise provided for. For his own enduring fame this change may have been of signal advantage, as it withdrew him from Court, to his residence at Garmylton, and devoting his leisure hours to literary aspirations, by meditating on the changes he had witnessed, and preparing his various addresses and complaints to the King. It was at the mature age of about thirty-seven that he commenced his poetical career by the publication of his DREAM, which Chalmers assigns to the year 1528. In the following year he produced his COMPLAYNT TO THE KING: and in 1530, the TESTAMENT AND COMPLAYNT OF THE KING'S PAPYNGO (or Parrot).

In these Poems, he not only sets forth his personal claims for long and faithful service, but he exposes

with great truth and boldness, the prevailing dis-
orders, the usurpation of the nobles, the party factions
and family feuds which divided and ruined the country,
and the licentious lives of the clergy.

The prelates before this time had become alarmed,
not at the irregularities in their own body, or among
the inferior clergy, but at the prospect of heresy find-
ing its way into a country which had always been
sound in the faith. An act was passed in Parliament,
17th July 1525, denouncing " the damnable opinions
of heresy spread in divers countreis be the heretic
Luther and his disciples," and as this realm has ever
" bene clene of all sic filth and vice," prohibiting
under the severest penalties " that na maner of person
to bring with thame ony bukis or warkis of the said
Lutheris his discipillis or seruandis, etc."[1]   But copies
of Tyndale's New Testament, and other books of the
new faith printed abroad found their way to Scotland,
and were eagerly read.   Two years later that noble-
minded youth Patrick Hamilton, infected with these
heresies, returned from Germany, and, in the words
of Knox, " the brycht beames of the trew licht,
which by Goddis grace was planted in his hearte,
began moste aboundantlye to burst furth, alse well in
publick as in secret."[2]   His zeal in avowing and
proclaiming such doctrines, brought him to the stake

[1] Acts of Parl., vol. ii.. p. 295.   On the margin of this Act,
in the Register, an additional clause was written by the Lord
Chancellor. Archbishop Dunbar, on the 5th September 1527.
This Act against heretics, with the said clause was renewed
in Parliament 12th June 1535. Ib. vol. ii., p. 341.

[2] History of the Reformation. Works vol. i., p. 15.

as the proto-martyr of the Reformation in Scotland,
on the last of February 1527-8.

Soon after this, in July 1528, another change took
place in the Government which brought Lyndsay more
prominently forward, during the rest of his life, as a
public character. The young King, who felt his ambition increasing with his growth, became impatient
and indignant under the control of the Earl of
Angus and the Douglasses, and resolved to free himself
from the restraint under which he was placed. At last
he contrived at night to escape from Falkland Palace
and to reach Stirling Castle, where he acted with
great and prompt decision. His keepers, in the
morning, hearing of his escape, were also on the alert.
But James immediately assembled a Council, and
issued a proclamation, 5th of July, commanding that
neither the Earl of Angus nor any of his kindred
should approach within six miles of the king's person, under the pains of high treason.

The King, it may be presumed, on becoming his
own master, did not overlook the services of his early
instructors. As already stated, Dunbar was pro-
moted to the See of Glasgow, and also obtained the
office of Lord High Chancellor, in 1532; and Sir
James Inglis, the Abbacy of Culross; while Lyndsay,
not later than 1529, became Chief Herald, or, as it
was called, Lyon King of Arms. On his inaugura-
tion, he received the honour of knighthood; and had
assigned to him, as his ordinary fee, an annual grant
of victual out of the King's lands of Luthrie, in Fife.

Lyndsay's appointment was one of peculiar import-

ance at this period, bringing him into active life. It
was then customary to employ the Lyon King in
royal messages and embassies as a recognized official.
He might well therefore, towards the close of his life,
apply the words of the Courteour in the Dialog on
the Monarchies, appropriately to himself, and say,

> I have, quod I, bene to this hour
> Sen I could ryde, ane Courteour,
>
> . . . . .
>
> Oft have I salit ouer the strandis,
> And travellit throuch divers landis
> Baith South, and North, East and West.

Perhaps his first visit to foreign parts, was the
political mission to Flanders in April 1531, on which
occasion he received a new Dress, as we learn from
the following payments in the Treasurer's Accounts,
(Oct. 1530 to Sept. 1531) as among those who received "leveray claithes (or dresses) at the feast of
Zule, there is entered to Dauid Lyndesay, Herald,
3 elnis of black velvet, £8, 5s., and 6 elnis paris black,
£12, 9s." On the 20th of May following "David
Lyndesay, Herald, be the Kingis precept (received xiij
elnis blak satyne to be him ane gown, £20, 16s.
Item, iij elnis black velvit to begarie the samyn
gown, £7, 16s. Summa of this liffray, £28, 12s."

The object of this mission was, to renew a commercial treaty between Scotland and the Netherlands concluded by King James the First, in 1430,
for a century which had now expired. Margaret,
Governess of the Netherlands, who died in November 1530, was succeeded by her niece the Queen of

Hungary, sister of the Emperor Charles the Fifth. In the Parliament held 27th April 1531, the Lords of Articles ordained Sir John Campbell of Lundy, to deliver the Contract, so lately made by the Emperor and Mistress Margaret, as Ambassador, concerning privileges, peace, and other things, to be sent with expedition under our Sovereign Lord's Seal. In this embassy, Campbell was accompanied by Lyndsay, and David Paniter as Secretary.

The Scottish Ambassadors were received with great state and solemnity by the Princess and the Emperor, at Brussels. Their mission was successful. Lyndsay had thus a favourable opportunity of seeing the splendour of the Emperor's Court, and of witnessing a grand tournament. These triumphs were not lost on him; and the letter he addressed to the Secretary from Antwerp on the 23d of August, is still preserved, and a copy of it may be here given as the only authentic specimen of his prose composition that seems to have reached our time. One might almost think, from the orthography, that the writer's own education had been somewhat neglected.

"My Lord,—I recommend my hartly servis onto your Lordship. Plesis your Lordship to wit, that I com to Brusselles the iij day of Julij, quhar I fand the Empriour, and gat presens of his Majeste the iij day efter my cummin, and hes gottin gud expedition of the prencipall erandis that I was send for ; and hes gottin the auld aliansis, and confederationis, confermit for the space of ane hundret yeiris. The quhilk confirmation I haiff raisit in dowbyl form, ane to deliver to the Conseruatour, and ane wther to bring with me in Scotland, bayth onder the Emperor's gret seill; and hes deliverit to his majeste the Kyng, our sowerainis part, wnder his gracis gret seill, for the said space of ane hundret yeirs.

"My Lord, ye sall understand that Sir Don Pedir De le Cowe wes not in the court, lang tym efter that I com thair, to quham I deliverit your Lordships writtinis, quhilk rasavit tham rycht thankfully, and schew me gret hwmanite for your Lordships saik; bot he gaiff me na answar of your writtins, quhill I was reddy to depart furth of the Cowrt Imperiell, quhais letter ye sall rasaiff fra this berrar. I remanit in the cowrt vii. owiks, and od dayis, apon the materis pertenyn to the marchans. Item, the brut was heir owyr all this contre, quhen I com to the cowrt, that the Kyngis grace, our sowerain was deid. For the quhilk caws the Quein of Wngare send for me, and inquirit diligentle of that mater at me, and was rycht glaid, quhen I schew hir the werrite, of the Kyngis grace our sowerains prosperrite. It was schawin to me that the Empriouris majeste gart all the Kyrk men in Brusselles pray for his Gracis saul. Thai nowelles war send for werrite furth of Ingland; and war haldin for effect, ay quhill my cumin to the Cowrt.

"My Lord, it war to lang to me to writ to your Lordship the triwmphis that I haiff sein, sen my cumin to the court Imperall; that is to say the triwmphand justynis, the terribill turnements, the feychtyn on fut in barras, the naymis of lords and knychts that war hurt the day of the gret towrnament; quhais circum-

stans I haiff writtin at lenth, in articles, to schaw the
Kyngis grace at my haym cumin. Item, the Empriour
purposis to depart at the fyn of this moneth, and passis
wp in Almanye for reformation of the Luteriens : the
Quein of Wngare ramanis heir Regent of all their
contres : and was confermit Regent be the iii. Estattis
in the town of Brussellis, the v. day of Julij. And as
for uther nowellis, I rafer to the berar. Writtin
with my hand, at Handwarp, the xxiii. day of August
by your Serviteur, at his power,

(Directed on the back)
   To my special Lord,
   my Lord, the gret Sacretar
   to our Sowerain Lord of Scotland.

The account of the Tournament and Articles
written for the purpose of showing to the King, are
unfortunately not preserved. Mr Tytler, trusting too
implicitly to Chalmers, says, that " On his return from
this mission, Lyndsay's mind was occupied with two
great subjects, his marriage, and his celebrated 'Satire
of the Thrie Estates.' His marriage (he adds) was
unhappy, originating probably in ambition, for he
united himself to a daughter of the house of Douglas,

and ending in disappointment. He had no children,
and from the terms in which he commonly talks of
the sex, it may be plausibly conjectured that the
Lady Lioness was not possessed of a very amiable
disposition. His 'Satire of the Three Estates,' was
a more successful experiment, and is well deserving
of notice, as the first approach to the regular Drama
which had yet been made in Scotland."

But such "plausible conjectures" are not confirmed
either in the one case or the other. There is no
evidence to show that the Play was of so early a date;
and as for the marriage, it has already been seen that
this event in our Poet's life had taken place several
years previously; and ambition could have had no
influence in the matter. The advent of the Douglasses
to power was then not so much as dreamt of, and
at this period (1532), they had lost all the power and
influence which they acquired. Even while in power,
the Poet was as loud as any one in denouncing their
proceedings, until their downfall in 1528. Neither
can we admit that the marriage was "unhappy," ex-
cepting the want of issue, when we find her husband,
at successive intervals, in 1531, 1535, and in 1542,
granting and confirming his spouse Jonet Douglas
in the conjunct fee of his lands of Garmylton and the
Mount. The following extract may also be quoted :—

" Ane lettre maid to Jonet Douglas Lady of the
Month, hir airis and assignais ane or ma of the gift
of the nonentreis malis fermes profflittis and dewiteis
of all and hale the twa aikeris of land liand on the
Mylne-hill besyd the burgh of Cowpar of the quhilkis

that ane is now occupiit be Johne Brown, and that
uther be Johne Wiliamsoun and David Gudsir equalie
betuix thame, and of half an aiker of land liand betuix the Mylnis of Cowpar now occupiit be the said
Johne Brown, &c.

. . . . . .

At Edinburgh the xix day of August the zeir of
God j^m v^e xxxi zeris.

Per signaturam manu S. D. N. Regis subscript."[1]

It may be noticed that Sir David's Register of
Arms, concludes with the Blazon of his own arms,
1542, which Nisbet thus describes: *Gules* a fesse
chequé *argent* and *azure*, between three stars in chief,
and a man's heart in base, *argent*." He says nothing
of the crest, a helmet, and a bloody heart, (for
Douglas,) or the supporters. See the reduced copy,
facing page vii.

It appears that the Ambassadors while at the
Court of the Emperor, had been instructed to see and
report on the subject of a matrimonial alliance.
Buchanan relates that Charles the Fifth was most
desirous that the League between Scotland and
France should not be maintained, and wished to contract another alliance besides that of the commercial
treaty ; and by his letter, in 1534, he gave the King
his choice of three Marys, all of them of his own blood ;
Mary, the Duchess of Hungary, his sister, then a
widow; Mary of Portugal, the daughter of his sister

[1] Reg. Secr. Sig. vol. ix., fol. 38, and repeated in the same
vol. at fol. 187.

Lemora ; and Mary of England, the daughter of his
Aunt, Queen Catherine, and of Henry the Eighth.
But this offer was not accepted ; and the young King
continuing his licentious intrigues, had at least three
sons, by ladies of high rank.

The honours conferred about this time on the
Scottish Monarch, gave occasion to the Lyon King,
or his Depute, to other visits abroad. In December
1531, James was chosen a Knight of the Order of the
Golden Fleece, by the Emperor ; about the same time,
of the Order of St Michael, by Francis the First ;
and of the Order of the Garter, 20th January 1534-5,
by his uncle Henry the Eighth.

In the summer of 1536, the Lyon King accompanied the ambassadors to France to conclude a treaty
of marriage with Marie de Bourbon, the daughter of
the Duke de Vendosme. The King, impatient at the
delay of his envoys, determining himself to fetch
home his betrothed bride, set sail and landed at
Dieppe. Wishing incognito to see the lady while the
treaty was in the course of negotiation, he disguised
himself, as one of the retinue, but the Princess at
once recognized him from his portrait which she had
secretly obtained from Scotland. But notwithstanding the gracious reception he met with from the
young lady and her parents, the King, after eight
days of sumptuous entertainment, must have felt
dissatisfied with the choice that had been made,
as he departed somewhat abruptly, on the ground
that it was his duty to consult the French monarch regarding his marriage, being then within his
Realm. Francis the First urged him to marry Marie

de Bourbon; but James eagerly desired to be united with the King's eldest daughter, the Princess Magdalene. Her father reluctantly gave his consent, owing to her delicate state of health, and averse to exposing her to the dangers of a long sea voyage, for a continued residence in what was deemed to be an inhospitable climate.

In sending notice of his approaching marriage, the King commanded that certain of the Lords, both Spiritual and Temporal, and some of the great Barons should "come to France, and compear at Paris at the day appointed to the said marriage, in their best array, for the honour of Scotland, as they would do him pleasure and service." [1]

The marriage was celebrated with great splendour in the Cathedral Church of Nostre Dame, the 1st of January 1536-7. After four months, when preparing to return home, Pitscottie details at great length, not only the triumphs and rejoicings at the time of the marriage, but the arrangements made by the French King in furnishing large vessels and costly presents before their departure. They sailed from Dieppe, with a fair wind, and in five days the gallant fleet of fifty ships reached Leith on the 28th of May. They passed to the Palace of Holyrood, until the preparations were ready for the King and Queen's triumphant progress through the chief towns of Scotland.

But within forty days of the Queen's landing, the universal joy was turned to sadness and lamentation by her death. "And also (says the same historian)

[1] Robert Lindesay of Pitscottie's History.

the King's heavy moan that he made for her, was greater than all the rest.

It was on this occasion that Lyndsay composed his poem "The Deploration of the Death of Quéne Magdalene," on the 7th of July, describing how this sad event put a stop to the splendid triumphs and ceremonies prepared for her Coronation. But we will let her rest with God (he adds) and return again to France, to the Duke of Vendome's daughter, who took such displeasure [distress] and melancholy for the King of Scotland's marriage, that she, within short while, took sickness, and died.[1] Quhairat when the King of Scotland got wit. he was heighlie displeased [distressed] thinkand that he was the occasion of that gentlewoman's death also."

James who was then in the prime of life, was the last of his line; and after a short while, a second French alliance was projected with the hope of having an heir to the throne. An embassy was accordingly sent, to propose a marriage with Mary, daughter of the Duke de Guyse, the widow of the Duke de Longueville. The arrangements and betrothal were speedily concluded with the advice and approbation of Francis the First and his Council, 23d May 1578. Lord Maxwell as Admiral of the Fleet, along with Cardinal Beaton and a large retinue, were sent to solemnize the marriage, and convoy the bride to Scotland, so soon as wind and weather might

---

[1] Piscottie here, as usual, is inaccurate in his dates. The Princess Marie died on the 28th September 1538. (Papiers d'Etat, par A. Teulet, vol. i., p. 109. Bannatyne Club publication.)

serve. Having embarked as usual at the Newhaven,
near Dieppe, and reaching the coast of Fife, they
landed near Balcomie Castle, and rested until horses
could be procured from St Andrews.

On such public occasions, it formed part of the
duty of the Lyon King to marshall processions, and
to superintend the pageants exhibited. For all this,
besides exercising his own inventive genius, in preparing speeches and salutations for the different
characters, the genius of Lynsday was peculiarly
adapted. The pageants he had devised for Queen
Magdalene, were now turned to some account. Here
we again quote from Pitscottie, the only description preserved, of the manner in which the Queen
was welcomed.

" Alwayis the Quein landit verrie plesantlie, in
ane pairt of Fyfe callit Fyfenesse besyd Balkomie
quhair sche remanit quhill horses come to her. But
the Kyng wes in Sanctandrois for the tyme withe
mony of the nobilitie, waiting upon her hamecuming :
Quha, quhen hee hard word that the Quein wes
landit at sik ane pairt, incontinent hee raid furth
withe his haill Lords, boith Speirituall and Temporall,
with many Barons, Lairds, and Gentlemen, who were
convened for the time at St Andrews, in their best array,
and met the Quein, and receveit hir withe greyt joy
and mirrines of fersis and playis, maid and preparit
for hir. And first, sche was receivit at the New Abbay
yet [gate] ; upon the eist syd thairof thair wes maid to
hir ane triumphand arch be Sir David Lindsay of the
Mount knicht alias Lyon Kyng at Armis, quha caussit
ane greyt cloud to cum out of the hevins down

abone the ӡeit [gate]; out [of] the quhilk cloude come
downe ane fair Lady most lyk ane angell having
the Keyis of Scotland in hir hand, and delyverit
thayme to the Queinis grace in signe and taikin that
all the harts of Scotland wer opin for the receveing
of hir Grace; withe certane Oratiouns maid be the
said Sir David to the Quein's grace, desyring hir
to feir hir God, and to serve him, and to reverence
and obey hir husband, and keip hir awin body clein,
according to God's will and commandment."

In connexion with these pageants we may notice
his poem on the burlesque Tournament betwixt the
King's "twa mediciners," Watson and Barbour.

The most remarkable, however, by far of Lyndsay's
productions was his play entitled, "THE SATYRE OF
THE THREE ESTATES." How long he was engaged in
preparing it, cannot be ascertained. No authority at
least can be adduced, to support the commonly received statement that it was completed and represented at Cupar-Fife, in the year 1535. I do not hesitate
to assert that it was first exhibited at Linlithgow,
at the feast of Epiphany on 6th January 1539-40, in
the presence of the King, Queen, the ladies of the
Court, the Bishops, and a great concourse of people
of all ranks. The supposed early date proceeds on
the assumption that it must have been prior to the
King's marriage. Had this been so, and had James
been introduced on the stage, under the character of
REX HUMANITAS, the play would never have been
repeated at intervals, at least three times in its original state.

d

The notes of "the Interlude," as then represented, transmitted to England, do not materially differ from the Play in its printed form. Its prominent object was the reformation of abuses, by exposing the abuses that prevailed both in Church and State, the ignorance of the priests, the grievances of tithes, and other clerical exactions, the profligate lives of the prelates, and the evils which abounded in the King's minority and encouraged him in idleness and vice by the influence of such attendants as Flattery, Falsehood, and Sensuality, usurping the places of Verity, Chastity, and Divine Correction. In the proclamation of the Play, Diligence or the Messenger says,

> Prudent Peopill, I pray you all
> Take na more grief in special ;
> *For we shall speik in general*
> For pastime and for play.

John Row, in his History of the Church, states that it was also acted in the amphitheatre of Perth, in the presence of the King, Queen, &c. It is not improbable Row has substituted the name of St. Johnstone or Perth, for Linlithgow.

In the subsequent representations of the Play at Cupar-Fife about 1552; and at Edinburgh in 1554, there may have been numerous changes and alterations which we have no means of ascertaining, by the omission or introduction of short Interludes. But it is obvious, considering the protracted time for the performance, that such Interludes of a coarse and indelicate character were meant for the amusement of the lower classes, during the intervals when the chief auditory had retired for refreshments. See, for instance, the note at page 196 and page 214, where Diligence drives the Pardoner and Pauper away. Also the interlude of the Auld Man and his Wife, when the Play was acted at Cupar-Fife. Some of these in fact, may have been written by Lyndsay years before, when, to amuse the youthful monarch, he exercised his own inventive powers, by performing short interludes, farces, and plays.

Leaving any further remarks on this singular production, a work of a totally different character requires special notice. This is the REGISTER OF ARMS, of the Scottish Nobility and Gentry, compleated under his direction, as Lyon Herald, during the King's life, in the year 1542. This official Register of Arms was submitted by Sir James Balfour, one of his successors as Lyon King, to the Lords of Privy Council, at Holyrood-house, on the 9th December 1630, and approven as an authentic Register. It is preserved in the Library of the Faculty of Advocates, Edinburgh, having been acquired with Balfour's valuable Manuscript Collections in 1698.

The volume consists of 133 leaves, of which 111 (only 106 specified by the Privy Council) belong to the original work. It had remained with the Heralds apparently till the Reign of Charles the First, and has on the additional leaves, the arms, with supporters of the intermediate Lyon Kings of Arms. The drawing of the arms, so carefully executed and properly blazoned, are creditable to the state of the

Heraldic Art in Scotland. Those of the Queens of
Scotland beginning with St Margaret and ending with
the Queens of James the Fifth, are impaled with the
royal arms. A limited number of copies of an exact
facsimile of the original Register, was published at
Edinburgh by W. & D. Laing, in 1821, folio.

The death of King James the Fifth at Falkland, on
the 14th of December 1542, was another of those sad
calamities which so grievously affected the prosperity
of Scotland. He was an accomplished Prince, although
his education had been neglected, active, high spirited,
but passionate and implacable in his resentment. He
was unfortunate in many of his measures, and his political relations with France, brought him into constant
strangement and opposition to his uncle the English
monarch. Lyndsay, who had been with James from
"the day of his nativity," also witnessed the prema-
ture termination of his career in the 31st year of his
age. Two infant sons had died within a short time of
each other; and in his last illness, broken-hearted at
his misfortunes, it is related that when the messenger
from Linlithgow arrived at Falkland, to inform him
of the Queen's safe delivery, to his eager inquiry, the
messenger said, "it was ane fair dochter," the King
answered and said, " Fairweill, it cam with ane lass,
and it will pass with ane lass:" reflecting on the
alliance which placed the Stewart family on the
throne : "and so he commendit himselff to the Al-
mightie God, and spak litle from thensforth, bot turned
his back to his lordis and his face to the wall." [1]

[1] Pitscottie's History.

The succession to the throne of an infant of a few days old (the ill-fated Mary, Queen of Scots) was an event which increased the political divisions and miseries of Scotland. Lyndsay had deprecated the chance of witnessing another protracted minority, which as it proved, entailed on this country an unusual share of misfortunes even compared with what he lamented when, in 1528, he exclaimed :—

I see richt weill that Proverb is richt trew,
' Wo to the Realme, that hath an our young King.'

Owing to this distracted state of public affairs, nearly two years elapsed before the Lyon King was sent officially to deliver the books of Statutes and the Orders of knighthood that had been conferred on the late king. In these were the Order of the Golden Fleece restored to the Emperor Charles the Fifth : of St Michael, sometimes called the Cockle, to Francis the First ; and of the Garter, to Henry the Eighth. The latter acknowledged this to the Earl of Arran, the Governor, in the following letter, which is interesting as mentioning the Lyon King in laudatory terms :—

" HENRY R.

" Right trustye and right welbeloued Cousin, we grete yo⁰ well, And whereas vpon the deceasse of o⁰ nephew the late King of Scottis, whose soule God pardoune being in his lieftyme ane of the Compaignions of o⁰ Ordre, yo⁰ sent vnto vs by this berar Sir Dauid Lyndsay, knight alias Lyon principal King of Armes of Scotlande, the Statutes of the said ordre

w^t the colar and garter of the same whiche we haue
receyved by thandes of the right Reuerend father in
god, our right trustye and right welbeloued Coun-
seylo^r, the bisshopp of Wynchestre, prelate of our
said Ordre, We haue thought good by these o^r letres to
signifie the same vnto yo^u with this also, that the
said Lyon in the deliuery thareof hath vsed himself
right discreatelye and moche to o^r contentation gevin
vnder o^r Signet at o^r hono^r of Hamptencorte, the
xxiiijth of Maye the xxxvth yere of o^r Reigne.

(Indorsed, Letre from K. Henry ye aucht K. of England to the erll of Arran, 1544.) A facsimile of the
original will appear in Part III. of that valuable and
handsome publication, "The National Manuscripts
of Scotland.

The eventful year 1546, commenced inauspiciously
with the trial and condemnation of George Wishart
for heresy. It signally failed in its object to arrest
the alarming progress of heretical opinions. He
suffered martyrdom on the 2d March 1545-6, in
front of the Castle of St Andrews, where Cardinal
Beaton and other Prelates in their gorgeous robes were
seated to witness his execution; and he predicted,
as some writers assert, the speedy fate that would
overtake the Cardinal amidst all his pride and power.
Such a statement is readily accepted by those who
impute to the martyr a knowledge of a preconcerted
scheme by a band of conspirators who were pensioned
by Henry. That some of the discontented Scots were
pensioned appears from the English records, but
except where blinded prejudice exists, it is clear that

the Cardinal's fate was mainly owing to the feelings excited to avenge such cruelty.

Norman Lesley, the eldest son of the Earl of Rothes may have had cause of private resentment against the Cardinal; but that the others were actuated by mercenary motives, let those believe who will. Under the circumstances it was a bold measure for sixteen persons to undertake to surprise his Castle of St Andrews, which was strongly fortified, and to assassinate himself; and their success was certainly equal to the boldness of the attempt. Chalmers says, "The odious assassination of this great, but obnoxious prelate, was achieved by a band of ruffians, who were in the pay of Henry VIII., on the 28th of May 1546. Lyndsay, immediately sat down to gratify his prejudice, by satirizing the memory of Beaton, and incidentally protecting the lives of the assassins." [1]

When Lyndsay sat down with this object is not stated, but if he had prejudices to gratify, Chalmers might have remembered it was not 'immediate,' by looking at "The Tragedie of the Cardinall" itself, where (line 266) these words are put in the Cardinal's mouth :—

Thay saltit me, syne closit in a kist,
I lay unburyit serin monethis, and mair,
Or I was borne to closter, kirk, or queir.

in reference to the fact that his body lay unburied from May 1546 till about January 1547. In devis-

[1] Lyndsay's Works, vol. i., p. 73.

ing the Cardinal's death, Lyndsay could not be said
to have had any participation.   In the note to this
poem (p. 274) I have inadvertently said, "During the
time that this Castle was besieged, it was resorted to
as a place of safety by Knox, Lyndsay, and various
persons who had not been concerned in the slaughter,
but were under suspicion of favouring the Reformers."
So far as Lyndsay was concerned this statement is
erroneous ; and it is important that what may be
called a vulgar error, should be corrected.   As Com-
missioner for the borough of Cupar, he was in his seat
in Parliament on the 4th of August when the summons
of treason was issued against Norman Lesley and the
other persons charged with this act of atrocity ; and
on the 14th of the month, the Lyon King and his
deputies were directed to see this duly executed.
—The number of persons in the Castle at no time
exceeded one hundred and fifty, yet the Governor
after five months spent in the vain attempt to reduce
it, (the garrison obtaining supplies of money and pro-
visions, by sea, from England) concluded a truce, and
raised the siege at the end of December or in January
following, until a Papal absolution was obtained.
Now it appears that on the 17th December " the Lyon
Herald with one trumpet, was sent to us from the
Governor and Counsale, and desyred speaking ; to
whom we made no answer.   Then he departed and
told the Governor he could have no speaking (or conference) of us, &c. (in the Castle)." [1]   No satisfactory
remission for a crime that was declared to be irremis-

[1] State Papers, Henry VIII., vol. v., p. 581.

sible could be obtained ; and the death of Henry VIII. on the 28th January 1546-7, blasted all the hopes of "the Castilians." Yet the garrison seem to have enjoyed an interval of rest for a few months, holding communications with the inhabitants of St Andrews, until the siege was renewed by a body of troops sent from France to the Governor's assistance.

The only time, therefore, when Lyndsay was in communication with the Castle, but not as a resident, was in the Spring of 1547, when his name is mentioned on a memorable occasion. John Knox, at that time, wearied (he tells us) with wandering about with his young pupils entered the Castle as a place of refuge at Easter, (the 10th April) 1547. In his account of the unexpected public call given him in the Parish Church of St Andrews to undertake the office of the ministry, he states that this was after private conference with John Rough, Henry Balnavis, and some others, towards the end of May, they having with thame in council "SCHIR DAVID LYNDESAY of the Mount."[1] It is to be observed, this scene took place, not in the Castle, but in the great Church of St Andrews.

Henry the Second of France having about this time ascended the throne of France, he agreed to send the troops mentioned under the command of Leon Strozzi. The French galleys arrived in the Bay of St Andrews on the 29th June ; and with his artillery, he compelled the Castle to surrender the 30th July ; but disregarding the terms of capitulation, the chief persons were

[1] See notes to Knox's Hist. of the Reformation : Works, vol. i., pp. 187, 188.

put on board the galleys and carried prisoners to France.[1] Had Lyndsay remained in the Castle during the siege, he doubtless would have shared the fate of Knox and Balnavis, and others, who were chained to the oars, as galley-slaves, and for many months suffered great hardship.

The subsequent events in Lyndsay's life are not very important, and have been related so well and concisely by Mr George Chalmers, that I cannot do better than quote his words :—

"Sir David, as Lion Herald, was dispatched in 1548 to Christian, King of Denmark, to solicit ships, for protecting the Scottish coasts against the English, and to negotiate a free trade, for the Scottish merchants, particularly in grain.[2] The ships were not granted ; but the free trade, as it was convenient to both parties, was more easily yielded to the persuasive instances of our Lion King. At Copenhagen, Lyndsay became acquainted with his countryman Dr Macabæus, and the other literati of reformed Denmark.

"Lyndsay at length returned to his usual occupations, and was probably no more employed in such distant embassies. About this time, he published the most pleasing of all his poems, THE HISTORIE AND TESTAMENT OF SQUYER MELDRUM. He, on this

[1] See notes to Knox's Hist. of the Reformation : Works, vol. i., pp. 205-208.

[2] "MS. Letters, which had been collected by Lesley, the famous bishop of Ross, and which were communicated to me by the late bishop Geddes, who cannot be enough praised for his ingenuity, and his friendliness."

occasion, tries to amuse as well as to reform ; but he shows his own coarseness by addressing his 'trifling jests and fulsom ribaldry' to 'companies unlettered, rude, and shallow." In 1553 our poet finished his last, and greatest work, THE MONARCHIE, which, from its elaboration, and extent, could not have been the labour of a week, a month, or a year. When he put his last hand to this employment of years, Lyndsay cried out :—

> Go hence, pure Buke, quhilk I have done indyte
> In rural ryme, in maner of dispyte,
>   Contrar the Warldis variatioun :
> Of Rethorick heir I proclame thee quyte.
> Idolatouris, I feir, sall with thee flyte,
>   Because of thame thow makis narratioun :
>   Bot cure thow nocht the indignatioun
> Of Hypocritis, and fals Pharisience,
> Quhowbeit on thee thay cry ane lowde vengence.'

" It is apparent that Lyndsay, during times of some difficulty, and great danger, was not afraid of *hypocritis* and *pharisience*. His name and titles were prefixed to the first edition of the work, while much artifice was used to protect the printer from the severe penalties of a recent Act of Parliament. In the midst of all those labours Lyndsay was not neglectful of his duties, as the chief of the Heralds. Some time after the year, wherein Mackenzie and his followers suppose him to have died, he acted with great precision and dignity as Lion King. On the 16th of January 1554-5, he held a chaptour of Heralds, *chaptourly* convened, in the Abbey of Halyrood-house, for the trial and punishment of William Crawar, a messenger, for abuse of his office.

" At the age of sixty-five Lyndsay saw his great work of Reformation gradually advance. He perceived the Queen-Mother procure the pardon of the assassins of Beaton ; to gratify even a more influential passion than revenge. Her ambition wished to supersede the Regent ; and her intrigues acquired this desire of her heart on the 12th of April 1554. On this occasion Lyndsay witnessed, if he did not manage, the acting of his SATYRE OF THE THREE ESTAITIS, on the Play-field at Edinburgh, before the Queen, the Court, and the Commons. Lyndsay had seen Acts of Parliament passed for reforming abuses throughout the reign of James V. He now saw Ecclesiastical Councils assemble, for reforming ecclesiastical persons and things. But, under an infant Queen, and a female Regent, temperate reform was not to be expected, amidst a rude and corrupt people. Sir David saw John Knox return to Scotland in 1555, and preach without apprehension. He beheld the assassins of Beaton return, in safety, during the subsequent years. He observed, in 1557, several persons of great consideration, ' who were ready to jeopard lives and goods for the setting forward of the work of reformation." But it is remarkable, considering the temperament of Lyndsay, that he never appeared personally at any meeting of the early Reformers, when they began to avow their purpose and to defy the established power. Whether he were alive on the 3d of December 1557, when *the Congregation* took a formal shape, by the signature of a Bond of Association, is uncertain."[1]

It is, however, quite certain that Lyndsay died some time previous to the 18th of April 1555, as will appear from an extract to be quoted from the Privy Seal Register; and consequently he could neither have witnessed Knox's return, the pardon of Beaton's assassins, nor been present at any meeting of the early Reformers. But nothing has been discovered of the circumstances of his death, or the place where he died and where his mortal remains were deposited. At this time the Lords of the Congregation were unknown; no Bond of Association had been prepared or signed; the Reformation was making but small progress; and the name of Protestant had not been assumed, there being at that time neither churches nor ministers, nor the face of a congregation in any part of the country. The visit of John Knox in September 1555 was only temporary, nor did he arrive again till May 1559, when his presence inspired fresh courage in the hearts of those who, in the interim had assumed the name of THE CONGREGATION.

The following extract from the Privy Council Register, is here given as it not only fixes the period of Lyndsay's decease, but proves his successor, as heir of tailzie, to have been his younger brother, who stands second in the deed of entail in 1542. As no mention is made of his wife, who had the lands by the same deed in conjunct-fee, there can be no

[1] Works of Sir David Lyndsay, by Chalmers, vol. i., pp. 36-42.

doubt that she had predeceased her husband the Lyon
King :—

"Ane lettre maid to Alexander Lyndesay of the
gift of the said Alexanderis mariage now beand in hir
Hieness handis be ressoun of deceis of vmquhile Sir
Dauid Lyndesay of the Mont knycht brother to the
said Alexander, to quhome the said Alexander is
nerrest and to be seruit air of tailzie vnto his heri-
tage And siclike of the releif, quhen it sal happin, of
the landis of Pratris throw sesing to be gevin to the
said Alexander as air foirsaid with power, &c. At
Striniling the xviij day of Aprile the zeir of God
foirsaid, &c.—g. [J^m v^c and lv zeris.   Gratis.]

Per signaturam.[1]

The Armorial Register of 1542 is already noticed
at p. xxxvi. Another heraldic MS. called "Collec-
tanea" has been ascribed to Sir David Lyndsay, but
it obviously belongs to the time of the younger or
third Sir David Lyndsay, 1592.

Robert Forman, who had for many years acted as
Ross Herald, became Lyndsay's immediate successor as
Lyon King; and, from their connexion with the Poet,
the names of other successors may be briefly added :—

SIR ROBERT FORMAN of Luthrie, 1555-1567.
SIR WILLIAM STEWART, February, 1567-8, deposed,
and executed for alleged crimes.[2]
SIR DAVID LYNDSAY of Rathillet, the Poet's
youngest brother, August 1568.   Died in 1591.

[1] Reg. Secr. Sig. vol. xxvii., fol. 105, b.
[2] Knox's Works, vol. vi., p. 692.

SIR DAVID LYNDSAY of the Mount, son of Alexander Lyndsay of the Mount, May 1592. Resigned in favour of his son-in-law,

SIR JEROME LYNDSAY of Annatland, created Lyon King, June 1621.

It only remains to offer a few remarks on two points, the one, regarding Lyndsay's character as a Reformer, the other, as a Poet.

The name of the Lyon King has always been reckoned among the earliest adherents of the Scottish Reformation. This requires some modification. All his writings had for their object an unmistakeable attempt to expose and reform abuses whether in Church or State. That they had a powerful effect in promoting such reforms is sufficiently obvious. In no other respect can he be called a Reformer. In his addresses to James, among all his varied attainments he urges him, not only

> Among the rest, SCHIR, LERNE TO BE ANE KING.
> Kyith on that craft, thy pregnant fresch ingyne
> Grantit to thee be influence Divyne.

but also to have regard to his own personal conduct,

> For quhow suld Prencis governe gret regionis
> That cannot dewlie guyde their awin personis.

In his earlier Complaynt to the King, he says—

> Swa is thare nocht, I understand
> Without gude ordour in this land,
> *Except the Spiritualitie:*
> Prayand thy Grace thareto have ee.

In his latest work, the Dialog (1552) when he introduces an Exclamation against Idolatrie, he says—

> I truist to se gude reformatione
> From tyme we gett ane faithfull prudent King.
> Quhilk knawis the treuth and his vocatione.

Had Lyndsay survived for a few years beyond the actual term of his life, we need scarcely doubt he would have joined himself to the Lords of the Congregation in the abjuration of Popery; but it cannot be said that, at any period of his life, he had actually renounced his general adherence to the Romish Faith. In his earliest poem, for instance, The Dreme (1528) his Mariolatry is exhibited, in the place assigned to the Virgin Mary, when describing "The Hevin Impyre," he says—

> Nyxt to the throne we saw the Quene of Quenis,
> Well cumpanyit with ladyis of delyte.
> Sich was the song of these blyssit Virgines,
> Na mortall man thair solace may indite.

In pointing out the ordinary evils of Idolatrous figures, in persons falling upon their knees and worshipping stocks and stones, he admits that some good might result from seeing and admiring such representations,

> Or, quhen thow seeis ane portrature
> Of blyssit Marie, Virgene pure,
> With one bony Babe upon her knee.

having, no doubt, in his mind the recollection of such a favourite subject by the greatest artists of his day, among the Italian, Flemish, and other schools of painting.

In the Epistle Nuncupatory of his Dialog on the Monarchies, in 1552, he says,

> . . . the straucht way sal thou wende
> To thame quhilk hes the realme in governance,
> Declare thy mynde to thame with circumstance :
> Go first tyll James, our Prince and Protectour,
> And his Brother, our Spirituall Governour,
> And Prince of Preistis in this Natioun.
> Efter reverend recommendatioun,
> Under their feit thow lowlye thee submyt, &c.

That is, to James, Earl of Arran, afterwards Duke de Chattelherault, and his bastard brother, John Hamilton, Archbishop of St Andrews, the successor of Cardinal Beaton. In this work, the Lyon King strongly urges the necessity of suppressing all kinds of idolatry, and to advance the sincere word of God. Yet, while presuming to offer sage advices to "Our Holie Father the Pope," he still continued to the last in styling his Holiness,

> . . . This potent Pope of Rome,
> The Soverane King of Christindome,
>
> .   .   .   .   .
>
> So gret ane Prince quhare sall thow fynd
> That Spiritually may lowse and bind ;
> Nor be quhame Synnis ar forgyffin,
> Be thay with his Disciplis schrevin ?

But it is a remarkable fact, that in such troublous times, and using the strongest language in condemning the Romish Clergy, Lyndsay should have been allowed to escape persecution in some of its varied

forms, whether of deprivation of property, imprison-
ment, torture, or death.

We cannot therefore but admire his boldness in
openly acknowledging himself the author of such
productions; and if we do not reckon him as one of
the Protestant Reformers, it would be a greater mis-
take should we hesitate for one moment in asserting
that his satirical writings had a powerful effect
in preparing the minds of his countrymen, by his
exposure of the manifold corruptions and errors of
Popery, for the final triumph of the Reformation,
accomplished mainly by the dauntless energy of our
great Reformer, John Knox.

In estimating the literary character of Lyndsay, we
cannot claim for him the name of a Great Poet.
Without either 'the language at large,' which he
assigns to Dunbar, or his inventive genius, our Author
is nevertheless entitled to no ordinary place among
our ancient Makaris. He exhibits (without the least
scruple in altering words to suit the rhyme) a great
command of versification, a fine feeling for the beauties of external nature, and a fund of what may be
called, low genuine humour and keen satire; while
for a vivid conception and delineation of individual
character, even in his impersonations of abstract
Virtues and Vices, he displays great Dramatic power,
and in this respect he far surpasses any one of the
early Scottish Poets.

Of Lyndsay's personal appearance we have no description. In the quarto edition of his Poems
published in France in 1558, there is a woodcut of a

figure in a herald's dress, repeated two or three
times, and of which a facsimile is given on the title
of the present volume. On that of the Second volume,
is a similar facsimile from the Edinburgh edition of
1634 of a portrait inscribed with his name. Both
cuts may be held as imaginary; yet the later one has
such a sly comical expression, that rude as it is, I feel
inclined to suggest it might have been taken from an
authentic original. But no such original is known to
exist. Several years ago, a residenter in the neighbourhood of Cupar, told me that an interesting discovery had been made of an original portrait of Sir
David Lyndsay. It had remained, he said, undis-
covered in a house near The Mount, but had been re-
moved to Rankeillor House by the proprietor: that
it was intended for Lyndsay, appeared from the peculiar dress, and the crown on his head. This excited
my curiosity, and, to lose no time, I arranged to cross
over to Fife within a few days, that we might
examine it together, and judge of its authenticity.
The first glance I had of the portrait satisfied me
I had come on rather a fool's errand, and that any
such discovery had still to be made. In the portrait
itself, I had no difficulty in recognizing one of those
that were painted by George Jamesone of Sir Thomas
Hope of Craighall,[1] Lord Advocate to Charles the
First, in his official costume, with a peculiar em-
broidered cap, mistaken by my informant for the
crown of the Lyon King.

[1] Engraved from the portrait at Hopetoun House, in Pink-
erton's " Scotish Gallery," 1799. Two other portraits of Sir
Thomas Hope are known.

In " Marmion," Sir Walter Scott, using a poetical license, has introduced Lyndsay at the Court of James the Fourth, in the character of Lyon Herald sixteen years before he obtained that office, in a spirited sketch, from which, in conclusion, the following lines may be quoted :—

> He was a man of middle age;
> In aspect manly, grave, and sage,
>   As on King's errand come ;
> But in the glances of his eye,
> A penetrating, keen, and sly
>   Expression found its home ;
> The flash of that satiric rage,
> Which, bursting on the early stage,
> Branded the vices of the age,
>   And broke the keys of Rome.
> On milk-white palfrey forth he paced ;
> His cap of maintenance was graced
>   With the proud heron-plume.
> From his steed's shoulder, loin, and breast,
>   Silk housings swept the ground,
> With Scotland's arms, device, and crest,
>   Embroidered round and round.
> The double tressure might you see,
>   First by Achaius borne,
> The Thistle, and the Fleur-de-lis,
>   And gallant Unicorn.
> So bright the KING's armorial coat,
> That scarce the dazzled eye could note,
>   In living colours, blazoned brave,
>   THE LION, which his title gave.

THE MINOR POEMS

OF

SIR DAVID LYNDESAY.

VOL. I.   A

THE DREME

OF SCHIR DAVID LYNDESAY.

THE EPISTIL TO THE KINGIS GRACE.

RYCHT potent Prince, of hie Imperial blude,
  Unto thy Grace I traist it be weill knawin
My servyce done unto your Celsitude,
  Quhilk nedis nocht at lenth for to be schawin ;
  And thocht my youtheid now be neir ouer blawin,
Excerst in servyce of thyne Excellence,
Hope hes me hecht ane gudlie recompense.

Quhen thow wes young, I bure thee in myne arme
  Full tenderlie, tyll thow begouth to gang ;
And in thy bed oft happit thee full warme,
  With lute in hand, syne, sweitlie to thee sang :
  Sumtyme, in dansing, feiralie I flang ;
And sumtyme, playand farsis on the flure ;
And sumtyme, on myne office takkand cure :

And sumtyme, lyke ane feind, transfigurate,
   And sumtyme, lyke the greislie gaist of Gye;
In divers formis oft tymes disfigurate,
   And sumtyme, dissagyist full plesandlye.
    So, sen thy birth, I have continewalye
Bene occupyit, and aye to thy plesoure,
And sumtyme, Seware, Coppare, and Carvoure;

Thy purs maister and secreit Thesaurare,
   Thy Yschare, aye sen thy natyvitie,
And of thy chalmer cheiffe Cubiculare,
   Quhilk, to this hour, hes keipit my lawtie;
    Lovyng be to the blyssit Trynitie!
That sic ane wracheit worme hes maid so habyll,
Tyll sic ane Prince to be so greabyll.

Bot now thow arte, be influence naturall,
   Hie of ingyne, and rycht inquisityve
Of antique storeis, and deidis marciall;
   More plesandlie the tyme for tyll ouerdryve,
    I have, at length, the storeis done, descryve
Of Hectour, Arthour, and gentyll Julyus,
Of Alexander, and worthy Pompeyus;

Of Jasone, and Medea, all at lenth,
   Of Hercules the actis honorabyll,
And of Sampsone the supernaturall strenth,
   And of leill luffaris storeis amiabyll;
    And oft tymes have I feinyeit mony fabyll,
Of Troylus, the sorrow, and the joye,
And Seigis all of Tyir, Thebes, and Troye.

The Propheceis of Rymour, Eeid, and Marlyng,
  And of mony uther plesand storye,
Of the Reid Etin, and the Gyir Carlyng,
  Confortand thee, quhen that I saw thee sorye :
  Now, with the supporte of the King of Glorye,
I sall thee schaw ane storye of the new,
The quhilk affore I never to thee schew.

But humilie I beseik thyne Excellence,
  With ornate termis thocht I can nocht express
This sempyll mater, for laik of eloquence ;
  Yit, nochtwithstanding all my besynes
  With hart and hand, my mynd I sall addres,
As I best can, and most compendious :
Now I begyn : the mater hapnit thus.

THE PROLOG.

In to the Calendis of Januarie,
  Quhen fresche Phebus, be movyng circulair,
Frome Capricorne wes enterit in Aquarie,
  With blastis that the branchis maid full bair,
  The snaw and sleit perturbit all the air,
And flemit Flora frome every bank, and bus,
Throuch supporte of the austeir Eolus.

Efter that I the lang wynteris nycht
  Had lyne walking, in to my bed, allone,
Throuch hevy thocht, that no way sleip I mycht,
  Rememberyng of divers thyngis gone :
  So, up I rose, and clethit me anone ;

Be this, fair Tytane, with his lemis lycht,
Ouer all the land had spred his baner brycht.

With cloke and hude I dressit me belyve,
   With dowbyll schone, and myttanis on my handis;
Howbeit the air was rycht penetratyve,
   Yit fure I furth, lansing ouirthorte the landis,
   Toward the see, to schorte me on the sandis ;
Because unblomit was baith bank and braye :
And so, as I was passing be the waye,

I met dame Flora, in dule weid dissagysit,
   Quhilk in to May wes dulce, and delectabyll ;
With stalwart stormis, hir sweitnes wes supprisit ;
   Hir hevynlie hewis war turnit in to sabyll,
   Quhilkis umquhile war to luffaris amiabyll.
Fled frome the froste, the tender flouris I saw,
Under dame Naturis mantyll, lurking law.

The small fowlis, in flokkis, saw I flee,
   To Nature makand greit lamentatioun :
Thay lychtit doun besyde me, on ane tree,
   Of thair complaynt I had compassioun,
   And, with ane pieteous exclamatioun,
Thay said, Blyssit be Somer, with his flouris ;
And waryit be thow, Wynter, with thy schouris.

Allace ! Aurora, the syllie Larke can crye,
   Quhare hes thou left thy balmy liquour sweit,
That us rejosit, we mounting in the skye ?
   Thy sylver droppis ar turnit in to sleit.

O fair Phebus ! quhare is thy hoilsum heit ?
Quhy tholis thow thy hevinlie plesand face
With mystic vapouris, to be obscurit, allace !

Quhar art thow May, with June thy syster schene
   Weill bordourit with dasyis of delyte ?
And gentyll Julie, with thy mantyll grene,
   Enamilit with rosis red and quhyte ?
   Now auld and cauld Januar, in dispyte,
Reiffis frome us all pastyme and plesour :
Allace ! quhat gentyll hart may this indure ?

Ouersylit ar with cloudis odious
   The goldin skyis of the Orient ;
Changeyng in sorrow our sang melodious,
   Quhilk we had wount to sing, with gude intent,
   Resoundand to the hevinnis firmament :
Bot now our daye is changeit in to nycht.
With that thay rais, and flew furthof my sycht.

Pensyve in hart, passing full soberlie,
   Unto the see, fordward I fure anone ;
The see was furth, the sand wes smooth and drye ;
   Then up and doun I musit myne allone,
   Tyll that I spyit ane lyttill cave of stone,
Heych in ane craig : upwart I did approche,
But tarying, and clam up in the roche :

And purposit, tor passing of the tyme,
   Me to defende from ociositie,
With pen and paper to register in ryme,

Sum mery mater of Antiquitie :
  Bot Idelnes, ground of iniquitie,
Scho maid so dull my spreitis, me within,
That I wyste nocht at quhat end to begin.

But satt styll in that cove, quhare I mycht see
  The wolteryng of the wallis, up and doun ;
And this fals Warldis instabilytie
  Unto that see makkand comparisoun,
  And of this Warldis wracheit variatioun,
To thame that fixis all thair hole intent
Consideryng quho most had suld most repent.

So, with my hude my hede I happit warme,
  And in my cloke I fauldit boith my feit ;
I thocht my corps with cauld suld tak no harme,
  My mittanis held my handis weill in heit ;
  The skowland craig me coverit frome the sleit :
Thare styll I satt, my bonis for to rest,
Tyll Morpheus, with sleip, my spreit opprest.

So, throw the bousteous blastis of Eolus,
  And throw my walkyng on the nycht before,
And throw the seyis movyng marvellous,
  Be Neptunus, with mony route and rore,
  Constrainit I was to sleip, withouttin more :
And quhat I dremit, in conclusioun
I sall you tell, ane marvellous Visioun.

    HEIR ENDIS THE PROLOG, AND FOLLOWIS
        THE DREME.

THE DREME.

Prophetias nolite spernere. Omnia autem probate: quod bonum est tenete.— THESSAL. V.

ME THOCHT ane Lady, of portratour perfyte,
  Did salus me, with benyng countynance ;
And I, quhilk of hir presens had delyte,
  Tyll hir agane maid humyl reverence,
  And hir demandit, savyng hir plesance,
Quhat wes hir name ? Scho answerit courtesly:
Dame Remembrance, scho said, callit am I.

Quhilk cummyng is for pastyme and plesoure
  Of thee, and for to beir thee companye,
Because I se thy spreit, withoute mesoure,
  So sore perturbit be malancolye ;
  Causyng thy corps to waxin cauld and drye ;
Tharefor, get up, and gang anone with me :
So war we both, in twynkling of ane ee,

Doun throw the Eird, in myddis of the center,
  Or ever I wyste, in to the lawest Hell.
In to that cairfull cove quhen we did enter,
  Yowtyng and yowlyng we hard, with mony yell
  In flame of fyre, rycht furious and fell,
Was cryand mony cairfull creature,
Blasphemand God, and waryand Nature.

Thare sawe we divers Papis, and Empriouris,
    Without recover, mony cairfull Kyngis ;
Thare saw we mony wrangous Conquerouris,
    Withouttin rycht, reiffaris of utheris ryngis ;
    The men of Kirk, lay boundin in to byngis ;
Thare saw we mony cairfull Cardinall,
And Archebischopis, in thair pontificall ;

Proude and perverst Prelatis, out of nummer,
    Priouris, Abbottis, and fals flatterand Freris ;
To specifye thame all, it wer ane cummer,
    Regular Channonis, churle Monkis and Chartereris,
    Curious Clerkis, and Preistis Seculeris :
Thare was sum parte of ilk Religioun,
In Haly Kirk quhilk did abusioun.

Than I demandit dame Remembrance
    The cause of thir Prelattis punytioun ?
Scho said, The cause of thair unhappy chance
    Was covatyce, luste, and ambitioun ;
    The quhilk now garris thame want fruitioun
Of God, and heir eternallie man dwell,
In to this painefull poysonit pytt of Hell.

Als they did nocht instruct the ignorant
    Provocand thame to penitence, be preicheing ;
Bot servit warldlie Prencis insolent,
    And war promovit be thair fenyeit fleicheing,
    Nocht for thair science, wysedome, nor teicheing ;
Be symonie, was thair promotioun,
More for deneiris, nor for devotioun.

Ane uther cause of the punytioun
  Of thir unhappy prelattis, imprudent,
Thay maid nocht equale distributioun
  Of haly Kirk the patrimonie and rent;
  Bot temporallie they have it all mispent,
Quhilkis suld have bene trypartit in to thrie;
First, to uphauld the Kirk in honestie;

The secund part, to sustene thair estaitis;
  The thrid part, to be gevin to the puris;
Bot thay dispone that geir all uther gaittis,
  On cartis, and dyce, on harllotrie, and huris;
  Thir catyvis tuke no compt of thair awin curis:
Thair kirkis reuin, thair ladyis clenelie cled
And rychelie rewlit, boith at burde and bed.

Thair bastarde bairnis proudely thay provydit;
  The Kirk geir larglie they did on thame spende;
In thair defaltis, thair subditis wer misgydit,
  And comptit nocht thair God for tyll offend,
  Quhilk gart thame want grace, at thair letter end.
Rewland that rowte, I sawe, in capis of bras,
Symone Magus, and byschope Cayphas;

Byschope Annas, and the treatour Judas,
  Machomete, that propheit poysonabyll,
Chore, Dathan, and Abirone thare was;
  Heretykis we sawe innumerabyll,
  It wes ane sycht rycht wonderous lamentabyll,
Quhow that thay lay in to thay flammis fleityng,
With cairfull cryis, girnyng, and greityng.

Religious men wer punyste panefullie,
   For vaine glore, als for inobedience,
Brekand thair Constitutiouns wyllfullie,
   Nocht haiffand thair onermen in reverence :
   To knaw thair Rewle thay maid no delygence,
Unleifsumlie thay usit propertie,
Passing the boundis of wylfull povertie.

Full sore wepyng, with vocis lamentabyll
   They cryit lowde, O Empriour Constantyne !
We may wyit thy possessioun poysonabyll
   Of all our gret punytioun and pyne :
   Quhowbeit thy purpose was, till ane gude fyne,
Thow baneist frome us trew devotioun,
Haiffand sie ee tyll our promotioun.

Than we beheld ane den full dolorous,
   Quhare that Prencis, and Lordis temporall,
War cruciate with painis rigorous :
   Bot to expreme thair panis, in speciall
   It dois exceid all my memoriall :
Importabyll paine they had, but confortyng ;
Thare blude royall maid them no supportyng.

Sum catyve Kingis, for creuell oppressioun,
   And uther sum, for thair wrangous conquest,
War condampnit, thay, and thair Successioun ;
   Sum for publict adulterye, and incest ;
   Sum leit thair pepill never leif in rest,
Delyting so in plesour sensuall ;
Quharefor thair paine was thare perpetuall.

Thare was the cursit Empriour Nero
   Of everilk vice the horrabyll veschell ;
Thare was Pharo, with divers Prencis mo,
   Oppressouris of the barnis of Israell ;
   Herode, and mony mo than I can tell,
Ponce Pylat was thare, hangit be the hals,
With unjuste Jugis, for thair sentence fals.

Dukis, Merquessis, Erlis, Barronis, Knychtis,
   With thai Prencis, wer punyst panefullie ;
Participant thay wer of thair unrychtis.
   Fordwarte we went, and leit thir Lordis lye,
   And sawe quhere Ladyis lamentabyllie
Lyke wod lyonis, wer cairfullie cryand
In flam of fyre, rycht furiouslie fryand ;

Emprices, Quenis, and ladyis of honouris,
   Mony Duches, and Comptes, full of cair,
Thay peirsit myne hart, thai tender creaturis,
   So pynit, in that pytt, full of dispair,
   Plungit in paine, with mony reuthfull rair :
Sum for thair pryde, sum for adulterye :
Sum for thair tyisting men to lychorye ;

Sum had bene creuell, and malicious ;
   Sum for making of wrangous heretouris :
For to rehers thair lyffis vitious,
   It wer bot tarye to the auditouris ;
   Of lychorye thay wer the verray luris,
With thair provocatyve impudicitie,
Brocht mony ane man to infelicitie.

Sum wemen, for thair pussillanimytie,
  Ouerset with schame, thay did thame never schryve
Of secreit synnis, done in quietie;
  And sum repentit never in thair lyve :
  Quhairfor but reuth, thai ruffeis did thame ryve,
Rigorouslie, without compassioun;
Gret was thair dule and lamentatioun.

That we wer maid, thay cryit oft, Allace !
  Thus tormentit with panis intollerabyll,
We mendit nocht, quhen we had tyme and space,
  Bot tuke, in eird, our lustis delectabyll:
  Quharfor with feindis, ugly and horrabyll,
We are condampnit for ever more, allace !
Eternalie, withouttin hope of grace.

Quhar is the meit, and drynke delicious,
  With quhilk we fed our cairfull cariounis ?
Gold, sylver, sylk, with perlis precious,
  Our ryches, rentis, and our possessionis ?
  Withouttin hope of our remissionis.
Allace ! our panis ar insufferabyll,
And our tormentis, to compt, innumerabyll.

Than we beheld, quhare mony ane thousand
  Commoun pepill lay, flichterand in the fyre :
Of everilk stait, thare was ane bailfull band ;
  Thare mycht be sene mony sorrowfull syre ;
  Sum for invy sufferit, and sum for yre,
And sum for laik of restitutioun
Of wrangous geir, without remissioun.

Mausworne merchandis, for thair wrangous winning,
    Hurdaris of gold, and commoun occararis,
Fals men of law in cautelis rycht cunning,
    Theiffis, revaris, and publict oppressaris :
    Sum part thare was of unleill lauboraris ;
Craftismen, thare saw we, out of nummer ;
Of ilke stait to declare, it wer ane cummer.

And als langsum to me, for tyll indyte
    Of this presoun the panis in speciall :
The heit, the calde, the dolour, and dispyte,
    Quharefor I speik of thame in generall :
    That dully den, that furneis infernall,
Quhose reward is rew, without remede,
Ever deyand, and never to be dede.

Hounger and thrist, in steid of meit and drynk,
    And for thair clethyng, tadis and scorpionis :
That myrke mansioun is tapessit with stynk,
    Thay se nathing bot horrabyll visionis :
    Thay heir bot scorne, and derysionis
Of foule feindis, and blasphemationis ;
Thair feillyng is importabyll passionis.

For melody, miserabyll murnyng,
    Thare is na solace, bot dolour infinyte ;
In bailfull beddis, bitterlye burnyng,
    With sobbyng, syching, sorrow, and with syte ;
    Thair conscience thair hartis so did byte :
To heir thame flyte, it was ane cace of cair,
So in dispyte, plungeit in to dispair.

A lytill above that dolorous doungeoun,
   We enterit in ane countre full of cair,
Quhare that we saw mony ane legioun,
   Greitand and gowland, with mony reuthfull rair.
    Quhat place is this, quod I, of blys so bair?
Scho answerit, and said, Purgatorye,
Quhilk purgis saulis, or thay cum to glorye.

I se no plesour heir, bot mekle paine,
   Quharefor, said I, leif we this sorte in thrall:
I purpose never to cum heir agane;
   Bot yit I do beleve, and ever sall,
    That the trew Kirk can no waye erre at all:
Sic thing to be gret Clerkis dois conclude,
Quhowbeit my hope, standis most in Cristis blude.

Abufe that, in the thrid presoun, anone
   We enterit in ane place of perditioun,
Quhare mony babbis war, makand drery mone,
   Because thay wantit the fruitioun
    Of God, quhilk was ane gret punytioun:
Of Baptisme, thay wantit the ansenze:
Upwart we went, and left that myrthles menze.

In tyll ane volt, abone that place of paine,
   Unto the quhilk, but sudgeorne, we ascendit,
That was the Lymbe in the quhilk did remaine
   Our Forefatheris, becaus Adam offendit,
    Eitand the fruit, the quhilk was defendit:
Mony ane yeir, thay dwelt in that dungeoun
In myrknes, and in desolatioun.

Than, throuch the Erth, of nature cauld and dry,
  Glaid to eschaip those places perrelous,
We haistit us, rycht wounder spedalye ;
  Yit we beheld, the secreitis marvellous,
  The mynis of gold, and stonis precious,
Of sylver, and of everilk fyne mettell,
Quhilk to declare, it wer ouer lang to dwell.

Up throuch the Watter, schortlie we intendit,
  Quhilk invirons the Erth, withouttin doute :
Syne, throw the Air, schortlie we ascendit,
  His regionis throuch, behaldyng in and out,
  Quhilk erth and walter, closis round aboute ;
Syne, schortlie upwarte, throw the Fyre we went,
Quhilk wes the hiest and hotest Element.

Quhen we had all thir Elementis ouerpast ;
  That is to saye, Erth, Watter, Air, and Fyre,
Upwart we went, withouttin ony rest,
  To se the Hevynnis, was our maist desyre :
  Bot, or we mycht wyn to the hevin impyre,
We behuffit to passe the way, full evin,
Up throuch the Speris of the Planetis sevin.

First, to the Mone, and vesyit all hir Speir,
  Quene of the See, and bewtie of the nycht,
Of nature wak, and cauld, and no thyng clere ;
  For of hir self scho hes none uther lycht,
  Bot the reflex of Phebus bemes brycht :
The twelf signis, scho passis rounde aboute
In aucht and twenty dayis, withouttin dout.

    VOL. I.   B

Than, we ascendit to Mercurius,
   Quhilk Poetis callis God of Eloquence,
Rycht doctour-lyke, with termes delicious,
   In arte exparte, and full of sapience :
    It wes plesour to pans on his prudence :
Payntouris, Poetis, ar subject to his cure ;
And hote, and dry, he is of his nature.

And als, as cunnyng Astrologis sayis,
   He dois compleit his cours naturallie,
In thre houndreth and aucht and thretty dayis.
   Syne, upwart we ascendit, haistelye,
    To fair Venus, quhare scho rycht lustelie
Was set in to ane sait, of sylver schene
That fresche Goddes, that lustie Luffis Quene.

Thay piersit myne hart, hir blenkis amorous,
   Quhowbeit that, sumtyme, scho is changeabyll,
With countenance and cheir full dolorous,
   Quhylumis rycht plesand, glaid, and delectabyll ;
    Sumtyme constant, and sumtyme variabyll ;
Yit hir bewtie, resplendand as the fyre,
Swagis the wraith of Mars, that God of Yre.

This plesand Planeit, geve I can rycht discryve,
   Scho is baith hote and wak, of hir nature
That is the cause, scho is provocatyve
   Tyll all thame that ar subject to hir cure,
    To Venus werkis, tyll that thay may indure ;
Als scho completis hir coursis naturall
In twelf monethis, withouttin ony fall.

Than past we to the Speir of Phebus brycht,
  That lustie lampe and lanterne of the hevin,
And glader of the sterris, with his lycht :
  And principall of all the planetis sevin,
  And sett in myddis of thame all, full evin,
As Roye royall, rollyng in his Speir,
Full plesandlie, in to his goldin cheir ;

Quhose influence and vertew excellent
  Gevis the lyfe tyll everilk erthlie thyng :
That Prince of everilk planeit, precellent,
  Dois foster flouris, and garris heirbis spryng
  Throuch the cald eirth, and causis birdis syng :
And als his regulare movyng in the hevin,
Is juste under the Zodiack full evin.

For to discryve his diademe Royall,
  Bordourit aboute with stonis schyning brycht,
His goldin cairt, or throne Imperiall,
  The foure stedis that drawis it full rycht,
  I leif to Poetis, because I have no slycht ;
Bot, of his nature, he is hote and drye,
Completand, in ane yeir, his cours, trewlie.

Than up to Mars, in hye, we haistit us,
  Wounder hote, and dryer than the tounder ;
His face flamand, as fyre rycht furious :
  His bost and brag, more aufull than the thounder,
  Maid all the hevin most lyk to schaik in schonder.
Quha wald behald his countynance, and feir,
Mycht call hym weill the god of men of weir :

With colour reid, and luke malicious,
   Rycht colerick of his complexioun,
Austeir, angrye, sweir, and seditions,
   Principall cause of the destructioun
   Of mony gude and nobyll Regioun :
War nocht Venus his yre dois mitigate,
This warld of peace wald be full desolate.

This god of greif, withouttin sudgeornyng,
   In yeris twa his cours he doith compleit.
Than past we up quhare Jupiter, the kyng,
   Satt in his speir, rycht amiabyll and sweit,
   Complexionate with waknes and with heit.
That plesand Prince, fair, dulce, and delicate,
Provokis peace and banesis debait.

The auld Poetis, be superstitioun,
   Held Jupiter the Father principall
Of all thair goddes, in conclusioun,
   For his prerogatyvis in speciall :
   Als, be his vertew, in to generall,
To auld Saturne he makis resistance,
Quhen, in his malice, he walde wyrk vengeance.

This Jupiter, withouttin sudgeornyng,
   Passis throw all the twelf Planetis, full evin,
In yeiris tweif : and, than, but tarying,
   We past unto the hiest of the sevin
   Tyll Saturnus, quhilk trublis all the hevin,
With hevy cheir, and cullour paill as leid.
In hym we sawe bot dolour to the deid :

And cauld and dry he is, of his nature,
    Foule lyke ane oule, of evyll conditioun :
Rycht unplesand he is of portrature.
    His intoxicate dispositioun,
    It puttis all thyng to perditioun,
Ground of seiknes, and malancolious,
Perverst and pure, baith fals and invyous.

His qualitie I can nocht love, bot lack.
    As for his movyng, naturalie, but weir,
About the signis of the Zodiack,
    He dois compleit his cours in thretty yeir :
    And so we left him in his frosty Speir.
Upwarte we did ascend, incontinent,
But rest, tyll we come to the Firmament,

The quhilk was fixit full of sterris brycht,
    Of figour round, rycht plesand and perfyte,
Quhose influence, and rycht excellent lycht,
    And quhose nummer, may nocht be put in wryte.
    Yit, cunnyng Clerkis dois naturallye indyte,
How that he dois compleit his cours, but weir,
In space of sevin and thretty thousand yeir.

Than the nynt Speir, and movare principall
    Of all the laif, we vesyit, all that hevin
Quhose daylie motioun is contyneuall :
    Baith firmament and all the planetis sevin,
    From eist to west, garris thame turne, full evin,
In to the space of four and twenty houris.
Yit, be the myndis of the Astronomouris.

The sevin Planetis, in to thair proper speris,
　From west to eist, thay move, naturallie,
Sum swyft, sum slaw, as to thair kynde afferis,
　As I have schawin, afore, speciallie,
　Quhose motioun causis contyneuallie
Rycht melodious harmonie and sound,
And all throw movyng of those Planetis round.

Than montit we, with rycht fervent desyre,
　Up throw the hevin callit Christallyne ;
And so we enterit in the Hevin impyre,
　Quhilk to discryve it passis myne ingyne ;
　Quhare God, in to His holy throne devyne,
Ryngis, in to his glore inestimabyll,
With Angellis cleir, quhilkis ar innumerabyll.

In Ordouris nyne thir spreitis glorious
　Ar devydit, the quhilkis excellentlye
Makis lovyng, with sound melodious,
　Syngand Sanctus rycht wounder ferventlye.
　Thir Ordouris nyne thay are full plesandlye
Devydit in to Hierarcheis three,
And three Ordouris in everilk Hierarchie.

The lawest Ordoure ar of Angelis brycht,
　As messingeris send unto this law regioun ;
The secund Ordour, Archangelis, full of mycht,
　Virtues, Potestatis, Principatis of renoun;
　The saxt is callit Dominatioun ;
The sevint, Thronus ; the auchtin, Cherubin ;
The nynt and hieast, callit Seraphin.

And, nyxt, unto the blyssit Trynitie,
   In his tryumphant throne imperiall :
Thre in tyll One, and One substance in Thre,
    Quhose indivisabyll essens eternall
    The rude ingyne of mankynd is too small
Tyll comprehend, quhose power infinyte
And devyne nature no creature can wryte.

So, myne ingyne is nocht sufficient
   For to treit of his heych Devinitie :
All mortal men ar insufficient
    Tyll considder thai Thre in Unitie.
    Sic subtell mater I man, on neid, lat be :
To study on my Creid it war full fair,
And lat Doctouris of sic hie materis declare.

Than we beheld the blyste Humanitie
   Of Christe, sittand in to His sege royall,
At the rycht hand of the Devynitie,
    With ane excelland courte Celestiall,
    Quhose exercitioun contyneuall
Was in lovyng thair Prince with reverence ;
And on this wyse thay kepit ordinance.

Nyxt to the Throne we saw the Quene of Quenis,
   Weill cumpanyit with Ladyis of delyte :
Sweit was the sang of those blyssit Virginnis ;
    No mortall man thair solace may indyte.
    The Angellis brycht, in nummer infinyte,
Everilk Ordour in thair awin degre,
War officiaris unto the Deitie.

Patriarkis and Prophetis honorabyll,
  Collaterall counsalouris in his consistorye,
Evangellistis, Apostolis venerabyll,
  War capitanis unto the Kyng of Glorye,
  Quhilk Christane lyke had woun the victorye.
Of that tryumphand courte celestiall
Sanct Peter was lufetenand-general.

The Martyris war as nobyll stalwart Knychtis,
  Discomfatouris of creuell battellis thre,
The flesche, the warld, the feind, and all his mychtis;
  Confessouris, Doctouris in Divinitie,
  As chapell clerkis unto His Deitie:
And, last, we sawe infinyte multytude
Makand servyce unto his Celsitude,

Quhilkis, be the hie Devyne permissioun,
  Felicitie they had invariabyll,
And of His Godhed cleir cognitioun;
  And compleit peace they had, interminabyll:
  Thair glore and honoure was inseparabyll.
That plesand place, repleit of pulchritude,
Innumerabyll it was of magnitude.

Thare is plentie of all plesouris perfyte,
  Evident brychtnes, but obscuritie;
Withouttin dolour, dulcore and delyte;
  Withouttin rancour, perfyte cheritie;
  Withouttin hunger, satiabilitie.
O happy ar those saulis predestinate,
Quhen saule and body sall be glorificate!

Thir marvellous myrthis for to declare,
  Be arithmatik thay ar innumerabyll ;
The portratour of that palace preclare,
  By Geomatre it is immesurabyll ;
  By Rethorike, als inpronunciabyll :
Thare is none eiris may heir, nor eine may see,
Nor hart may thynk, thair greit felycitie.

Quhare to suld I presume for tyll indyte,
  The quhilk Sanct Paule, that doctour sapient,
Can nocht expres, nor in to paper wryte,
  The hie excelland worke indeficient,
  And perfyte plesoure, ever parmanent,
In presens of that mychtie Kyng of Glore,
Quhilk was, and is, and sall be ever more !

At Remembrance humilye I did inquyre,
  Geve I mycht in that plesour styll remane.
Scho said, Aganis reasoun is thy desyre ;
  Quharefor, my freind, thow mon returne agane,
  And, for thy synnis, be pennance, suffer paine,
And thole the dede, with creuell panis sore,
Or thow be ding to ryng with hym in glore.

Than we returnit, sore aganis my wyll,
  Doun throw the Speris of the hevinnis cleir.
Hir commandiment behuffit I fulfyll,
  With sorye hart, wyt ye, withouttin weir.
  I wald full faine haif taryit thare all yeir ;
Bot scho said to me, Thare is no remede,
Or thow remane heir, first thow mon be dede.

Quod I : I pray yow hartfullye, madame,
  Sen we have had sic Contemplatioun
Of hevinlye plesouris, yit or we passe hame,
  Lat us have sum consideratioun
  Of Eirth, and of his situatioun.
Scho answerit and said, That sall be done.
So wer we boith brocht in the air, full sone,

Quhare we mycht se the Eirth all at one sycht,
  Bot lyke one moit, as it apperit to me,
In to the respect of the hevinnis brycht.
  I have marvell, quod I, quhow this may be :
  The Eirth semis of so small quantitie,
The leist sterne fixit in the Firmament
Is more than all the Eirth, be my jugement.

THE QUANTITIE OF THE EIRTH.

Scho sayis, Sonne, thow hes schawin the veritie :
  The smallest sterne fixit in the Firmament,
In deid it is of greter quantytie
  Than all the Eirth, efter the intent
  Of wyse and cunnyng Clerkis sapient.
Quhat quantytie is than the Eirth? quod I.
That sall I schaw, quod scho, to thee schortlie.

Efter the myndis of the Astronomouris,
  And, speciallie, the Auctour of the Speir,
And uther divers gret Philosophouris,
  The quantytie of the Eirth circuleir

Is fyftie thousand liggis, withouttin weir,
Sevin houndreth, and fyftie, and no mo,
Devyding, aye, ane lig in mylis two :

And everilk myle in aucht stagis devyde ;
    Ilk staige, ane hundrith pais, twenty, and fyve ;
Ane pais, fyve fute, quha wald tham weil decyde ;
    Ane fute, four palmes, geve I can rycht discryve ;
    Ane palme, four inche ; and, quha sa wald belyve
The circuit of the Eirth passe round aboute,
Man be considderit on this wyse, but doute.

Suppone that thare war none impediment,
    Bot that the eirth but perrell wer, and plane,
Syne, that the persoun wer rycht deligent,
    And yeid, ilk day, ten liggis in certane,
    He mycht pas round aboute, and cum agane,
In four yeris, saxtene oulkis, and dayis two :
Go, reid the Auctour, and thow sall fynd it so.

THE DEVISIOUN OF THE EIRTH.

THEN, certanlye, scho tuke me be the hand,
    And said, My sone, cum on thy wayis with me.
And so scho gart me cleirly understand
    How that the Eirth trypartit wes in thre ;
    In Affrik, Europe, and Asie,
Efter the myndis of the Cosmographouris,
That is to say, the Warldis descriptouris :

First, Asia contenis in the Orient,
   And is weill more than baith the uther twane;
Affrik, and Europe, in the Occident,
   And ar devydit be ane see, certane,
   And that is callit the See Mediterrane,
Quhilk at the strait of Marrok hes entre,
That is betuix Spanye and Barbarie.

Towart the southwest lyis Africa;
   And, in the northwest, Europa doith stand;
And all the eist contenis Asia:
   On this wyse is devydit the ferme land.
   It war mekle to me, to tak on hand
Thir regionis to declare in speciall;
Yit, sall I schaw thair names in generall.

In mony divers famous Regionis
   Is devydit this part of Asia,
Weill plenischit with cieteis, towris, and townis:
   The gret Ynde, and Mesopotamia,
   Penthapolis, Egypt, and Syria,
Capadocia, Seres, and Armenye,
Babilone, Caldea, Parth, and Arabye:

Sidone, Judea, and Palestina,
   Over Scithia, Tyir, and Galilie,
Hiberia, Bactria, and Philestina,
   Hircanea, Compagena, and Samarie.
   In lytill Asia standis Galathie,
Pamphilia, Isauria, and Leid,
Rhegia, Arethusa, Assyria, and Meid.

Secundlie, we considderit Africa,
   With mony fructfull famous regioun,
As Ethiope, and Tripolitana,
   Zewges, quhare standis the tryumphant toun
   Of nobyll Carthage, that ciete of renoun ;
Garamantes, Nadabar, Libia,
Getulia, and Mauritania,

Fezensis, Numidie, and Thingitane :
   Of Affrick, thir ar the principall.
Than Europe we considderit, in certane,
   Quhose Regionis schortlie rehers I sall.
   Foure principallis I fynd abone thame all,
Quhilkis ar Spanye, Italie, and France,
Quhose subregionis wer mekle tyll avance :

Nether Scithia, Trace, and Carmanie,
   Thusia, Histria, and Pannonia,
Denmark, Gotland, Grunland, and Almanie,
   Pole, Hungarie, Boeme, Norica, Rethia,
   Teutonia, and mony divers ma.
And was in foure devidit Italie,
Tuskane, Ethruria, Naiplis, and Champanye

And subdevydit sindry uther wayis,
   As Lumbardie, Veneis, and uther ma,
Calaber, Romanie, and Janewayis.
   In Grece, Epyrus, and Dalmatica,
   Tessalie, Athica, and Illyria,
Achaya, Boeotia, and Macedone,
Archadie, Pierie, and Lacedemone.

And France we sawe devydit in to three,
   Belgica, Rethia, and Aquitane,
And subdevydit in Flanderis, Picardie,
   Normandie, Gasconye, Burguinye, and Bretane,
   And utheris divers Duchereis, in certane,
The quhilks wer too lang for to declair ;
Quharefor, of thame as now I speik na mair.

In Spanye lyis Castelye and Arragone,
   Naverne, Galice, Portingall, and Granate.
Than sawe we famous Ylis mony one,
   Quhilks in the Occiane sey was situate.
   Thame to discryve my wyt wes desolate ;
Of Cosmographie I am nocht expart,
For I did never study in that art ;

Yit I sall sum of thair names declare,
   As Madagascar, Gaides, and Taprobane,
And utheris divers Ylis gude and fair,
   Situate into the See Mediterrane ;
   As Cyper, Candie, Corsica, and Sardane,
Crete, Abidos, Thoes, Cecilia,
Tapsone, Eolie, and mony uther ma.

Quho wald at lenth heir the discriptioun
   Of everilk Yle, als weill as the ferme land,
And properteis of everilk Regioun,
   To study, and to reid, man tak on hand,
   And the attentike werkis understand,
Of Plinius, and worthy Ptholomie,
Quhilkis war expart in to Cosmographie :

Thare sall thay fynd the names and properteis
　　Of every Yle, and of ilke Regioun.
Than I inquirit of eirthly Paradyce,
　　Of the quhilk Adam tynt possessioun.
　　Than schew scho me the situatioun
Of that precelland place, full of delyte,
Quhose properteis wer lang for to indyte.

OF PARADYCE.

THIS Paradyce, of all plesouris repleit,
　　Situate I saw in to the Orient.
That glorious gairth of every flouris did fleit :
　　The lusty lillyis, the rosis redolent,
　　Fresche holesum fructis indeficient,
Baith herbe and tree, thare growis ever grene,
Throw vertew of the temperat air serene.

The sweit hailsum arromatyke odouris,
　　Proceidyng frome the herbis medicinall,
The hevinlie hewis of the fragrant flouris,
　　It was ane sycht wounder celestiall.
　　The perfectioun to schaw, in speciall,
And joyis, of that Regioun Devyne,
Of mankynd it exceidis the ingyne :

And als so hie, in situatioun,
　　Surmountyng the myd Regioun of the air,
Quhare no maner of perturbatioun
　　Of wodder may ascend so hie as thare :

Four fludis flowyng from ane fontane fair,
As Tygris, Ganges, Euphrates, and Nyle,
Quhilk, in the cist, transcurris mony ane myle.

The countre closit is aboute, full rycht,
    With wallis hie, of hote and birnyng fyre,
And straitly kepit be ane Angell brycht,
    Sen the departyng of Adam, our grandschyre ;
    Quhilk, throw his cryme, incurrit Goddis yre,
And of that place tynte the possessioun,
Baith frome hym self and his successioun.

Quhen this lufesum lady Remembrance
    All this foresaid had gart me understand,
I prayit hir, of hir benevolence,
    To schaw to me the countre of Scotland.
    Weill, Sonne, scho said, that sall I tak on hand.
So, suddanlie scho brocht me, in certane,
Evin juste abone the braid Yle of Bretane,

Quhilk standis northwest, in the Occiane see,
    And devydit in famous regionis two,
The south part, Ingland, ane full ryche countre,
    Scotland, be north, with mony Ylis mo.
    Be west Ingland, Yreland doith stand, also,
Quhose properteis I wyll nocht tak on hand
To schaw at lenth, bot only of Scotland.

OF THE REALME OF SCOTLAND.

QUHILK, efter my sempyll intendiment,
   And as Remembrance did to me report,
I sall declare the suith and verrayment,
   As I best can, and in to termis schort.
     Quharfor, effecteouslie I yow exhorte,
Quhowbeit my wrytting be nocht tyll avance,
Yit, quhare I faill, excuse myne ignorance.

Quhen that I had ouersene this Regioun,
   The quhilk, of nature, is boith gude and fair,
I did propone ane lytill questioun,
   Beseikand hir the same for to declare.
     Quhat is the cause our boundis bene so bair?
Quod I : or quhat dois mufe our miserie?
Or quhareof dois proceid our povertie?

For, throw the supporte of your hie prudence,
   Of Scotland I persave the properteis,
And als considderis, be experience,
   Of this countre the gret commoditeis :
     First, the haboundance of fyschis in our seis,
And fructuall montanis for our bestiall,
And, for our cornis, mony lusty vaill ;

The ryche ryveris, pleasand and profitabyll ;
   The lustie lochis, with fysche of sindry kyndis :
Huntyng, halkyng. for nobyllis convenabyll ;
   Forestis full of da, ra, hartis, and hyndis ;

VOL. I.   C

The fresche fontanis, quhose holesum cristal strandis
Refreschis so the fair fluriste grene medis,
So laik we no thyng that to Nature nedis,

Of every metal, we have the ryche mynis,
    Baith gold, sylver, and stonis precious,
Howbeit we want the spyces and the wynis,
    Or uther strange fructis delycious,
    We have als gude, and more neidfull for us.
Meit, drynk, fyre, clathis, thar mycht be gart abound
Quhilkis als is nocht in al the Mapamound :

More fairer peple, nor of gretar ingyne,
    Nor of more strenth, gret dedis tyll indure.
Quharefor, I pray yow that ye wald defyne
    The principall cause quharefor we ar so pure ;
    For I marvell gretlie, I yow assure,
Considderand the peple, and the ground,
That ryches suld nocht in this Realme redound.

My Sonne, scho said, be my discretioun,
    I sall mak answeir, as I understand.
I say to thee, under confessioun,
    The falt is nocht, I dar weill tak on hand,
    Nother in to the peple nor the land.
As for the land, it lakis na uther thyng
Bot laubour, and the pepyllis governyng.

Than quharein lyis our inprosperitie ?
    Quod I, I pray yow hartfullie, Madame,
Ye wald declare to me the veritie ;
    Or quho sall beir, of our barrat the blame ?

For, be my treuth, to see I thynk gret schame
So plesand peple, and so fair ane land,
And so few verteous dedis tane on hand.

Quod scho, I sall, efter my jugement,
　Declare sum causis, in to generall,
And, in to termes schorte, schaw myne intent ;
　And syne, transcend more in to speciall.
　So, this is myne conclusioun fynall,
Wantyng of justice, polycie, and peace,
Ar cause of thir unhappynes, allace !

It is deficill ryches tyll incres,
　Quhare Polycie makith no residence ;
And Polieye may never have entres,
　Bot quhare that Justice dois delygence
　To puneis quhare thare may be found offence.
Justice may nocht have dominatioun,
But quhare Peace makis habitatioun.

Quhat is the cause, that wald I understand,
　That we sulde want Justice and Polycie
More than dois France, Italie, or Ingland ?
　Madame, quod I, schaw me the veritie ;
　Sen we have lawis in to this countre,
Quhy want we lawis exercitioun,
Quho suld put justice tyll exccutioun ?

Quharein dois stand our principall remeid,
　Or quha may mak mendis of this myscheif ?
Quod scho, I fynd the falt in to the heid ;
　For thay, in quhome dois ly our hole releif,

I fynd thame rute and grund of all our greif;
For, quhen the heidis ar nocht delygent,
The membris man, on neid, be negligent.

So, I conclude, the causis principall
    Of all the trubyll of this Natioun
Are in to Prencis, in to speciall,
    The quhilkis hes the gubernatioun,
    And of the peple dominatioun;
Quhose contynewall exerscitioun
Sulde be in justice executioun.

For, quhen the sleuthful hird dois sloug and sleip,
    Taking no cure, in kepyng of his floke,
Quho wyll go sers amang sic heirdis scheip,
    May habyll fynd mony pure scabbit crok,
    And goyng wyll at large, withouttin lok;
Than Lupis cumis, and Lowrance, in ane lyng,
And dois, but reuth, the sely scheip dounthryng.

Bot the gude hird, walkryfe, and delygent,
    Doith so, that all his flokis are rewlit rycht,
To quhose quhissill all are obedient;
    And, geve the wolfis cumis, daye or nycht,
    Thame to devore, than are they put to flycht,
Houndit, and slane be thair weill dantit doggis;
So are thay sure, baith yowis, lambis, and hoggis.

So, I conclude, that, throw the negligence
    Of our infatuate heidis insolent,
Is cause of all this Realmis indigence,
    Quhilkis, in justice, hes nocht bene delygent,

Bot to gude counsall inobedient,
Havand small ee unto the commoun weill,
Bot to thair singulare profect everilk deill.

For, quhen thir wolfis, be oppressioun,
   The pure peple, but piete, doith oppres;
Than sulde the prencis mak punisioun,
   And cause thai rebauldis for to mak redres,
   That ryches mycht be policye incres:
Bot rycht difficill is to mak remeid,
Quhen that the falt is so in to the heid.

COMPLAYNT OF THE COMMOUNWEILL
OF SCOTLAND.

AND thus as we wer talking, to and fro,
   We saw a bousteous berne cum ouir the bent,
Bot hors, on fute, als fast as he mycht go,
   Quhose rayment wes all raggit, revin, and rent;
   With visage leyne, as he had fastit Lent:
And fordwart fast, his wayis he did advance,
With ane rycht melancolious countynance:

With scrip on hip, and pyikstaff in his hand,
   As he had purposit to passe fra hame.
Quod I, Gude man, I wald faine understand,
   Geve that ye plesit, to wyt quhat wer your name?
   Quod he, My Sonne, of that I think gret schame:
Bot, sen thow wald of my name have ane feill,
Forsuith, thay call me John the Commounweill.

Schir Commounweill, quho hes yow so disgysit?
    Quod I : or quhat makis yow so miserabyll?
I have marvell to se yow so supprysit,
    The quhilk that I have sene so honorabyll.
    To all the warld ye have bene profitabyll,
And weill honourit in everilk natioun :
How happinnis, now, your tribulatioun?

Allace ! quod he, thow seis how it dois stand
    With me, and quhow I am disherisit
Of all my grace, and mon pass of Scotland,
    And go, afore quhare I was cherisit.
    Remane I heir, I am bot perysit ;
For thare is few to me that takis tent,
That garris me go so raggit, rewin, and rent :

My tender freindis are, all, put to the flycht ;
    For Policye is fled agane in France.
My syster, Justice, almaist haith tynt hir sycht,
    That scho can nocht hald evinly the ballance.
    Plane wrang is clene capitane of ordinance,
The quhilk debarris laute and reasoun ;
And small remeid is found for open treasoun.

In to the South, allace ! I was neir slane ;
    Ouer all the land I culd fynd no releif :
Almoist betuix the Mers and Lowmabane
    I culde nocht knaw ane leill man be ane theif.
    To schaw thair reif, thift, murthour, and mischeif,
And vicious workis, it wald infect the air ;
And als langsum to me, for tyll declair.

In to the Hieland, I could fynd no remeid,
  Bot suddantlie I wes put to exile :
Thai sweir swyngeoris thay tuke of me non heid,
  Nor amangs thame lat me remaue ane quhyle.
  Als, in the Oute Ylis, and in Argyle,
Unthrift, sweirnes, falset, povertie, and stryfe
Pat Policye in dainger of hir lyfe.

In the Lawland I come to seik refuge,
  And purposit thare to mak my residence ;
Bot Singulare profeit gart me soune disluge,
  And did me gret injuries and offence,
  And said to me, Swyith, harlote, hy thee hence ;
And in this countre see thow tak no curis,
So lang as my auctoritie induris.

And now I may mak no langer debait ;
  Nor I wate nocht quhome to I suld me mene ;
For I have socht throw all the Spirituall stait,
  Quhilkis tuke na compt for to heir me complene :
  Thair officiaris, thay held me at disdene ;
For Symonie, he rewlis up all that rowte ;
And Covatyce, that Carle, gart bar me oute.

Pryde haith chaist far frome thame Humilitie ;
  Devotioun is fled unto the Freris ;
Sensuale plesour hes baneist Chaistitie ;
  Lordis of Religioun, thay go lyke Seculeris,
  Taking more compt in tellyng thair deneris,
Nor thai do of thair constitutioun,
Thus are thay blyndit be ambitioun.

Our gentyll men are all degenerat ;
   Liberalitie and Lawte boith ar lost ;
And Cowardyce with Lordis is laureat ;
   And knychtlie Curage, turnit in brag and boast ;
   The Civele weir misgydis everilk oist.
Thare is nocht ellis bot ilk man for hym self,
That garris me go, thus baneist lyke ane elf.

Tharefor, adew : I may no langer tarye.
   Fair weill, quod I, and with sanct Jhone to borrow.
Bot, wyt ye weill, my hart was wounder sarye,
   Quhen Comounweill so sopit was in sorrow ;
   Yit, efter the nycht, cumis the glaid morrow.
Quharefor, I pray yow, schaw me, in certane,
Quhen that ye purpose for to cum agane.

That questioun, it sall be sone decydit,
   Quod he, thare sall na Scot have confortyng
Of me, tyll that I see the countre gydit
   Be wysedome of ane gude auld prudent Kyng,
   Quhilk sall delyte hym maist, abone all thyng,
To put Justice tyll executioun,
And on strang traitouris mak punitioun.

Als yit to thee I say ane uther thyng :
   I see rycht weill, that proverbe is full trew,
Wo to the realme that hes ouer young ane King.
   With that he turnit his bak, and said, Adew.
   Ouer firth and fell rycht fast fra me he flew,
Quhose departyng to me was displesand.
With that, Remembrance tuk me be the hand

And sone, me thocht, scho brocht me to the roche,
    And to the cove, quhare I began to sleip.
With that, one schip did spedalye approche,
    Full plesandlie saling apone the deip,
    And, syne, did slake hir salis, and gan to creip,
Towart the land, anent quhare that I lay:
Bot, wyt ye weill, I gat ane fellown fray.

All hir cannounis sche leit craik of at onis:
    Down schuke the stremaris frome the topcastell;
Thay sparit nocht the poulder, nor the stonis;
    Thay schot thair boltis, and doun thair ankeris fell;
    The Marenaris, thay did so youte and yell,
That haistalie I stert out of my Dreme,
Half in ane fray, and spedalie past hame.

And lychtlie dynit, with lyste and appetyte,
    Syne efter, past in tyll ane Oratore,
And take my pen, and thare began to wryte
    All the Visioun that I have schawin afore:
    Schir, of my Dreme, as now thou gettis no more.
Bot I beseik God for to send thee grace,
To rewle thy realme in unitie, and peace.

ANE EXHORTATIOUN TO THE KYNGIS GRACE.

Schir, sen that God, of his preordinance,
Haith grantit thee to have the governance
 Of his peple, and create thee ane Kyng;
Faill nocht to prent in thy rememberance,
That he wyll nocht excuse thyne ignorance,
 Geve thow be rekles, in thy governyng:
 Quharefor, dress thee, above all uther thyng,
Of his lawis to keip the observance,
 And thou schaip lang in Royaltie to ryng.

Thank Hym that hes commandit dame Nature
To prent thee of so plesand portrature:
 Hir gyftis may be cleirly on thee knawin.
Tyll dame Fortune thow nedis no procurature;
For scho hes lairglie kyith on thee hir cure,
 Hir gratytude sche hes unto thee schawin:
 And, sen that thow mon scheir as thow hes sawin,
Have all thy hope in God, thy Creature,
 And aske Hym grace, that thow may be his awin.

And syne, considder thy vocatioun,
That for to have the gubernatioun
 Of this Kynrik, thow art predestinate.

Thow may weill wyt, be trew narratioun,
Quhat sorrow, and quhat trubulatioun,
  Haith bene in this pure realme infortunate.
  Now conforte thame that hes bene desolate;
And of thy peple have compassioun,
  Sen thow be God art so preordinate.

Tak manlie curage, and leif thyne insolence,
And use counsale of nobyll dame Prudence;
  Founde thee firmelie on Faith, and Fortytude;
Drawe to thy courte Justice and Temperance;
And to the Commounweill have attendance.
  And also, I beseik thy Celsitude,
  Hait vicious men, and lufe thame that ar gude;
And ilke flattrer thou fleme frome thy presence,
  And fals reporte out of thy Courte exclude.

Do equale justice boith to gret and small;
And be exampyll to thy peple all,
  Exercing verteous deidis honorabyll.
Be nocht ane wrache, for oucht that may befall:
To that unhappy vice and thow be thrall,
  Tyll all men thow sall be abhominabyll.
  Kyngis nor knychtis ar never convenabyll
To rewle peple, be thay nocht lyberall:
  Was never yit na wrache to honour habyll.

And tak exempyll of the wracheit endyng
Quhilk maid Mydas of Trace, the mychtie king,
  That to his Goddis maid invocatioun
Throw gredines, that all substanciall thing
That ever he twycheit suld turne, but tarying,

In to fyne gold : he gat his supplicatioun ;
All that he twychit, but delatioun,
Turnit in gold, boith meit, drynk, and clethyng ;
And deit of hounger, but recreatioun.

Als, I beseik thy Majestie serene,
Frome lychorie thow keip thy body clene ;
Taist never that intoxicat poysoun :
Frome that unhappy sensuall syn abstene,
Tyll that thow get ane lusty, plesand Quene :
Than tak thy plesour, with my benesoun.
Tak tent how prydful Tarquyne tynt his croun,
For the deforsyng of Lucres, the schene,
And was depryvit, and baneist Romis toun.

And, in dispyit of his lycherous levyng,
The Romanis wald be subject to no kyng,
Mony lang yeir, as storyis doith recorde,
Tyll Julyus, throw verteous governyng
And princelie curage, gane on thame to ryng,
And, chosin of Romanis, Empriour and lord.
Quharfor, my Soverane, in to thy mynd remord,
That vicious lyfe makis oft ane evyll endyng,
Without it be throw speciall grace restord.

And geve thow wald thy fame, and honour, grew,
Use counsall of thy prudent Lordis trew,
And see thow nocht presumpteouslie pretend
Thy awin perticulare weill for tyll ensew :
Wyrk with counsall, so sall thou never rew.
Remember of thy freindis the fatell end,
Quhilks to gude counsall wald not condescend,

Tyll bitter deith, allace! did thame persew.
　Frome sic unhap, I pray God thee defend!

And fynalie, remember thow mon dee,
And suddanlie pass of this mortall see:
　And art nocht sicker of thy lyfe two houris;
Sen thare is none frome that sentence may flee,
Kyng, Quene, or Knycht, of lawe estait, nor hie,
　Bot all mon thole of Deith the bitter schouris:
　Quhar bene thay gone, thir Papis and Empriouris?
Bene thay nocht dede? so sall it fair on thee:
　Is no remeid, strenth, ryches, nor honouris.

　　　　And so, for conclusioun,
　　　　Mak our provisioun,
　　　　To get the infusioun
　　　　　　　　Of His hie grace:
　　　　Quhilk bled, with effusioun,
　　　　With scorne and derisioun,
　　　　And deit, with confusion,
　　　　　　　　Confirmand our peace.　AMEN!

THE COMPLAYNT

OF SCHIR DAVID LYNDESAY TO THE KINGIS GRACE.

Schir, I beseik thyne Excellence,
Heir my Complaynt with pacience :
My dolent hart dois me constrane
Of my infortune to complane,
Quhowbeit I stand in gret dowtance
Quhome I sall wyte of my mischance ;
Quhidder Saturnis creueltie,
Ryngand in my Natyvitie,
Be bad aspect, quhilk wyrkis vengeance ;
Or utheris hevinlye influence :
Or geve I be predestinate,
In Courte, to be infortunate,
Quhilk hes so lang in servyce bene,
Contynewallie with Kyng and Quene,
And enterit to thy Majestie
The day of thy Natyvitie :
Quharethrow my freindis bene eschamit,
And with my fais I am defamit,
Seand that I am nocht regardit,
Nor with my brether, in Courte rewardit ;

Blamand my sleuthfull neclygence,
That seikis nocht sum recompence ;
Quhen divers men dois me demand,
Quhy gettis thow nocht sum peis of land,
Als weill as uther men hes gottin ?
Than wys I to be dede, and rottin,
With sic extreme discomfortyng,
That I can mak no answeryng.
I wald sum wyse man did me teche
Quhidder that I suld flatter, or fleche :
I will nocht flyte, that I conclude,
For crabyng of thy Celsitude ;
And to flatter I am defamit :
Want I reward, then am I schamit.
Bot I hope thow sall do als weill
As did the Father of fameill,
Of quhome Christ makis mentioun,
Quhilk, for ane certane pensioun,
Feit men to wyrk in his wyne-yaird,
But quho come last gat first rewaird,
Quharethrow the first men wer displesit :
Bot he thame prudentlie amesit ;
For, thocht the last men first wer servit,
Yit gat the first that thay deservit.
So, am I sure thy Majestie
Sall anis rewarde me, or I de,
And rub the ruste off my ingyne,
Quhilk bene, for langour, lyke to tyne.
Althocht I beir nocht lyke ane baird,
Lang servyce yarnis ay rewaird.
I can nocht blame thyne Excellence,

That I so lang want recompence.
Had I solistit, like the laif,
My rewarde had nocht bene to craif;
Bot now I may weill understand,
Ane dum man yit wan never land,
And, in the court, men gettis na thyng
Withoute inopportune askyng.
Allace! my sleuth and schamefulnes,
Debarrit fra me all gredynes.
Gredie men, that ar delygent,
Rycht oft obtenis thair intent,
And failyeis nocht to conqueis landis,
And namelye, at young Prencis handis.
But I tuke never non uther cure,
In speciall, bot for thy plesour.
Bot now I am na mair dispaird,
Bot I sall get Princely rewaird ;
The quhilk, to me, sall be mair glore
Nor thame thow did reward afore.
Quhen men dois aske ocht at ane kyng,
Sulde aske his grace ane nobyll thyng,
To his Excellence honorabyll,
And to the asker proffitabyll.
Thocht I be, in my askyng, lidder,
I praye thy Grace for to considder ;
Thow hes maid baith lordis and lairdis,
And hes gevin mony ryche rewardis
To thame that was full far to seik,
Quhen I lay nychtlie be thy cheik.

    I tak the Quenis Grace, thy mother,
My Lord Chancelare, and mony uther,

Thy Nowreis, and thy auld Maistres,
I tak thame all to beir wytnes;
Auld Willie Dillie, wer he on lyve,
My lyfe full weill he could discryve:
Quhow, as ane chapman beris his pak,
I bure thy Grace upon my bak,
And sumtymes, strydlingis on my nek,
Dansand with mony bend and bek.
The first sillabis that thow did mute
Was PA, DA LYN, upon the lute
Than playit I twenty spryngis, perqueir,
Quhilk wes gret piete for to heir.
Fra play thow leit me never rest,
Bot Gynkartoun thow lufit ay best;
And ay, quhen thow come frome the scule,
Than I behuffit to play the fule:
As I at lenth, in to my Dreme,
My sindry servyce did expreme.
Thocht it bene better, as sayis the wyse,
Hape to the court nor gude servyce,
I wate thow luffit me better, than,
Nor, now, sum wyfe dois hir gude man.
Than men tyll uther did recorde,
Said Lyndesay wald be maid ane lorde:
Thow hes maid lordis, Schir, be Sanct Geill,
Of sum that hes nocht servit so weill.

　　To yow, my Lordis, that standis by,
I sall you schaw the causis quhy:
Geve ye lyst tary, I sall tell,
Quhow my infortune first befell;
I prayit daylie, on my knee,

My young maister that I mycht see,
Of eild, in his Estait Royall,
Havand power imperyall :
Than traistit I without demand,
To be promovit, to sum land.
Bot my askyng, I gat ouer soun,
Because ane clips fell in the mone,
The quhilk all Scotland maid on steir,
Than did my purpose ryn arreir,
The quhilk war langsum to declare ;
And als my hart is wounder sare,
Quhen I have in remembrance
The suddand cheange, to my myschance.
  The Kyng was bot twelf yeris of aige,
Quhen new rewlaris come, in thair raige,
For Commounweill makand no cair,
Bot for thair proffeit singulair.
Imprudentlie, lyk wytles fuilis,
Thay tuke that young Prince frome the scuilis,
Quhare he, under obedience,
Was lernand vertew, and science,
And haistelie platt in his hand
The governance of all Scotland ;
As quho wald, in ane stormye blast,
Quhen marinaris bene all agast
Throw dainger of the seis raige,
Wad tak ane chylde of tender aige,
Quhilk never had bene on the sey,
And to his biddyng all obey,
Gevyng hym haill the governall
Of schip, marchand, and marinall,

For dreid of rockis and foreland,
To put the ruther in his hand :
Without Goddis grace, is no refuge :
Geve thare be dainger, ye may juge.
I gyf thame to the Devyll of hell,
Quhilk first devysit that counsell,
I wyll nocht say, that it was treassoun ;
Bot I dar sweir, it was no reassoun.
I pray God, lat me never se ryng,
In to this realme, so young ane Kyng.

    I may nocht tary to decyd it,
Quhow than the Court, ane quhyle, was gydit
Be thame, that peirtlye tuke on hand
To gyde the Kyng, and all Scotland :
And als langsum, for to declare
Thair facound flatteryng wordis fair.

    Schir, sum wald say, your Majestie
Sall now go to your lybertie ;
Ye sall to no man be coactit,
Nor to the scule no more subjectit :
We thynk thame verray naturall fulis,
That lernis ouir mekle at the sculis.
Schir, ye mon leir to ryn ane speir,
And gyde yow lyke ane man of weir ;
For we sall put sic men aboute yow,
That all the warld and mo sall doute yow.
Than, to his Grace, they put ane gaird,
Quhilk haistelie gat thair rewaird.
Ilk man, eftir thair qualitie,
Thay did solyst his Majestie.
Sum gart hym raiffell at the rakkat ;

Sum harld hym to the hurly hakkat ;
And sum, to schaw thair courtlie corsis,
Wald ryid to Leith, and ryn thair horsis,
And wychtlie wallope ouer the sandis :
Yea nother spairit spurris, nor wandis ;
Castand galmoundis, with bendis and beckis,
For wantones, sum brak thair neckis.
Thare was no play bot cartis and dyce :
And ay Schir Flatterie bure the pryce ;
Roundand and rowkand, ane tyll uther,
Tak thow my part, quod he, my bruther,
And mak betuix us sicker bandis,
Quhen ocht sall vaik, amangs our handis,
That ilk man stand to help his fallow.
I hald thareto, man, be Alhallow,
Swa thou fysche nocht within my boundis.
That sall I nocht, be Goddis woundis,
Quod he, bot eirar tak thy part.
Swa sall I thyne be Goddis hart ;
And geve the Thesaurair be our friend,
Than sall we get baith tak, and teind.
Tak he our part, than quha dar wrang us ?
Bot we sall part the pelf amang us :
Bot haist us, quhill the Kyng is young,
And lat ilk man keip weill ane toung,
And in ilk quarter have ane spye
Us tyll adverteis haistelie,
Quhen ony casualiteis
Sall happin in tyll our countreis :
Lat us mak sure provisioun,
Or he cum to discretioun.
No more he wate nor dois ane Sanct,

Quhat thyng it bene to have, or want :
So, or he be of perfyte aige,
We sall be sicker of our waige ;
And syne, lat ilk ane carle craif uther ;
That mouth speik mair, quod he, my brother.
For God, nor I rax in ane raipe,
Thow mycht geve counsale to the Pape.
Thus lauborit thay within few yeiris,
That thay become no pagis peiris,
Swa haistelye thay maid ane hand :
Sum gadderit gold, sum conqueist land.
Schir, sum wald say, be Sanct Dionyce
Geve me sum fat benefyce,
And all the proffet ye sall have ;
Geve me the name, tak yow the lave :
Bot, be his bowis war weill cumit hame,
To mak servyce, he wald thynk schame ;
Syne slyp awaye, withouttin more,
Quhen he had gottin that he sang fore.
    Me thocht it was ane pieteous thyng,
To se that fair, young, tender Kyng,
Of quhome thir gallandis stude no awe,
To play with hym, pluke at the crawe.
Thay become ryche, I yow assure,
Bot aye the Prence remanit pure.
Thare wes few of that garnisoun
That lernit hym ane gude lessoun ;
Bot sum to crak, and sum to clatter,
Sum maid the fule, and sum did flatter.
Quod ane, The Devyll stik me with ane knyfe,
  Bot Schir, I knaw ane maid in Fyfe,

Ane of the lusteiest wantoun lassis,
Quhare to, Schir, be Goddis blude, scho passis.
Hald thy toung, brother, quod ane uther,
I knaw ane fairar, be fyftene futher :
Schir, quhen ye pleis to Lythgow pass,
Thare sall ye se ane lustie lass.
Now trittyll, trattyll, trolylow.
Quod the thrid man ; thow dois bot mow,
Quhen his Grace cumis to fair Sterlyng,
Thare sall he se ane dayis derlyng.
Schir, quod the fourt, tak my counsall,
And go all to the hie bordall ;
Thare may we loupe at lybertie,
Withouttin ony gravitie.
    Thus every man said for hym self,
And did amangis thame part the pelf ;
Bot I, allace ! or ever I wyste,
Was trampit doun in to the duste,
With hevy charge, withouttin more,
Bot I wyst never yit quharefore ;
And haistellie, before my face,
Ane uther slippit in my place,
Quhilk rychelie gat his rewaird,
And stylit was the Ancient laird.
That tyme I mycht mak no defence,
Bot tuke, perforce, in pacience ;
Prayand to send thame ane myschance
That had the Court in governance,
The quhilkis aganis me did malyng,
Contrar the plesour of the Kyng ;
For weill I knew his Grace's mynd

Was ever to me trew and kynd;
And, contrar thair intentioun,
Gart pay me, weill, my pensioun.
Thocht I, ane quhyle, wantit presence,
He leit me have no indigence :
Quhen I durst nother peip nor luke,
Yit wald I hyde me in ane nuke,
To se those uncouth vaniteis,
Quhow thay, lyke ony beisy beis,
Did occupy thair goldin houris,
With help of thair new governouris.
Bot, my Complaynt for to compleit,
I gat the soure, and thay the sweit :
Als Jhone Makrery, the kyngis fule,
Gat dowbyll garmoundis agane the Yule,
Yit, in his maist tryumphant glore,
For his rewarde, gat the grandgore ;
Now in the court seindell he gois,
In dreid men stramp upon his tois ;
As I, that tyme, durst nocht be sene
In oppin court, for baith my eine.
    Allace ! I have no tyme to tary,
To schaw yow all the fery fary :
Quhow those that had the governance
Amangis thame selfis raisit variance ;
And quho maist to my skaith consentit,
Within few yeris full sore repentit,
Quhen thay could mak me no remeid ;
For they war harlit out be the heid,
And utheris tuke the governyng,
Weill wors than thay, in alkin thyng.

Thay lordis tuke no more regaird,
Bot quho mycht purches best rewaird :
Sum to thair friendis gat benefyceis,
And uther sum gat Byschopreis.
For every lord, as he thocht best,
Brocht in ane bird to fyll the nest ;
To be ane wacheman to his marrow,
Thay gan to draw at the cat harrow.
The proudest Prelatis of the Kirk
Was faine to hyde thame in the myrk,
That tyme, so failyeit wes thair sycht.
Sen syne thay may nocht thole the lycht
Of Christis trew Gospell to be sene,
So blyndit is thair corporall ene
With warldly lustis sensuall,
Takyng in Realmes the governall,
Baith gyding Court, and Sessioun,
Contrar to thair professioun ;
Quhareof I thynk thay sulde have schame,
Of spirituall preistis to tak the name.
For Esayas, in to his wark,
Callis thame lyke doggis that can nocht bark,
That callit ar preistis, and can nocht preche,
Nor Christis law to the pepill teche.
Geve for to preche bene thair professioun,
Quhy sulde thay mell with Court, or Sessioun,
Except it war in Spirituall thyngis ;
Referryng unto lordis and kyngis
Temporall causis to be decydit :
Geve thay thair spirituall office gydit,
Ilke man mycht say, thay did thair partis :

Bot, geve thay can play at the cairtis,
And mollet moylie on ane mule,
Thocht thay had never sene the scule,
Yit, at this day, als weill as than,
Wyll be maid sic ane spirituall man.
Prencis that sic prelatis promofis
Accompt thareof to geve behuflis,
Quhilk sall nocht pas but puneischement,
Without thay mend, and sore repent,
And, with dew ministratioun,
Wyrk efter thair vocatioun.
I wys that thyng quhilk wyll nocht be,
Thir perverst Prelatis ar so hie:
Frome tyme that thay bene callit Lordis,
Thay ar occasioun of discordis,
And lairglie wyll propynis hecht,
To gar ilk lord with uther fecht:
Geve for thair part it may availl,
Swa, to the purpose of my taill.
    That tyme, in court, rais gret debait,
And everilk lord did stryve for stait,
That all the realme mycht mak no reddyng,
Quhill on ilk side thare was blude scheddyng,
And feildit uther, in land and burgh,
At Lythgow, Melros, and Edinburgh.
Bot, to deplore I thynk greit paine
Of nobyll men that thare was slane,
And, als, langsum to be reportit
Of thame quhilk to the court resortit;
As tyrranis, tratouris, and transgressouris,
And commoun publict plaine oppressouris,

Men murdreisaris, and commoun theiffis,
In to that court gat all releiflis.
Thare was few lordis, in all thir landis,
Bot tyll new Regentis maid thair bandis.
Than rais ane reik, or ever I wyste,
The quhilk gart all thair bandis bryste:
Than thay allone quhilk had the gyding,
Thay culde nocht keip thair feit frome slyding;
Bot of thair lyflis thay had sic dreid,
That thay war faine tyll trott ouer Tweid.

Now, POTENT PRINCE, I say to thee,
I thank the Haly Trinitie,
That I have levit to se this daye,
That all that warld is went awaye,
And thow to no man art subjectit,
Nor to sic counsalouris coactit.
The foure gret Vertues cardinalis,
I see thame, with the principalis:
For Justice haldis hir sweird on hie,
With hir ballance of equitie,
And, in this realme, hes maid sic ordour,
Baith throw the Heland and the Bordour,
That Oppressioun and all his fallowis
Ar hangit heych apon the gallowis.
Dame Prudence hes thee be the heid,
And Temperance dois thy brydill leid;
I see dame Force mak assistance,
Berand thy targe of assurance;
And lusty lady Chaistitie
Hes baneist Sensualitie;

Dame Ryches takis on thee sic cure,
I pray God, that scho lang indure,
That Povertie dar nocht be sene
In to thy hous, for baith hir ene,
Bot fra thy Grace fled mony mylis,
Amangis the hountaris in the Ylis;
Dissimulance dar nocht schaw hir face,
Quhilk wount was to begyill thy Grace;
Foly is fled out of the toun,
Quhilk ay was contrair to ressoun:
Polycie and Peace begynnis to plant,
That verteous men can no thyng want;
And, as for sleuthfull idyll lownis,
Sall fetterit be in the gailyeownis:
Jhone Upeland bene full blyith, I trow,
Because the rysche bus kepis his kow;
Swa is thare nocht, I understand,
Withoute gude ordour in this land,
Except the Spiritualitie:
Prayand thy Grace thareto have ee,
Cause thame mak ministratioun
Conforme to thair vocatioun,
To preche with unfenyeit intentis,
And trewly use the Sacramentis,
Eftir Christis institutionis,
Levyng thair vaine traditiounis,
Quhilkis dois the syllie scheip illude,
Quhame for Christ Jesus sched his blude,
As superstitious pylgramagis,
Prayand to gravin ymagis,
Expres aganis the Lordis command.

I do thy Grace tyll understand,
Geve thow to mennis lawis assent,
Aganis the Lordis commandiment,
As Jeroboam, and mony mo,
Prencis of Israell also,
Assentaris to ydolatrie,
Quhilkis puncist war rycht pieteouslie,
And frome thair realmes wer rutit oute;
So sall thow be, withouttin doute,
Baith heir and hyne, withouttin more,
And want the everlestyng glore;
Bot, geve thow wyll thy hart inclyne,
And keip his blyssit law devyne,
As did the faithfull Patriarkis,
Boith in thair wordis, and thair warkis,
And as did mony faithfull kyngis
Of Israell, duryng thair ryngis,
As kyng David and Salomone,
Quhilkis ymagis wald suffer none
In thair ryche tempillis for to stand,
Because it was nocht Goddis command;
Bot, distroyit all ydolatrie,
As in the Scripture thow may see;
Quhose ryche rewarde was hevinly blys,
Quhilk sall be thyne, thow doand this.
    Sen thow hes chosin sic ane gaird,
Now am I sure to get rewaird;
And, sen thow art the rychest Kyng
That ever in this Realme did ryng,
Of gold, and stonis precious,
Maist prudent, and ingenious,

And hes thy honour done avance,
In Scotland, Ingland, and in France,
Be merciall deidis honourabyll,
And art tyll every vertew abyll,
I wat thy Grace wyll nocht misken me,
Bot thow wyll uther geve, or len me.
  Wald thy Grace len me, to ane day,
Of gold ane thousand pound, or tway,
And I sall fix, with gude intent,
Thy Grace ane daye of payment,
With seillit oblygatioun,
Under this protestatioun,
Quhen the Basse and the Yle of Maye
Beis sett vpon the Mont Senaye;
Quhen the Lowmound, besyde Falkland,
Beis lyftit to Northumberland;
Quhen kirkmen yairnis no dignitie,
Nor wyffis no soveranitie;
Wynter but frost, snaw, wynd, or rane;
Than sall I geve thy gold agane;
Or, I sall mak the payment
Efter the Daye of Jugement,
Within ane moneth, at the leist,
Quhen Sanct Peter sall mak ane feist
To all the fyscharis of Aberladye,
Swa thow have myne aquittance reddye;
Failyeand thareof, be Sanct Phillane,
Thy Grace gettis never ane grote agane.
  Geve thow be nocht content of this,
I man requeist the Kyng of blys,
That he to me have sum regaird,

And cause thy Grace me to rewaird :
For David, Kyng of Israell,
Quhilk was the gret Propheit Royall,
Sayis, God hes haill at his command
The hartis of Prencis in his hand :
Even as he lyste thame for to turne,
That mon thay do withoute sudgeorne ;
Sum tyll exault to dignitie,
And sum to depryve in povertie ;
Sum tyme of layid men to mak lordis,
And, sum tyme, lordis to bynd in cordis,
And thame alutterlye distroye,
As plesis God, that ryall roye.
For thow art bot ane instrument
To that gret Kyng, Omnipotent :
So, quhen plesis his Excellence,
Thy Grace sall mak me recompence ;
Or He sall cause me stand content
Of quiet lyfe, and sober rent,
And tak me, in my latter aige,
Unto my sempyll herytage,
And spend it that my eldaris woun,
As did Diogenes in his toun.
Of this COMPLAYNT, with mynd full meik,
Thy Grace's Answeir, Schir, I beseik.

QUOD LYNDESAY TO THE KING.

THE TESTAMENT AND COMPLAYNT

OF OUR SOVERANE LORDIS PAPYNGO,
KYNG JAMES THE FYFT,

QUHILK LYITH SORE WOUNDIT, AND MAY NOT DEE,
TYLL EVERY MAN HAVE HARD QUHAT SCHO SAYIS :
QUHAREFOR GENTYLL REDARIS, HAIST YOW, THAT
SCHO WER OUT OF PAINE.

THE PROLOG.

SUPPOSE I had ingyne Angelicall,
With sapience more than Salamonicall,
  I not quhat mater put in memorie ;
The Poeitis auld, in style heroycall,
In breve subtell termes rethoryeall,
  Of everlike mater, tragedie, and storie,
  So ornatlie, to thair heych laude and glorie,
Haith done indyte, quhose supreme sapience
Transcendith far the dull intellygence

Of Poeitis now, in tyll our vulgare toung :
For quhy? the bell of rethorick bene roung
  Be Chauceir, Goweir, and Lidgate laureate
Quho dar presume thir Poeitis tyll impnug,

Quhose sweit sentence throuch Albione bene sung?
  Or quho can now the workis countrafait
  Of Kennedie, with termes aureait?
Or of Dunbar, quhilk language had at large,
As may be sene in tyll his Goldin Targe?

Quintyn, Merser, Rowle, Henderson, Hay, and Holland,
Thocht thay be deid, thair libellis bene levand,
  Quhilkis to reheirs makeith redaris to rejose.
Allace! for one, quhilk lampe wes of this land,
Of Eloquence the flowand balmy strand,
  And in our Inglis rethorick, the rose,
  As of rubeis the charbunckle bene chose!
And, as Phebus dois Cynthia precell,
So Gawane Dowglas, Byschope of Dunkell,

Had, quhen he wes in to this land on lyve,
Abufe vulgare Poëitis prerogatyve,
  Boith in pratick and speculatioun.
I saye no more, gude Redaris may descryve
His worthy workis, in nowmer mo than fyve;
  And speciallye, the trew Translatioun
  Of Virgill, quhilk bene consolatioun
To cunnyng men, to knaw his gret ingyne,
Als weill in naturall science as devyne.

And, in the Courte, bene present, in thir dayis,
That ballattis brevis lustellie, and layis,
  Quhilkis tyll our Prince daylie thay do present.
Quho can say more than Schir James Inglis sayis,
In ballattis, farses, and in plesand playis;
  Bot Culrose hes his pen maid impotent.

Kyd, in cunnyng and pratick, rycht prudent;
And Stewarte, quhilk desyrith ane staitly style,
Full ornate werkis daylie dois compyle.

Stewart of Lorne wyll carpe rycht curiouslie;
Galbraith, Kynlouch, quhen thay lyst tham applie
    In to that art, ar craftie of ingyne.
Bot, now of lait, is starte up haistelie,
Ane cunnyng Clerk, quhilk wrytith craftelie,
    Ane plant of Poeitis, callit Ballendyne,
    Quhose ornat workis my wytt can nocht defyne:
Gett he in to the courte auctoritie,
He wyll precell Quintyn and Kennedie.

So, thocht I had ingyne, as I have none,
I watt nocht quhat to wryt, be sweit Sanct Jhone;
    For quhy? in all the garth of eloquence,
Is no thyng left, bot barrane stok and stone:
The poleit termes are pullit everilk one,
    Be thir fornamit Poeitis of prudence;
    And sen I fynd none uther new sentence,
I sall declare, or I depart yow fro,
The Complaynt of ane woundit Papingo.

Quharefor, because myne mater bene so rude
Of sentence, and of rethorike denude,
    To rurall folke, myne dyting bene directit,
Far flemit frome the sycht of men of gude;
For cunnyng men, I knaw, wyll soune conclude,
    It dowe no thyng, bot for to be dejectit:
    And, quhen I heir myne mater bene detractit,

Than sall I sweir, I maid it bot in mowis,
To landwart lassis, quhilks kepith kye and yowis.

THE COMPLAYNT OF THE PAPYNGO.

QUHO clymmis to hycht, perforce his feit mon faill :
  Expreme I sal that be Experience,
Geve that yow pleis to heir one pieteous taill ;
  How one fair Bird be fatall violence
  Devorit was, and mycht mak no defence
Contrare the deth, so failyeit naturall strenth,
As efter, I sall schaw yow at more lenth.

One Papyngo, rycht plesand and perfyte,
  Presentit was tyll our moist nobyll Kyng,
Of quhome his grace one lang tyme had delyte,
  More fair of forme, I wat, flew never on wyng ;
  This proper bird, he gave in governyng
To me, quhilk wes his simpyll servitoure,
On quhome, I did my dilygence and cure,

To lerne hir language artificiall,
  To play Platfute, and quhissill Fute before :
Bot, of hir inclynatioun naturall,
  Scho countrafaitit all fowlis, les and more :
  Of hir curage, scho wald, without my lore,
Syng lyke the merle, and crawe lyke to the cocke,
Pew lyke the gled, and chant lyke the laverock,

Bark lyk ane dog, and kekell lyke ane ka,
　Blait lyke ane hog, and buller lyke ane bull,
Gaill lyke ane goik, and greit quhen scho wes wa ;
　Clym on ane corde, syne lauch, and play the fule :
　Scho mycht have bene ane Menstrall agane Yule.
This blyssit bird wes to me so pleasand,
Quhare ever I fure, I bure hir on my hand.

And so befell, in tyll ane myrthfull morrow,
　In to my garth I past me to repose,
This bird and I, as we wer wount aforrow :
　Amang the flowris fresche, fragrant, and formose.
　My vitale spretis dewlie did rejose,
Quhen Phebus rose, and rave the cloudis sabyll,
Throuch brychtnes of his bemys amyabyll.

Without vapour was weill purificate
　The temperat air, soft, sober, and serene ;
The Erth, be Nature, so edificate
　With holsum herbis, blew, quhyte, reid and grene ;
　Quhilk elevate my spreitis from the splene.
That daye, Saturne, nor Mars, durst nocht appeir,
Nor Eole, of his cove he durst nocht steir.

That daye perforce behuffit to be fair,
　Be influence and cours celestiall :
No planete preisit for to perturbe the air ;
　For Mercurius, be movyng naturall,
　Exaltit wes, in to the throne tryumphall
Of his mansioun, unto the fyftene gre,
In his awin soverane signe of Virginee.

That daye did Phebus plesandlie depart
　　Frome Geminie, and enterit in Cancer ;
That daye Cupido did extend his dart ;
　　Venus, that daye, conjunit with Jupiter ;
　　That daye Neptunus hid hym, lyke one sker ;
That daye dame Nature, with gret besynes,
Fortherit Flora to keyth hir craftynes :

And retrograde wes Mars in Capricorne ;
　　And Cynthia in Sagittar asseisit ;
That daye dame Ceres, goddes of the corne,
　　Full joyfullie Johne Uponland appleisit ;
　　The bad aspect of Saturne wes appeisit,
That daye, be Juno, of Jupiter the joye,
Perturband spreitis causyng to hauld coye.

The sound of birdis surmontit all the skyis,
　　With melodie of notis musycall ;
The balmy droppis of dew Tytane updryis,
　　Hyngande upone the tender twystis small.
　　The hevinlie hew, and sound angelicall,
Sic perfyte plesoure prentit in myne hart,
That with gret pyne, frome thyne I mycht depart.

So, styll amang those herbis amyabyll,
　　I did remane one space, for my pastance :
Bot wardlie plesour bene so variabyll,
　　Myxit with sorrow, dreid, and inconstance,
　　That thare in tyll is no contynuance.
So mycht I saye, my schorte solace, allace !
Was drevin in dolour, in one lytill space.

For, in that garth, amang those fragrant flouris
  Walkyng allone, none bot my birde and I,
Unto the tyme that I had said myne Houris,
  This Bird I sett upon one branche me bye :
  But scho began to speill, rycht spedalie,
And in that tree scho did so heych ascende,
That, be no waye, I mycht hir apprehende.

Sweit Bird, said I, be war, mont nocht ouer hie ;
  Returne in tyme, perchance thy feit may failye ;
Thou art rycht fat, and nocht weill usit to flie ;
  The gredie gled, I dreid, scho thee assailye.
  I wyll, said scho, ascend, vailye quod vailye,
It is my kynd to clym ; aye to the hycht
Of fether and bone, I watt weill, I am wycht.

So, on the heychest lytill tender twyste,
  With wyng displayit, scho sat full wantounlie ;
Bot Boreas blew one blast, or ever scho wyst,
  Quhilk braik the branche, and blew hir suddantlie
  Doun to the ground with mony cairfull crye :
Upon ane stob scho lychtit on hir breist,
The blude ruschit out, and scho cryit for a preist.

God wat, gyff than my hart wes wo begone,
  To see that fowle flychter amang the flouris,
Quhilk, with gret murnyng, gan to mak hir mone :
  Now cumyng ar, said scho, the fatall houris ;
  Of bitter deth now mon I thole the schouris :
O dame Nature, I pray thee, of thy grace,
Len me layser to speik one lytill space,

For to complene my fait infortunate,
  And to dispone my geir, or I depart;
Sen of all conforte I am desolate,
  Allone, except the Deth, heir with his darte.
  With anfull cheir, reddy to peirs myne hart.
And, with that word, scho tuke one passioun,
Syne flatlyngis fell, and swappit in to swoun.

With sory hart, peirsit with compassioun,
  And salt teiris disteilyng frome myne eine,
To heir that birdis lamentatioun,
  I did approche, under ane hauthorne grene,
  Quhare I mycht heir and se, and be unsene;
And, quhen this bird had swounit twyse or thryse,
Scho gan to speik, saying on this wyse:

O! fals Fortune, quhy hes thou me begylit?
  This day, at morne, quho knew this cairfull cace?
Vaine hope, in thee my reasoun haith exilit,
  Havyng sic traist in to thy fenyeit face:
  That ever I wes brocht in to the court, allace!
Had I, in forrest, flowin amang my feris,
I mycht full weill have levit mony yeris.

Prudent counsell, allace! I did refuse,
  Agane reassoun usyng myne appetyte:
Ambitioun did so myne hart abuse,
  That Eolus had me in gret dispyte:
  Poeitis of me haith mater to indyte,
Quhilk clam so heych: and wo is me tharefore,
Nocht doutyng that the deth durste me devore.

This daye, at morne, my forme and feddrem fair,
 Abufe the proude pacocke, war precelland :
And now, one catyve carioun, full of cair,
 Baithand in blude, doun from my hart distelland !
 And in myne eir, the bell of deith bene knelland.
O fals warld ! fy on thy felycitie,
Thy pryde, avaryce, and immundicitie !

In thee, I see, no thyng bene permanent ;
 Of thy schort solace sorrow is the ende ;
Thy fals infortunate gyftis bene bot lent :
 This day ful proude, the morne no thyng to spend.
 O ye that doith pretende, aye till ascend,
My fatale end have in rememberance,
And yow defende, frome sic unhappy chance.

Quhydder that I wes strickin in extasie,
 Or throuch one stark imagynatioun,
Bot, it apperit, in myne fantasie,
 I hard this dolent Lamentatioun.
 Thus dullit in to desolatioun,
Me thocht this bird did breve, in hir maneir,
Hir Counsale to the Kyng, as ye sall heir.

THE FIRST EPYSTYLL OF THE PAPYNGO
DIRECT TILL OUR SOVERANE LORD
KYNG JAMES THE FYFT.

PREPOTENT PRINCE, peirles of pulchritude !
 Glore, honour, laude, tryumphe, and victorie,

Be to thy heych excellent Celsitude,
    With marciall dedis, dygn of memorie.
    Sen Atropus consumit haith my glorie,
And dolente deith, allace! mon us depart,
I leif to thee my trew unfenyeit hart;

To gydder with this cedull subsequent,
    With moist reverent recommendatioun:
I grant, thy Grace gettis mony one document,
    Be famous Fatheris predicatioun,
    With mony notabyll narratioun,
Be plesande Poeitis, in style heroycall,
Quhow thow suld gyde thy Seait Imperiall.

Sum doith deplore the gret calamiteis
    Of divers Realmes transmutatioun;
Sum picteouslie doith treat of Tragedeis,
    All for thy Graces informatioun:
    So I intend, but adulatioun,
In to my barbour rusticall indyte,
Among the reste, Schir, sum thyng for to wryte.

Soverane, consave this simpyll similytude
    Of officiaris, servyng thy Senyeorie:
Quho gydis thame weil gettis of thy Grace gret gude;
    Quho bene injuste, degradit ar of glorie,
    And canceillat out of thy memorie;
Providyng syne, more plesand in thair place:
Beleve rycht so, sall God do with thy Grace.

Considder weill, thow bene bot officiare
    And wassall to that Kyng incomparabyll:

Preis thou to pleis that puissant prince preclare,
   Thy ryche rewarde salbe inestimabyll,
   Exaultit heych, in glore interminabyll,
Abone Archangels, Virtues, Potestatis,
Plesandlie placit among the Principatis.

Of thy vertew, Poeitis perpetuallie
   Sall mak mentioun, unto the warld be endit :
So thow excers thyne office prudentlie,
   In hevin, and eirth, thy Grace salbe commendit :
   Quharefor afeir, that He be nocht offendit,
Quhilk hes exaultit thee to sic honour,
Of His people to be one Governour,

And, in the eirth, haith maid sic ordinance,
   Under thy feit all thyng terrestryall
Are subject to thy plesour, and pastance,
   Boith fowle, and fysche, and bestis pastorall,
   Men to thy servyce, and wemen, thay bene thrall :
Halkyng, hountyng, armes, and leiffull amour
Preordinat ar, be God, for thy plesour.

Maisteris of muscik to recreat thy spreit,
   With dantit voce, and plesande instrument.
Thus may thou be of all plesouris repleit,
   So in thyne office thou be deligent :
   Bot, be thou found sleuthfull, or negligent,
Or injuste, in thyne executioun,
Thou sall nocht faill devine puneissioun.

Quharefor, sen thou hes sic capacitie,
   To lerne to playe so plesandlie, and syng,

Ryde hors, ryn speris, with gret audacitie,
    Schute with hand-bow, crosbow, and culveryng,
    Among the rest, Schir, lerne to be ane Kyng:
Kyith on that craft, thy pregnant fresche ingyne,
Grantit to thee be influence Divine.

And sen the diffinitioun of ane Kyng
    Is, for to have of peple governance,
Addres thee first, abufe all uther thyng,
    Tyll put thy bodye tyll sic ordinance,
    That thyne vertew, thyne honour may avance:
For quhow suld Prencis governe gret regionis,
That can nocht dewlie gyde thair awin personis?

And, geve thy Grace wald leif rycht plesandlie,
    Call thy Counsale, and cast on thame the cure;
Thair juste decretis defend and fortyfie;
    But gude counsale, may no Prince lang indure:
    Wyrk with counsale, than sall thy work be sure:
Cheis thy Counsale of the most sapient,
Without regarde to blude, ryches, or rent.

Amang all uther pastyme, and plesour,
    Now, in thy adolescent yeris ying,
Wald thou, ilk day, study bot half one hour,
    The regiment of princelie governyng,
    To thy peple, it war ane plesande thyng;
Thare mycht thou fynd thyne awin vocatioun,
Quhow thou suld use thy sceptour, swerd, and croun.

The Cronecklis to knaw I thee exhorte,
    Quhilk may be myrrour to thy Majestie:

Thare sall thou fynd boith gude and evyll reporte
  Of everilk Prince, efter his qualytie :
  Thocht thay be dede, thair deidis sall nocht dee.
Traist weill thou salbe stylit, in that storie,
As thou deservis putt in memorie.

Requeist that Roye quhilk rent wes on the Rude,
  Thee to defend frome dedis of defame,
That no Poeite reporte of thee bot gude ;
  For Princes dayis induris bot one drame.
  Sen first kyng Fergus bure ane dyadame,
Thou art the last king, of fyve score and fyve;
And all ar dede, and none bot thou on lyve.

Of quhose number fyftie and fyve bene slane,
  And moist parte, in thair awin mysgovernance.
Quharefor, I thee bescik, my Soverane,
  Consydder of thair lyvis the circumstance,
  And quhen thou knawis the cause of thair mischance,
Of vertew than, exault thy saillis on hie,
Traistyng to chaip that faitale destanie.

Trait ilk trew Barroun, as he war thy brother,
  Quhilk mon at neid, thee and thy realme defende :
Quhen suddantlie one doith oppresse one uther,
  Lat Justice, myxit with mercy, thame amende.
  Have thou thair hartis, thou hes yneuch to spend;
And, be the contrar, thou are bot Kyng of Bone,
From tyme thyne hereis hartis bene from thee gone.

I have no laser, for to wryt at lenth
  Myne hole intent, untyll thyne Excellence,

Decressit so I am in wyt and strenth,
  My mortall wounde doith me sic violence.
  Peple of me maye have experience ;
Because, allace ! I wes inconnsolabyll,
Now mon I dee, ane catyve myserabyll.

THE SECUND EPISTYL OF THE PAPYNGO, DIRECTIT TO HIR BRETHER OF COURTE,

BRETHER of Court, with mynd precordiall
  To the gret God hartlie I commend yow :
Imprent my fall in your memoriall,
  Togidder with this cedull that I send yow.
  To preis ouer heych, I pray you not pretend yow :
The vaine ascens of court, quho wyll consydder,
Quho sittith moist hie, sal fynd the sait most slidder.

So ye, that now bene lansyng upe the ledder,
  Tak tent in tyme, fassinnyng your fingaris faste.
Quho clymith moist heych, moist dynt hes of the wedder,
  And leist defence aganis the bitter blast
  Of fals Fortune, quhilk takith never rest ;
Bot moste redouttit, daylie scho doun thryngis,
Nocht sparing Papis, Conquerouris, nor Kyngis.

Thocht ye be montit upe aboue the skyis,
  And hes boith kyng and court in governance,
Sum was als heych, quhilk now rycht lawly lyis,
  Complanyng sore the Courtis variance,
  Thair preterit tyme may be experience,

Quhilk, throuch vaine hope of courte, did clym so hie,
Syne wantit wyngis, quhen thay wend best to flie.

Sen ilke court bene untraist and transitorie,
 Changyng als oft as woddercok in wynd,
Sum maikand glaid, and uthir sum rycht sorie,
 Formaste this day, the morne may go behynd,
 Lat not vaine hope of court your reasone blynd :
Traist weill, sum men wyll gyf you laud, as lordis,
Quhilk wald be glaid to se you hang in cordis.

I durst declair the myserabilitie
 Of divers courtis, war nocht my tyme bene schort,
The dreidfull change, vain glore, and vilitie,
 The painfull plesour, as Pocitis doith reporte,
 Sum tyme in hope, sum tyme in disconforte ;
And how sum men dois spend thair youtheid haill
In court, syne endis in the hospytaill :

Quhow sum in court bene quyet counsalouris,
 Without regarde to commounweill, or kyngis,
Castyng thair cure, for to be Conquerouris ;
 And, quhen thay bene heych rasit, in thair ryngis,
 How change of court tham dulfully donn thringis ;
And, quhen thay bene from thair estait deposit,
Quhow mony of thair fall bene rycht rejosit :

And quhow fonde fenyeit fulis, and flatteraris
 For small servyce optenith gret rewardis ;
Pandaris, pykthankis, custronis, and clatteraris
 Loupis up, frome laddis, syne lychtis amang lardis ;
 Blasphematours, beggaris, and commoun bardis

Sum tyme, in courte, hes more auctoritie
Nor devote Doctouris in Divinitie ;

Quhow, in sum countre, bene barnes of Baliall,
    Full of dissimulit payntit flatterie,
Provocande, be intoxicat counsall,
    Prences tyll hurdome and tyll hasardrie :
    Quho dois in Prencis prent sic harlotrie,
I saye, for me, sic peirte provocatouris
Sulde puneist be abufe all strange tratouris.

Quhat travers, troubyll, and calamitie
    Haith bene, in courte, within thir houndreth yeris :
Quhat mortall changis, quhat miseritie !
    Quhat nobyll men bene brocht upon thair beiris !
    Traist weill, my ffreindis, follow ye mon your feiris :
So, sen in court bene no tranquillytie,
Sett nocht on it your hole felycite.

The courte changeith sumtyme, with sic outrage,
    That few or none may makyn resistance,
And spairis nocht the prince more than the paige,
    As weill apperith, be experience.
    The Duke of Rothesay mycht mak no defence,
Quhilk wes pertenand Roye of this regioun,
Bot, dulefully devorit in presoun.

Quhat dreid, quhat dolour had that nobyll kyng,
    Robert the Thride, frome tyme he knew the cace
Of his two Sonnis dolent departyng !
    Prince David deyid, and James captyve, allace !
    Tyll trew Scottis men, quhilk wes a cairful cace.

Thus, may ye knaw, the courte bene variand,
Quhen blude ryall the change may not ganestand.

Quho rang in court more hie and tryumphand
   Nor Duke Murdoke, quhill that his day indurit ?
Was he nocht gret Protectour of Scotland ?
   Yit of the court he was nocht weill assurit ;
   It changit so, his lang servyce wes smurit :
He and his sonne, fair Walter, but remede,
Forfaltit war, and put to dulefull dede.

Kyng James the First, the patroun of prudence,
   Gem of ingyne, and peirll of polycie,
Well of Justice, and flude of eloquence,
   Quhose vertew doith transcende my fantasie
   For tyll discryve ; yit, quhen he stude moste hie,
Be fals exhorbitant conspiratioun
That prudent prince wes piteouslie put doun.

Als, James the Secunde, roye of gret renoun,
   Beand in his superexcelland glore,
Throuch reakles schuttyng of one gret cannoun,
   The dolent deith, allace ! did hym devore.
   One thyng thare bene, of quhilk I marvell more,
That Fortune had at hym sic mortall feid,
Throuch fyftie thousand, to waill him by the heid.

My hart is peirst with panes, for to pance,
   Or wrytt, that courtis variatioun
Of James the Third, quhen he had governance,
   The dolour, dreid, and desolatioun,
   The change of court, and conspiratioun ;

And quhou that Cochrane, with his companye,
That tyme in courte clam so presumpteouslye.

It had bene gude, tha heirnes had bene unborne,
  Be quhome that nobyll Prince wes so abusit :
Thay grew, as did the weid abufe the corne,
  That prudent lordis counsall wes refusit,
  And held hym quyet, as he had bene inclusit.
Allace ! that Prince, be thair abusion,
Was fynalie brocht to confusioun.

Thay clam so heych, and gat sie audience,
  And with thair Prince grew so familiar,
His germane brother mycht get no presence ;
  The Duke of Albanie, nor the Erle of Mar,
  Lyke baneist men, was haldin at the bar,
Tyll in the Kyng thare grew sie mortall feid,
He flemit the Duke, and patt the Erle to dede.

Thus Cochrane, with his catyve companye,
  Forsit thame to flee ; bot yit thay wantit fedderis :
Abufe the heych cederis of Libanye.
  Thay clam so hie, tyll thay lape ouir thair ledderis;
  On Lawder bryge, syne keppit wer in tedderis,
Stranglit to deith, thay gat none uther grace,
Thair King captyve, quhilk wes ane cairful cace.

Tyl putt in forme that fait infortunat,
  And mortall change, perturbith myne ingyne ;
My wytt bene waik, my fyngaris fatigate,
  To dyte, or wryt, the rancour, and rewyne,
  The civyll weir, the battell intestyne :

How that the Sonne, with baner braid displayit
Agane the Fader, in battell, come arrayit.

Wald God that Prince had bene that day, confortit
   With sapience of the prudent Salomone,
And with the strenth of strang Sampsone supportit,
   With the bauld oste of gret Agamemnone !
   Quha suld I wys, remedie wes thare none :
At morne ane king, with sceptour, sweird, and croun ;
At evin, ane dede deformit carioun !

Allace ! quhare bene that rycht redoutit roye,
   That potent prince, gentyll king James the Feird ?
I pray to Christe his saule for to convoye :
   Ane greater nobyll rang nocht in to the eird.
   O Atropus ! warye we maye thy weird ;
For he wes myrrour of humylitie,
Lode sterne and lampe of liberalytie.

Duryng his tyme, so Justice did prevaill,
   The Savage Iles trymblit for terrour ;
Eskdale, Euisdale, Liddisdale, and Annerdale,
   Durste nocht rebell, doutyng his dyntis dour ;
   And of his Lordis had sic perfyte favour ;
So for to schaw, that he aferit no fone,
Out throuch his realme he wald ryde hym alone.

And of his court, throuch Europe sprang the fame,
   Of lustie Lordis and lufesum Ladyis ying,
Tryumphand tornayis, justyng, and knychtly game,
   With all pastyme, accordyng for ane kyng :
   He wes the glore of princelic governyng,
     VOL. I.   F

Quhilk, throuch the ardent lufe he had to France,
Agane Ingland did move his ordinance.

Of Floddoun Feilde the rewyne to revolve,
  Or that moste dolent daye for tyll deplore,
I nyll, for dreid that dolour yow dissolve,
  Schaw how that Prince, in his tryumphand glore,
  Distroyit was, quhat nedeith proces more ?
Nocht be the vertew of Inglis ordinance,
Bot, be his awin wylfull mysgovernance.

Allace ! that daye had he bene counsalabyll,
  He had obtenit laude, glore, and victorie ;
Quhose picteous proces bene so lamentabyll,
  I nyll at lenth it put in memorie.
  I never read in Tragedie nor storie,
At one journaye, so mony nobyllis slane,
For the defence and lufe of thair Soverane.

Now, brether, marke, in your remembrance,
  Ane myrroar of those mutabiliteis :
So may ye knaw the courtis inconstance,
  Quhen prencis bene, thus, pullit frome thair seis ;
  Efter quhose deith quhat strainge adversiteis,
Quhat gret mysreule, in to this regioun rang,
Quhen our young prince could noder spek nor gang !

During his tender youthe and innocence,   [chance !
  Quhat stouith, quhat reif, quhat murther, and my
Thare wes nocht ellis bot wrakyng of vengeance,
  In to that court thare rang sic variance.
  Divers rewlaris maid divers ordinance :

Sum tyme, our Quene rang in auctoritie,
Sum tyme, the prudent Duke of Albanie ;

Sum tyme, the realme was reulit be Regentis ;
    Sum tyme, lufetenentis, ledaris of the law :
Than rang so mony inobedientis,
    That few or none stude of ane uther aw :
    Oppressioun did so loud his bugyll blaw,
That none durst ryde bot in to feir of weir :
Jok Uponeland, that tyme, did mys his meir.

Quho was more heych in honour elevate,
    Nor was Margareit, our heych and mychtie princess?
Sic power was to hir appropriate,
    Of King, and Realme, scho wes governoress :
    Yit come one change, within ane schorte proces ;
That peirle preclare, that lusty plesand Quene,
Lang tyme durst nocht in to the Court be sene.

The Archebischop of Sanctandrous, James Betoun,
    Chancellare, and Primate in power pastorall,
Clam, nyxt the Kyng, moste heych in this regioun.
    The ledder schuke, he lap, and gat ane fall :
    Auctoritie, nor power spirituall,
Ryches, freindschip, mycht not that tyme prevaill,
Quhen dame Curia began to steir hir taill.

His heych prudence prevalit hym nocht ane myte,
    That tyme the courte bair hym sic mortall feid :
As presoneir thay keipt hym, in despyte ;
    And sum tyme wyst not quhare to hyde his heid,
    Bot, dissagysit, lyke Jhone the Reif, he yaid.

Had nocht bene hope bair hym sic companye,
He had bene stranglit be melancholye.

Quhat cummer and cair wes in the court of France,
    Quhen kyng Francis wes takin presoneir !
The Duke of Burboun, amyd his ordinance,
    Deit at ane straik, rycht bailfull brocht on beir.
    The court of Rome, that tyme, ran all arreir,
Quhen Pape Clement wes put in strang presoun,
The nobyll Citie put to confusioun.

In Ingland, quho had greter governance
    Nor thair tryumphand courtly Cardinall ?
The commounweill, sum sayis, he did avance,
    Be equale justice, both to gret and small,
    Thare wes no Prelate to hym peregall.
Inglismen sayis, had he roung langer space,
He had deposit Sanct Peter of his place.

His princely pompe, nor Papale gravitie,
    His palyce royall, ryche, and radious,
Nor yit the flude of superfluitie
    Of his ryches, nor travell tedious,
    Frome tyme dame Curia held hym odious,
Avalit hym nocht, nor prudence moste profound :
The ledder brak, and he fell to the ground.

Quhare bene the douchty Erlis of Dowglas,
    Quhilkis royallie in to this regioun rang ?
Forfalt, and slane, quhat nedith more proces !
    The Erle of Marche wes merschellit tham amang;
    Dame Curia thame dulefullie doun thrang ;

And, now of lait, quho clam more heych amang us,
Nor did Archebalde, umquhyle the Erle of Angous;

Quho, with his Prince, wes more familiar,
   Nor of his grace had more auctorie?
Was he nocht gret Wardane and Chancellar?
   Yit, when he stude upon the heychest gre,
   Traistyng no thyng bot perpetuitie,
Was suddanlie deposit frome his place,
Forfalt, and flemit, he gat non uther grace.

Quharefor, traist nocht in tyll auctoritie,
   My deir brether, I pray yow hartfullie:
Presume nocht in your vaine prosperitie;
   Conforme your traist in God alluterlie;
   Syne, serve your Prince with enteir hart trewlie;
And, quhen ye se the court bene at the best,
I counsall yow, than draw you to your rest.

Quhare bene the heych tryumphant court of Troy?
   Or Alexander, with his twelf prudent peiris?
Or Julius, that rycht redoutit Roye?
   Agamemnone, moste worthy in his weiris?
   To schaw thair fyne my frayit hart afeiris:
Sum murdreist war, sum poysonit pieteouslie,
Thair cairfull courtis dispersit dulefullie.

Traist weill, thare is no constant court bot one,
   Quhare Christ bene kyng, quhose tyme interminabyll
And heych triumphant glore beis nevir gone.
   That quyet court, myrthfull, and immutabyll,
   But variance, standith aye ferme and stabyll:

Dissimilance, flattry, nor false reporte
In to that court sall never get resorte.

Traist weill, my freindis, this is no fenyeit fare ;
   For quho that bene in the extreme of dede,
The veritie, but doute, thay sulde declare,
   Without regarde to favour or to fede.
   Quhill ye have tyme, deir brether, mak remede.
Adew ! for ever, of me ye get no more,
Beseikand God to bryng yow to his glore.

Adew, Edinburgh ! thou heych tryumphant toun,
   Within quhose boundis rycht blythfull have I bene,
Of trew merchandis the rute of this regioun,
   Moste reddy to resave Court, King, and Quene !
   Thy polecye, and justice may be sene :
War devotioun, wysedome, and honestie,
And credence, tynt, thay mycht be found in thee.

Adew, fair Snawdoun ! with thy touris hie,
   Thy Chapell Royall, park, and tabyll rounde !
May, June, and July walde I dwell in thee,
   War I one man, to heir the birdis sounde,
   Quhilk doith agane thy royall roche redounde.
Adew, Lythquo ! quhose Palyce of plesance
Mycht be one patrone in Portingall or France !

Fair weill, Falkland ! the fortrace of Fyfe,
   Thy polyte park, under the Lowmound Law !
Sum tyme in thee I led ane lusty lyfe,
   The fallow deir, to see thame raik on raw.
   Court men to cum to thee, thay stand gret awe,

Sayand, thy burgh bene, of all burrowis, baill,
Because, in thee, thay never gat gude aill.

THE COMMONYNG BETUIX THE PAPYNGO, AND HIR HOLYE EXECUTOURIS.

THE Pye persavit the Papyngo in paine,
    He lychtit doun, and fenyeit him to greit :
Sister, said he, alace ! quho hes yow slane ?
    I pray yow, mak provisioune for your spreit,
    Dispone your geir, and yow confes compleit :
I have power, be your contritioun,
Of all your mys, to geve yow full remissioun.

I am, said he, one Channoun regulare,
    And of my brether Pryour principall :
My quhyte rocket, my clene lyfe doith declare ;
    The blak bene of the deith memoriall :
    Quharefor, I thynk your gudis naturall
Sulde be submyttit hole into my cure ;
Ye know, I am ane holye creature.

The Ravin come rolpand, quhen he hard the rair ;
    So did the Gled, with mony pieteous pew ;
And fenyeitlye thay contrafait greit cair.
    Sister, said thay, your raklesnes we rew,
    Now, best it is our juste counsall ensew ;
Sen we pretend to heych promotioun,
Religious men, of gret devotioun.

I am ane blak Monk, said the rutlande Ravin;
    So said the Gled, I am ane holy freir,
And hes power to bryng yow quyke to hevin:
    It is weill knawin, my conscience bene full cleir,
    The blak Bybill, pronunce I sall perqueir,
So tyll our brether, ye will geve sum gude,
God wat geve we hes neid of lyves fude.

The Papyngo said, Father, be the Rude,
    Howbeit your rayment be religious lyke,
Your conscience, I suspect, be nocht gude;
    I did persave, quhen prevelye ye did pyke
    Ane chekin from ane hen, under ane dyke.
I grant, said he, that hen was my gude freind,
And I that chekin tuke, bot for my teind.

Ye knaw the faith be us mon be susteind;
    So be the Pope it is preordinate,
That spirituall men suld leve upon thair teind:
    Bot, weill wat I, ye bene predestinate,
    In your extremis to be so fortunate,
To have sic holy consultatioun;
Quharefore, we mak yow exhortatioun:

Sen dame Nature hes grantit yow sic grace,
    Layser to mak confessioun generall,
Schaw furth your syn in haist, quhil ye haif space;
    Syne of your geir mak one memoriall:
    We thre sal mak your feistis funerall,
And with gret blys, bury we sall your bonis,
Syne trentalls twenty trattyll all at onis.

The roukis sall rair, that men sall on thame rew,
  And crye *Commemoratio Animarum.*
We sall gar chehnis cheip, and geaslyngis pew,
  Suppose the geis and hennis suld crye alarum :
  And we sall serve *Secundum usum Sarum,*
And mak you saif : we fynd Sanct Blase to borgh,
Cryand for yow the cairfull corrynogh.

And we sall syng about your sepulture
  Sanct Mongois matynis, and the mekle creid ;
And syne devotely saye, I yow assure,
  The auld Placebo bakwart, and the beid ;
  And we sall weir, for yow, the murnyng weid :
And, thocht your spreit with Pluto war profest,
Devotelie sall your Diregie be addrest.

Father, said scho, your facunde wordis fair,
  Full sore I dreid, be contrar to your dedis :
The wyffis of the village cryis, with cair,
  Quhen thai persave your mowe ouirthort thar medis :
  Your fals consait, boith duke and draik sore dreidis ;
I marvell, suithlie, ye be nocht eschamit
For your defaltis, beyng so defamit.

It dois abhoir, my pure perturbit spreit,
  Tyll mak to yow ony confessioun :
I heir men saye, ye bene one ypocrite,
  Exemptit frome the Senye and the Sessioun :
  To put my geir in your possessioun,
That wyll I nocht, so help me Dame Nature !
Nor of my corps I wyll yow geve no cure.

Bot, had I heir the nobyll Nychtingall,
    The gentyll Ja, the Merle, and Turtur trew,
My obsequeis and feistis funerall,
    Ordour thay wald, with notis of the new.
    The plesand Pown, moste angellyke of hew :
Wald God I wer, this daye, with hym confest,
And my devyse dewlie be hym addrest !

The myrthfull Maveis, with the gay Goldspink,
    The lustye Larke, wald God thay war present :
My infortune, forsuith, thay wald forthink,
    And comforte me that bene so impotent.
    The swyft Swallow, in prattick moste prudent,
I wate scho wald my bledyng stem belyve,
With hir moste verteous stone restringityve.

Compt me the cace, under confessioun,
    The Gled said proudlye to the Papingo,
And we sall sweir, be our professioun,
    Counsall to keip, and schaw it to no mo :
    We thee beseik, or thou depart us fro,
Declare to us sum causis reasonabyll,
Quhy we bene haldin so abhominabyll.

Be thy travell, thou hes experience,
    First, beand bred in to the Orient,
Syne be thy gude servyce, and delygence,
    To Prencis maid heir in the Occident :
    Thow knawis the vulgare pepyllis jugement,
Quhare thou transcurrit the hote Meridionall,
Syne nyxt the Poill, the plaige Septentrionall.

So, be thyne heych ingyne superlatyve,
    Of all countreis thou knawis the qualiteis ;
Quharefore, I thee conjure, be God of lyve,
    The veritie declare, withouttin leis,
    Quhat thou hes hard, be landis, or be seis,
Of us Kirkmen, boith gude and evyll reporte ;
And quhow thay juge, schaw us, we thee exhorte.

Father, said scho, I catyve creature,
    Dar nocht presume with sic mater to mell ;
Of your caces, ye knaw, I have no cure,
    Demand thame quhilk in prudence doith precell ;
    I maye nocht pew, my panes bene so fell :
And als, perchance, ye wyll nocht stand content
To knaw the vulgare pepyllis jugement.

Yit, wyll the deith alyte withdrawe his darte,
    All that lyis in my memoryall,
I sall declare with trew unfenyeit hart ;
    And first, I saye to you, in generall,
    The commoun peple sayith, ye bene all,
Degenerit frome your holy pirmityvis,
As testyfeis the proces of your lyvis.

Of your peirles, prudent predecessouris
    The beginnyng, I grant, wes verray gude :
Apostolis, Martyres, Virgines, Confessouris,
    The sound of thair excellent Sanctitude
    Was hard ouer all the warld, be land and flude ;
Plantyng the faith, be predicatioun,
As Christe had maid to thame narratioun.

To fortyfie the faith thay tuke no feir,
    Afore Prencis, preching full prudentlie ;
Of dolorous deith thay doutit nocht the deir,
    The veritie declaryng ferventlie ;
    And martyrdome thay sufferit pacientlie :
Thay tuke no cure of land, ryches, nor rent ;
Doctryne and deid war boith equivolent.

To schaw at lenth thair workis, wer gret wunder,
    Thair myracklis, thay wer so manifest ;
In name of Christe thay hailit mony hounder,
    Rasyng the dede, and purgeing the possest,
    With perverst spreitis, quhilkis had bene opprest :
The crukit ran, the blynd men gat thair ene,
The deiff men hard, the lypper war maid clene.

The Prelatis spousit wer with Povertie,
    Those dayis, quhen so thay flurisit in fame,
And, with hir generit lady Chaistitie,
    And dame Devotioun, notabyll of name :
    Humyll thay wer, simpyll, and full of schame.
Thus Chaistitie and dame Devotioun,
Wer principall cause of thair promotioun.

Thus thay contynewit, in this lyfe devyne,
    Aye tyll thare rang, in Romes gret cietie,
Ane potent Prince was namit Constantyne
    Persavit the Kirk had spowsit Povertie,
    With gude intent, and movit of pietie,
Cause of divorce he fande betuix thame two,
And partit thame, withouttin wordis mo.

Syne, schortlie, with ane gret solempnitie,
   Withouttin ony dispensatioun,
The Kirk he spowsit with dame Propirtie,
   Quhilk haistelye, be proclamatioun,
   To Povertie gart mak narratioun,
Under the pane of peirsyng of hir eine,
That with the Kirk scho sulde no more be seine.

Sanct Sylvester, that tyme, rang Pope in Rome,
   Quhilk first consentit to the mariage
Of Propirtie, the quhilk began to blome,
   Taking on hir the cure, with heych corrage,
   Devotioun drew hir tyll one heremytage,
Quhen scho considerit lady Propirtie,
So heych exaltit in to dignitie.

O Sylvester, quhare was thy discretioun,
   Quhilk Peter did renounce thow did resave :
Androw, and Jhone, did leif thair possessioun,
   Thair schippis, and nettis, lynes, and all the lave ;
   Of temporall substance no thing wald thay have,
Contrarious to thair contemplatioun,
Bot soberlye thair sustentatioun.

Johne the Baptist went to the wyldernes.
   Lazarus, Martha, and Marie Magdalane,
Left heretage and guddis, more and les :
   Prudent Sanct Paule, thocht Propertie prophane,
   Frome toun to toun he ran, in wynde and rane,
Upon his feit, techeing the word of grace,
And never was subjectit to ryches.

The Gled said, Yit I heir no thyng bot gude :
    Proceid schortlye, and thy mater avance.
The Papyngo said, Father, be the Rude,
    It wer too lang to schaw the circumstance,
    Quhow Propertie, with hir new alyance,
Grew gret with chylde, as trew men to me talde,
And bure two dochteris, gudlie to behalde.

The eldest dochter named was Ryches,
    The secunde syster, Sensualytie ;
Quhilks did incres, within one schorte proces,
    Preplesande to the Spiritualytie,
    In gret substance, and excellent bewtie,
Thir Ladyis two grew so, within rew yeiris,
That in the warlde wer non mycht be thair peiris.

This royall Ryches and lady Sensuall
    Frome that tyme furth tuke hole the governance,
Of the moste part of the Stait Spirituall :
    And thay agane, with humbyll observance,
    Amorouslie thair wyttis did avance,
As trew luffaris, thair ladyis for to pleis :
God wate, geve than thair hartis war at eis.

Soune thay foryet to study, praye, and preche,
    Thay grew so subject to dame Sensuall,
And thocht bot paine pure pepyll for to teche ;
    Yit thay decretit, in thair gret Counsall,
    Thay wald no more to mariage be thrall,
Traistyng surely, tyll observe Chaistitie,
And all begylit, quod Sensualytie.

Apperandlye thay did expell thair wyffis,
  That thay mycht leif at large, without thirlage,
At libertie to lede thair lustie lyffis,
  Thynkand men thrall, that bene in mariage
  For new faces provokis new corrage :
Thus Chaistitie thay turne in to delyte ;
Wantyng of wyffis bene cause of appetyte.

Dame Chaistitie did steill away for schame,
  Frome tyme scho did persave thair proviance ;
Dame Sensuall, one letter gart proclame,
  And hir exilit Italy and France :
  In Inglande couthe scho get none ordinance :
Than to the Kyng and Courte of Scotlande
Scho markit hir, withouttin more demande.

Traistyng in to that Court to get conforte,
  Scho maid hir humyll supplycatioun.
Schortlye thay said, Scho sulde get na supporte,
  Bot bostit hir, with blasphematioun :
  To Preistis go mak your protestatioun :
It is, said thay, mony one houndreth yeir
Sen Chaistitie had ony entres heir.

Tyrit for travell, scho to the Preistis past,
  And to the rewlaris of religioun.
Of hir presens schortlye thay war agast,
  Sayand, thay thocht it bot abusion
  Hir to resave : so, with conclusion,
With one avyce, decretit, and gave dome,
Thay walde resset no rebell out of Rome.

Sulde we resave that Romanis hes refusit,
    And bancist Inglande, Italye, and France,
For your flattrye, than wer we weill abusit :
    Passe hyne, said thay, and fast your way avance,
    Amang the Nonnis, go seik your ordinance ;
For we have maid aith of fidelytie
To dame Ryches and Sensualytie.

Than, paciently, scho maid progressioun
    Towarde the Nonnis, with hart syching full sore.
Thay gaif hir presens, with processioun,
    Ressavand hir with honour, laud, and glore,
    Purposyng to preserve hir ever more.
Of that novellis come to dame Propertie,
To Ryches, and to Sensualytie ;

Quhilkis sped thame at the post, rycht spedalye,
    And sett ane seage proudlye about the place.
The sillye Nonnis did yeild thame haistelyé,
    And humyllye of that gylt askit grace,
    Syne gave thair bandis of perpetuall peace.
Ressavand thame, thay kest up wykkets wyde :
Than Chaistytie walde no langer abyde.

So for refuge, fast to the Freris scho fled,
    Quhilks said, Thay wald of ladyis tak no cure.
Quhare bene scho now, than said the gredy Gled ?
    Nocht amang yow, said scho, I yow assure :
    I traist scho bene, upon the Borrow-mure,
Besouth Edinburgh, and that rycht mony menis,
Profest amang the Systeris of the Schenis.

Thare hes scho found hir mother Povertie,
    And Devotioun, hir awin syster carnall ;
Thare hes scho found Faith, Hope, and Charitie,
    Togidder with the Vertues Cardinall :
    Thare hes scho, found ane Convent yit unthrall
To dame Sensuall, nor with ryches abusit,
So quietlye those ladyis bene inclusit.

The Pyote said, I dreid, be thay assailyeit,
    Thay rander thame, as did the holy Nonnis.
Doute nocht, said scho, for thay bene so artalyeit,
    Thay purpose to defend thame with thair gunnis
    Reddy to schute, thay have sax gret cannounnis,
Perseverance, Constancye, and Conscience,
Austerytie, Laubour, and Abstynance.

To resyste subtell Sensualytie,
    Strongly thay bene enarmit, feit and handis,
Be Abstynence, and keipith Povertie,
    Contrar Ryches, and all hir fals servandis :
    Thay have ane boumbard, braissit up in bandis,
To keip thair porte, in myddis of thair clois,
Quhilk is callit, *Domine custodi nos ;*

Within quhose schote thare dar no enemeis
    Approche thair place, for dreid of dyntis doure ;
Boith nycht and daye thay wyrk, lyke besye beis,
    For thair defence, reddye to stande in stoure,
    And hes sic watcheis on thair utter toure,
That dame Sensuall with seage dar not assailye,
Nor cum within the schote of thair artailye.

The Pyote said, Quhareto sulde thay presume
   For to resyste sweit Sensualytie,
Or dame Ryches, quhilkis reularis bene in Rome ?
   Ar thay more constant, in thair qualytie,
   Nor the prencis of Spiritualytie,
Quhilkis plesandlye, withouttin obstakle,
Haith thame resavit in their habitakle ?

Quhow long, traist ye, those ladyis sall remane
   So solytar, in sic perfectioun ?
The Papingo said, Brother, in certane,
   So lang as thay obey correctioun,
   Cheisyng thair heddis be electioun,
Unthrall to Ryches, or to Povertie,
Bot as requyrith thair necessitie.

O prudent Prelatis, quhare was your presciance,
   That tuke on hand tyll observe Chaistitie,
But austeir lyfe, laubour, and abstenance ?
   Persavit ye nocht the gret prosperitie,
   Apperandlye to cum of Propertie ?
Ye knaw gret cheir, great eais, and ydelnes
To Lychorie was mother and maistres.

Thow ravis unrockit, the Ravin said, be the Rude,
   So to reprove Ryches or Propertie.
Abraham, and Ysaac, war ryche, and verray gude ;
   Jacobe and Josephe had prosperitie.
   The Papingo said, That is verytie ;
Ryches, I grant, is nocht to be refusit,
Providyng alwaye, it be nocht abusit.

Than laid the Ravin ane Replycatioun,
   Syne said, Thy reasone is nocht worth ane myte,
As I sall prove, with protestatioun
   That no man tak my wordis in dispyte :
   I saye, the temporall Prencis hes the wyte,
That in the Kirk sic pastours dois provyde
To governe saulis, that not tham selfis can gyde.

Lang tyme efter the Kirk tuke Propertie,
   The Prelatis levit in gret perfectioun,
Unthrall to Ryches, or Sensualytie,
   Under the Holy Spreitis protectioun,
   Orderlye chosin, be electioun,
As Gregore, Jerome, Ambrose, and Augustyne,
Benedict, Bernard, Clement, Cleit, and Lyne.

Sic pacient Prelatis enterit be the porte,
   Plesand the peple be predicatioun.
Now dyke-lowparis dois in the Kirk resort :
   Be symonie, and supplycatioun
   Of Prencis be thair presentatioun ;
So sillye saulis, that bene Christis scheip,
Ar gevin to hungrye gormande wolfis to keip.

No marvell is, thocht we Religious men
   Degenerit be, and in our lyfe confusit :
Bot sing, and drynk, none uther craft we ken,
   Our Spirituall Fatheris hes us so abusit :
   Agane our wyll, those treukouris bene intrusit.
Lawit men hes now religious men in curis ;
Profest virgenis in keipyng of strong huris.

Prencis, prencis, quhar bene your heych prudence
    In dispositioun of your beneficeis ?
The guerdonyng of your courticience,
    Is sum cause of thir gret enormyteis.
    Thare is one sorte, wattand, lyke houngre fleis,
For Spirituall cure, thocht thay be no thing abyll,
Quhose gredie thristis bene insaciabyll.

Prencis, I pray yow, be no more abusit,
    To verteous men havyng so small regarde :
Quhy sulde vertew, throuch flattrye, be refusit,
    That men for cunnyng can get no rewarde ?
    Allace ! that ever one braggar, or ane barde,
Ane hure maister, or commoun hasarture,
Sulde, in the Kirk, get ony kynde of cure !

War I one man worthy to weir ane croun,
    Aye quhen thare vakit ony beneficeis,
I suld gar call ane Congregatioun,
    The principall of all the Prelaceis,
    Moste cunnyng clerkis of Universiteis,
Moste famous Fatheris of religioun,
With thair advyse, mak dispositioun.

I suld dispone all offices pastorallis
    Tyll Doctouris of Devynitie, or Jure ;
And cause daine Vertew pull up all hir sailis,
    Quhen cunnyng men had in the Kirk moist cure ;
    Gar Lordis send thair sonnes, I yow assure,
To seik science, and famous sculis frequent ;
Syne thame promove that wer moste sapient.

Gret plesour wer to heir ane Byschope preche,
   One Deane, or Doctour in Divinitie,
One Abbote quhilk could weill his Convent teche,
   One Persoun flowing in phylosophie :
   I tyne my tyme, to wys quhilk wyll nocht be ;
War nocht the preaching of the Begging Freris,
Tynt war the faith amang the Seculeris.

As for thair precheing, quod the Papingo,
   I thame excuse, for quhy, thay bene so thrall
To Propertie, and hir ding Dochteris two,
   Dame Ryches, and fair lady Sensuall,
   That may nocht use no pastyme spirituall ;
And in thair habitis, thay tak sic delyte,
Thay have renuncit russat and raploch quhyte.

Cleikand to thame skarlote, and crammosie,
   With menever, martrik, grice, and ryche armyne ;
Thair lawe hartis exaultit ar so hie,
   To see thair Papale pompe, it is ane pyne.
   More ryche arraye is now, with frenyeis fyne,
Upon the bardyng of ane Byscheopis mule,
Nor ever had Paule, or Peter, agane Yule.

Syne fair ladyis, thair chene may not eschape,
   Dame Sensuall so sic seid haith in tham sawin ;
Les skaith it war, with lycence of the Pape,
   That ilke Prelate one wyfe had of his awin,
   Nor se thair bastardis ouirthort the countre blawin ;
For now, be thay be weill cumin frome the sculis,
Thay fall to work, as thay war commoun bullis.

Pew, quod the Gled, thow prechis all in vaine :
    Ye Seculare floks hes of our cace no curis.
I grant, said scho ; yit men wyll speik agane,
    Quhow ye haif maid a hundreth thousand huris,
    Quhilkis nevir had bene, war not your lychorous
And geve I lee, hartlye I me repent ;   [luris
Was never bird, I watt, more penitent.

Than scho hir shrave, with devote contynance,
    To that fals Gled, quhilk fenyeit hym one freir ;
And quhen scho had fulfyllit hir pennance,
    Full subtellye at hir he gan inqueir :
    Cheis yow, said he, quhilk of us Brother heir
Sall have of all your naturall geir the curis :
Ye knaw none bene more holye creaturis.

I am content, quod the pure Papingo,
    That ye freir Gled, and Corby monk, your brother,
Have cure of all my guddis, and no mo,
    Sen at this tyme, freindschip I find non uther.
    We salbe to yow trew, as tyll our Mother,
Quod thay, and sweir tyll fulfyll hir intent.
Of that, said scho, I tak ane Instrument.

The Pyote said, Quhat sall myne office bee ?
    Ouirman, said scho, unto the tother two.
The rowpand Revin said, Sweit syster, lat see
    Your holy intent ; for it is tyme to go.
    The gredie Gled said, Brother, do nocht so ;
We wyll remane, and haldin up hir hede,
And never depart from hir till scho be dede.

The Papingo thame thankit tenderlye,
   And said, Sen ye have tane on yow this cure,
Depart myne naturall guddis equalye,
   That evir I had, or hes of dame Nature ;
   First, to the Howlet, indigent and pure,
Quhilk on the daye, for schame, dar nocht be sene,
Tyll hir I laif my gay galbarte of grene.

My brycht depurit ene, as christall cleir,
   Unto the Bak ye sall thame boith present ;
In Phebus presens quhilk dar nocht appeir,
   Of naturall sycht scho bene so impotent.
   My birneist beik I laif, with gude entent,
Unto the gentyll, pieteous Pellicane,
To helpe to peirs hir tender hart in twane.

I laif the Goik, quhilk hes no sang bot one,
   My musyke, with my voce angelycall ;
And, to the Guse, ye geve, quhen I am gone,
   My eloquence and toung rethoricall :
   And tak and drye my bonis, gret and small,
Syne, close thame in one cais of ebure fyne,
And thame present onto the Phenix syne,

To birne with hir, quhen scho hir lyfe renewis ;
   In Arabye, ye sall hir fynde but weir,
And sall knaw hir be hir moste hevinly hewis,
   Gold, asure, gowles, purpour, and synopeir.
   Hir dait is for to leif fyve houndreth yeir ;
Mak to that bird my commendatioun :
And als, I mak yow supplycatioun,

Sen of my corps I have yow gevin the cure,
  Ye speid yow to the court, but tareyng,
And tak my hart, of perfyte portrature,
  And it present unto my Soverane Kyng:
  I wat he wyll it clois in to one ryng.
Commende me to his Grace, I yow exhorte,
And of my passion, mak hym trew reporte.

Ye thre my trypes sall have, for your travell,
  With luffer and lewng, to part equale amang yow;
Prayand Pluto, the potent prince of hell.
  Geve ye failye, that in his feit he fang yow,
  Be to me trew, thocht I no thyng belang yow;
Sore I suspect, your conscience be too large.
Doute nocht, said thay, we tak it with the charge.

Adew, Brether! quod the pure Papingo;
  To talking more I have no tyme to tarye;
Bot, sen my spreit mon fra my body go,
  I recommend it to the Quene of Farye,
  Eternallye in tyll hir court to carye,
In wyldernes, among the holtis hore.
Than scho inclynit hir hed, and spak no more.

Plungit in tyll hir mortall passioun,
  Full grevouslie scho gryppit to the ground.
It war too lang to mak narratioun,
  Of sychis sore, with mony stang and stound,
  Out of hir wound the blude did so abound,
One compas round was with hir blude maid reid:
Without remeid, thare wes no thyng bot dede.

And he scho had, *In Manus tuas*, said,
   Extinctit wer hir naturall wyttis fyve ;
Hir heid full softlye on hir schulder laid,
   Syne yeild the spreit, with panes pungityve.
   The Ravin began rudely to rug and ryve,
Full gormondlyke, his emptie throte to feid.
Eit softlye, brother, said the gredy Gled :

Quhill scho is hote, depart hir evin amang us ;
   Tak thow one half, and reik to me ane uther :
In tyll our rycht, I wat, no wycht dar wrang us.
   The Pyote said, The feind resave the fouther.
   Quhy mak ye me stepbarne, and I your brother ?
Ye do me wrang, schir Gled, I schrew your harte.
Tak thare, said he, the puddyngis for thy parte.

Than, wyt ye weill, my hart wes wounder sair,
   For to behald that dolent departyng,
Hir angell fedderis fleying in the air ;
   Except the hart, was left of hir no thing.
   The Pyote said, This pertenith to the Kyng,
Quhilk tyll his Grace I purpose to present.
Thow, quod the Gled, sall faill of thyne entent.

The Revin said, God ! nor I rax in ane rape,
   And thow get this tyll outher kyng or duke !
The Pyote said, Plene I nocht to the Pape
   Than in ane smedie I be smorit with smuke.
   With that the Gled the pece claucht in his cluke,
And fled his way : the lave, with all thair mycht,
To chace the Gled, flew all out of my sycht.

Now have ye hard this lytill Tragedie,
  The sore Complent, the Testament, and myschance
Of this pure Bird, quhilk did ascend so hie.
  Beseikand yow, excuse myne ignorance,
  And rude indyte, quhilk is nocht tyll avance.
And to the quair, I geve commandiment,
Mak no repair quhair Poetis bene present :

        Because thow bene
          But Rethorike, so rude,
        Be never sene,
          Besyde none other buke,
        With Kyng, nor Quene,
          With Lord, nor man of gude ;
        With coit unclene,
          Clame kynrent to sum cuke ;
        Steil in ane nuke,
          Quhen thay lyste on thee luke ;
        For smell of smuke,
          Men wyll abhor to beir thee ;
        Heir I manesweir thee ;
          Quhairfor, to lurke go leir thee.

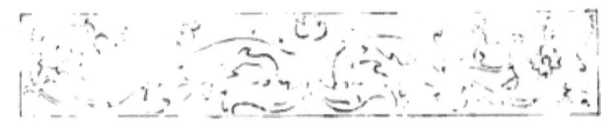

THE ANSWER

QUHILK SCHIR DAVID LYNDESAY MAID TO THE KINGIS FLYTING.

DEDOUTIT ROY, your ragment I haif red
   Quhilk dois perturb my dul intendement :
From your Flyting, wald God that I wer fred,
   Or ellis sum tygeris toung wer to me lent :
   Schir, pardone me, thocht I be impacient,
Quhilk bene so with your prunzeand pen detractit,
And rude report, from Venus court dejectit.

Lustie ladyis, that your libellis lukis,
   My cumpanie dois hald abhominable ;
Commandand me beir cumpanie to the cukis,
   Moist lyke ane devill, thay hald me detestable ;
   Thay baneis me, sayand, I am nocht able
Thame to compleis, or preis to thair presence :
Upon your pen, I cry ane loud vengeance.

Wer I ane Poeit, I suld preis with my pen,
   To wreik me on your vennemous wryting ;
Bot I man do, as dog dois in his den,
   Fald baith my feit, or fle fast frome your Flyting,
   The mekil Devil may nocht indure your dyting :

Quharefor, *Cor mundum crea in* me, I cry,
Proclamand yow the Prince of Poetry.

Schir, with my Prince, pertenit me nocht to pley,
   Bot, sen your Grace, hes gevin me sic command
To mak answer, it must neidis me obey :
   Thocht ye be now strang, lyke ane elephand,
   And in till Venus werkis maist vailzeand,
The day wyll cum, and that within few yeiris,
That ye will draw at laiser, with your feiris.

Quhat can ye say farther, bot I am failzeit
   In Venus werkis, I grant Schir, that is trew ;
The tyme hes bene, I was better artailzeit,
   Nor I am now, bot yit full sair I rew,
   That ever I did mouth-thankles so persew :
Quharefor, tak tent, and your fyne powder spare,
And waist it nocht, bot gyf ye wit weill quhare.

Thocht ye rin rudelie, lyke ane restles ram,
   Schutand your bolt at mony sindrie schellis,
Beleif richt weill, it is ane bydand gam :
   Quharefor be war, with dowbling of the bellis,
   For mony ane dois haist thair awin saule knellis ;
And speciallie, quhen that the well gois dry,
Syne can nocht get agane sic stufe to by.

I give your Counsale, to the feynd of Hell,
   That wald nocht of ane Princess yow provide ;
Tholand yow rin schutand frome schell to schell,
   Waistand your corps, lettand the tyme ouerslyde :
   For lyke ane boisteous bull, ye rin, and ryde.

Royatouslie, lyke ane rude rubeator,
Ay lukkand lyke ane furious fornicatour.

On ladronis for to loup, ye wyll nocht lat,
   Howbeit the caribaldis cry, the Corinoch :
Remember how, besyde the masking fat,
   Ye caist ane quene ouerthort ane stinking troch,
   That feynd, with fuffilling of hir roistit hoch,
Caist doun the fat, quharthrow drink, draf, and juggis,
Come rudely rinnand doun about your luggis.

Wald God, the lady, that luffit yow best,
   Had sene yow thare ly swetterand lyke twa swyne ;
Bot to indyte, how that duddroun wes drest,
   Drowkit with dreggis, quhimperand with mony
      quhryne,
   That process to report, it wer ane pyne :
On your behalf, I thank God, tymes ten score,
That yow preservit from gut, and from grandgore.

Now, Schir, fairweill, because I can nocht Flyte,
   And thocht I could, I wer nocht till avance
Aganis your ornate meter to indyte :
   Bot yit be war, with lawbouring of your lance,
   Sum sayis, thare cummis ane buckler furth of France,
Quhilk wyll indure your dintis, thocht thay be dour.
Fair weill, of flowand Rethorick the Flour.

      Quod Lyndesay, in his Flyting,
      Aganis the Kingis dyting.

THE COMPLAYNT

AND PUBLICT CONFESSIOUN OF THE KINGIS AULD HOUND, CALLIT BAGSCHE, DIRECTIT TO BAWTIE, THE KINGIS BEST BELOVIT DOG, AND HIS COMPANZEONIS.

ALLACE! quhome to sulde I complayne,
  In my extreme necessitie:
Or quhame to sall I mak my maine
  In court, na dog wyll do for me,
  Beseikand sum for cheritie,
To beir my Supplicatioun,
  To Scudlar, Luffra, and Bawtie,
Now, or the King pas off the town.

I have followit the court so lang,
  Quhill, in gude faith, I may no mair ;
The Countre knawis I may nocht gang,
  I am so crukit, auld, and sair,
  That I wait nocht quhare to repair ;
For, quhen I had authoritie,
  I thocht me so familiar,
I never dred necessitie.

I rew the race, that Geordie Steill,
   Brocht Bawtie to the Kingis presence,
I pray God, lat him never do weill,
   Sen syne I gat na audience;
    For, Bawtie now gettis sic credence,
That he lyis on the Kingis nycht gown,
   Quhare, I perforce, for my offence,
Man, in the clois, ly lyke ane loun.

For I haif bene, ay to this hour,
   Ane wirrear of lamb, and hog;
Ane tyrane, and ane tulzeour,
   Ane murdreissar of mony ane dog;
    Fyve foullis I chaist out throch ane scrog,
Quharefor thair motheris did me warie;
   For thay war drownit all in ane bog;
Speir at Jhone Gordoun of Pittarie,

Quhilk in his house, did bryng me up,
   And usit me to slay the deir;
Sweit milk, and meill, he gart me sup,
   That craft I leirnit sone perqueir;
    All uther vertew ran arreir,
Quhen I began to bark and flyte;
   For thare was nother monk, nor freir,
Nor wyfe, nor barne, bot I wold byte.

Quhen to the King the cace was knawin
   Of my unhappy hardines,
And all the suth unto hym schawin,
   How everilk dog I did oppres;
    Than, gaif his Grace command expres,

I suld be brocht to his presence ;
  Nochtwithstanding my wickitnes,
In Court I gat greit audience.

I schew my greit ingratitude,
  To the capitane of Badzeno,
Quhilk, in his house, did find me fude
  Twa yeir, with other houndis mo :
  Bot quhen I saw that it was so,
That I grew heich into the court,
  For his reward I wrocht hym wo,
And cruellie I did hym hurt.

So thay that gave me to the King,
  I was thair mortall enemie,
I tuke cure of na kynd of thyng,
  Bot pleis the Kingis Majestie ;
  Bot quhen he knew my crueltie,
My falset, and my plane oppressioun,
  He gave command, that I suld be,
Hangit, and that without confessioun.

And yit because that I was auld,
  His Grace thocht petie for to hang me,
Bot leit me wander quhare I wald ;
  Than set my fais for to fang me,
  And every bouchour dog doun dang me ;
Quhen I trowit best to be ane laird,
  Than, in the court, ilk wicht did wrang me ;
And this I gat for my rewaird.

I had wirreit black Makesoun,
    Wer nocht that rebaldis come, and red ;
Bot he was flemit of the toun,
    From tyme the king saw how I bled ;
He gart lay me upon ane bed,
For with ane knife I was mischevit ;
    This Makesoun, for feir, he fled,
Ane lang tyme or he was relevit.

And Patrik Strivling in Ergyle,
    I bure him bakwart to the ground,
And had him slane, within ane quhyle ;
    War nocht the helping of ane hound :
Yit, gat he mony bludie wound,
As yit his skyn wyll schaw the markis ;
    Find me ane dog quhare ever ye found
Hes maid sa mony bludie sarkis.

Gude brother Lanceman, Lyndesayis dog,
    Quhilk ay hes keipit thy lautie,
And never wirryit lamb, nor hog ;
    Pray Luffra, Scudlar, and Bawtie,
    Of me Bagsche to have pitie,
And provide me ane portioun,
    In Dumfermeling, quhare I may dre
Pennance, for my extortioun :

Get, be thair solistatioun,
    Ane letter frome the Kingis Grace,
That I may have collatioun,
    With fyre and candil, in the place,
    Bot I wyll leif schort tyme allace !
        VOL. I.   H

Want I gude fresche flesche for my gammis;
    Betuix Ashwednisday, and Paice,
I man have leave to wirrie lambis.

Bawtie, considder weill this bill,
    And reid this cedull, that I send yow,
And everilk poynt thareof fulfill,
    And now in tyme of mys amend yow;
    I pray yow that ye nocht pretend yow,
To clym ower hie, nor do na wrang,
    Bot frome your fais with rycht defend yow,
And tak exemple quhow I gang.

I was that na man durst cum neir me,
    Nor put me furth of my lugeing;
Na dog durst fra my denner sker me,
    Quhen I was tender with the King :
    Now everilk tyke dois me doun thring,
The quhilk before be me war wrangit,
    And sweris, I serve na uther thing,
Bot, in an helter, to be hangit.

Thocht ye be hamelie with the King,
    Ye Luffra, Scudlar, and Bawtie,
Be war that ye do nocht doun thring
    Your nychtbouris throw authoritie;
    And your exemple mak be me,
And beleve weill ye are bot doggis,
    Thocht ye stand in the hiest gre,
Se ye byte nother lambis, nor hoggis.

Thocht ye have now greit audience,
    Se that be yow be nane opprest;
Ye wylbe punischit for your offence,
    Frome tyme the King be weill confest;
    Thare is na dog, that has transgrest
Throw crueltie, and he may fang him,
    His Majestie wyll tak na rest,
Tyll on ane gallous he gar hang him.

I was anis als far ben as ye ar,
    And had in Court als gret credence,
And ay pretendit to be hiear;
    Bot, quhen the Kingis Excellence,
    Did knaw my falset, and offence,
And my prydefull presumptioun,
    I gat nane uther recompence,
Bot hoyit, and houndit, of the toun.

Was never sa unkynd ane corce,
    As quhen I had authoritie:
Of my freindis, I tuke na force,
    The quhilkis afore had done for me.
    This proverb, is of veritie,
Quhilk I hard red, in tyll ane letter:
    Hiest in Court nixt the widdie,
Without he gyde hym all the better.

I tuke na mair compt of ane lord,
    Nor I did of ane keitching knaif,
Thocht everilk day I maid discord,
    I was set up abone the laif,

The gentill hound was to me slaif,
And with the Kingis awin fingeris fed,
   The sillie rachis wald I raif;
Thus, for my evil deidis, wes I dred :

Tharefor, Bawtie, luke best about,
   Quhen thou art hiest with the King,
For then thou standest in greitest dout,
   Be thou nocht gude of governing :
   Put na pure tyke frome his steiding.
Nor yit na sillie rachis raif;
   He sittis abone that seis all thing,
And of ane knicht can mak ane knaif.

Quhen I cam steppand ben the flure,
   All rachis greit roume to me red ;
I of na creature tuke cure,
   Bot lap upon the Kingis bed,
   With claith of gold thocht it wer spred ;
For feir, ilk freik wald stand on far,
   With everilk dog I was so dred,
Thay trimblit quhen thay hard me nar.

Gude brother Bawtie, beir thee evin,
   Thocht with thy Prince thow be potent ;
It cryis ane vengeance frome the hevin,
   For till oppres ane innocent :
   In welth be than maist vigilent,
And do na wrang to dog, nor beiche,
   As I have, quhilk I now repent,
Na messane reif, to mak thee riche.

Nor for augmenting of thy boundis,
  Ask na reward, schir, at the King,
Quhilk may do hurt to uther houndis,
  Expres aganis Goddis bidding :
  Chais na pure tyke from his midding,
Throw cast of Court, or Kingis requeist ;
  And of thyself presume no thing,
Except thow art ane brutall beist.

Traist weill thare is none oppressour,
  Nor boucheour dog, drawer of blude,
Ane tyrane, nor ane transgressour,
  That sall now of the King get gude ;
  From tyme furth, that his Celsitude
Dois cleirlie knaw the veritie,
  Bot he is flemit, for to conclude,
Or hangit heych upon ane tre.

Thocht ye be cuplit all togidder,
  With silk, and swoulis of sylver fyne ;
Ane dog may cum furth of Balquhidder,
  And gar yow leid ane lawer tryne ;
  Than sall your plesour turne in pyne,
Quhen ane strange hounter blawis his horne,
  And all your treddingis gar yow tyne ;
Than sall your labour be forlorne.

I say no more, gude freindis, Adew !
  In dreid we never meit agane :
That ever I kend the Court, I rew,
  Was never wycht so will of wane :
  Lat no dog serve our Soverane,

Without he be of gude conditioun ;
　Be he perverst, I tell yow plane,
He hes neid of ane gude remissioun.

That I am on this way mischevit,
　The Erle of Hountlie I may warie,
He wend I had bene weill relevit
　Quhen to the Courte he gart me carie ;
　Wald God, I war now in Pittarie,
Because I have bene so evil deidie :
　Adew ! I dar na langer tarie,
In dreid, I waif in tyll ane widdie.

THE DEPLORATIOUN OF

THE DEITH OF QUENE MAGDALENE.

O CREWELL Deith! too greit is thy puissance,
    Devorar of all erthlie levyng thingis:
Adam, we may thee wyit of this mischance,
    In thy default, this cruell tyrane ringis;
    And sparis nother Empryour, nor Kingis:
And now, allace! hes reft furth of this land,
The flour of France, and confort of Scotland.

Father Adam, allace! that thow abusit
    Thy fre wyll, being inobedient
Thow chesit deith, and lestyng lyfe refusit:
    Thy successioun, allace! that may repent,
    That thow hes maid mankynd so impotent;
That it may mak to deith no resistance,
Exemple of our Quene, the flour of France.

O dreidfull dragoun! with thy dulefull dart,
    Quhilk did nocht spair of femynine the flour;
Bot, crewellie, did perse hir throuch the hart,

And wald nocht give hir respite for ane hour,
  To remane with hir Prynce, and paramour,
That scho at laiser, mycht have tane licence :
Scotland on thee, may cry ane loud vengeance.

Thow leit Methusalem leif nine houndreth yeir,
  Thre score and nyne, bot in thy furious rage
Thow did devore this young Princess, but peir,
  Or scho was compleit sevintene yeir of age.
  Gredie gorman ! qnhy did thow nocht assuage
Thy furious rage, contrair that lustie Quene,
Till we sum fruct had of hir bodye sene.

O dame Nature ! thow did na deligence,
  Contrair this theif, quhilk all the warld confoundis;
Had thow with naturall targis maid defence,
  That brybour had nocht cummit within hir boundis,
  And had been savit, frome sic mortall stoundis,
This mony ane yeir, bot quhare was thy discretioun
That leit hir pas, till we had sene successioun.

O Venus ! with thy blind sone, Cupido,
  Fy on yow baith ! that maid na resistance ;
In to your court, ye never had sic two,
  So leill luffaris, without dissimulance,
  As James the Fyft and Magdalene of France,
Discendyng baith of blude Imperiall,
To quhome in lufe, I find na paregall.

For, as Leander swame outthrow the flude,
  To his fair Lady Hero, mony nichtis,
So did this Prynce, throw bulryng stremis wode,

With erlis, baronis, squyaris, and with knychtis,
  Contrair Neptune, and Eoll, and thair mychtis,
And left his Realme, in greit disesperance,
To seik his lufe, the first Dochter of France.

And scho, like prudent Quene Penelope,
  Full constantlie wald change him for none uther,
And for his plesour left hir awin countre,
  Without regard to Fader, or to Mother,
  Taking no cure of sister, nor of brother ;
Bot schortlie tuke hir leif, and left thame all,
For lufe of him to quhom lufe maid hir thrall.

O dame Fortune ! quhare was thy greit confort
  Till hir, to quhome thow was so favorabill ?
Thy slyding giftis maid hir na support,
  Hir hie lynage, nor riches intellebill,
  I se thy puissance bene bot variabill ;
Quhen hir Father, the maist hie Cristin King,
Till his deir chyld, micht mak no supportyng.

The potent prince, hir lustye lufe, and knycht,
  With his maist hardie Noblis of Scotland,
Contrair that bailfull bribour had no micht,
  Thocht all the men had bene at his command
  Of France, Flanderis, Italie, and Ingland,
With fiftie thousand millioun of tresour,
Micht nocht prolong that Lady is lyfe ane hour.

O Paris ! of all citeis principall,
  Quhilk did resave our Prince, with laud, and glorie
Solempnitlie throw arkis triumphall,

Quhilk day bene digne, to put in memorie ;
  For as Pompey, efter his victorie,
Was into Rome resavit, with greit joy,
So thow resavit our richt redoutit Roy.

Bot, at his mariage, maid upon the morne,
  Sic solace, and solempnizatioun
Was never sene afore, sen Christ was borne,
  Nor to Scotland sic consolatioun ;
  Thare selit was the confirmatioun
Of the weill keipit ancient Alliance,
Maid betuix Scotland and the realme of France.

I never did se one day mair glorious,
  So mony, in so riche abilzementis
Of silk, and gold, with stonis precious,
  Sic bankettyng, sic sound of instrumentis,
  With sang, and dance, and martiall tornamentis.
Bot, lyke ane storme, efter ane plesand morrow,
Sone was our solace changit in to sorrow.

O traytour Deith ! quhome none may contramand,
  Thow mycht have sene the preparatioun
Maid be the Thre Estaitis of Scotland,
  With greit confort and consolatioun
  In everilk cietie, castell, toure, and towr,
And how ilk Nobill set his haill intent,
To be excellent in abilzement.

Theif ! saw thow nocht the greit preparatyvis
  Of Edinburgh, the nobill famous toun,
Thow saw the peple, labouring for thair lyvis,

To mak triumphe, with trump, and clariou ;
  Sic plesour was never, in to this regioun,
As suld have bene the day of hir entrace ;
With greit propynis, gevin till hir Grace.

Thow saw makand rycht costlie scaffalding,
  Depayntit weill, with gold and azure fine,
Reddie preparit for the upsetting,
  With fontanis, flowing watter cleir, and wyne,
  Disagysit folkis, lyke creaturis divyne,
On ilk scaffold, to play ane syndrie storie,
Bot, all in greiting turnit thow that glorie.

Thow saw mony ane lustie fresche galland,
  Weill ordourit for resaving of thair Quene :
Ilk craftisman, with bent bow, in his hand,
  Full galzeartlie in schort clething of grene :
  The honest Burges, cled thow suld have sene,
Sum in scarlot, and sum in claith of grane,
For till have met thair Lady Soverane.

Provest, Baillies, and Lordis of the toun,
  The Senatouris, in ordour consequent,
Cled into silk of purpure, blak, and brown ;
  Syne the greit Lordis of the Parliament,
  With mony knychtlie Barroun, and Banrent,
In silk, and gold, in colouris confortable ;
Bot, thow, allace ! all turnit into sable.

Syne all the Lordis of Religioun,
  And Princes of the preistis venerable,
Full plesandlie in thair processioun,

With all the cunnyng Clerkis honorable ;
    Bot, thiftuouslie, thow tyrane tresonable,
All thair greit solace, and solempniteis,
Thow turnit in till dulefull Diregeis.

Syne nixt, in ordour, passing throw the toun,
    Thow suld have hard the din of instrumentis,
Of tabrone, trumpet, schalme, and clarioun,
    With reird redoundand, throw the elementis :
    The Herauldis, with thair awful vestimentis,
With Maseris, upon ather of thair handis,
To rewle the preis, with burneist silver wandis.

Syne, last of all, in ordour triumphall,
    That most illuster Princess honorable,
With hir the lustie ladyis of Scotland,
    Quhilk suld have bene ane sicht most delectable ;
    Hir rayment to rehers, I am nocht able,
Of gold, and perle, and precious stonis brycht,
Twinklyng lyke sterris, in ane frostie nycht.

Under ane pall of gold, scho sulde have past,
    Be burgessis borne, clothit in silkis fyne,
The greit maister of housholde, all thare laste,
    With hym, in ordour, all the Kingis tryne,
    Quhais ordinance war langsum to defyne ;
On this maner, scho passing throw the toun
Suld have resavit mony benisoun,

Of virginis, and of lustie burges wyiffis ;
    Quhilk suld have bene ane sicht celestiall ;
Vice la Royne ! cryand for thair lyiffis,

With ane harmonious sound angelicall ;
    In everilk corner, myrthis musicall :
Bot thow tyrane, in quhome is found no grace,
Our Alleluya hes turnit in Allace !

Thow sulde have hard the ornate Oratouris,
    Makand hir Hienes salutatioun,
Baith of the Clergy, Toun, and Counsalouris,
    With mony notable narratioun :
    Thow suld have sene hir Coronatioun,
In the fair Abbay of the Haly Rude,
In presence of ane myrthfull multitude.

Sic banketting, sic awfull tornamentis,
    On hors, and fute, that tyme quhilk suld haif bene ;
Sic Chapell Royall, with sic instrumentis,
    And craftie musick, singing from the splene,
    In this countre, was never hard, nor sene :
Bot, all this greit solempnitie, and gam,
Turnit thow hes, *In Requiem æternam.*

Inconstant warld ! thy freindschip, I defy ;
    Sen strenth, nor wisdome, riches, nor honour,
Vertew, nor bewtie, none may certefy,
    Within thy boundis, for to remane ane hour ;
    Quhat vailith to be Kyng, or Empryour,
Sen pryncely puissance may nocht be exemit
From deith, quhais dolour can nocht be expremit !

Sen man in erth hes na place permanent,
    Bot all mon passe be that horrible port ;
Lat us pray to the Lord Omnipotent,

That dulefull day to be our greit confort,
  That in His realme, we may with Him resort,
Quhilkis from the hell, with His blude ransomit bene,
With Magdalene, umquhyle of Scotland Quene.

O Deith! thocht thow the bodie may devore
  Of every man, yit hes thow na puissance,
Of thair vertew, for to consume the glore,
  As salbe sene of Magdalene of France,
  Umquhyle our Quene, quhome Poetis shall avance,
And put hir in perpetuall memorie,
So sall hir fame of thee haif victorie.

Thocht thow hes slane the hevinly Flour of France,
  Quhilk impit was in to the Thrissill kene,
Quhairin all Scotland saw thair haill plesance,
  And maid the Lyoun rejoysit frome the splene:
  Thocht rute be pullit frome the levis grene,
The smell of it sall, in despyte of thee,
Keip ay twa Realmes in peace, and amitie.

THE JUSTING BETUIX

JAMES WATSOUN AND JHONE BARBOUR,
SERVITOURIS TO KING JAMES THE FYFT.

In Sanct Androis, on Whitsoun Monnunday
Twa campionis thair manheid did assay :
Past to the barres, enarmit heid and handis,
Was never sene sic justing in no landis.
In presence of the Kingis Grace, and Quene,
Quhare mony lustie lady mycht be sene :
Mony ane knicht, barroun, and banrent,
Come for to se that awfull Tornament.
The ane of thame was gentill James Watsoun,
And Jhone Barbour, the uther campioun ;
Unto the King thay wer familiaris,
And of his chalmer boith cubicularis :
James was ane man of greit intelligence,
Ane medicinar ful of experience ;
And Jhone Barbour, he was ane nobill leche,
Crukit carlinnis, he wald gar thame get speche.
    From tyme thay enterit war into the feild,
Full womanlie thay weildit speir and scheild,

And wichtlie waifflit in the wynd thair heillis,
Hobland lyke cadgeris rydand on thair creillis;
But ather ran at uther with sic haist,
That they could never thair speir get in the reist;
Quhen gentill James trowit best with Jhone to meit,
His speir did fald among his horsis feit:
I am richt sure, gude James had bene undone,
War nocht that Jhone his marke tuke be the Mone.
Quod Jhone, Howbeit thou thinkis my leggis lyke
My speir is gude, now keip ye fra my knokkis. [rokkis,
Tary, quod James, ane quhyle, for be my thrift
The feind ane thing I can se bot tho lift.
No more can I, quod Jhone, be Goddis breid,
I se na thing except the steipill heid;
Yit, thocht thy braunis be lyk twa barrow trammis,
Defend thee, man! Than ran thay to, lyk rammis.
At that rude rink, James had bene strykin down,
War nocht that Jhone, for feirsnes fell in swoun;
And rycht sa James to Jhone had done greit deir,
Wer not amangis his hors feit he brak his speir.
Quod James to Jhone, Yit for our ladyis saikis,
Lat us togidder straik three market straikis.
I had, quod Jhone, that sall on thee be wrokin;
Bot or he spurrit his hors, his speir was brokin.
From tyme with speiris nane could his marrow meit;
James drew ane swerd, with ane richt awfull spreit,
And ran til Jhone, til haif raucht him ane rout;
Johnis swerd was roustit, and wald no way cam out.
Than James leit dryfe at Jhone, with boith his fistis,
He mist the man, and dang upon the lystis;
And with that straik, he trowit that Jhone was slane,

His swerd stak fast, and gat it never agane.
Be this, gude Jhone had gottin furth his sword,
And ran to James with mony awfull word :
My furiousness, for suith, now sall thou find !
Straikand at James his swerd flew in the wind.
Than, gentill James began to crack greit wordis ;
Allace ! quod he, this day for falt of swordis.
Than ather ran at uther with new raicis
With gluifis of plait thay dang at utheris facis.
Quha wan this feild, na creature culd ken,
Till at the last Johne cryit, Fy ! red the men :
Yea ! red, quod James, for that is my desyre,
It is ane hour sen I began to tyre.

 Sone be thay had endit that royall rink,
Into the feild micht no man stand for stink :
Than every man, that stude on far, cryit, Fy !
Sayand Adew ! for dirt partis company.
Thair hors, harnis, and all geir, wes so gude,
Lovyng to God ! that day was sched no blude.

QUOD LYNDESAY, AT COMMAND OF KING
JAMES THE FYFT.

ANE SUPPLICATIOUN
DIRECTIT TO THE KINGIS GRACE, IN CONTEMPTIOUN OF SYDE TAILLIS.

Schir! thocht your Grace hes put gret ordour,
Baith in the Hieland, and the Bordour;
Yit mak I Supplicatioun,
Till have sum reformatioun
Of ane small falt, quhilk is nocht tressoun,
Thocht it be contrarie to ressoun.
Because the mater bene so vyle,
It may nocht have ane ornate style;
Quharefor, I pray your Excellence,
To heir me with greit patience:
Of stinkand weidis maculate,
Na man may mak ane rois chaiplate.
Soverane, I mene of thir Syde Taillis,
Quhilk throw the dust, and dubbis traillis,
Thre quarteris lang behynd thair heillis,
Expres agane all Commounweillis.
Thocht Bischopis, in thair pontificallis,
Have men for to beir up thair taillis,
For dignitie of thair office;
Richt so ane Quene, or ane Emprice;
Howbeit thay use sic gravitie,
Conformand to thair Majestie:
Thocht thair rob royallis be upborne,

I think it is ane verray scorne,
That every lady of the land
Suld have hir taill so syde trailland;
Howbeit thay bene of hie estait
The Quene, thay suld nocht counterfait.
Quhare ever thay go, it may be sene,
How kirk, and calsay, thay soup clene;
The imagis in to the Kirk,
May think of thair syde taillis irk:
For quhen the wedder bene maist fair,
The dust fleis hiest in the air,
And all thair facis dois begarie,
Gif thay culd speik, thay wald thame warie.
    To se I think ane plesand sicht,
Of Italie the ladyis bricht,
In thair clething maist triumphand,
Above all other Christin land:
Yit, quhen thay travell throw the townis,
Men seis than feet beneth thair gownis,
Four inche abone thair proper heillis,
Circulat about als round as quheillis;
Quhare throw thare dois na poulder ryis,
Thair fair quhyte lymmis to suppryis.
Bot, I think maist abusioun,
To se men of religioun,
Gar beir thair taillis throw the streit,
That folkis may behald thair feit,
I trow Sanct Bernard, nor Sanct Blais,
Gart never man beir up thair clais;
Peter, nor Paule, nor Sanct Androw,
Gart never beir up thair taillis, I trow.

Bot, I lauch best to se ane Nun,
Gar beir hir taill abone hir bun,
For no thing ellis, as I suppois,
Bot for to schaw hir lillie quhyte hois :
In all thair Rewlis, they will nocht find,
Quha suld beir up thair taillis behind.
Bot I have maist in to despyte,
Pure claggokis cled in roiploch quhyte,
Quhilk hes skant twa markis for thair feis,
Will have twa ellis beneath thair kneis :
Kittok, that clekkit wes yestrene,
The morne, wyll counterfute the Quene :
Ane mureland Meg, that milkit the yowis,
Claggit with clay abone the howis,
In barn, nor byir, scho wyll nocht byde,
Without hir kyrtyll taill be syde.
In burrowis, wantoun burges wyiflis,
Quha may have sydest taillis stryiflis,
Weill bordourit with velvoit fyne :
Bot following thame it is ane pyne,
In somer quhen the streittis dryis,
Thay rais the dust abone the skyis ;
None may ga neir thame at thair eis,
Without thay cover mouth and neis,
Frome the powder to keip thair ene,
Considder gif thair cloiflis be clene.
Betuixt thair cleving and thair kneis,
Quha micht behald thair sweitie theis,
Begairit all with dirt, and dust,
That were aneuch to stanche the lust
Of ony man that saw thame naikit :

I think sic giglottis ar bot glaikit
Without profite to have sye pryde
Harland thair claggit taillis so syde :
I wald thae Borrowstounis barnis had breikkis,
To keip sic mist fra malkinnis cheikkis ;
I dreid rouch malkin die for drouth,
Quhen sic dry dust blawis in hir mouth.
I think maist pane efter ane rane,
To se thame towkit up agane ;
Than, quhen thay step furth throw the streit,
Thair faldingis flappis about thair feit,
Thair laithlie lyning furthwart flypit,
Quhilk hes the muk and midding wypit ;
Thay waist mair claith, within few yeiris,
Nor wald cleith fyftie score of freiris.
Quhen Marioun from the midding gois,
Frome hir morne turne, scho strypis the nois,
And all the day, quhare ever scho go,
Sic liquour scho likkith up also :
The turcumis of hir taill, I trow,
Micht be ane supper till ane sow.
I ken ane man, quhilk swoir greit aithis,
How he did lift ane Kittokis claithis,
And wald have done, I wat nocht quhat,
Bot sone remeid of lufe he gat ;
He thocht na schame to mak it wittin,
How hir syde taill was all beschittin ;
Of filth sic flewer straik till his hart,
That he behovit for till depart.
Quod scho, Sweit schir, me think ye rew.
Quod he, Your taill makis sic ane stew,

That be Sanct Bryde, I may nocht byde it,
Ye were nocht wyse, that wald nocht hyde it,
  Of Taillis I will no more indyte,
From dreid sum duddroun me despyte :
Nochtwithstanding, I wyll conclude,
That of syde taillis can cum na gude,
Syder nor may thair hanclethis hyde,
The remanent proceidis of pryde,
And pryde proceidis of the devill,
Thus alway thay proceid of evill.
  Ane uther falt, Schir, may be sene,
Thay hyde thair face all bot the ene,
Quheu gentill men biddis thame gude day,
Without reverence thay slyde away,
That none may knaw, I you assure,
Ane honest woman, be ane hure ;
Without thair naikit face I se,
Thay get na mo Gude dayis of me.
Haile ane Frence lady quhen ye pleis,
Scho wyll discover mouth, and neis ;
And with one humill countenance,
With visage bair, mak reverence.
Quhen our ladyis dois ryde in raine,
Suld no man have thame at disdane,
Thocht thay be coverit mouth and neis :
In that case thay will nane displeis,
Nor quhen thay go to quiet places,
I thame excuse, to hyde thair faces,
Quhen thay wald mak collatioun,
With ony lustie companyeoun,
Thocht thay be hid than to the ene,

Ye may considder quhat I mene ;
Bot, in the Kirk, and market placis,
I think thay suld nocht hide thair facis :
Without this faltis be sone amendit,
My Flyting, Schir, sall never be endit.
Bot wald your Grace my counsall tak,
Ane proclamatioun ye suld mak,
Baith throw the Land, and Borrowstounis,
To schaw thair face, and cut thair gounis ;
Nane suld fra that exemptit be,
Except the Quenis Majestie :
Because this mater is nocht fair,
Of rethorik it man be bair.
Wemen will say, this is no bourdis,
To wryte sick vyle and filthy wordis ;
Bot wald thay clenge thair filthy taillis,
Quhilk ouir the myris and middingis traillis,
Than suld my wryting clengit be,
None uther mendis thay get of me ;
The suith suld nocht be holden clos,
Veritas non quærit angulos.
I wait gude wemen that bene wyse,
This rurall ryme wyll nocht dispyse ;
None wyll me blame, I you assure
Except ane wanton glorious hure,
Quhais flyting I feir nocht ane fle :
Fair weill ! ye get no more of me.

QUOD LYNDESAY, IN CONTEMPT OF THE SYDE TAILLIS,
THAT DUDDROUNIS, AND DUNTIBOURIS, THROW THE
    DUBBIS TRAILLIS.

KITTEIS CONFESSIOUN.

THE CURATE, AND KITTIE.

THE Curate Kittie culd confesse,
And scho tald on baith mair and lesse.
  Quhen scho was telland as scho wist,
The Curate Kittie wald have kist ;
Bot yit ane countenance he bure
Degeist, devote, daine, and demure ;
And syne began hir to exempne :
He wes best at the efter game.
Quod he, Have ye na wrangous geir ?
Quod scho, I staw ane pek of beir.
Quod he, That suld restorit be,
Tharefor, delyver it to me ;
Tibbie, and Peter bad me speir,
Be my conscience, thay sall it heir.
Quod he, Leve ye in lecherie ?
Quod scho, Will Leno mowit me.
Quod he, His wyfe that sall I tell,
To mak hir acquentance with my sell.
Quod he, Ken ye na heresie ?
I wait nocht quhat that is, quod sche.

Quod he, Hard ye na Inglis bukis?
Quho scho, My maister on thame lukis.
Quod he, The bischop that sall knaw,
For I am sworne, that for to schaw.
Quod he, What said he of the King?
Quod scho, Of gude he spak na thing.
Quod he, His Grace of that sall wit;
And he sall lose his lyfe for it.
    Quhen scho in mynd did mair revolve;
Quod he, I can nocht you absolve,
Bot, to my chalmer cum at even
Absolvit for to be, and schrevin.
Quod scho, I wyll pas tyll ane uther:
And I met with Schir Andro, my brother,
And he full clenely did me schryve,
Bot he wes sumthing talkatyve;
He speirit mony strange case,
How that my lufe did me inbrace,
Quhat day, how oft, quhat sort, and quhare?
Quod he, I wald I had bene thare.
He me absolvit for ane plak,
Thocht he na pryce with me wald mak,
And mekil Latyne he did mummill,
I hard na thing bot hummill bummill.
He schew me nocht of Goddis word,
Quhilk scharper is than ony sword,
And deip intill our hart dois prent,
Our syn quharethrow we do repent;
He pat me na thing into feir,
Quharethrow I suld my syn forbeir;
He schew me nocht the maledictioun

Of God for syn, nor the afflictioun ;
And in this lyfe the greit mischeif
Ordanit to punische hure and theif ;
Nor schew he me of hellis pane,
That I mycht feir, and vice refraine ;
He counsalit me nocht till abstene,
And leid ane holy lyfe, and clene :
Of Christis blude na thing he knew,
Nor of His promisses full trew,
That saifis all that wyll beleve,
That Sathan sall us never greve.
He teichit me nocht for till traist,
The confort of the Haly Ghaist ;
He bad me nocht to Christ be kynd,
To keip His law with hart and mynd,
And lufe and thank His greit mercie,
Fra syn and hell that savit me ;
And lufe my nichtbour as my sell,
Of this na thing he culd me tell.
Bot gave me pennance, ilk ane day
Ane *Ave Marie* for to say :
And Fridayis fyve na fische to eit,
Bot butter and eggis ar better meit ;
And with ane plak to buy ane Messe,
Fra drounkin Schir Jhone Latynclesse.
Quod he, Ane plak I wyll gar Sandie
Give thee agane, with handie dandie
Syne into pilgrimage to pas :
The verray way to wantounes.
Of all his pennance, I was glaid,
I had them all perqueir, I said ;

To mow and steill, I ken the pryce,
I sall it set on cincq and syce;
Bot he my counsale culd nocht keip,
He maid him be the fyre to sleip;
Syne cryit, Colleris, beif, and coillis,
Hois, and schone with dowbill soillis,
Caikis, and candill, creische, and salt,
Curnis of meill, and luitlillis of malt,
Wollin and linning, werp and woft;
Dame ! keip the keis of your woll loft:
Throw drink and sleip maid him to raif,
And swa with us thay play the knaif.

   Freiris sweiris, be thair professioun,
Nane can be saif, but this Confessioun,
And garris all men understand,
That it is Goddis awin command;
Yit it is nocht but mennis drame,
The pepill to confound and schame.
It is nocht ellis but mennis law,
Maid mennis mindis for to knaw,
Quharethrow thay syle thame as thay will,
And makis thair law conforme tharetill;
Sittand in mennis conscience,
Abone Goddis magnificence;
And dois the pepill teche and tyste
To serve the Pape the Antechriste.

   To the greit God Omnipotent
Confess thy syn, and sore repent;
And traist in Christ, as wrytis Paule,
Quhilk sched his blude to saif thy saule,
For nane can thee absolve bot He,

Nor tak away thy syn frome thee.
Gif of gude counsall thow hes neid,
Or hes nocht leirnit weill thy Creid,
Or wickit vicis regne in thee,
The quhilk thow can nocht mortifie,
Or be in desperatioun,
And wald have consolatioun;
Than till ane preichour trew thow pas,
And schaw thy syn and thy trespas;
Thow neidis nocht to schaw him all,
Nor tell thy syn, baith greit and small,
Quhilk is unpossible to be;
Bot schaw the vice that troubillis thee:
And he sall of thy saule have reuth,
And thee instruct in to the treuth,
And with the Word of Veritie,
Sall confort, and sall counsall thee:
The Sacramentis schaw thee at lenth,
Thy lytle faith to stark and strenth;
And how thow suld thame richtlie use,
And all hypocrisie refuse.
  Confessioun first wes ordanit fre,
In this sort, in the Kirk, to be:
Swa to confes, as I descryve,
Wes in the gude Kirk primityve;
Swa wes confessioun ordanit first,
Thocht Codrus kyte suld cleve and birst.

THE TRAGEDIE OF

THE MAIST REVEREND FATHER DAVID, BE
THE MERCY OF GOD, CARDINALL, ARCH-
BISCHOP OF SANCTANDROIS, AND OF THE
HAILL REALME OF SCOTLAND PRIMATE,
LEGATE, AND CHANCELLOR, &c.

Mortales cum nati sitis, ne supra Deum vos crereritis.

THE PROLOG.

NOCHT lang ago, efter the hour of pryme,
 Secreitly sittyng in mine Oratorie,
I tuk ane Buke, till occupy the tyme,
 Quhare I fand mony Tragedie and Storie,
 Quhilk Jhone Bochas had put in memorie ;
Quhow mony Prencis, Conquerours, and Kingis
War dulfullie depossit frome thair ringis.

Quhow Alexander, the potent Conquerour,
 In Babilone was poysonit pietcouslie ;
And Julius the mychtie Empriour,
 Murdreist at Rome, causles and cruellie ;
 Prudent Pompey, in Egypt schamefullie
He murdreist was : Quhat nedith proces more ?
Quhose Tragedeis war pietie tyll deplore.

I sittyng so, upon my Buke redyng,
   Rycht suddantlie afore me did appeir
Ane woundit man, aboundantlie bledyng,
   With vissage paill, and with ane deidlye cheir;
   Semand ane man of two and fyftie yeir;
In rayment reid cloithit full curiouslie,
Of vellvoit, and of satyn crammosie.

With febyll voce, as man opprest with paine,
   Soiftlye he made me supplycatioun,
Sayand, My friend, go reid and reid againe,
   Geve thow can fynde, by true narratioun,
   Of ony paine lyke to my passioun :
Rycht sure I am, war Jhone Bochas on lyve,
My Tragedie at lenth he wald discryve.

Sen he is gone, I pray thee tyll indyte
   Of my infortune sum remembrance ;
Or at the leist, my Tragedie to wryte,
   As I to thee sall schaw the circumstance,
   In termes breve, of my unhappy chance,
Sen my beginnyng tyll my fatall ende,
Quhilk I wald tyll all creature war kende.

I not, said I, mak sic memoriall,
   Geve of thy name I had intelligence.
I am David, that cairfull Cardinall,
   Quhilk doith appeir, said he, to thy presens,
   That umquhyle had so gret preeminens :
Than he began his dedis tyll indyte,
As ye sall heir, and I began to wryte.

THE TRAGEDIE.

I, DAVID BETOUN, umquhyle Cardinall,
  Of nobyll blude, be lyne, I did descend :
During my tyme, I had no paregall ;
  Bot now is cum, allace ! my fatall end.
  Aye, gre by gre, upwart I did ascende ;
Swa that in to this realme did never ryng
So greit one man as I, under ane kyng.

Quhen I was ane young joly gentyll man,
  Prencis to serve I sett my hole intent.
First tyll ascende, at Arbroith I began,
  Ane Abacie of greit ryches and rent,
  Of that estait, yit was I nocht contente :
To get more ryches, dignitie, and glore,
My hart was set : allace ! allace ! tharefore.

I maid sic servyce tyll our Soverane kyng,
  He did promove me tyll more hie estait,
One Prince abufe all preistis for tyll ryng,
  Archebyschope of Sanctandrois consecrat.
  Tyll that honour quhen I wes elevate,
My prydefull hart was nocht content at all,
Tyll that I create wes ane Cardinall.

Yit preisit I tyll have more auctoritie,
  And fynalie was chosin Chancelare.

And for uphalding of my dignitie
   Was maid Legate; than had I no compare.
   I purcheist for my proffect singulare,
My boxis and my threasure tyll avance,
The Byschopreik of Merapose, in France.

Of all Scotland I had the Governall;
   But my avyse, concludit wes no thyng:
Abbot, Byschope, Archebyschope, Cardinall,
   In to this Realme no hiear could I ryng,
   Bot I had bene Pape, Emperour, or Kyng.
For schortnes of the tyme, I am nocht abyll
At lenth to schaw my actis honorabyll.

For my moste princelye prodigalytie,
   Amang prelatis in France, I bure the pryse,
I schew my lordlye lyberalitie,
   In banketting, playing at cartis, and dyse;.
   In to sic wysedome I was haldin wyse.
And sparit nocht to play, with Kyng nor Knycht,
Three thousand crownis of gold, upon ane nycht.

In France I maid seir honest voyagis,
   Quhare I did actis ding of remembrance.
Throuch me war maid triumphand mariagis
   Tyll our Soverane boith proffet and plesance.
   Quene Magdalene, the first Dochter of France,
With greit ryches, was in to Scotland brocht:
That mariage throuch my wysedome wes wrocht.

Efter quhose deith, in France I paste agane:
   The secunde Quene homwart I did convoye,

That lustye Princes, Marie de Lorane,
  Quhilk wes resavit with greit tryumphe and joye.
  So servit I our rycht redouttit Roye.
Sone efter that, Harye of Ingland Kyng,
Of our Soverane desyrit ane commonyng.

Of that metyng our Kyng wos weill content,
  So that in York was sett boith tyme and place :
Bot our Prelatis nor I wald never consent
  That he sulde se Kyng Harye in the face ;
  Bot we wer weill content, quhowbeit his Grace
Had saylit the sey to speik with ony uther,
Except that Kyng, quhilk was his Mother Brother.

Quhair throuch thar rose greit weir and mortal stryfe,
  Greit heirschipps, hounger, darth, and desolatioun ;
On ather syde did mony lose thair lyfe,
  Geve I wald mak ane trew narratioun,
  I causit all that trybulatioun :
For tyll mak peace I never wald consent,
Without the Kyng of France had bene content.

Duryng this weir war takin prisoneris,
  Of nobyll men fechtyng full furiouslie,
Mony one lorde, barrone, and bachileris,
  Quhair throuch our Kyng tuke sic melancolie
  Quhilk drave hym to the dede, rycht dulefullie.
Extreme dolour ouirset did so his hart,
That frome this lyfe, allace ! he did depart.

Bot, efter that boith strenth and speche wes lesit,
  Ane paper blank his Grace I gart subscryve,
    VOL. I.   K

In to the quhilk I wrait all that I plesit,
  Efter his deith, quhilk lang war tyll descryve,
  Throuch that wrytting I purposit, belyve,
With supporte of sum Lordis benevolens,
In this regioun tyll have preemynens.

As for my Lord, our rychteous Governour :
  Geve I wald schortlie schaw the veritie,
Tyll hym I had no maner of favour.
  Duryng that tyme, I purposit that he
  Suld nevir cum to none Auctoritie :
For his supporte, tharefor, he brocht amang us,
Furth of Ingland, the nobyll Erle of Angus.

Than was I put abak frome my purpose,
  And suddantlie caste in captyvitie,
My prydefull hart to dant, as I suppose,
  Devysit by the heich Divinitie :
  Yit in my hart sprang no humylitie.
Bot now the Word of God full weill I knaw,
Quho dois exault hym self, God sall hym law.

In the meine tyme, quhen I wes so subjectit,
  Ambassadouris war sent in to Ingland,
Quhair thay boith peace and mariage contractit ;
  And more surelie for tyll observe that band,
War promeist divers pleagis of Scotland.
Of that contract I wes no way content,
Nor nevir wald thareto geve my consent.

Tyll Capytanis that kepit me in waird,
  Gyftis of gold I gave thame greit plentie ;

Rewlaris of court I rychelie did rewaird,
   Quhair throuch I chapit frome captivitie :
   Bot quhen I wes free at my libertie,
Than, lyke ane lyone lowsit of his caige,
Out throuch this realme I gan to reill and rage.

Contrare the Governour, and his companie,
   Oft tymes maid I insurrectioun,
Purposyng for tyll have hym haistelie
   Subdewit unto my correctioun,
   Or put hym tyll extreme subjectioun.
Duryng this tyme, geve it war weill decydit,
This realme by me was utterlie devydit.

The Governour purposyng to subdew,
   I raisit ane oyste of mony bald Barroun,
And maid ane raid, quhilk Lythgow yit may rew ;
   For we distroyit ane myle about the town :
   For that I gat mony blak malysoun :
Yit, contrare the Governouris intent,
With our Young Princess, we to Strivilyng went.

For heich contemptioun of the Governour,
   I brocht the Erle of Lennox furth of France :
That lustie Lord, levand in gret plesour,
   Did lose that land and honest ordinance.
   Bot he and I fell sone at variance,
And throuch my counsall was within schort space,
Forfaltit and flemit, he gat none uther grace.

Than throuch my prudens, practyke, and ingyne,
   Our Governour I causit to consent

Full quyetlie, to my counsale inclyne ;
  Quhareof his Nobyllis war nocht weill content :
  For quhy ? I gart dissolve in plane Parliament,
The band of peace contractit with Ingland,
Quharthrouch come harme and heirschip to Scotland.

That peace brokin, arose new mortall weiris,
  Be sey, and land, sie reif without releif,
Quhilk to report my frayit hart affeiris :
  The veritie to schaw, in termes breif,
  I was the rute of all that gret myscheif.
The South Countre may saye, it had bene gude
That my noryce had smorit me in my cude.

I wes the cause of mekle more myschance,
  For uphald of my glore, and dignitie,
And plesour of the potent Kyng of France :
  With Ingland wald I have no unitie :
  Bot, quho consydder wald the veritie,
We mycht full weill have levit in peace and rest,
Nyne or ten yeiris, and than playit louse or fast.

Had we with Ingland keipit our contrackis,
  Our nobyll men had levit in peace and rest ;
Our marchandis had nocht lost so mony packis,
  Our commoun peple had nocht bene opprest :
  On ather syde, all wrangis had bene redrest ;
Bot Edinburgh sen syne, Leith, and Kynghorne,
The day and hour may ban, that I was borne.

Our Governour, to mak hym to me sure,
  With sweit and subtell wordis, I did hym syle,

Tyl I his sone and air gat in my cure ;
 To that effect, I fand that craftye wyle,
 That he no maner of waye mycht me begyle :
Than leuch I, quhen his liegis did allege
Quhow I his sone had gottin in to plege.

The Erle of Angus, and his germane Brother,
 I purposit to gar thaim lose thair lyfe ;
Rycht so tyll have destroyit mony uther,
 Sum with the fyre, sum with the sword and knyfe ;
 In speciale mony gentyll men of **Fyfe** ;
And purposit tyll put to gret torment
All favoraris of the Auld and New Testament.

Than every freik thay tuke of me sic feir,
 That tyme quhen I had so greit governance,
Greit Lordis dreidyng, I sulde do thame deir,
 Thay durst nocht cum tyll court, bot assurance :
 Sen syne thare hes nocht bene sic variance.
Now, tyll our Prince, barronis obedientlie,
But assurance, thay cum full courteslie.

My hope was moste in to the Kyng of France,
 Togiddir with the Popis holynes,
More nor in God, my worschipe tyll avance.
 I traistit so into thair gentylnes,
 That no man durste presume me tyll oppres :
Bot, quhen the day come, of my fatall houre,
Far was frome me thair supporte and succoure.

Than to preserve my ryches, and my lyfe,
 I made one strenth, of wallis heych and braid,

Sic ane Fortres wes never found in Fyfe,
  Belevand thare durst no man me invaid.
  Now fynd I trew the saw, quhilk David said,
Without God of ane hous be Maister of wark,
He wyrkis in vaine, thocht it be never so stark.

For I was, throuch the hie power Divine,
  Rycht dulefullye doung down amang the ass,
Quhilk culd not be throuch mortall mannis ingyne:
  Bot, as David did slay the gret Golyas,
  Or Helopherne be Judith killit was,
In myd amang his tryumphant armye,
So was I slane into my cheiff Cictie.

Quhen I had gretest dominatioun,
  As Lucifer had, in the Hevin impyre,
Came suddantlye my deprivatioun,
  Be thame quhilk did my dolent deith conspyre.
  So cruell was thair furious byrnand yre,
I gat no tyme, laser, nor lybertie,
To saye, *In manus tuos Domine.*

Behald my fatall infylicitie:
  I beand in my strenth incomparabyll,
That dreidfull dungeoun maid me no supplye
  My gret ryches, nor rentis profitabyll,
  My sylver work, jowellis inestimabyll,
My Papall pompe, of golde my ryche thresoure,
My lyfe and all, I loste in half ane hour.

To the pepill wes maid ane spectakle
  Of my dede and deformit carioun.

Sum said, it was ane manifest myrakle ;
   Sum said it was Divine punitioun
   So to be slane, in to my strang dungeoun :
Quhen every man had judgit as hym lyste,
Thay saltit me, syne closit me in ane kyste.

I lay unburyit seven monethis and more,
   Or I was borne to closter, kirk, or queir,
In ane mydding, quhilk paine bene tyll deplore,
   Without suffrage of chanoun, monk, or freir :
   All proud Prelatis at me may lessonis leir,
Quhilk rang so lang, and so triumphantlie,
Syne, in the dust doung doun so dulefullie.

TO THE PRELATIS.

O ye my Brether ! Prencis of the Preistis,
   I mak yow hartly supplycatioun,
Boith nycht and day revolve in to your breistis,
   The proces of my deprivatioun.
   Consydder quhat bene your vocatioun :
To follow me, I pray yow nocht pretend yow,
Bot reid at lenth this cedull that I send yow.

Ye knaw quhow Jesus his disciplis sent,
   Ambassadouris tyll every natioun,
To schaw his law, and his commandement
   To all pepill, by predycatioun ;
   Tharefor I mak to yow narratioun,

Sen ye to thame ar verray successouris,
Ye aucht tyll do, as did your predecessouris.

Quhow dar ye be so bauld tyll tak on hand,
    For to be herraldis to so greit ane Kyng,
To beir his message boith to burgh and land,
    Ye beand dum, and can pronunce no thyng,
    Lyke Menstralis, that can nocht play nor sing!
Or quhy suld men geve to sic hirdis hyre,
Quhilk can not gyde thair scheip about the myre.

Eschame ye nocht to be Christis servitouris,
    And for your fee, hes gret temporall landis :
Syne of your office can nocht take the curis,
    As Cannone Law and Scripture yow commandis !
    Ye wyll nocht want teind scheif, nor offerandis,
Teind woll, teind lambe, teind calf, teind gryce, and
        guse ;
To mak servyce ye ar all out of use.

My deir Brether, do nocht as ye war wount,
    Amend your lyfe, now quhill your day induris;
Traist weill, ye sall be callit to your count
    Of everilk thyng belanging to your curis.
    Leif hasartrie, your harlotrie, and huris,
Remembring on my unprovisit deid :
For efter deith may no man mak remeid.

Ye Prelatis, quhilkis hes thousandis for to spende,
    Ye send ane sempyll Freir for yow to preiche :

It is your craft, I mak it to yow keud,
   Your selfis iu your Templis for to teiche.
   Bot ferlye nocht, thocht, syllie freris fleiche ;
For, and thay planelie schaw the veritie,
Than wyll thay want the Byschopis charitie.

Quharefor bene gevin yow sic Royall rent,
   Bot for tyll fynd the pepill Spirituall fude,
Prechand to thame the Auld and New Testament ?
   The Law of God doith planely so conclude.
   Put nocht your hope in to no warldly gude,
As I have done : behauld my gret thresoure
Maid me no helpe, at my unhappye houre.

That day quhen I was Byschope consecrait,
   The great Byble wes bound upon my bak ;
Quhat wes tharein, lytill I knew, God wait !
   More than ane beist berand ane precious pak.
   Bot haistelie my covenant I brak ;
For, I wes oblyssit, with my awin consent,
The Law of God to preiche with gude intent.

Brether, rycht so, quhen ye wer consecrait,
   Ye oblyssit yow all on the samyn wyse.
Ye may be callit Byschoppis countrefait,
   As gallandis buskit for to mak ane Gyse.
   Now thynk I, Prencis ar no thyng to pryse,
Tyll geve ane famous office tyll ane fule ;
As quho walde putt ane myter on ane mule.

Allace ! and ye that sorrowfull sycht hade sene,
   Quhow I lay bullerand, baithit in my blude,

To mend your lyfe, it had occasioun bene,
  And leif your auld corruptit consuetude :
    Failyeing thareof, than, schortlie I conclude,
Without ye frome your rebaldrye aryse,
Ye sall be servit on the samyn wyse.

TO THE PRENCIS.

Imprudent Prencis, but discretioun,
  Havyng in erth power Imperiall,
Ye bene the cause of this transgressioun :
  I speik to yow all, in to generall,
    Quhilk doith dispone all office Spiritnall,
Gevand the saulis, quhilkis bene Chrystis scheip,
To blynd pastouris but conscience to keip.

Quhen ye, Prencis, doith laik ane officiar,
  Ane baxster, browster, or ane maister cuke,
Ane trym tailyeour, ane counnyng cordynar,
  Ouir all the land at lenth, ye wyll gar luke
    Most abyll men sic officis tyll bruke :
Ane browster quhilk can brew most hoilsum aill,
Ane cunnyng cuke, quhilk best can sessoune caill.

Ane tailyeour, quhilk hes fosterit bene in France,
  That can mak garmentis, on the gayest gyse.
Ye Prencis bene the cause of this myschance,
  That, quhen thare doith vaik ony benefyse,
    Ye aucht tyll do upone the samyn wyse,

Gar scars and seik, baith in to burgh and lande,
The law of God quho best can understand.

Mak hym Byschope, that prudentlie can preche,
  As dois pertene tyll his vocatioun;
Ane Persone, quhilk his parischoun can teche :
  Gar Vicaris mak dew mynistratioun.
  And als, I mak you supplicatioun,
Mak your Abbotis of rycht religious men,
Quhilk Christis law can to thair Convent ken :

But not to rebaldis, new cum frome the roste,
  Nor of ane stuffat stollin out of ane stabill,
The quhilk in to the scule maid never na coste,
  Nor never was tyll Spirituall science abill ;
  Except the cartis, the dyce, the ches, and tabill,
Of Rome rakaris, nor of rude ruffianis,
Of calsay paikaris, nor of publycanis.

Nor to fantastyke fenyeit flatteraris,
  Most meit to gather mussillis in to Maye,
Of cowhubeis, nor yit of clatterraris,
  That in the Kirk can nother sing, nor saye,
  Thocht they be clokit up in clerkis arraye,
Lyke doytit Doctoris new cum out of Athenis,
And mummyll ouer ane pair of maiglit matenis.

Nocht qualyfeit to bruk ane benefyse,
  Bot throuch Schir Symonis solysitatioun,
I was promovit on the samyn wyse,
  Allace ! throuch Prencis supplycatioun,
  And maid in Rome, throuch fals narratioun,

Byschope, Abbote, bot no Religious man :
Quho me promovit I now thair banis ban.

Quhowbeit I was Legat, and Cardinall,
   Lytill I knew tharein quhat suld be done ;
I understude no science Spirituall,
    No more than did blynd Alane of the Mone.
   I dreid the Kyng that syttith heych abone,
On yow Prencis sall mak sore punischement,
Rycht so, on us, throuch rychteous judgement :

On yow Prencis, for undiscreit gevyng
   Tyll ignorantis sic officis tyll use ;
And we, for our inoportune askyng,
    Quhilk sulde have done sic dignitie refuse.
   Our ignorance hes done the warld abuse,
Throuch Covatyce of ryches, and of rent.
That ever I was ane Prelate, I repent

O Kyngis, mak ye no cair to geve in cure,
   Virginis profest in to Religioun,
In tyll the keipyng of ane commoun hure !
    To mak, think ye nocht gret derisioun,
   Ane woman Persone of ane parischoun,
Quhare thare bene two thousand saulis to gyde,
That from harlottis can not hir hyppis hyde ?

Quhat ! and Kyng David levit in thir dayis,
   Or out of hevin, quhat and he lukit down,
The quhilk did found so mony fair Abbayis ?
    Seand the gret abhominatioun
   In mony Abbayis of this Natioun,

He wald repent, that narrowit so his boundis,
Of yeirly rent three score of thousand poundis.

Quharefor I counsale everyilk Christinit Kyng,
　　Within his realme mak Reformatioun,
And suffer no mo rebaldis for to ryng
　　Abufe Christis trew Congregatioun :
　　Failyeing thareof, I mak narratioun,
That ye Prencis, and Prelatis, all at onis,
Sall bureit be in hell, saule, blude and bonis.

That ever I brukit benefice I rew,
　　Or to sic hycht so proudely did pretend ;
I man depart, tharefor, my friends, adew !
　　Quhare ever it plesith God, now man I wend.
　　I pray thee tyll my freindis me recommend,
And failye nocht, at lenth, to put in wryte
My TRAGEDIE, as I have done indyte.

ANE DESCRIPTIOUN

OF PEDDER COFFEIS HAVING NA REGAIRD TIL HONESTIE IN THAIR VACATIOUN.

It is my purpose to discryve
  This holy perfyte genolagie
Of Pedder Knavis superlatyve
  Pretendland to awtoretie,
  That wait of nocht but beggartie.
Ye burges sonis prevene thir lownis,
  That wald distroy nobilitie,
And baneiss it all Borrow townis.

Thay ar declarit, in Sevin Pairtis;
  Ane scroppit coffe, quhen he begynnis
Sornand all and sindry airtis,
  For to by hennis reidwood he rynnis,
  He lokis thame up in to his innis
Unto ane deth, and sellis thair eggis,
  Regraitandly on thame he wynnis,
And secondly his meit he beggis.

Ane swyngeour coffe, amangis the wyvis,
    In landwart dwellis with subteill menis,
Exponand thame, auld sanctis lyvis,
    And sanis thame with deid mennis banis ;
    Lyk Rome rakaris, with awsterne granis,
Speikand curlyk ilk ane till uder
    Peipand peurly with peteouss granis,
Lyk fenyeit Symmye and his bruder.

Thir cur coffeis that sailis ouer sone,
    And thretty sum abowt ane pak,
With bair blew bonattis and hobbeld schone,
    And beir bonnokkis with thame thay tak ;
    Thay schamed schrewis, God gif thame lak.
At none quhen merchantis makis gud cheir,
    Steilis doun, and lyis behind ane pak.
Drinkand bot dreggis and barmy beir.

Knaifatica coff misknawis him sell,
    Quhen he gettis in a furrit goun :
Grit Lucifer, maister of hell,
    Is nocht sa helie as that loun ;
    As he cummis brankand throw the toun.
With his keis clynkand on his arme,
    That calf clovin futtit fleid custroun,
Will mary nane bot a burges bairne.

Ane dyvour coffe, that wirry hen,
    Distroyis the honor of our natioun,
Takis gudis to frist fra fremit men,
    And brekis his obligatioun,

Quhilk dois the marchandis defamatioun,
Thay ar reprevit for that regratour ;
  Thairfoir we gif our declaratioun,
To hang and draw that common tratour.

Ane curloreous coffe, that hege skraper,
  He sittis at hame quhen that thay baik,
That pedder brybour, that scheip keipar,
  He tellis thame ilk ane caik by caik ;
  Syne lokkis thame up, and takis a faik,
Betuix his dowblett and his jackett,
  And eitis thame in the buth, that smaik ;
God that he mort into ane rakkett !

Ane cathedrall coffe, he is ouir riche,
  And hes na hap his gude to spend,
Bot levis lyk ane wareit wreche,
  And trestis nevir till tak ane end ;
  With falsheid evir dois him defend,
Proceding still in averice,
  And leivis his saule na gude commend,
Bot walkis ane wilsome wey, I wiss.

I yow exhort all that is heir,
  That reidis this bill, ye wald it schaw
Unto the Provest, and him requeir,
  That he will geif thir Coffeis the law,
  And baneiss thame the Burgess raw,
And to the Scho streit ye thame ken ;
  Syne cutt thair luggis, that ye may knaw
Thir Peddir Knavis be Burges men.

THE HISTORIE AND TESTAMENT

OF SQUYER WILLIAM MELDRUM

OF CLEISCHE AND BYNNIS.

VOL. I.   L

THE HISTORIE AND TESTAMENT

OF SQUYER WILLIAM MELDRUM,

OF CLEISCHE AND BYNNIS.

QUHO that antique storeis reidis,
Considder may the famous deidis
Of our nobill progenitouris;
Quhilk suld to us be richt mirrouris,
Thair verteous deidis to ensew,
And vicious leving to eschew.
Sic men bene put in memorie,
That deith suld not confound thair glorie,
Howbeit thair bodie bene absent,
Thair verteous deidis bene present.
Poetis thair honour to avance
Hes put thame in rememberance;
Sum wryt of preclair conquerouris,
And sum of vailyeand empriouris;
And sum of nobill michtie kingis,
That royallie did reull their ringis;
And sum of campiounis, and of knichtis,
That bauldlie did defend thair richtis;
Quhilk vailyeandlie did stand in stour,
For the defence of thair honour;
And sum of squyeris douchtie deidis.

That wounders wrocht in weirlie weidis;
Sum wryt of deidis amorous;
As Chauceir wrait of Troilus,
How that he luiflit Cressida;
Of Jason, and of Medea.
   With help of Cleo I intend,
Sa Minerve wald me sapience send,
Ane nobill Squyer to discryfe,
Quhais douchtines, during his lyfe,
I knaw myself, thairof I wryte,
And all his deidis I dar indyte:
And secreitis that I did not knaw,
That nobill Squyer did me schaw.
Sa I intend the best I can,
Descryve the deidis and the man;
Quhais youth did occupie in lufe,
Full plesantlie, without reprufe.
Quhilk did as monie douchtie deidis,
As monie ane, that men of reidis,
Quhilkis poetis puttis in memorie,
For the exalting of thair glorie:
Quhairfoir I think, sa God me saif!
He suld have place amangis the laif.
That his hie honour suld not smure,
Considering quhat he did indure,
Oft times for his ladeis sake;
I wait Sir Lancelote du Lake,
Quhen he did lufe king Arthuris wyfe,
Faucht never better with sword, nor knyfe,
For his ladie in no battell,
Nor had not half so just querrell.

The veritie quha list declair,
His lufe was ane adulterair,
And durst not cum into hir sicht,
Bot lyke ane houlet on the nicht :
With this Squyer it stude not so,
His ladie luifit him and no mo ;
Husband, nor lemman, had scho none,
And so he had hir lufe alone.
I think it is no happy lyfe,
Ane man to jaip his maisteris wyfe,
As did Lancelote, this I conclude,
Of sic amour culd cum na gude.
  Now to my purpois will I pas,
And shaw ye how the Squyer was :
Ane gentilman of Scotland borne,
So was his father him beforne :
Of nobilnes lineallie discendit,
Quhilkis thair gude fame hes ever defendit.
Gude WILLIAME MELDRUM he was namit,
Quhilk in his honour was never defamit :
Stalwart and stout, in everie stryfe,
And borne within the schyre of Fyfe,
To Cleishe and Bynnis richt heritour,
Quhilk stude for lufe in monie stour.
  He was bot twentie yeiris of age,
Quhen he began his vassalage :
Proportionat weill, of mid stature,
Feirie, and wicht, and micht indure,
Ouirset with travell, both nicht and day,
Richt hardie baith in ernist and play :
Blyith in countenance, richt fair of face,

And stude weill ay in his ladies grace :
For, he was wounder amiabill,
And in all deidis honorabill ;
And aye his honour did avance,
In Ingland first, and syne in France :
And thair his manheid did assaill,
Under the Kingis greit Admirall,
Quhen the greit Navie of Scotland,
Passit to the sey aganis Ingland.

And as thay passit be Ireland coist,
The Admirall gart land his oist,
And set Craigfergus into fyre,
And saifit nouther barne nor byre.
It was greit pietie for to heir,
Of the pepill the bailfull cheir,
And how the land folk wer spuilyeit,
Fair wemen under fute wer fuilyeit.

Bot this young Squyer bauld and wicht
Savit all wemen quhair he micht :
All preistis and freiris he did save ;
Till at the last he did persave
Behind ane garding amiabill,
Ane womanis voce richt lamentabill ;
And on that voce he followit fast,
Till he did see her, at the last,
Spuilyeit, naikit as scho was borne ;
Twa men of weir wer hir beforne,
Quhilk wer richt cruell men and kene,
Partand the spuilyie thame betwene.
Ane fairer woman nor scho wes,
He had not sene in onie place.

Befoir him on hir kneis scho fell,
Sayand, For him that heryit Hell !
Help me, sweit Sir, I am ane mayd.
Than softlie to the men he said :
I pray yow give againe hir sark,
And tak to yow all other wark.

Hir kirtill was of scarlot reid,
Of gold ane garland on hir heid,
Decorit with enamelyne ;
Belt and brochis of silver fyne,
Of yallow taftais wes hir sark,
Begaryit all with browderit wark,
Richt craftelie, with gold and silk.
Than said the Ladie, quhyte as milk,
Except my sark no thing I crave,
Let thame go hence with all the lave.
Quod thay to hir, Be Sanct Fillane,
Of this ye get nathing agane.

Than said the Squyer courteslie,
Gude friendis I pray yow hartfullie,
Gif ye be worthie men of weir,
Restoir to hir againe hir geir,
Or be greit God that all hes wrocht,
That spuilyie sall be full deir bocht.
Quod thay to him, We thee defy :
And drew thair swordis haistely,
And straik at him with sa greit ire,
That from his harnes flew the fyre ;
With duntis sa derflie on him dang,
That he was never in sic ane thrang.
Bot he him manfullie defendit,

And with ane bolt on thame he bendit,
And hat the ane upon the heid,
That to the ground he fell doun deid ;
For to the teith he did him cleif.
Lat him ly thair with ane mischeif !
Than with the uther hand for hand,
He beit him with his birneist brand :
The uther was baith stout and strang,
And on the Squyer derflie dang.
And than the Squyer wrocht greit wonder
Ay tyll his sword did shaik in sunder :
Than drew he furth ane sharp dagair,
And did him cleik be the collair,
And evin in at the collerbane,
At the first straik he hes him slaine ;
He founderit fordward to the ground ;
Yit was the Squyer haill and sound :
For quhy ? he was sa weill enarmit,
He did escaip fra thaime unharmit.

    And quhen he saw thay wer baith slane,
He to that Ladie past agane :
Quhair scho stude naikit on the bent,
And said, Tak your abulyement.
And scho him thankit full humillie,
And put hir claithes on spedilie.
Than kissitt he that Ladie fair,
And tuik his leif at hir but mair :
Be that the taburne, and trumpet blew,
And everie man to shipburd drew.
    That Ladie was dolent in hart,
From tyme scho saw he would depart,

That hir relevit from hir harmes :
And hint the Squyer in hir armes ;
And said, Will ye byde in this land.
I sall yow tak to my husband :
Thocht I be cassin now in cair,
I am, quod scho, my fatheris air,
The quhilk may spend of pennies round,
Of yeirlie rent ane thowsand pound.
With that hartlie scho did him kis,
Are ye, quod scho, content of this ?
Of that, quod he, I wald be fane,
Gif I micht in this Realme remane :
Bot I mon first pas into France ;
Sa quhen I cum agane, perchance,
And efter that the peice be maid,
To marie yow, I will be glaid :
Fair weill ! I may no langer tarie ;
I pray God keip yow, and sweit sanct Marie.
     Than gaif scho him ane lufe taking,
Ane riche rubie set in ane ring.
I am, quod scho, at your command,
With yow to pas into Scotland.
I thank yow hartfullie, quod he,
Ye ar ouir young to saill the see,
And speciallie with men of weir.
Of that, quod scho, tak ye na feir :
I sall me cleith in mennis clais,
And ga with yow quhair evir ye pleis :
Suld I not lufe him paramour,
That saifit my lyfe and my honour ?
Ladie, I say yow in certane,

Ye sall have lufe for lufe agane,
Trewlie unto my lyfis end :
Fairweill ! to God I yow commend.
　　With that into his boit he past,
And to the ship he rowit fast.
Thay weyit thair ankeris, and maid saill,
This navie with the Admirall,
And landit in bauld Brytane.
This Admirall was Erle of Arrane,
Quhilk was baith wyse and vailyeand,
Of the blude royall of Scotland :
Accompanyit with monie ane knicht,
Quhilk wer richt worthie men and wicht.
Among the laif, this young Squyar,
Was with him richt familiar :
And throw his verteous diligence,
Of that lord he gat sic credence,
That quhen he did his courage ken,
Gaif him cure of fyve hundreth men ;
Quhilkis wer to him obedient,
Reddie at his commandement.
　　It wer too lang for to declair,
The douchtie deidis that he did thair ;
Becaus he was sa courageous,
Ladies of him wes amorous.
He was ane munzeoun for ane dame,
Meik in chalmer lyk ane lame,
Bot in the feild ane campioun
Rampand lyke ane wyld lyoun ;
Weill practikit with speir and scheild,
And with the formest in the feild.

No Chiftane was amangis thame all,
In expensis mair liberall.
In everilk play he wan the pryse:
With that he was verteous and wyse;
And so, becaus he was weill pruifit,
With everie man he was weill luifit,

HARY the Aucht King of Ingland,
That tyme at Caleis wes lyand:
With his triumphand ordinance,
Makand weir on the realme of France.
The King of France his greit armie
Lay neir hand by in Picardie:
Quhair aither uther did assaill.
Howbeit thair was na sic battaill:
Bot thair wes daylie skirmishing,
Quhare men of armis brak monie sting.
Quhen to the Squyer Meldrum
Wer tauld thir novellis all and sum,
He thocht he wald vesie the weiris;
And waillit furth ane hundreth speiris,
And futemen quhilk wer bauld and stout,
The maist worthie of all his rout.
  Quhen he come to the King of France,
He wes sone put in ordinance:
Richt so was all his companie,
That on him waitit continuallie.
Thair was into the Inglis oist,
Ane campioun that blew greit boist:
He was ane stout man and ane strang,
Quhilk oist wald with his conduct gang,

Outthrow the greit armie of France,
His valiantnes for to avance :
And Maister Talbart was his name ;
Of Scottis and Frenche quhilk spak disdane.
And on his bonnet usit to beir,
Of silver fine, takinnis of weir ;
And proclamationnis he gart mak,
That he wald for his ladies saik,
With any gentilman of France,
To fecht with him with speir or lance.
Bot no Frenche man in all that land,
With him durst battell hand for hand.
Than lyke ane weriour vailyeand,
He enterit in the Scottis band :
And quhen the Squyer Meldrum
Hard tell this campioun wes cum,
Richt haistelie he past him till,
Demanding him quhat was his will ;
Forsuith I can find none, quod he,
On hors, nor fute, dar fecht with me.
Than said he, It wer greit schame,
Without battell ye suld pass hame ;
Thairfoir to God I mak ane vow,
The morne my self sall fecht with yow !
Outher on horsback or on fute,
Your crakkis I count thame not ane cute :
I sall be fund into the feild,
Armit on hors with speir and scheild.
Maister Talbart said, My gude chyld,
It wer maist lyk that thow wer wyld :
Thow art too young and hes no micht,

To fecht with me that is so wicht ;
To speik to me thow suld have feir,
For I have sik practik in weir,
That I wald not effeirit be,
To mak debait aganis sic three :
For I have stand in monie stour,
And ay defendit my honour ;
Thairfoir, my barne, I counsell thee,
Sic interprysis to let be.
   Than said this Squyer to the Knicht,
I grant ye ar baith greit and wicht :
Young David was far les than I,
Quhen with Golias manfullie,
Withouttin outher speir or scheild,
He faucht, and slew him in the feild.
I traist that God sal be my gyde,
And give me grace to stanche thy pryde :
Thocht thow be greit like Gowmakmorne,
Traist weill I sall yow meit the morne :
Beside Montruill upon the grene,
Befoir ten houris I sal be sene.
And gif ye wyn me in the feild,
Baith hors and geir I sall yow yeild :
Sa that siclyke ye do to me.
That I sall do be God ! quod he,
And thairto I give thee my hand.
And swa betwene thame maid ane band,
That thay suld meit upon the morne.
Bot, Talbart maid at him bot scorne ;
Lychtlyand him with wordis of pryde,
Syne hamewart to his oist culd ryde.

And shew the brethren of his land,
How ane young Scot had tane on hand,
To fecht with him beside Montruill;
Bot I traist he sall prufe the fuill.
Quod thay, The morne that sall we ken
The Scottis are haldin hardie men.
Quod he, I compt thame not ane cute,
He sall returne upon his fute,
And leif with me his armour bricht,
For weill I wait he has no micht,
On hors nor fute, to fecht with me.
Quod thay, The morne that sall we se.

    Quhan to Monsieour De Obenie
Reportit was the veritie,
How that the Squyer had tane on hand.
To fecht with Talbart hand for hand.
His greit courage he did commend,
Syne haistelie did for him send.
And quhen he come befoir the Lord,
The veritie he did record,
How for the honour of Scotland,
That battell he had tane on hand;
And sen it givis me in my hart,
Get I ane hors to tak my part,
My traist is sa in Goddis grace,
To leif hym lyand in the place:
Howbeit he stalwart be and stout,
My Lord, of him I have no dout.

    Than send the Lord out throw the land,
And gat ane hundreth hors fra hand:
To his presence he brocht in haist,

And bad the Squyer cheis him the best.
Of that the Squyer was rejoisit,
And cheisit the best as he suppoisit,
And lap on hym delyverlie ;
Was never hors ran mair plesantlie,
With speir and sword at his command,
And was the best of all the land.

He tuik his leif, and went to rest ;
Syne airlie in the morne him drest,
Wantonlie in his weirlyke weid,
All weill enarmit, saif the heid :
He lap upon his cursour wicht,
And straucht him in his stirroppis richt,
His speir and scheild and helme wes borne
With squyeris that raid him beforne ;
Ane velvot cap on heid he bair,
Ane quaif of gold to heild his hair.

This Lord of him tuik sa greit joy,
That he himself wald hym convoy :
With him ane hundreth men of armes,
That thair suld no man do hym harmes.
The Squyer buir into his scheild,
Ane otter in ane silver feild,
His hors was bairdit full richelie,
Coverit with satyne cramesie.
Than fordward raid this campioun,
With sound of trumpet and clarioun,
And spedilie spurrit ouir the bent,
Lyke Mars the God armipotent.

Thus leif we rydand our Squyar,
And speik of Maister Talbart mair :

Quhilk gat up airlie in the morrow,
And no manner of geir to borrow :
Hors, harnes, speir, nor scheild,
Bot was ay reddie for the feild ;
And had sic practik into weir,
Of our Squyer he tuik na feir.
And said unto his companyeoun,
Or he come furth of his pavilyeoun,
This nicht I saw into my dreame,
Quhilk to reheirs I think greit schame :
Me thocht I saw cum fra the see,
Ane greit otter rydand to me,
The quhilk was blak, with ane lang taill,
And cruellie did me assail ;
And bait me till he gart me bleid,
And drew me backwart fra my steid.
Quhat this suld mene I cannot say,
Bot I was never in sic ane fray.
His fellow said, Think ye not schame,
For to gif credence till ane dreame ?
Ye knaw it is aganis our faith ;
Thairfoir go dres yow in your graith,
And think weill throw your hie courage,
This day ye sall wyn vassalage.
    Then drest he him into his geir,
Wantounlie like ane man of weir,
Quhilk had baith hardines and fors ;
And lichtlie lap upon his hors.
His hors was bairdit full bravelie,
And coverit was richt courtfullie
With browderit wark, and velvot grene :

Sanct George's croce thare micht be sene
On hors, harnes, and all his geir.
Than raid he furth withouttin weir,
Convoyit with his Capitane,
And with monie ane Inglisman,
Arrayit all with armes bricht,
Micht no man see ane fairer sicht.
 Than clariounis and trumpettis blew ;
And weriouris monie hither drew :
On everie side come monie man,
To behald quha the battell wan :
The feild wes in the medow grene,
Quhair everie man micht weill be sene.
The heraldis put thame sa in ordour,
That no man passit within the bordour,
Nor preissit to cum within the grene,
Bot heraldis and the campiounis kene.
The ordour and the circumstance
Wer lang to put in remembrance.
Quhen thir twa nobilmen of weir,
Wer weill accowterit in their geir,
And in their handis strang burdounis;
Than trumpettis blew and clariounis,
And heraldis cryit hie on hicht,
Now let tham go! God shaw the richt !
 Than spedilie thay spurrit thair hors,
And ran to uther with sic fors,
That baith thair speiris in sindrie flaw ;
Than said thay all that stude on raw,
Ane better cours, than they twa ran,
Wes not sene sen the warld began.

Than baith the parties wer rejoisit ;
The campiounis ane quhyle repoisit,
Till they had gottin speiris new,
Than with triumph the trumpettis blew
And they with all the force thay can
Wounder rudelie at aither ran,
And straik at uther with sa greit ire,
That fra thair harnes flew the fyre.
Thair speiris wer sa teuch and strang,
That aither uther to eirth doun dang.
Baith hors, and man, with speir and scl
Than flatlingis lay into the feild.
Than Maister Talbart was eschamit,
Forsuith for ever I am defamit !
And said this, I had rather die,
Without that I revengit be.

 Our young Squyer, sie was his hap,
Was first on fute ; and on he lap
Upon his hors, without support :
Of that the Scottis tuke gude comfort.
Quhen thay saw him sa feirelie
Loup on his hors sa galyeardlie.
The Squyer liftit his visair,
Ane lytill space to take the air.
Thay bad him wyne, and he it drank,
And humillie he did thame thank.
Be that Talbart on hors wes mountit,
And of our Squyer lytill countit.
And cryit, Gif he durst undertak,
To run anis for his ladies saik ?
The Squyer answerit hie on hicht,

That sall I do be Marie bricht !
I am content all day to ryn,
Tyll ane of us the honour wyn.
Of that Talbart was weill content,
And ane greit speir in hand he hent.
The Squyer in his hand he thrang
His speir, quhilk was baith greit and lang,
With ane sharp heid of grundin steill,
Of quhilk he wes appleisit weill.
That plesand feild was lang and braid,
Quhair gay ordour and rowme was maid :
And everie man micht have gude sicht,
And thair was mony weirlyke knicht.
Sum man of everie natioun,
Was in that congregatioun.

   Than trumpettis blew triumphantlie,
And thai twa campiounis egeirlie,
Thai spurrit thair hors with speir on breist
Pertlie to preif thair pith thay preist :
That round, rink roume wes at utterance ;
Bot Talbartis hors with ane mischance
He outterit, and to ryn was laith ;
Quhairof Talbart was wonder wraith.
The Squyer furth his rink he ran,
Commendit weill with everie man ;
And him dischargeit of his speir,
Honestlie lyke ane man of weir.
Becaus that rink thay ran in vane ;
Than Talbart wald not ryn agane,
Till he had gottin ane better steid ;
Quhilk was brocht to him with gude speid.

Quhairon he lap, and tuik his speir,
As brym as he had bene ane beir.
And bowtit fordward with ane bend,
And ran on to the rinkis end,
And saw his hors was at command;
Than wes he blyith, I understand,
Traistand na mair to ryn in vane:
Than all the trumpettis blew agane.
Be that with all the force thay can,
Thay rycht rudelie at uther ran.
Of that meiting ilk man thocht wounder,
Quhilk soundit lyke ane crak of thunder;
And nane of thame thair marrow mist.
Sir Talbartis speir in sunder brist,
Bot the Squyer with his burdoun,
Sir Talbart to the eirth dang doun.
That straik was with sic micht and fors, ˙
That on the ground lay man and hors;
And throw the brydell hand him bair,
And in the breist ane span and mair.
Throw curras, and throw gluifis of plait,
That Talbart micht mak na debait,
The trencheour of the Squyeris speir,
Stak still into Sir Talbartis geir.

    Than everie man into that steid
Did all beleve that he was deid.
The Squyer lap rycht haistelie,
From his cursour deliverlie,
And to Sir Talbart maid support,
And humillie did him comfort.
Quhen Talbart saw into his scheild,

Ane otter in ane silver feild,
This race, said he, I may sair rew,
For I see weill my dream wes trew :
Me thocht yone otter gart me bleid,
And buir me backwart from my steid ;
Bot heir I vow to God soverane,
That I sall never just agane.
And sweitlie to the Squyer said,
Thow knawis the cunning that we maid,
Quhilk of us twa suld tyne the feild,
He suld baith hors and armour yield,
Tili him that wan : quhairfoir I will,
My hors and harnes geve thee till.
    Then said the Squyer courteouslie,
Brother, I thank yow hartfullie.
Of yow forsuith nathing I crave,
For I have gottin that I wald have.
With everie man he was commendit,
Sa vailyeandlie he him defendit.
The Capitane of the Inglis band
Tuke the young Squyer be the hand ;
And led him to the pailyeoun,
And gart him mak collatioun,
Quhen Talbartis woundis wes bund up fast,
The Inglis capitane to him past :
And prudentlie did him comfort,
Syne said, Brother, I yow exhort
To tak the Squyer be the hand.
And sa he did at his command ;
And said, This bene but chance of armes :
With that he braisit him in his armes ;

Sayand, Hartlie I yow forgeve.
And then the Squyer tuik his leve ;
Commendit weill with everie man.
Than wichtlie on his hors he wan ;
With monie ane nobyll man convoyit.
Leve we thair Talbart sair annoyit ;
Some sayis of that discomfitour,
He thocht sic schame and dishonour,
That he departit of that land,
And never wes sene into Ingland.

  Bot our Squyer did still remane
Efter the weir, quhill peice wes tane.
All capitanes of the Kingis gairdis
Gaif to the Squyer rich rewairdis :
Becaus he had sa weill debaitit,
With everie nobill he wes weill traitit.
Efter the weir he tuke licence,
Syne did returne with diligence,
From Pycardie to Normandie,
And thare ane space remanit he ;
Becaus the Navie of Scotland
Wes still upon the coist lyand.

  Quhen he ane quhyle had sojornit,
He to the court of France returnit :
For to decore his vassalage,
From Bartanze tuke his voyage :
With aucht scoir in his companie
Of waillit wicht men and hardie ;
Enarmit weill lyke men of weir,
With hakbut, culvering, pik, and speir ;
And passit up throw Normandie,

Til Ambiance in Pycardie ;
Quhair nobill Lowes, the King of France,
Was lyand with his ordinance :
With monie ane prince and worthie man :
And in the court of France wes than
Ane mervellous congregatioun,
Of monie ane divers natioun ;
Of Ingland monie ane prudent lord,
Efter the weir makand record.
  Thare wes than ane Ambassadour,
Ane lord, ane man of greit honour :
With him was monie nobill knicht
Of Scotland, to defend their richt :
Quhilk guydit thame sa honestlie,
Inglismen had thame at invie,
And purposit to mak thame cummer,
Becaus they wer of greiter number,
And sa quhairever thay with thame met,
Upon the Scottis thay maid onset,
And lyke wyld lyounis furious,
Thay layd ane seige about the hous,
Thame to destroy, sa thay intendit :
Our worthie Scottis thame weill defendit.
The Sutheroun wes ay fyve for ane,
Sa on ilk syde thare wes men slane ;
The Inglismen grew in greit ire,
And cryit swyith, Set the house in fyre.
Be that the Squyer Meldrum
Into the market streit wes cum,
With his folkis in gude array,
And saw the toun wes in ane fray ;

He did inquyre the occasioun ;
Quod thay, The Scottis ar all put doun,
Be Inglismen, into thair innis.
Quod he, I wald give all the Bynnis,
That I micht cum or thay departit.
With that he grew sa cruell hartit,
That he was lyke ane wyld lyoun,
And rudelie ran outthrow the toun,
With all his companie weill arrayit,
And with baner full braid displayit.
And quhen thay saw the Inglis route,
Thay set upon thame with ane schout :
With reird sa rudelie on thame ruschit,
That fiftie to the eirth thay duschit :
Thair was nocht ellis but tak and slay.
This Squyer wounder did that day ;
And stoutlie stoppit in the stour,
And dang on thame with dintis dour :
Wes never man buir better band ;
Thare micht na buckler byde his brand,
For it was weill sevin quarter lang.
With that sa derflie on thame dang,
That lyke ane worthie campioun,
Ay at ane straik he dang ane doun :
Sum was evill hurt, and sum wes slane,
Sum fell, quhilk rais not yit agane.
Quhen that the Sutheroun saw his micht,
Effrayitlie thay tuke the flicht ;
And wist not quhair to flie for haist,
Thus throw the toun he hes thame chaist ;
Wer not Frenchemen come to the redding,

Thar had bene mekill mair blude shedding.
    Of this journey I mak ane end,
Quhilk everie nobill did commend.
Quhen to the King the cace wes knawin,
And all the suith unto him shawin ;
How this Squyer sa manfullie,
On Sutheroun wan the victorie,
He put him into ordinance,
And sa he did remane in France,
Ane certane tyme for his plesour,
Weill estemit in greit honour,
Quhair he did monie ane nobill deid.
With that, richt wantoun in his weid,
Quhen ladies knew his hie courage,
He was desyrit in mariage
Be ane ladie of greit rent ;
Bot youth maid him sa insolent,
That he in France wald not remane,
Bot come to Scotland hame agane :
Thocht Frenche ladies did for him murne,
The Scottis wer glaid of his returne.
At everie lord he tuke his leve,
Bot his departing did thame greive ;
For he was luifit with all wichtis,
Quhilk had him sene defend his richtis ;
Scottis capitanes did him convoy,
Thocht his departing did thame noy.
    At Deip he maid him for the saill,
Quhair he furnischit ane gay veschaill,
For his self and his men of weir,
With artailyie, hakbut, bow, and speir ;

And furneist hir with gude victuaill,
With the best wyne that he could waill.
And quhen the schip was reddie maid,
He lay bot ane day in the raid,
Quhill he gat wind of the southeist,
Than thay thair ankeris weyit on haist ;
And syne maid saill, and fordwart past.
Ane day at morne, till at the last
Of ane greit saill thay gat ane sicht ;
And Phœbus schew his bemis bricht,
Into the morning richt airlie.
Than past the skipper richt spedelie,
Up to the top with richt greit feir,
And saw it wes ane man of weir ;
And cryit, I see nocht ellis, perdie !
Bot we mon outher fecht or fle.

  The Squyer wes in his bed lyand,
Quhen he hard tell this new tydand.
Be this the Inglis artailye,
Lyke hailschot maid on thame assailye ;
And sloppit throw thair fechting saillis,
And divers dang out ouir the waillis.
The Scottis agane with all thair micht,
Of gunnis than thay leit fle ane flicht :
That thay micht weill see quhair they wair,
Heidis and armes flew in the air.
The Scottis schip scho wes sa law,
That monie gunnis out ouir hir flaw,
Quhilk far beyond thame lichtit doun ;
Bot the Inglis greit galyeoun,
Fornent thame stude, lyke ane strang castell,

That the Scottis gunnis micht na way faill,
Bot hat hir ay on the richt syde,
With monie ane slop, for all hir pride,
That monie ane beft wer on thair bakkis;
Than rais the reik with uglie crakkis,
Quhilk on the sey maid sic ane sound,
That in the air it did redound :
That men micht weill wit on the land,
That shippis wer on the sey fechtand.

 Be this, the Gyder straik the shippis,
And ather on uther laid thair clippis ;
And than began the strang battell,
Ilk man his marrow did assaill ;
So rudelie thay did rushe togidder,
That nane micht hald thair feit for slidder.
Sum with halbert, and sum with speir,
Bot hakbuttis did the greitest deir ;
Out of the top the grundin dartis
Did divers peirs outthrow the hartis :
Everie man did his diligence,
Upon his fo to wirk vengeance ;
Ruschand on uther routtis rude,
That ouir the waillis ran the blude.
The Inglis Capitane cryit hie,
Swyith yeild yow, doggis ! or ye sall die ;
And do yow not, I make ane vow,
That Scotland sal be quyte of yow.
Than peirtlie answerit the Squyar,
And said, O tratour Tavernar !
I lat thee wit, thow hes na micht,
This day to put us to the flicht.

Thay derflie ay at uther dang,
The Squyer thristit throw the thrang,
And in the Inglis schip he lap,
And hat the Capitane sic ane flap
Upon his heid, till he fell doun,
Welterand intill ane deidlie swoun.
And quhen the Scottis saw the Squyer,
Had strikkin doun that rank Rever,
Thay left thair awin schip standand waist,
And in the Inglis schip, in haist,
Thay followit all thair capitane ;
And sone wes all the Southeroun slane :
Howbeit thay wer of greiter number.
The Scottismen put thame in sic cummer ;
That they wer fane to leif the feild,
Cryand Mercie, than did thame yeild.

Yit wes the Squyer straikand tast
At the Capitane till at the last ;
Quhen he persavit no remeid,
Outher to yeild, or to be deid,
He said, O gentill Capitane,
Thoill me not for to be slain.
My lyfe to yow sal be mair pryse.
Nor sall my deith ane thowsand syse.
For ye may get, as I suppois,
Three thousand nobillis of the rois
Of me, and of my companie ;
Thairfoir I cry yow loud mercie !
Except my life, nothing I craif :
Tak yow the schip and all the laif.
I yeild to yow baith sword and knyfe ;

Thairfoir, gude maister, save my lyfe !
  The Squyer tuik him be the hand,
And on his feit he gart him stand ;
And traittit him richt tenderlie,
And syne unto his men did cry,
And gaif to thame richt strait command,
To straik no moir, bot hald thair hand.
Than baith the Capitanes ran and red,
And so thair wes na mair blude sched.
Than all the laif thay did thame yeild,
And to the Scottis gaif sword and sheild.

  Ane nobill leiche the Squyer had,
Quhairof the Inglismen wes full glaid,
To quhome the Squyer gaif command,
The woundit men to tak on hand :
And so he did with diligence,
Quhairof he gat gude recompence.
Than quhen the woundit men wer drest,
And all the deand men confest,
And deid men cassin in the see,
Quhilk to behald wes greit pietie ;
Thare wes slane of Inglis band
Fyve scoir of men, I understand,
The quhilk wer cruell men and kene ;
And of the Scottis wer slane fyftene.
And quhen the Inglis capitane
Saw, how his men wer tane and slane,
And how the Scottis, sa few in number,
Had put thame in sa greit ane cummer ;
He grew intill ane frenesy,
Sayand, Fals Fortoun ! I thee defy ;

For I belevit this day at morne,
That he wes not in Scotland borne,
That durst have met me hand for hand,
Within the boundis of my brand.
The Squyer bad him mak gud cheir,
And said, it was bot chance of weir.
Greit conquerouris, I yow assure,
Hes hapnit siclike adventure :
Thairfoir mak merrie, and go dyne,
And let us preif the michtie wyne.
Sum drank wyne, and sum drank aill ;
Syne pat the shippis under saill.
And waillit furth of the Inglis band,
Twa hundreth men, and put on land,
Quyetlie on the coist of Kent,
The laif in Scotland with him went.
The Inglis Capitaine, as I ges,
He wairdit him in the Blaknes,
And treitit him richt honestlie,
Togither with his companie ;
And held thame in that garnisoun,
Till thay had payit thair ransoun.

   Out throw the land than sprang the fame,
That Squyer Meldrum wes cum hame.
Quhen thay hard tell how he debaitit,
With everie man he was sa treitit :
That quhen he travellit throw the land,
Thay bankettit him fra hand to hand,
With greit solace ; till at the last,
Out throw Straitherne the Squyer past ;
And as it did approch the nicht,

Of ane castell he gat ane sicht,
Beside ane montane in ane vaill ;
And than eftir his greit travaill,
He purpoisit him to repois,
Quhair ilk man did of him rejois.
Of this triumphant plesand place,
Ane lustie Ladie wes maistres,
Quhais lord was deid schort tyme befoir,
Quhairthrow hir dolour wes the moir :
Bot yit scho tuke sum comforting,
To heir the plesant dulce talking,
Of this young Squyer, of his chance,
And how it fortunit him in France.
    This Squyer, and the Ladie gent,
Did wesche, and then to supper went.
During that nicht thare was nocht ellis,
But for to heir of his novellis :
Eneas quhen he fled from Troy,
Did not quene Dido greiter joy ;
Quhen he in Carthage did arryve,
And did the seige of Troy discryve.
The wonderis that he did reheirs
Wer langsum for to put in vers ;
Of quhilk this ladie did rejois.
They drank, and syne went to repois.
He fand his chalmer weill arrayit,
With dornik work on buird displayit.
Of venisoun he had his waill,
Gude aquavite, wyne, and aill,
With nobill confeittis, bran, and geill ;
And swa the Squyer fuir richt weill.

Sa to heir mair of his narratioun,
This Ladie came to his collatioun,
Sayand, he was richt welcum hame.
Grandmercie than, quod he, Madame!
Thay past the tyme with ches and tabill,
For he to everie game was abill.
Than unto bed drew everie wicht,
To chalmer went this Ladie bricht;
The quhilk this Squyer did convoy:
Syne till his bed he went with joy.
That nicht he sleipit never ane wink,
But still did on the Ladie think;
Cupido, with his fyrie dart,
Did peirs him so out throw the hart,
Sa all that nicht he did but murnit;
Sum tyme sat up, and sum tyme turnit.
Sichand with monie gant and grane,
To fair Venus makand his mane:
Sayand, Ladie, quhat may this mene?
I was ane fre man lait yistrene:
And now ane cative bound and thrall,
For ane that I think flour of all.
I pray God sen scho knew my mynd,
How for hir saik I am sa pynd:
Wald God I had bene yit in France,
Or I had hapnit sic mischance:
To be subject or serviture
Till ane, quhilk takis of me na cure.
    This Ladie ludgit neirhand by,
And hard the Squyer prively
With dreidfull hart makand his mone,

With monie cairfull gant and grone :
Hir hart fulfillit with pietie,
Thocht scho wald haif of him mercie :
And said, Howbeit I suld be slane,
He sall have lufe for lufe agane.
Wald God I micht with my honour
Have him to be my paramour !

   This was the mirrie tyme of May !
Quhen this fair Ladie, freshe and gay,
Start up to take the hailsum air,
With pantonis on hir feit ane pair :
Airlie into ane cleir morning,
Befoir fair Phœbus uprising :
Kirtill alone withouttin clok,
And saw the Squyeris dure unlok,
Scho slippit in or ever he wist,
And fenyeitlie past till ane kist ;
And with hir keyis oppinit the lokkis,
And maid hir to take furth ane boxe.
Bot that was not hir erand thare ;
With that this lustie young Squyar
Saw this Ladie so plesantlie,
Cum to his chalmer quyetlie,
In kyrtill of fyne damais broun,
Hir goldin traissis hingand doun ;
Hir pappis wer hard, round, and quhyte,
Quhome to behald was greit delyte ;
Lyke the quhyte lyllie wes hir lyre,
Hir hair was like the reid gold wyre,
Hir schankis quhyte withouttin hois ;
Quhairat the Squyer did rejois ;

   VOL. I.   N

And said than, Now vailye quod vailye,
Upon the Ladie thow mak ane sailye.
　　Hir courlyke kirtill was unlaist,
And sone into his armis hir braist,
And said to hir, Madame, gude-morne,
Help me your man, that is forlorne :
Without ye mak me sum remeid,
Withouttin dout, I am bot deid ;
Quhairfoir ye mon relief my harmes.
With that he hint hir in his armes,
And talkit with hir on the flure,
Syne quyetlie did bar the dure.
Squyer, quod scho, quhat is your will ?
Think ye my womanheid to spill ?
Na, God forbid ! it wer greit syn,
My lord and ye wes neir of kyn :
Quhairfoir I mak yow supplicatioun,
Pas, and seik ane dispensatioun ;
Than sall I wed yow with ane ring,
Than may ye leif at your lyking :
For ye ar young, lustie and fair ;
And als ye ar your fatheris air ;
Thare is na ladie in all this land,
May yow refuse to hir husband.
And gif ye lufe me, as yow say,
Haist to dispens the best ye may ;
And thair to yow I geve my hand,
I sall yow take to my husband.
　　Quod he, Quhill that I may indure,
I vow to be your serviture ;
Bot I think greit vexatioun,

To tarrie upon dispensatioun,
Than in his armis he did hir thrist,
And aither uther sweitlie kist ;
And wame for wame thay uther braissit,
With that hir kirtill wes unlaissit :
Than Cupido with his fyrie dartis,
Inflammit sa thir luiferis hartis,
Thay micht na maner of way dissever ;
Nor ane micht not part fra ane uther ;
Bot like wodbind thay wer baith wrappit,
Thair tenderlie he has hir happit,
Full softlie, up intill his bed,
Judge ye, gif he hir schankis shed.
Allace ! quod scho, quhat may this mene ?
And with hir hair scho dicht hir ene.

   I can not tell how thay did play,
Bot I beleve scho said not nay.
He pleisit hir sa, as I hard sane,
That he was welcum ay agane.
Scho rais, and tenderlie him kist,
And on his hand ane ring scho thrist ;
And he gif hir ane lufe dowrie,
Ane ring set with ane riche rubie ;
In takin that their lufe for ever,
Suld never frome thir twa dissever.

   And than scho passit unto hir chalmer,
And fand hir madinnis sweit as lammer,
Sleipand full sound, and nothing wist,
How that thair ladie past to the kist.
Quod thay, Madame, quhare have ye bene ?
Quod scho, Into my gardine grene,

To heir thir mirrie birdis sang.
I lat you wit, I thocht not lang,
Thocht I had taryit thair quhile none.
Quod thai, Quhair wes your hose and schone?
Quhy yeid ye with your bellie bair?
Quod scho, The morning wes sa fair,
For be him that deir Jesus sauld,
I felt na wayis ony maner of cauld.
Quod thay, Madame, me think ye sweit.
Quod scho, Ye see I sufferit heit;
The dew did sa on flouris fleit,
That baith my lymmis ar maid weit:
Thairfoir ane quhyle I will heir ly,
Till this dulce dew be fra me dry:
Ryse, and gar mak our denner reddie.
That sall be done, quod thay, my ladie.

    Efter that scho had tane hir rest,
Scho rais, and in hir chalmer hir drest:
And efter Mes to denner went;
Than was the Squyer diligent,
To declair monie sindrie storie,
Worthie to put in memorie.

    Quhat sall we of thir luferis say?
Bot all this tyme of lustie May,
Thay past the tyme with joy and blis,
Full quietlie with mony ane kis:
Thair was na creature that knew
Yit of thir luferis chalmer glew.
And sa he levit plesandlie,
Ane certane tyme with his Ladie.
Sum tyme halking and hunting,

Sum time with wantoun hors rinning ;
And sum time like ane man of weir,
Full galzardlie wald ryn ane speir :
He wan the pryse above thame all,
Baith at the buttis and the futeball :
Till everie solace he was abill,
At cartis, and dyce, at ches and tabill ;
And gif ye list I sall yow tell
How that he seigit ane castell.

Ane messinger come spedilie,
From the Lennox to that Ladie ;
And schew how that Makfagon,
And with him mony bauld baron,
Hir castell had tane perfors,
And nouther left hir kow nor hors :
And heryit all that land about,
Quhairof the Ladie had greit dout.
Till hir Squyer scho passit in haist,
And schew him how scho wes opprest :
And how he wastit monie ane myle,
Betuix Dunbartane and Argyle.
And quhen the Squyer Meldrum
Had hard thir novellis all and sum ;
In till his hart thare grew sic ire,
That all his bodie brint in fyre ;
And swoir it suld be full deir sald,
Gif he micht find him in that hald.
He and his men did thame addres,
Richt haistelie in thair harnes ;
Sum with bow and sum with speir,
And he like Mars the god of weir,

Come to the Ladie, and tuke his leif;
And scho gaif him hir richt hand gluif,
The quhilk he on his basnet bure,
And said, Madame, I yow assure,
That worthie Lanclot du Laik
Did never mair for his ladies saik,
Nor I sall do, or ellis dé,
Without that ye revengit be.
Than in hir armes scho him braist,
And he his leif did take in haist :
And raid that day, and all the nicht,
Till on the morne he gat ane sicht
Of that castell, baith fair and strang :
Than in the middis his men amang,
To michtie Mars his vow he maid,
That he suld never in hart be glaid ;
Nor yit returne furth of that land,
Quhill that streuth wer at his command.
All the tennentis of that Ladie
Come to the Squyer haistelie,
And maid aith of fidelitie,
That thay suld never fra him flie.
   Quhen to Makferland, wicht and bauld,
The veritie all haill wes tauld,
How the young Squyer Meldrum
Wes now into the cuntrie cum,
Purpoisand to seige that place ;
Than vittaillit he that fortres,
And swoir he suld that place defend,
Bauldlie, untill his lyfis end.
Be this the Squyer wes arrayit,

With his baner bricht displayit,
With culvering, hakbut, bow, and speir ;
Of Makfarland he tuke na feir.
And like ane campioun courageous,
He cryit and said, Gif ouir the house !
The Capitane answerit heichly,
And said, Tratour, we thee defy :
We sall remane this hous within,
In to despyte of all thy kin.
With that the archeris bauld and wicht,
Of braid arrowis let fle ane flicht
Amang the Squyeris companie ;
And thay agane richt manfullie,
With hakbute, bow, and culveryne,
Quhilk put Makferlandis men to pyne ;
And on their colleris laid full sikker ;
And thair began ane bailfull bikker.
Thair was bot schot and schot agane,
Till on ilk side thair wes men slane.
Than cryit the Squyer courageous,
Swyith lay the ledderis to the hous ;
And sa thay did, and clam belyfe,
As busie beis dois to thair hyfe.
Howbeit thair wes slane monie man,
Yit wichtlie ouir the wallis thay wan.
    The Squyer formest of them all,
Plantit the banir ouir the wall :
And than began the mortall fray,
Thair wes nocht ellis bot tak and slay.
Than Makferland that maid the prais,
From time he saw the Squyeris face,

Upon his kneis he did him yeild,
Deliverand him baith speir and schield :
The Squyer hartilie him resavit,
Commandand that he suld be savit :
And sa did slaik that mortall feid,
Sa that na man wes put to deid.
In fre waird was Makferland seisit,
And leit the laif gang quhair thay pleisit.

    And sa this Squyer amorous,
Seigit and wan the ladies hous.
And left thairin ane capitane,
Syne to Stratherne returnit agane :
Quhair that he with his fair Ladie,
Ressavit wes full plesantlie,
And to tak rest did him convoy,
Judge ye gif thair wes mirth and joy.
Howbeit the chalmer dure wes cloisit,
They did bot kis, as I suppoisit.
Gif uther thing wes them betwene,
Let them discover that luiferis bene :
For I am not in lufe expart,
And never studyit in that art.
Thus thay remainit in merines,
Beleifand never to have distress,
In that meine time this Ladie fair,
Ane douchter to the Squyer bair :
Nane fund wes fairer of visage.

    Than tuke the Squyer sic courage,
Agane the merrie time of May,
Threttie he put in his luferay,
In scarlot fyne, and of hew grene ;

Quhilk wes ane semelie sicht to sene.
The Gentilmen in all that land,
Wer glaid with him to mak ane band ;
And he wald plainelie tak thair partis,
And not desyring bot thair hartis.
Thus levit the Squyer plesandlie,
With musick and with menstralie :
Of this Ladie he wes sa glad,
Thair micht na sorrow mak him sad ;
Ilk ane did uther consolatioun,
Taryand upon dispensatioun.
Had it cum hame, he had hir bruikit,
Bot or it come, it was miscnikit ;
And all this game he bocht full deir,
As ye at lenth sall efter heir.

Of warldlie joy it wes weill kend,
That sorrow bene the fatall end ;
For jelousie and fals invie,
Did him pursew richt cruellie.
I mervell not thocht it be so,
For they wer ever luiferis fo :
Quhairthrow he stude in monie ane stour,
And ay defendit his honour.

Ane cruell Knicht dwelt neir hand by,
Quhilk at this Squyer had invy,
Imaginand intill his hart,
How he thir luiferis micht depart ;
And wald have had hir maryand
Ane gentilman within his land,
The quhilk wes neir to him in bluid :
Bot finallie for to conclude,

Thairto scho wald never assent :
Quhairfoir the Knicht set his intent,
This nobill Squyer for to destroy
And swore, he suld never have joy
In till his hart, without remeid,
Till ane of thame wer left for deid.
This vailyand Squyer manfully,
In ernest or play did him defy ;
Offerand himself for to assaill,
Bodie for bodie in battaill.
The Knicht thairto not condiscendit,
Bot to betrais him ay intendit.
    Sa it fell anis upon ane day,
In Edinburgh, as I hard say,
This Squyer and the Ladie trew,
Was thair just matteris to persew :
That cruell Knicht full of invy,
Gart hald on thame ane secreit spy,
Quhen thai suld pas furth of the Toun,
For this Squyeris confusioun ;
Quhilk traistit no man suld him greive,
Nor of tressoun had no beleive.
And tuik his licence from his oist,
And liberallie did pay his coist ;
And sa departit blyith and mirrie,
With purpois to pas ouir the Ferrie.
He wes bot auchtsum in his rout,
For of danger he had no dout.
The spy came to the Knicht anone,
And him informit how thay wer gone,
Than gadderit he his men in hy,

With thrie scoir in his company ;
Accowterit weill in feir of weir,
Sum with bow, and sum with speir ;
And on the Squyer followit fast,
Till thay did see him at the last ;
With all his men richt weill arrayit,
With cruell men nathing effrayit.

And quhen the Ladie saw the rout,
God wait gif scho stude in greit dout.
Quod scho, Your enemies I see,
Thairfoir, sweit hart, I reid yow fle ;
In the cuntrey I will be kend,
Ye ar na partie to defend.
Ye knaw yone Knichtis crueltie,
That in his hart hes no mercie :
It is bot ane that thay wald have,
Thair foir deir hart, yourself ye save ;
Howbeit thay tak me with this trane,
I sal be sone at yow agane :
For ye war never sa hard staid.
Madame, quod he, be ye not raid,
For, be the Halie Trinitie,
This day ane fute I will not fle.

And be he had endit this word,
He drew ane lang twa handit sword :
And put his aucht men in array,
And bad that thay suld tak na fray.
Than to the Squyer cryit the Knicht,
And said, Send me the Ladie bricht :
Do ye not sa, be Goddis corce,
I sall hir tak away perforce.

The Squyer said, Be thow ane knicht,
Cum furth to me and schaw the richt,
Bot hand for hand without redding,
That thair be na mair blude shedding.
And gif thow winnis me in the field,
I sall my Ladie to thee yield.
The Knicht durst not for all his land,
Fecht with this Squyer hand for hand.
    The Squyer than saw na remeid,
Bot outher to fecht, or to be deid :
To hevin he liftit up his visage,
Cryand to God with hie courage,
To Thee my quarrell I do commend !
Syne bowtit fordwart with ane bend ;
With countenance baith bald and stout,
He rudelie rushit in that rout :
With him his litill companie,
Quhilk thame defendit manfullie.
The Squyer with his birneist brand,
Amang his fa men maid sic hand :
That Gaudefer, as sayis the letter,
At Gadderis Ferrie faucht no better :
His sword he swappit sa about,
That he greit roum maid in the rout :
And like ane man that was dispairit,
His wapoun sa on thame he wairit,
Quhome ever he hit, as I hard say,
Thay did him na mair deir that day ;
Quha ever come within his boundis,
He chaipit not but mortall woundis ;
Sum mutilate wer, and sum wer slane,

Sum fled, and come not yit agane.
He hat the Knicht abone the breis,
That he fell fordwart on his kneis;
Wer not Thome Giffard did him save,
The Knicht had sone bene in his grave:
Bot than the Squyer with his brand,
Hat Thomas Giffard on the hand:
From that time furth during his lyfe,
He never weildit sword nor knyfe.
Than come ane sort as brim as beiris,
And in him festnit fyftene speiris,
In purpois to have borne him doun,
Bot he as forcie campioun,
Amang thai wicht men wrocht greit wounder.
For all thair speiris he schure in sunder:
Nane durst cum neir him hand for hand,
Within the boundis of his brand.

   This worthie Squyer courageous,
Micht be comparit to Tydeus:
Quhilk faucht for to defend his richtis,
And slew of Thebes fyftie knichtis.
Rolland with Brandwell his bricht brand,
Faucht never better hand for hand;
Nor Gawin aganis Golibras;
Nor Olyver with Pharambras;
I wait he faucht that day als weill,
As did Sir Gryme aganis Graysteill;
And I dar say, he was als abill,
As ony Knicht of the Round Tabill;
And did his honour mair avance,
Nor onie of thay knichtis perchance:

The quhilk I offer me to preif,
Gif that ye pleis, Sirs, with your leif.
  Amang thay knichts wes maid ane band,
That thay suld fecht bot hand for hand,
Assurit that thai suld come no mo;
With this Squyer it stude not so:
His stalwart stour quha wald discryfe,
Aganis ane man their come ay fyfe.
Quhen that this cruell tyrane Knicht
Saw the Squyer sa wounder wicht,
And had no micht him to destroy,
Into his hart thair grew sic noy,
That he was abill for to rage,
That no man micht his ire asswage.
Fy on us! said he to his men,
Ay aganis ane sen we are ten;
Chaip he away, we are eschamit,
Like cowartis we sall be defamit:
I had rather be in hellis pane,
Or he suld chaip fra us unslane.
And callit thrie of his companie,
Said, Pas behind him quyetlie.
And sa thay did richt secretlie,
And came behind him cowartlie,
And hackit on his hochis and theis,
Till that he fell upon his kneis:
Yit quhen his schankis wer schorne in sunder,
Upon his kneis he wrocht greit wounder;
Sweipand his sword round about,
Not haifand of the deith na dout:
Durst nane approche within his boundis,

Till that his cruell mortall woundis
Bled sa, that he did swap in swoun ;
Perforce behuifit him than fall doun,
And quhen he lay upon the ground,
They gaif him monie cruell wound ;
That men on far micht heir the knokkis,
Like boucheouris hakkand on thair stokkis ;
And finallie without remeid,
Thay left him lyand thair for deid,
With ma woundis of sword and knyfe,
Nor ever had man that keipit lyfe.

Quhat suld I of thir traitouris say ?
Quhen thay had done thay fled away.
Bot than this lustie Ladie fair,
With dolent hart scho maid sic cair ;
Quhilk wes greit pietie for to rehears,
And langsum for to put in vers.
With teiris scho wuische his bludie face,
Sichand with manie loud allace.
Allace ! quod scho, that I was borne !
In my querrell thow art forlorne ;
Sall never man eftir this hour,
Of my bodie have mair plesour ;
For thow wes gem of gentilnes,
And werie well of worthines.
Than to the eirth scho rushit doun,
And lay into ane deidlie swoun.

Be that the Regent of the land,
Fra Edinburgh come fast rydand :
Sir Anthony Darsie wes his name,
Ane knicht of France and man of fame,

Quhilk had the guiding haillilie,
Under Johne Duke of Albanie;
Quhilk wes to our young King tutour,
And of all Scotland Governour.
Our King was bot fyve yeiris of age,
That time quhen done wes the outrage.
Quhen this gude Knicht the Squyer saw,
Thus lyand in till his deid thraw,
Wo is me! quod he, to see this sicht,
On thee, quhilk worthie wes and wicht.
Wald God that I had bene with thee,
As thow in France was anis with me;
Into the land of Picardy,
Quhair Inglis men had greit invy,
To have me slane, sa thay intendit,
Bot manfullie thow me defendit,
And vailyeandlie did save my lyfe;   .
Was never man with sword nor knyfe,
Nocht Hercules, I dar weill say,
That ever faucht better for ane day;
Defendland me within ane stound,
Thow dang seir Sutheroun to the ground.
I may thee mak no help, allace;
Bot I sall follow on the chace,
Richt spedilie baith day and nicht,
Till I may get that cruell Knicht.
I mak ane vow, gif I may get him,
Intill ane presoun I sall set him,
And quhen I heir that thow beis deid,
Than sall my handis straik off his head.
    With that he gave his hors the spurris,

And spedelie flaw ouir the furris.
He and his gaird with all thair micht,
Thay ran till thai ouirtuik the Knicht.
Quhen he approcht he lichtit doun,
And like ane vailyeand campioun,
He tuk the tyrane presonar,
And send him backward to Dumbar ;
And thair remainit in presoun,
Ane certaine time in that dungeoun.
   Let him ly thair with mekil cair,
And speik we of our heynd Squyar :
Of quhome we cannot speik bot gude ;
Quhen he lay bathand in his blude,
His freindis and his Ladie fair,
Thay maid for him sic dule and cair ;
Quhilk wer greit pietie to deploir,
Of that mater I speik no moir.
Thay send for Leichis haistelie,
Syne buir his bodie tenderlie,
To ludge into ane fair ludgyne,
Quhair he ressavit medicyne.
The greitest Leichis of the land,
Come all to him without command.
And all practikis on him provit,
Becaus he was sa weill belovit.
Thay tuik on hand his life to save,
And he thame gaif quhat thay wald have.
Bot he sa lang lay into pane.
He turnit to be ane Chirurgiane :
And als be his naturall ingyne,
He lernit the art of medicyne.
   VOL. I.   O

He saw thame on his bodie wrocht,
Quhairfoir the Science wes deir bocht.
Bot efterward quhen he was haill,
He spairit na coist nor yit travaill,
To preif his practikis on the pure,
And on thame previt monie ane cure,
On his expensis, without rewaird,
Of money he tuik na regaird.

    Yit sum thing will we commoun mair
Of this Ladie, quhilk maid greit cair,
Quhilk to the Squyer wes mair pane
Nor all his woundis in certane.
And than his freindis did conclude,
Becaus scho micht do him na gude,
That scho suld tak hir leif and go,
Till hir cuntrie, and scho did so :
Bot thir luiferis met never agane,
Quhilk wes to thame ane lestand pane :
For scho aganis hir will wes maryit,
Quhairthrow hir weird scho daylie waryit.
Howbeit hir bodie wes absent,
Hir tender hart wes ay present,
Baith nicht and day with hir Squyar,
Wes never creature that maid sic cair :
Penelope for Ulisses,
I wait, had never mair distres ;
Nor Cresseid for trew Troylus,
Wes not tent part sa dolorous :
I wait it wes aganis hir hart,
That scho did from hir Lufe depart ;
Helene had not sa mekill noy,

Quhen scho perforce wes brocht to Troy.
I leif hir than with hart full sore,
And speik now of this Squyer more.
   Quhen this Squyer wes haill and sound,
And softlie micht gang on the ground,
To the Regent he did complane ;
Bot he, allace ! wes richt sone slane
Be David Hume of Wedderburne :
The quhilk gart mone Frenchemen murne.
For thair was nane mair nobill knicht,
Mair vailyeand, mair wyse, mair wicht :
And sone efter that crueltie,
The Knicht was put to libertie,
The quhilk the Squyer had opprest :
Sa wes his matter left undrest.
Becaus the King was young of age,
Than tyrannis rang into thair rage.
Bot efterward, as I hard say,
On Striviling brig upon ane day,
This Knight was slane with crueltie,
And that day gat na mair mercie,
Nor he gaif to the young Squyar ;
I say na mair, let him ly thair.
For cruell men ye may weill see,
They end oft times with crueltie ;
For Christ to Peter said this word,
Quha ever straikis with ane sword,
That man sal be with ane sword slane,
That saw is suith, I tell you plane :
He menis quha straikis cruellie,
  Aganis the Law without mercie.

Bot this Squyer to nane offendit.
Bot manfullie him self defendit.
Wes never man with sword nor knyfe,
Mycht saif thair honour and thair lyfe ;
As did the Squyer all his dayis,
With monie terribill effrayis.
Wald I at lenth his lyfe declair,
I micht weill writ ane uther quair ;
Bot at this tyme I may not mend it,
Bot schaw you how the Squyer endit.

Thair dwelt in Fyfe ane agit Lord,
That of this Squyer hard record,
And did desire richt hartfullie,
To have him in his companie :
And send for him with diligence,
And he come with obedience ;
And lang tyme did with him remane,
Of quhome this agit Lord was fane.
Wyse men desiris commounlie
Wyse men into thair companie.
For he had bene in monie ane land,
In Flanderis, France, and in Ingland ;
Quhairfoir the Lord gaif him the cure,
Of his houshold I yow assure ;
And in his hall cheif Merschall
And auditour of his comptis all.

He was ane richt courticiane,
And in the law ane practiciane ;
Quhairfoir during this Lordis lyfe,
Schyref Depute he wes in Fyfe :
To everie man ane equal judge,

And of the pure he was refuge ;
And with justice did thame support,
And curit thair sairis with greit comfort :
For as I did reheirs before,
Of medicine he tuke the lore,
Quhen he saw the chirurgience
Upon him do thair diligence.
Experience maid him perfyte,
And of the Science he tuke sic delyte,
That he did mony thriftie cure,
And speciallie upon the pure ;
Without rewaird for his expensis,
Without regaird or recompensis,
To gold, to silver, or to rent,
This nobill Squyer tuke litill tent :
Of all this warld na mair he craifit,
So that his honour micht be saifit.
And ilk yeir for his Ladie's saik,
Ane banket royall wald he maik ;
And that he maid on the Sonday
Precedand to Aschwednisday.
With wyld foull, venisoun and wyne :
With tairt, and flam, and frutage fyne :
Of bran and geill thair wes na skant,
And ipocras he wald not want
I have sene sittand at his tabill,
Lordis and lairdis honorabill,
With knichtis, and monie ane gay squyar,
Quhilk wer too lang for to declair :
With mirth, musick and menstrallie.
All this he did for his Ladie :

And for hir saik during his lyfe,
Wald never be weddit to ane wyfe.
   And quhen he did declyne to age,
He faillit never of his courage.
Of ancient storyis for to tell,
Above all other he did precell.
Sa that everilk creature,
To heir him speik thay tuke plesure.
   Bot all his deidis honorabill,
For to descryve I am not abill:
Of everie man he was commendit,
And as he levit, sa he endit.
Plesandlie till he micht indure,
Till dolent deith come to his dure;
And cruellie with his mortall dart,
He straik the Squyer throw the hart:
His saull with joy angelicall,
Past to the hevin Imperiall.
Thus at the Struther into Fyfe,
This nobill Squyer loist his lyfe.
I pray to Christ for to convoy
All sic trew luiferis to his joy.
Say ye AMEN, for Cheritie.
Adew! ye sall get na mair of me.

THE TESTAMENT OF THE NOBILL AND VAILYEAND SQUYER WILLIAME MELDRUM OF THE BYNNIS.

The holie man Job, ground of pacience,
  In his gret trubill trewlie did reporte,
Quhilk I persave now be Experience,
  That mennis lyfe in eirth bene wounder short.
  My youth is gane, and eild now dois resort ;
My time is gane, I think it bot ane dreame,
Yit efter deith remane sall my gude fame.

I persave shortlie, that I man pay my det,
  To me in eirth no place bene permanent :
My hart on it no mair now will I set,
  Bot with the help of God omnipotent,
  With resolute mind go mak my Testament :
And tak my leif at cuntriemen, and kyn,
And all the warld, and thus I will begyn.

Thrie Lordis to me sall be Executouris.
  Lindesayis all thrie in surname of renoun :
Of my Testament thay sall have haill the curis ;
  To put my mind till executioun.
  That Surname failyeit never to the Croun,
Na mair will thay to me I am richt sure,
Quhilk is the cause that I give thame the cure.

First David Erll of Craufuird wise and wicht,
  And Johne Lord Lindesay my maister special,
The thrid sal be ane nobill travellit Knicht,
  Quhilk knawis the coistis of feistis funeral :
  The wise Sir Walter Lindesay they him call.
Lord of Sanct Johne, and Knicht of Torfichane,
Be sey and land ane vailyeand capitane.

Thocht age hes maid my bodie impotent,
  Yit in my hart hie courage doeth precell :
Quhairfoir I leif to God, with gude intent,
  My spreit, the quhilk he hes maid immortell ;
  Intill his Court perpetuallie to dwell :
And nevir moir to steir furth of that steid
Till Christ descend and judge baith quick and deid.

I yow beseik, my Lordis Executouris,
  My geir geve till the nixt of my kynrent :
It is well kend, I never tuik na cures,
  Of conquessing of riches nor of rent ;
  Dispone as ye think maist expedient :
I never tuik cure of gold more than of glas ;
Without honour, fy ! fy upon riches !

I yow requeist, my freindis ane and all,
  And nobill men of quhome I am descendit :
Faill not to be at my feist funerall,
  Quhilk throw the warld I traist sal be commendit,
  Ye knaw how that my fame I have defendit,
During my life, unto this latter hour,
Quhilk suld to yow be infinite plesour.

First of my bowellis clenge my bodie clene,
  Within and out, syne weische it weill with wyne :
Bot honestlie see that nothing be sene,
  Syne clois it in an coistlie carvit schryne,
  Of cedar treis, or of cyper fyne :
Anoynt my corpis with balme delicious,
With cynamome and spycis precious.

In twa caissis of gold and precious stanis,
  Inclois my hart and toung richt craftelie ;
My sepulture syne gar mak for my banis,
  Into the tempell of Mars triumphandlie,
  Of marvill stanis carvit richt curiouslie ;
Quhairin my kist and banis ye sall clois
In that triumphand tempill to repois.

Mars, Venus, and Mercurius, all thre,
  Gave me my natural inclinatiounis ;
Quhilk rang the day of my nativitie,
  And sa thair hevinlie constellatiounis
  Did me supporte in monie Nationnis ;
Mars maid me hardie like an feirs lyoun,
Quhairthrow I conqueist honour and renoun.

Quho list to knaw the actis bellicall,
  Let thame ga reid the Legend of my life ;
Thare sall thai find the deidis martiall,
  How I have stand in monie stalwart strife ;
  Victoriouslie with speir, sheild, sword, and knife :
Quhairfoir to Mars the god armipotent,
My corps incloisit ye do till him present.

Mak offering of my toung rhetoricall,
  Till Mercurius quhilk gaif me eloquence,
In his tempill to hing perpetuall,
  I can mak him na better recompence ;
  For quhen I was brocht to the presence
Of kingis in Scotland, Ingland and in France,
My ornate toung my honour did avance.

To fresche Venus my hart ye sall present,
  Quhilk hes to me bene ay comfortabill ;
And in my face sic grace scho did imprent,
  All creatures did think me amiabill.
  Women to me scho maid sa favorabill :
Wes never Ladie that luikit in my face,
But honestlie I did obtene hir grace.

My freind Sir David Lyndsay of the Mont
  Sall put in ordour my Processioun ;
I will that thair pas formest in the front
  To beir my penseil ane wicht campioun,
  With him ane band of Mars his religioun,
That is to say, in steid of monkis and freiris,
In gude ordour ane thowsand hagbutteris.

Nixt them ane thowsand futemen in ane rout,
  With speir and sheild, with buckler, bow and brand,
In ane luferay young stalwart men and stout.
  Thridlie in ordour thair sall cum ane band,
  Of nobill men, abill to wraik thair harmes,
Thair Capitane with my standard in his hand,
On bairdit hors ane hundreth men of armes.

Amang that band, my baner sal be borne,
   Of silver schene, thrie otteris into sabill :
With tabroun, trumpet, clarioun, and horne,
   For men of armes very convenabill :
   Nixt after thame ane campioun honorabill,
Sall beir my basnet with my funerall,
Syne efter him in ordour triumphall,

My arming sword, my gluifis of plait, and sheild
   Borne be ane forsie campioun, or ane knicht,
Quilk did me serve in monie dangerous feild.
   Nixt efter him, ane man in armour bricht,
   Upon ane jonet or ane cursour wicht :
The quhilk sal be ane man of greit honour,
Upon ane speir to beir my coit armour.

Syne nixt my beir sal cum my corspresent,
   My bairdit hors, my harnes, and my speir ;
With sum greit man of my awin kynrent,
   As I wes wont on my bodie to beir,
   During my time quhen I went to the weir ;
Quhilk sal be offerit with ane gay garment,
To Mars his preist at my interrement.

Duill weidis I think hypocrisie and scorne,
   With huidis heklit doun ouirthort thair ene,
With men of armes, my bodie sal be borne,
   Into that band see that no blak be sene :
   My luferay sal be reid, blew, and grene,
The reid for Mars, the grene for freshe Venus,
The ble, for lufe of god Mercurius.

About my beir, sall ryde ane multitude,
    All of ane luiferay of my cullouris thrie ;
Erles, and Lordis, Knichtis, and men of gude ;
    Ilk Barroun beirand in his hand on hie,
    Ane lawrer branche, insigne of victorie,
Becaus I fled never out of the feild,
Nor yit as presoner unto my fois me yeild.

Agane that day, faill not to warne and call
    All men of musick, and of menstrallie ;·
About my beir with mirthis musicall,
    To dance and sing with hevinlie harmonie,
    Quhais plesand sound redound sall in the sky ;
My spreit I wait sal be with mirth and joy,
Quhairfoir with mirth my corps ye sal convoy.

Thus beand done, and all things reulit richt,
    Than plesandlie mak your progressioun,
Quhilk I beleif sal be ane pleasand sicht ;
    Se that ye thoill na priest in my processioun.
    Without he be of Venus professioun,
Quhairfoir gar warne all Venus chapel clarkis,
Quhilk hes bene most exercit in hir warkis.

With ane Bischop of that religioun,
    Solemnitlie gar thame sing my saull mes,
With organe, timpane, trumpet, and clarioun,
    To shaw thair musick, dewlie them addres,
    I will that day, be heard no hevines :
I will na service of the Requiem,
Bot Alleluya, with melodie and game.

Efter the Evangell, and the Offertour,
  Throw all the tempill, gar proclame silence :
Than to the pulpet gar ane Oratour,
  Pas up and shaw in oppin audience,
  Solempnitlie with ornate eloquence ;
At greit laser, the Legend of my life,
How I have stand in monie stalwart strife.

Quhen he hes reid my buik fra end till end,
  And of my life maid trew narratioun ;
All creature I wait will me commend,
  And pray to God for my salvatioun ;
  Than efter this solempnizatioun,
Of service trew, and all brocht to ane end ;
With gravitie than with my bodie wend.

And clois it up into my sepulture,
  Thair to repois till the Greit Judgement ;
The quhilk may not corrupt I yow assure,
  Be vertew of the precious oyntment,
  Of balme, and uther spyces redolent.
Let not be rung for me, that day, saull knellis
Bot greit cannounis gar them crak for bellis.

Ane thousand hakbuttis gar schute al at anis,
  With swesche, talburnis, and trumpettis awfullie ;
Lat never spair the poulder nor the stanis,
  Quhais thundring sound redound sall in the sky,
  That Mars may heir quhair he triumphandlie
Above Phebus is situate full evin,
Maist awfull god, under the sternie hevin.

And syne hing up above my sepulture,
   My bricht harnes, my shield, and als my speir ;
Togidder with my courtlie coit armour.
   Quhilk I wes wont upon my bodie beir,
   In France, in Ingland, being at the weir ;
My baner, basnet, with my temperall,
As bene the use of feistis funerall.

This beand done, I pray yow tak the pane,
   My Epitaphe to writ upon this wyis,
Above my grave, in golden letteris fyne :
   THE MAIST INVINCIBILL WEIRIOUR HEIR LYIS,
   DURING HIS TIME, QUHILKWAN SIC LAUD AND PRYIS,
THAT THROW THE HEVINIS SPRANG HIS NOBLE FAME :
VICTORIOUS WILLIAM MELDRUM WES HIS NAME.

Adew, my Lordis, I may na langer tarie,
   My Lord Lindesay, adew abone all uther ;
I pray to God, and to the Virgine Marie,
   With your lady to leif lang in the Struther ;
   Maister Patrik, with young Normond your brother;
With my ladeis, your sisteris, all adew !
My departing I wait weill ye will rew.

Bot maist of all the fair Ladies of France,
   Quhen thai heir tell but dout that I am deid ;
Extreme dolour will change thair countenance,
   And for my saik will wear the murning weid ;
   Quhen thir novellis dois into Ingland spread,
Of Londoun than the lustie ladies cleir,
Will for my saik mak dule and drerie cheir.

Of Craigfergus my dayis darling adew,
  In all Ireland of feminine the flour :
In your querrell twa men of weir I slew,
  Quhilk purposit to do yow dishonour ;
  Ye suld have bene my spous and paramour,
With rent and riches for my recompence,
Quhilk I refusit throw youth and insolence.

Fair weill ! ye lemant lampis of lustines
  Of fair Scotland, adew my Ladies all ?
During my youth with ardent besines,
  Ye knaw how I was in your service thrall,
  Ten thowsand times adew above thame all ;
Sterne of Stratherne, my Ladie Soverane !
For quhome I sched my blud with mekill pane.

Yit wald my Ladie luke at evin and morrow
  On my legend at length scho wald not mis,
How for hir saik I sufferit mekill sorrow,
  Yit give I micht at this time get my wis,
  Of hir sweit mouth, deir God, I had ane kis ;
I wis in vane, allace we will dissever,
I say na mair, Sweit hart, Adew for ever !

Brether in armes, Adew in generall,
  For me, I wait your hartis bene full soir ;
All trew companyeounis into speciall,
  I say to yow, Adew for evermoir !
  Till that we meit agane with God in gloir ;
Sir Curat, now gif me incontinent
My crysme, with the holie Sacrament.

My spreit hartlie I recommend
  In manus tuas, Domine :
My hoip to thee is till ascend,
  Rex, quia redemisti me ;
  Fra syn *resurrexisti me ;*
Or ellis my saull had bene forlorne :
  With sapience *docuisti me :*
Blist be the hour that Thow wes borne.

ANE DIALOG BETUIX

EXPERIENCE AND ANE COURTEOUR.

ANE DIALOG

BETUIX EXPERIENCE AND ANE COURTEOUR

OF THE MISERABYLL ESTAIT

OF THE WORLD.

Absit Gloriari, nisi in Cruce Domini nostri Jesu Christi.

THE EPISTIL TO THE REDAR.

Thou lytill Quair, of mater miserabyll,
Weil auchtest thou coverit to be with sabyll,
  Renunceand grene, the purpur, reid, and quhit :
To delicat men thou art nocht delectabyll,
Nor yit tyll amorous folkis amiabyll :
  To reid on thee thai wyl haif no delite ;
  Warldlye peple wyll have at thee dispyte,
Quhilk fyxit hes thare hart and hole intentis
On sensuall luste, on dignitie, and rentis.

We have no Kyng thee to present, allace !
Quhilk to this countrie bene ane cairfull cace ;

And als our Quene, of Scotland Heretour,
Sche dwellith in France : I pray God saif hir Grace.
It war too lang for thee to ryn that race,
    And far langar or that young tender Flour
    Bryng home tyll us ane Kyng and Governour.
Allace, tharefor, we may with sorrow syng,
Quhilk muste so long remane without one Kyng.

I nott quhome to thy simpylnes to sende :
With cunnyng men, from tyme that thou be kende,
    Thy vaniteis no waye thay wyll advance,
Thynkand thee proude sic thyngis to pretende ;
Nochtwithstanding, the straucht way sal thou wende
    To thame quhilk hes the realme in governance :
    Declare thy mynde to thame with circumstance.
Go first tyll James, our Prince and Protectour,
And his Brother, our Spirituall Governour,

And Prince of Priestis in this Natioun :
Efter reverend recommendatioun,
    Under thare feit thow lawlye thee submyt,
And mak thame humyll supplicatioun,
Geve thay in thee fynd wrang narratioun,
    That thay wald pleis thy faltis to remyt :
    And of thare grace geve thay do thee admyt,
Than go thy waye quhare ever thow plesis best ;
Be thay content, mak reverence to the rest :

To faithfull prudent Pastouris Spirituall,
To nobyll Erlis, and Lordis Temporall,
    Obedientlye tyll thame thow thee addres,

Declaryng thame this schort memoriall,
Quhow Mankynd bene to miserie maid thrall.
    At lenth to thame the cause plainlie confesse,
    Beseikand thame all lawis to suppresse
Inventit be mennis traditioun,
Contrar to Christis institutioun :

And cause them cleirlye for tyll understand
That, for the brekyng of the Lordis command,
    His thrynfald wande of flagellatioun
Hes scurgit this pure Realme of Scotland,
Be mortall weris baith be say and land,
    With mony terrabyll trybulatioun.
    Tharefor, mak to thame trew narratioun,
That all thir weiris, this derth, huuger, and pest,
Was nocht bot for our synnis manifest.

Declare to thame quhow, in the tyme of Noye,
Allvterlye God did the warld destroye,
    As Holy Scripture maketh mentioun ;
Sodom, Gomor, with thare regioun and roye ;
God sparit nother man, woman, nor boye ;
    But all were brynt for thare offensioun.
    Jherusalem, that moste tryumphaut town,
Distroyit was for thare iniquity,
As in the Scripture planelye thay may se.

Declare to thame, this mortal miserie,
Be sweird and fyre, derth, pest, and povertie,
    Procedis of syn, gyf I can rycht discryve,
For laik of faith, and for idolatrye,

For fornicatioun, and for adultrye,
   Of Princis, Prelatis, with mony ane man and wyve,
Expell the cause, than the effect belyve
Sall cease : quhen that the peple doith repent,
Than God sall slak his bow, quhilk yit is bent.

Mak thame requeist quhilk hes the Governance
The sinceir word of God for tyll avance
   Conforme to Christis institution.
Without hypocrisie or dissimulance :
Causying Justice hauld evinlye the ballance :
   On Publicanis making punyssioun ;
   Commendyng thame of gude conditioun.
That beyng done, I dout nocht bot the Lorde
Sall of this countrie have misericorde.

Thocht God with mony terrabyll effrayis
Hes done this countrie scurge by divers wayis ;
   Be juste jugement, for our grevous offence,
Declare to thame they sall have mery dayis,
Efter this trubyll, as the Propheit sayis,
   Quhen God sall se our humyll repentance :
   Tyll strange pepyll thocht he hes gevin lycence
To be our scurge induryng his desyre,
Wyll, quhen he lyste, that scurge cast in the fyre.

Pray thame that thay putt nocht thare esperance
In mortall men onelye, thame tyll advance,
   Bot principallye in God Omnipotent :
Than neid thai not to charge the realme of France
With gounnis, galayis, nor uther ordinance,

So that they be to God obedient ;
 In thir premyssis be thay nocht negligent,
Displayand Christis banar hie on heycht,
Thair ennimeis of thame sall have no mycht.

Go hence, pure Buke, quhilk I have done indyte
In rurall ryme, in maner of dispyte,
  Contrar the Warldis variatioun :
Of Rethorick heir I proclame thee quyte.
Idolatouris, I feir, sall with thee flyte,
  Because of thame thow makis narratioun :
  Bot cure thow nocht the indignatioun
Of Hypocritis, and fals Pharisience,
Quhowbeit on thee thay cry ane lowde vengence.

Requeist the Gentyll Reder that thee redis,
Thocht ornat termes in to thy park not spredis,
  As thay in thee may have experience :
Thocht barran feildis beris nocht but weidis,
Yit brutall beistis sweitlye on thame feidis :
  Desyre of thame none uther recompence
  Bot that thay wald reid thee with pacience :
And, geve thay be in ony way offendit,
Declare to thame, it salbe weill amendit.

HEIR ENDIS THE EPISTIL AND FOLLOWIS THE
PROLOG.

THE PROLOG

OF THE MISERABILL ESTAIT OF THIS WARLD.

Musing and marvelling on the miserie
    Frome day to day on erth quhilk dois incres,
And of ilk stait the instabilitie
    Proceding of the restless besynes
    Quhare on the most part doith thair mynd addres
Inordinatlie, on houngrye covatyce,
Vaine glore, dissait, and uther sensuall vyce :

Bot tumlyng in my bed I mycht nocht lye ;
    Quharefore I fuir furth, in ane Maye mornyng,
Conforte to gett of my malancolye,
    Sumquhat affore fresche Phebus uprysing,
    Quhare I mycht heir the birdis sweitlye syng :
In tyll ane park I past, for my plesure
Decorit weill be craft of dame Nature.

Quhow I resavit confort naturall
    For tyll discryve at lenth it war too lang ;
Smelling the holsum herbis medicinall,
    Quhare on the dulce and balmy dew down dang,
    Lyke aurient peirles on the twistis hang ;
Or quhow that the aromatic odouris
Did proceid frome the tender fragrant flouris ;

Or quhow Phebus, that king etheriall,
    Swyftlie sprang up in to the Orient,
Ascending in his throne imperiall,
    Quhose brycht and beriall bemes resplendent
    Illumynit all on to the Occident,
Confortand everye corporall creature
Quhilk formit war, in erth, be dame Nature;

Quhose donke impurpurit vestiment nocturnall,
    With his imbroudit mantyll matutyne,
He lefte in tyll his regioun aurorall,
    Quhilk on hym waitit quhea he did declyne
    Towarte his Occident palyce vespertyne,
And rose in habyte gaye and glorious,
Brychtar nor gold or stonis precious.

Bot Synthea, the hornit nychtis quene,
    Scho loste hir lychte and lede ane lawar saill,
Frome tyme hir soverane lorde that scho had sene,
    And in his presens waxit dirk and paill,
    And ouer hir visage kest ane mistye vaill;
So did Venus, the goddes amorous,
With Jupiter, Mars, and Mercurius.

Rycht so the auld intoxicat Saturne,
    Persaving Phebus powir, his beymes brycht,
Abufe the Erth than maid he no sudgeourne,
    Bot suddandlye did lose his borrowit lycht,
    Quhilk he durst never schaw bot on the nycht.
The Pole Artick, Ursis, and Sterris all
Quhilk situate ar in the Septentrionall,

Tyll errand schyppis quhilks ar the souer gyde,
　　Convoyand thame upone the stormye nycht,
Within thare frostie circle, did thame hyde.
　　Howbeit that sterris have none uthir lycht
　　Bot the reflex of Phebus bemes brycht,
That day durst none in to the hevin appeir,
Till he had circuit all our Hemispheir.

Me thocht it was ane sycht celestiall,
　　To sene Phebus so angellyke ascend
In tyll his fyrie chariot triumphall,
　　Quhose bewtie brychte I culd nocht comprehend.
　　All warldlie cure anone did fro me wend,
Quhen fresche Flora spred furth hir tapestrie,
Wrocht be dame Nature, quent and curiouslie

Depaynt with mony hundreth heviniie hewis;
　　Glaid of the rysing of thair royall Roye,
With blomes breckand on the tender bewis,
　　Quhilk did provoke myne hart tyl natural joye.
　　Neptune, that day, and Eoll held thame coye,
That men on far mycht heir the birdis sounde,
Quhose noyis did to to the sterrye hevin redounde.

The plesand powne prunycand his feddrem fair;
　　The myrthfull mavcs maid gret melodie:
The lustye lark ascending in the air,
　　Numerand his naturall notis craftelye;
　　The gay goldspiuk; the merll rycht myrralye:
The noyis of the nobyll nychtingalis;
Redoundit throuch the montans, meids,

Contempling this melodious armonye,
   Quhow everilke bird drest thame for tyl advance,
To saluss Nature with thare melodye,
   That I stude gasing, halfingis in ane trance,
   To heir thame mak thare naturall observance,
So royallie, that all the roches rang,
Throuch repurcussioun of thare suggurit sang.

I lose my tyme, allace! for to rehers
   Sic unfruitful and vaine discriptioun,
Or wrytt, in to my raggit rurall vers,
   Mater without edificatioun;
   Consydering quhow that myne intentioun
Bene tyll deplore the mortall misereis,
With continuall cairfull calamiteis,

Consisting in this wracheit vaill of sorrow:
   Bot sad sentence sulde have ane sad indyte;
So termes brycht I lyste nocht for to borrow.
   Of murnyng mater men hes no delyte:
   With roustye termes, tharefor, wyl I wryte,
With sorrowful seychis, ascending from the splene,
And bitter teris distellyng from myne ciue;

Withoute ony vaine invocatioun
   To Minerva, or to Melpominee:
Nor yitt wyll I mak supplicatioun
   For help to Cleo nor Calliopee:
   Sic marde Musis may mak me no supplee.
Proserpyne I refuse, and Apollo,
And rycht so Ewterp, Jupiter, and Juno,

Quhilkis bene to pleasand Poetis conforting :
   Quharefor, because I am nocht one of tho,
I do desyre of thame no supporting.
   For I did never sleip on Pernasso,
   As did the Poetis of lang tyme ago,
And, speciallie, the ornate Ennius ;
Nor drank I never with Hysiodus,

Of Grece the perfyte poet soverane,
   Of Hylicon, the sors of eloquence,
Of that mellifluons, famous, fresche fontane :
   Quharefor I awe to thame no reverence.
   I purpose nocht to mak obedience
To sic mischeand Musis nor Malmontrye
Afore tyme usit in to Poetrye.

Raveand Rhamnusia, goddés of dispýte,
   Mycht be to me ane Muse rycht convenabyll,
Gyff I desyrit sic help for tyll indyte
   This murnyng mater, mad and miserabyll.
   I mon go seik ane Muse more comfortabyll,
And sic vaine superstitioun to refuse,
Beseikand the gret God to be my Muse ;

Be quhose wysdome all maner of thing bene wrocht,
   The heych hevinnis, with all thair ornamentis ;
And without mater maid all thing of nocht :
   Hell in myd centir of the Elementis.
   That hevinlye Muse to seik my hole intent is,
The quhilk gaif sapience to king Salomone,
To David grace, strenth to the strang Sampsone,

And of pure Peter maid ane prudent precheour;
   And, be the power of his Deitee,
Of creuell Paule he maid ane cunnyng techeour.
   I mon beseik, rycht lawly on my knee,
   His heych superexcellent Majestie,
That with his hevinlye spreit he may inspyre
To wrytt no thyng contrarye his desyre.

Beseikand als his Soverane Sonne, Jesu,
   Quhilk wes consavit be the Holy Spreit,
Incarnat of the purifyit Virgin trew,
   In to the quhome the Prophicie was compleit,
   That Prince of Peace, most humyll and mansweit,
Quhilk onder Pylate sufferit passioun,
Upon the Croce, for our salvatioun.

And be that creuell deith intollerabyll
   Lowsit we wer frome bandis of Belyall;
And mairattour, it wes so proffitabyll
   That to this hour come nevir man, nor sall,
   To the tryumphant joye imperiall
Of lyfe, quhowbeit that thay war nevar sa gude,
Bot be the vertew of that precious blude.

Quharefor, in steid of the Mont Pernaso,
   Swyftlie I sall go seik my Soverane,
To Mont Calvarie the straucht way mon I go,
   To gett ane taist of that moist fresche fontane.
   That sors to seik my hart may nocht refrane
Of Hylicone, quhilk wes boith deip and wyde,
That Longeous did grave in tyll his syde.

From that fresche fontane sprang a famous flude,
  Quhilk redolent rever throuch the warld yit
    rynnis,
As christall cleir, and mixit bene with blude ;
  Quhose sound abufe the heyest hevinnis dinnis,
  All faithfull pepil purgeing frome thare sinnis,
Quharefor I sall beseik his Excellence,
To grant me grace, wysedome, and eloquence ;

And baythe me with those dulce and balmy strandis
  Quhilk on the Croce did spedalie out spryng
Frome his moste tender feit and hevinly handis ;
  And grant me grace to wrytt nor dyte no thyng
  Bot tyll his heich honour and loude lovyng ;
Bot quhose support thare may na gud be wrocht
Tyll his plesure, gude workis, word, nor thocht.

Tharefor, O Lorde, I pray thy Majestie,
  As thow did schaw thy heych power Divyne,
First plainlie in the Cane of Galelee,
  Quhare thow convertit cauld watter in wyne,
  Convoye my mater tyll ane fructuous fyne,
And save my sayingis baith frome schame and syn:—
Tak tent, for now I purpose to begyn.

HEIR ENDIS THE PROLOG AND BEGINNIS
THE MATER.

ANE DIALOG

BETUIX EXPERIENCE AND ANE COURTEOUR.

THE FIRST BUKE.

IN TO that Park I sawe appeir
One ageit Man, quhilk drew me neir,
Quhose beird wes weill thre quarter lang;
His hair doun ouer his schulders hang,
The quhilk as ony snaw wes quhyte;
Quhome to behald I thocht delyte;
His habitt Angellyke of hew,
Of culloure lyke the sapheir blew,
Onder ane hollyng he reposit,
Of quhose presens I was rejosit.
I did hym saluss reverendlye;
Sa did he me, rycht courteslye.
To sitt down he requeistit me,
Onder the schaddow of that tre,
To saif me frome the sonnis heit,
Amangis the floweris softe and sweit;
For I wes werye for walking.
Than we began to fall in talking:
   I sperit his name, with reverence!
   I am, said he, EXPERIENCE.

COURTEOUR.

Than, Schir, said I, ye can nocht faill
To gyff ane desolate man counsaill.
Ye do appeir ane man of fame ;
And, sen Experience bene your name,
I praye yow, Father venerabyll,
Geve me sum counsell confortabill.

EXPERIENCE.

Quhat bene, quod he, thy vocatioun,
Makand sic supplycatioun ?

COURTEOUR.

I haif, quod I, bene to this hour,
Sen I could ryde, ane Courteour ;
Bot now, Father, I thynk it best,
With your counsell, to leif in rest,
And frome thyne furth to tak myne cais,
And quyetlie my God to pleais,
And renunce curiositie,
Levyng the Court, and lerne to dé.
Oft have I sailit ouer the strandis,
And travalit throuch divers landis,
Foith South, and North, and Est, and West ;
Yitt can I never fynd quhare Rest
Doith mak his habitatioun,
Withoute your supportatioun.
Quhen I belief to be best easit,
Most suddantlye I am displeasit ;
Frome trubbyll quhen I fastest fle,

Than fynd I most adversatie.
Schaw me, I pray you hartfullye,
Quhow I may leif most pleasandlie,
To serve my God, of kyngis Kyng,
Sen I am tyrit for travellyng ;
And lerne me for to be content
Of quyet lyfe, and sobir rent,
That I may thank the Kyng of Glore,
As thocht I had ane mylyeoun more.
Sen everilk Court bene variant,
Full of invy, and inconstant :
Mycht I, but trubbyll, leif in rest
Now in my aige, I thynk it best.

EXPERIENCE.

  Thow art ane gret fuill, Sonne, said he,
Thyng to desyre quhilk may not be,
Yarnyng to have prerogatyve
Above all Creature on lyfe.
Sen Father Adam creat bene
In to the campe of Damascene,
Mycht no man say, on to this hour,
That ever he fand perfyte plesour,
Nor never sall, tyll that he se
God in his Divyne Majestie :
Quharefore prepair thee for travell,
Sen mennis lyfe bene bot battell.
All men begynnis for tyll de
The day of thare Nativitie ;
And journelly thay do proceid,
Tyll Atrops cut the fatell threid ;

And, in the breif tyme that thay have
Betuix thare byrth on to thare grave;
Thow seis quhat mutabiliteis,
Quhat miserabyll calamiteis;
Quhat trubbyll, travell, and debait
Seis thow in everie mortall stait!
Begyn at pure lawe Creaturis,
Ascending, syne, to Senaturis,
To gret Princis and Potestatis,
Thow sall nocht fynd in non estatis,
Sen the begynning, generallie,
Nor in our tyme now, speciallie,
Bot teddious, restles besynes
Bot ony maner of sickernes.

COURTEOUR.

Prudent Father, quod I, allace!
Ye tell to me one cairfull cace;
Ye say, that no man to this hour,
Hes found in erth perfyte plesour,
Without infortunat variance:
Sen we bene thrall to sic myschance,
Quhy do we set so our intentis
On ryches, dignitie, and rentis?
Sen in the Erth bene no man sure
One day but trubbyll tyll indure;
And, werst of all, quhen we leist wene,
The cruell deith we mon sustene,
Geve I your Fatherheid durst demand,
The cause I wald faine understand;
And als, Father, I yow implore,
Schaw me sum trubbyll gone afore:

That, heryng utheris indigence,
I may the more haif patience.
Marrowis in trybulatioun
Bene wracheis consolatioun.

EXPERIENCE.

Quod he, Efter my small cunnyng
To thee I sall mak answeryng.
Bot, ordourlie for to begyn,
This misarie procedis of syn.
Bot it wer lang for to defyn it
Quhow all men ar to syn inclynit.
Quhen syn aboundantlye doith ryng,
Justly God makith punyssing :
Quharefor gret God in to his handis,
To dant the warld, hes divers wandis ;
Efter our evyll conditioun
He makis on us punytioun,
With hunger, darth, and indigens ;
Sum tyme gret plagis, and pestilens,
And sum tyme with his bludy wand,
Throw creuell weir be sey and land :
Concludyng, all our misarie
Proceidis of syn, alluterlie.

COURTEOUR.

Father, quod I, declare to me
The cause of this fragyllitie,
That we bene all to syn inclynde,
In werk, in word, and in our mynde.
I wald the veritie wer schawin,
Quho hes this seid amang us sawin ?

And quhy we ar condampnit to dede?
And quhow that we may get remede?

EXPERIENCE.

  Quod he, The Scripture hes concludit
Men frome felicitie wer denudit
Be Adam, our progenitour,
Unquhyle of Paradyse possessour;
Be quhose most wylfull arrogance
Wes Mankynd brocht to this myschance;
Quhen he was inobedient,
In breking Godis commandiment.
Be solystatioun of his wyfe
He loste that hevinlye plesand lyfe;
Etand of the forbiddin tre,
Thare began all our miserie.
So Adam wes cause radicall
That we bene fragyll synnaris all.
Adam brocht in this natioun
Syn, Deith, and als dampnatioun.
Quho wyll say he is no synnar,
Christ sayis, he is ane gret lear.
Mankynde sprang furth of Adamis loynis,
And tuke of hym flesche, blude, and bonis;
And so, efter his qualytie
All ar inclynit synnaris to be.

  Bot yit, my Sonne, dispare thow nocht;
For God, that all the warld hes wrocht,
Hes maid ane Soverane remede,
To saif us boith frome syn and dede,
And frome etarne dampnatioun:
Tharefore tak consolatioun.

For God, as Scripture doith recorde,
Haveyng of man misericorde,
Send doun his onelye Sonne, Jesu,
Quhilk lychtit in one Virgin trew,
And cled his heych Divynitie
With our pure vyle Humanytie ;
Syne frome our synnis, to conclude,
He wysche us with his precious blude.
Quhowbeit throw Adam we mon dee,
Throuch that Lord we sall rasit bee ;
And everilk man he sall releve
Quhilk in his blude doith ferme beleve ;
And bryng us all into his glore
The quhilk throw Adam bene forlore ;
Without that we, throw laik of faith,
Of his Godheid incur the wraith :
Bot quho in Christ fermely belevis
Sall be relevit frome all myschevis.

COURTEOUR.

Quhat Faith is that that ye call ferme ?
Schir, gar me understand that terme.

EXPERIENCE.

Faith without Hope and Charitie
Avalit nocht, my Sonne, said he.

COURTEOUR.

Quhat Charitie bene, that wald I knaw.

EXPERIENCE.

Quod he, My Sonne, that sall I schaw :

First, lufe thy God above all thyng,
And thy nychtbour but fenzeyng ;
Do none injure nor villanie,
Bot as thow wald wer done to thee :
Quyk faith but cheritabyll werkis
Can never be, as wryttis Clerkis,
More than the fyre, in tyli his mycht,
Can be but heit, nor Sonne but lycht ;
Geve Charitie into thee failis,
Thy Faith nor Hope no thyng availis.
The Devyll hes Faith, and tryulis for dreid ;
Bot he wantis Hope and Lufe in deid.
Do all the gude that may be wrocht,
But Charitie, all availis nocht.
Quharefor pray to the Trinitie
For tyll support thy Charitie.

  Now have I schawin thee as I can,
Quhow Father Adam, the first man,
Brocht in the warld boith Syn and Dede,
And quhow Christ Jesu maid remede,
Quhilk, on the day of Jugement,
Sall us delyver frome torment,
And bryng us to his lestyng glore,
Quhilk sall indure for ever more.
Bot in this warld thow gettis no rest,
I mak it to thee manifest ;
Tharefore, my Sonne, be diligent,
And lerne for to be patient :
And in to God sett all thy traist :
All thyng sall than cum for the best.

COURTEOUR.

Father, I thank yow hartfullye
Of your conforte and cumpanye,
And hevinlye consolatioun ;
Makand yow supplicatioun,
Geve I durst put yow to sic pyne,
That ye wald pleis for to defyne,
And gar me cleirlye understand,
Quhow Adam brak the Lordis command ;
And quhow, throw his transgressioun,
Wer punyst his successioun.

EXPERIENCE.

My Sonne, quod he, wald thow tak cure
To luke on the Divyne Scripture,
In to the Buke of Genesis
That storye thare thow sall nocht mis.
And alswa syndrie cunnyng Clerkis
Hes done rehers, in to thare werkis,
Of Adamis fall, full ornatly,
Ane thousand tymes better nor I
Can wrytt of that unhappy man.
Bot I sall do the best I can
Schortlie to schaw that cairfull cace,
With the support of Goddis grace.

ANE EXCLAMATIOUN TO THE REDAR, TWYCHEYNG THE WRYTTING OF VULGARE AND MATERNALL LANGUAGE.

GENTYL Redar, haif at me non dispyte,
    Thynkand that I presumptuously pretend,
In vulgair toung so heych mater to writ ;
    Bot quhair I mys I pray ye tyll amend.
    Tyll unlernit I wald the caus were kend
Of our most miserabyll travell and torment,
And quhow, in erth, no place bene permanent.

Quhowbeit that divers devote cunnyng Clerkis
    In Latyne toung hes wryttin syndrie bukis,
Our unlernit knawis lytill of thare werkis,
    More than thay do the ravyng of the rukis.
    Quharefore to colyearis, cairtaris, and to cukis,
To Jok and Thome, my rhyme sall be directit,
With cunnyng men quhowbeit it wylbe lackit.

Thocht every Commoun may nocht be one Clerk,
    Nor hes no leid except thare toung maternall,
Quhy suld of God the marvellous hevinly werk
    Be hid from thame ? I thynk it nocht fraternall.
    The Father of Hevin, quhilk wes and is Eternall,
To Moyses gaif the Law, on Mont Senay,
Nocht into Greik nor Latyne, I heir say.

He wrait the Law, in Tablis hard of stone,
 In thare awin vulgare language of Hebrew,
That all the bairnis of Israell, every one,
 Mycht knaw the Law, and so the same ensew.
 Had he done wryt in Latyne or in Grew,
It had to thame bene bot ane sawrles jest :
Ye may weill wytt God wrocht all for the best.

Arristotyll nor Plato, I heir sane,
 Wrait nocht thare hie Philosophie naturall
In Duche, nor Dence, nor toung Italiane,
 Bot in thare most ornate toung maternall,
 Quhose fame and name doith ryng perpetuall.
Famous Virgill, the Prince of Poetrie,
Nor Cicero, the flour of Oratrie,

Wrait nocht in Caldye language, nor in Grew,
 Nor yit into the language Sarazene,
Nor in the naturall language of Hebrew,
 Bot in the Romane toung, as may be sene,
 Quhilk wes thair proper language, as I wene.
Quhen Romanis rang dominatoris in deid,
The ornat Latyne wes thare proper leid.

In the mene tyme, quhen that thir bauld Romanes,
 Over all the warld had the dominioun,
Maid Latyne scolis thare glore for tyll avance,
 That thair language mycht be over all commoun ;
 To that intent, be my opinioun,
Traisting that thare Impyre sulde ay indure :
Bot of fortune alway thay wer nocht sure.

Of Languagis the first diversytie
   Wes maid be Goddis maledictioun.
Quhen Babilone was beildit in Calde,
   Those beildaris gat none uther afflictioun :
   Affore the tyme of that punyssioun
Wes bot one toung, quhilk Adam spak hym self,
Quhare now of toungis thare bene thre score and twelf.

Nochtwithstandyng, I thynk it gret plesour,
   Quhare cunnyng men hes languagis anew,
That, in thare youth, be deligent laubour,
   Hes leirnit Latyne, Greik, and ald Hebrew :
   That I am nocht of that sorte sore I rew ;
Quharefore I wald all bukis necessare
For our faith were in tyll our toung Vulgare.

Christ, efter his glorious Ascentioun,
   Tyll his Disciplis send the Holy Spreit,
In toungis of fyre, to that intentioun,
   Thay, beand of all languagis repleit,
   Throuch all the warld, with wordis fair and sweit,
Tyll every man the faith thay suld furth schaw
In thare awin leid, delyverand thame the Law.

Tharefore I thynk one gret dirisioun,
   To heir thir Nunnis and Systeris nycht and day
Syngand and sayand Psalmes and Orisioun,
   Nocht understandyng quhat thay syng nor say,
   Bot lyke one Stirlyng or ane Papingay,
Quhilk leirnit ar to speik be lang usage :
Thame I compair to byrdis in ane cage.

Rycht so childreyng and ladyis of honouris
  Prayis in Latyne, to thame ane uncuth leid,
Mumland thair Matynis, Evinsang, and thair Houris,
  Thare Pater Noster, Ave, and thare Creid.
  It wer als plesand to thare spreit, in deid,
GOD HAVE MERCY ON ME, for to say thus,
As to say, *Miserere mei Deus.*

Sanct Jerome in his propir toung Romane
  The Law of God he trewlie did translait,
Out of Hebrew and Greik, in Latyne plane,
  Quhilk hes bene hid from us lang tyme, God wait,
  Onto this tyme : bot, efter myne consait,
Had Sanct Jerome bene borne in tyll Argyle,
In to Yrische toung his bukis had done compyle.

Prudent Sanct Paull doith mak narratioun
  Twycheyng the divers leid of every land,
Sayand, thare bene more edificatioun
  In fyve wordis that folk doith understand,
  Nor to pronounce of wordis ten thousand
In strange langage, sine wait not quhat it menis :
I thynk sic pattryng is not worth twa prenis.

Unlernit peple, on the holy day,
  Solemnitlye thay heir the Evangell sung,
Nocht knawyng quhat the Preist dois sing nor say,
  Bot as ane bell quhen that thay heir it rung :
  Yit, wald the Preistis in to thare mother toung
Pas to the pulpitt and that doctryne declare
Tyll lawid pepyll, it wer more necessare.

I wald Prelattis and Doctouris of the Law
  With us lawid peple wer nocht discontent,
Thocht we in to our vulgare toung did knaw
  Of Christ Jesu the lyfe and Testament
  And quhow that we sulde keip commandiment ;
Bot in our language lat us pray and reid
Our Pater Noster, Ave, and our Creid.

I wald sum Prince of gret discretioun
  In vulgare language planelye gart translait
The neidfull Lawis of this Regioun :
  Than wald thare nocht be half so gret debait
  Amang us peple of the law estait.
Geve every man the verytie did knaw,
We nedit nocht to treit thir Men of law.

Tyll do our nychtbour wrang we wald be war,
  Gyf we did feir the lawis punysment :
Thare wald nocht be sic brawlyng at the bar,
  Nor Men of law loup to sic royall rent.
  To keip the law gyf all men war content,
And ilk man do as he wald be done to,
The Jugis wald get lytill thyng ado.

The Propheit David, Kyng of Israell,
  Compyld the plesand Psalmes of the Psaltair
In his awin propir toung, as I heir tell ;
  And Salomone, quhilk wes his sone and air,
  Did mak his buke in tyll his toung Vulgare.
Quhy suld nocht thare saying be tyll us schawin
In our language ? I wald the caus wer knawin.

Lat Doctoris wrytt thare curious questionis,
 And argumentis sawin full of sophistrye,
Thare Logick, and thare heych opinionis,
 Thare dirk jugementis of Astronomye,
 Thare Medecyne, and thare Philosophye;
Latt Poetis schaw thare glorious ingyne,
As ever thay pleis, in Greik or in Latyne;

Bot lat us haif the Bukis necessare
 To Commoun weill and our Salvatioun
Justlye translatit in our toung Vulgare.
 And als I mak thee Supplicatioun
 O gentyll Redar, haif none indignatioun,
Thynkand I mell me with so hie matair.
Now to my purpose fordwart wyll I fair.

FINIS.

HEIR FOLLOWIS THE CREATIOUN OF ADAM AND EVE.

Quhen God had maid the hevinis brycht,
The Sone and Mone for to geve lycht,
The Sterry Hevin and Christellyne,
And, be his Sapience Divyne,
The Planetis, in thair circlis round
Quhirling about with merie sound,
Of quhome Phebus was principall,
Juste in his lyne Eclipticall ;
And gave, be Divyne Sapience,
Tyll every Ster thare influence,
With motioun continuall,
Quhilk doith indure perpetuall ;
And, farrest frome the Hevin impyre.
The Erth, the Walter, Air, and Fyre :
He cled the Erth with herbis and treis ;
All kynd of fysches in the seis,
All kynd of beist, he did prepair,
With fowlis fleying in the air.
Thus, be his word all thyng was wrocht
Without materiall, maid of nocht :
So, be His wysedome infinyte
All wes maid plesand and perfyte.
  Quhen Hevin and Erth, and thare contentis,
Wer endit, with thare ornamentis,
Than, last of all, the Lord began

Of most vyle erth to mak the Man.
Nocht of the lillie, nor the rose,
Nor syper tre, as I suppose,
Nother of gold, nor precious stonis ;
Of erth he maid flesche, blude, and bonis.
To that intent God maid hym thus,
That man sulde nocht be glorious,
Nor in hym selfe no thyng suld se
Bot matere of humylitie.
Quhen Man wes maid, as I have tald,
God in his face did hym behald,
Breithand in hym ane lyflie spreit.
Quhen all thir werkis wer compleit,
He maid Man, to his simylitude,
Precelland in to pulchritude,
Dotit with giftis of Nature
Above all erthlye creature ;
Syne plesandlye did hym convoye
To ane regioun repleit with joye,
Of all plesour quhilk bair the pryce.
And callit Erthly Paradyce ;
And brocht, be Divyne providence,
All beistis and byrdis tyll his presence.
Adam did craftely impone
Ane speciall name tyll every one,
And to all thyngis materiall,
He namyt thame in speciall :
Quhow he thame namyt yitt bene kend,
And salbe to the warldis end.
In to that Gardyng of plesance
Two treis grew most tyll avance,

Above all uther quhilk bair the pryce,
In myddis of that Paradyce.
The one wes callit the Tre of lyfe ;
The uther tre began our stryfe,
The tre to knaw boith gude and evyll,
Quhilk, be perswatioun of the Devyll,
Began our misarie and wo.
Bot lat us to our purpose go.
   Quhow God gave Adam strait commande
That tre to twyche nocht with his hand :
All uther fructis of Paradyce
He bad hym eit at his devyce ;
Sayand, Gyf thow eit of this tre,
With dowbyll deith than sall thow dee :
Tharefor I thé command, be war,
And frome this tree thow stand afar.
Yitt Father Adam wes allone,
But cumpanye of ony one :
Than thocht the Lord it necessare
Tyll hym to creat ane helpare.
   God putt in Adam sic sapour
That for to sleip he tuke plesour,
And laid hym down apone the grounde ;
And quhen Adam wes slepand sounde,
He tuke ane rib furth of his syde,
Syne fyld it up with flesche and hyde,
And maid ane Woman of that bone :
Fairar of forme wes never none.
Than tyll Adam incontinent
That fair Ladye he did present,
Quhilk schortlye said, for to conclude,

Thow art my flesche, my bonis, and blude ;
And Virago he callit hir, than,
Quhilk is, interpreit, maid of man,
Quhilk Eva efterwart was namyt,
Quhen, for hir falt, sche was diffamyt.
Than did the Lord thame sanctyfie,
Saying, Incres and multiplie.
Be this men suld leif all thair kyn,
And with thare wyflis mak dwellyn,
And, for thare saik, leif Father and Mother,
And lufe thame best above all uther :
For God has ordanit thame, trewlye,
To be two saulis in one bodye.

My wytt is waik for tyll indyte
Thaire heavinlye plesouris infinyte,
Wes never none erthlye creature
Sen syne had sic perfyte plesoure.
Thay had puyssance imperiall
Above all thyng materiall.
Als cunnyng Clerkis dois conclude,
Adam preceld in pulchritude
Most naturall, and the farest Man
That evir wes, sen the warld began,
Except Christ Jesu, Goddis Sonne,
To quhome wes no comparisone ;
And Eva, the fairest Creature
That ever wes formit be nature.
Thocht thay wer nakit as thay wer maid,
No schame ather of uther haid :
Quhat plesour mycht ane man haif more
Nor haif his Lady hym before,

So lustye, plesand, and perfyte,
Reddy to serve his appetyte !
Thay had none uther cure, I wys,
Bot past thare tyme with joye and blys.
Wyld beistis did to thame repair ;
So did the fowlis of the air,
With noyis most angelycall
Makand thame myrthis musicall ;
The fyschis soumand in the strandis
Wer holelye at thair commandis :
All Creaturis, with ane accorde,
Obeyit hym as thare soverane Lorde.
Thay sufferit nother heit nor cald,
With every plesour that thay wald.
Als, to the deith thay wer nocht thrall ;
And rychtso suld we have bene all :
For he and all his successouris
Suld have possedit those plesouris,
Syne frome that joye materiall
Gone to the glore imperiall.
Thay had, geve I can rycht discryve,
Gret joy in all thare wyttis fyve,
In heiryng, seying, gustyng, smellyng,
Induryng thare delytesum dwellyng ;
Heiryng the byrdis armoneis,
Taistyng the fructis of divers treis,
Smellyng the balmye dulce odouris
Quhilk did proceid frome fragrant flowris,
Seying so mony hevinlye hewis
Of blomes brekyng on the bewis ;
Of twycheyng, als thay had delyte

Of utheris bodeis soft and quhyte ;
But doute, induryng that plesour,
Thay luffit uther Paramour ;
No marvell bene thoucht swa suld be,
Cousyderyng thare gret bewte.
Als, God gave thame command expres
To multiplie and tyll incres,
That thare seid and successioun
Mycht plencis every Natioun.

   I lyst nocht tary tyll declare
All properteis of that place preclare ;
Quhow herbis and treis grew ay grene,
Nor of the temperat air serene ;
Quhow fructis indeficient,
Ay alyke rype and redolent ;
Nor of the fontane, nor the fludis,
Nor of the flowris pulchritudis.
That mater Clerkis dois declare ;
Quharefore I speik of thame na mare.
The Scripture makis no mentioun
Quhow lang thay rang in that Regioun ;
Bot I beleve the tyme wes schorte,
As divers Doctouris dois reporte.

FINIS.

OF THE MISERABILL TRANSGRESSIOUN
OF ADAM.

COURTEOUR.

FATHER, How happinit that mischance?
Quod I; schaw me the circumstance,
Declaryng me that carefull cace.
Quhow Adam lost that plesand place
Frome hym and his successioun.
Quhow did proceid that transgressioun?

EXPERIENCE.

Quod he, Efter my rude ingyne
I sall rehers thee that rewyne.
Quhen God, the Plasmatour of all,
In to the Hevin imperiall
Did creat all the Angellis brycht,
He maid one Angell most of mycht,
To quhome he gave preheminence,
Above thame all, in sapience.
Becaus all uther he did prefer,
Namit he wes brycht Lucifer.
He wes so plesand and so fair
He thocht hymself without compair,
And grew so gay and glorious
He gan to be presumptuous,
And thocht that he wald sett his sait
In to the North, and mak debait
Agane the Majestie Divyne;
Quhilk wes the cause of his rewyne.

For he incurrit Goddis ire,
And banyst frome the Hevin impyre,
With Angellis mony one legioun,
Quhilkis wer of his opinioun,
Innumerabyll with hym thare fell :
Sum lychtit in the lawest Hell,
Sum in the Sey did mak repair,
Sum in the Erth, sum in the Air,
   That most unhappy cumpanye
At Father Adam had invye,
Parsaveyng Adam and his seid
In to thare places to succeid.
The Serpent wes the subtellest
Above all beistis and craftyest.
Than Sathan with ane fals intent,
Did enter in to that Serpent ;
Imagenyng sum craftye wyle,
Quhow he mycht Adam best begyle,
And gar hym brek commandiment.
Bot to the Woman first he went ;
Traistyng the better to prevaill,
Full subtellye did hir assaill.
With facund wordis, fals and fair,
He grew with hir familiair,
That he his purpose mycht avance ;
Belevand in hir inconstance.
   Quhat is the cause, Madame, said he,
That ye forbeir yone plesand tre,
Quhilk bene, but peir, moste pretious,
Quhose fruct bene moste delytious ?
   I nyll, quod sche, thare to accord :

We ar forbyddin be the Lord,
The quhilk hes given us lybertie
Tyll eit of every fruct and tre
Quhilk growis in to Paradyse :
Brek we command, we ar nocht wyse.
He gave tyll us ane strait command
That tre to twyche nocht with our hand ;
Eit we of it, without remede,
He said, but dout, we sulde be dede.

   Beleve nocht that, said the Serpent :
Eit ye of it, incontinent
Repleit ye sall be with science,
And haif perfyte intelligence,
Lyke God hym self, of evyll and gude.

   Than, haistellye for to conclude,
Heiryng of this prerogatyve,
Sche pullit doun the fruct belyvé,
Throw counsall of the fals Serpent,
And eit of it to that intent,
And patt hir Husband in beleve,
That plesand fruct gyf he wald preve,
That he suld be als sapient
As the gret God Omnipotent.
Thynk ye nocht that ane plesand thyng,
That we, lyke God, suld ever ryng ?

   He, herand this narratioun,
And be hir solistatioun,
Movit be prydefull ambitioun,
He eit, on that conditioun.
The principall poyntis of this offence
War pryde and inobedience,

ingredienti

Desyring for to be equall
To God, the Creatour of all.
   Allace ! Adam quhy did thow so ?
Quhy causit thow this mortall wo ?
Had thow bene constant, firme, and stabyll,
Thy glore had been incomparabyll.
Quhare wes thy consyderatioun,
Quhilk had the dominatioun
Of every levyng creature
That God had formit be Nature,
Tyll use thame at thy awin devyse ?
Wes thow nocht prince of Paradyse ?
Wes never man, sen syne, on lyve
That God gave sic prerogatyve :
He gave thee strenth above Sampsone,
And sapience more than Salomone ;
Young Absolone, in his tyme moste fair,
To thy bewtie wes no compair ;
Arestotyll thow did precall
In to phylosophie naturell ;
Virgill, in tyll his poetrye,
Nor Cicero, in tyll oratrye,
War never half so eloquent.
Quhy brak thow Goddis commandiment ?
Quhare wes thy wytt, that wald nocht flee
Far frome the presens of that tree ?
Gaif nocht thy Maker thee free wyll
To take the gude and leif the evyll ?
Quhow mycht thy forfalt be excusit,
That Goddis commandiment refusit,
Throuch thy wyfis perswasioun ?

Quhilk hes bene the occasioun,
Sen syne, that mony nobyll men,
Be the evyll counsall of wemen,
Alluterlye distroyit bene,
As in the Storeis may be sene,
Quhilk now we neid nocht tyll declair,
Bot fordwart tyll our purpose fair.
   Quhen thay had eaitin of the frute,
Of joye than wer thay destitute.
Than gan thay boith for to thynk schame,
And to be naikit thocht defame,
⤏And maid thame breikis of levis grene,
That thair secreitis suld nocht be sene.
Bot in the stait of Innocence
Thay had none sic experience ;
Bot, quhen thay war to Syn subjectit,
To schame and dreid thay war coáctit.
And in ane busk thay hid thame clois,
Aschamit of the Lordis voice,
Quhilk callit Adam be his name.
   Quod he, My Lord, I thynk gret schame
Naikit to cum to thy presence.
Thow had none sic experience,
Quod God, quhen thow wes innocent :
Quhy brake thow my commandiment ?
Allace ! quod Adam to the Lorde,
The veritie I sall recorde ;
This Woman that thow gaif to me
Gart me eit of yone plesand tre.
Rycht so the Woman hir excusit,
And said, the Serpent me abusit.

Than to the Serpent God said thus,
O thow Dissaver venimous,
Because the Woman thow begylit,
Frome thynefurth sall thow be exylit :
Curst and waryit sall thow be,
So sall thy seid be, efter thee :
Cauld erth salbe thy fude, also,
And creipand on thy breist sall go :
Als, I sall put inamitie
Betuix the woman ever and thee :
Betuix thy seid and womanis seid
Salbe continuall mortall feid.
Quhowbeit thow hes wrocht thir myschevis,
It sall nocht be as thow belevis :
Sic seid salbe in woman sawin,
That thy power salbe doun thrawin ;
Treddyng thy heid that thow may feill,
And thow sall tred hym on the heill.
This was his promys and menyng,
That the Immaculat Virgyng
Sulde beir the Prince Omnipotent,
Quhilk suld tred doun that fals Serpent,
Sathan, and all his companye,
And thame confunde alluterlye.

COURTEOUR.

Quod I, Geve Sathan, prince of Hell,
Spak in the Serpent, as ye tell,
And beistis can no way syn at all,
Quhy wes the Serpent maid so thrall ?
I heir men say, affore that hour

The Serpent had ane fair figour,
And yeid straucht up upone his feit,
And had his membris all compleit,
As utheris beistis upone the bent.

EXPERIENCE.

Quod he, For he wes instrument
To Sathan, in this miserie,
Puneist he wes, as ye may se ;
As, be experience, thow may knaw,
Expres in to the Commoun Law,
Ane man convickit for bewgrye,
The beist is brynt, als weill as he,
Quhowbeit the beist be innocent ;
And so befell of the Serpent.
It was the Feynd, full of dispyte,
Of Adamis fall quhilk had the wyte,
As he has had of mony mo :
Bot tyll our purpose let us go.
   Than to the Woman, for hir offence,
God did pronunce this sore sentence,
All plesour that thow had afforrow
Sall cheangit be in lestyng sorrow :
Quhare that thow suld with myrth and joy
Have borne thy byrth, but pane or noy,
Now all thy bairnis sall thow bair
With dolour and continuall cair :
And thow salbe, for oucht thow can,
Ever subjectit to the Man.
   Be this sentence, God did conclude
Wemen frome lybertie denude,

Quhilk be experience, ye may se,
Quhow Quenis of most hie degre
Ar under moste subjectioun,
And sufferis moste correctioun ;
For thay lyke byrdis in tyll ane cage,
Ar keipit ay under thirlage ;
So all wemen, in thare degre,
Suld to thair men subjectet be.
Quhowbeit sum yit wyll stryve for stait,
And for the maistrye mak debait,
Quhilk gyf thay want, boith ewin and morrow
Thare men wyll suffer mekle sorrow.
Of Eve thay tak that qualitie,
To desyre Soveranitie.

    And than tyll Adam, said the Lord,
Because that thow hes done accord
Thy wyll, and harknit to thy wyfe,
Now sall thow lose this plesand lyfe :
Thow wes tyll hir obedient,
Bot thow brake my commandiment ;
Curste and barren the erth salbe,
Quhare ever thow gois, tyll that thow de :
But labour, it sall beir no corne,
Bot thrisyll, nettyll, breir, and thorne :
For fude thow gettis none uther beild,
Bot eait the herbis upone the feild :
Sore laubouryng, tyll thy browis sweit,
Frome thyne furth sall thow wyn thy meit :
I maid thee of the erth, certane,
And thow in erth sall turne agane.
Than maid he thame abilzement,

Of skynnis ane raggit rayment,
Thame to preserve frome heit and cauld :
Than grew thare dolour mony fauld.
Now, Adam, are ye lyke tyll us,
With your gay garment glorious ?
To thame thir wordis said the Lorde.
Then cryit thay boith Misericorde,
    Quhen frome that Garth, with hartis sore,
Baneist thay wer, for ever more,
On to this wracheit vaill of sorrow,
With daylie laubour, evin and morrow.
Efter quhose dolorous departyng,
The Lorde gave Paradyce in kepying
Tyll ane Angell of Cherubin.
That none sulde have entres thare in ;
Att the quhilk entres he did stand,
With flammand fyrie sweird in hand,
To keip that Adam and his wyfe
Sulde nocht taist of the tre of lyfe :
For, geve thay of that tre had previt,
Perpetuallye thay mycht have levit.
So Adam and his Successioun
Of Paradyce tynt possessioun ;
And be this syn Originall
War men to miserie maid thrall.
    My Sonne, now may thow cleirly se,
This Warld began with miserie ;
With miserie it doith proceid,
Quhose fyne sall dolour be and dreid.

COURTEOUR.
Father, quod I, quhat kynd of lyfe

Led Adam with his lusty wyfe,
Efter thare bailfull banesyng?

EXPERIENCE.

Quod he, Continuall womentyng :
My heart has yitt compassioun,
Quhow thay went wandryng up and doun,
Weipyng, with mony lowde Allace !
That thay had lost that plesand place ;
In wyldernes to be exilde,
Quhare thay fand nocht bot beistis wylde,
Manesyng thame for tyll devore,
Quhilkis all obedient war affore.

COURTEOUR.

Father, quod I, in quhat countrie
Did leif Adam, efter that he
Was banesit from that delyte?

EXPERIENCE.

Clerkis, quod he, hes put in wryte
Quhow Adam dwelt, with mekle baill,
In Mamber, in that lusty vaill,
Quhilk efter was the Jowis land ;
Quhare yit his Sepulture dois stand.
I lyste nocht tary tyll discryve
The wo of Adam nor his Wyve ;
Nor tell quhen thay had sonnis two,
Cayn and Abell, and no mo ;
Nor quhow curst Cayn, for invy,
Did slay his Brother creuelly ;

Nor of thare murnyng, nor thare mone,
Quhen thay, but sonnis, wer left allone,
Abell lay slane upone the ground,
Curst Cayn flemit and vagabound ;
Nor quhow God, of his speciall grace,
Send thame the thrid sonne, fair of face,
Most lyke Adam of flesche and blude,
Seth was his name, gratious and gude ;
Nor quhow blynd Lameth raikleslye
Did slay Cayn, unhappelye.

   Adam, as Clerkis dois discrive,
Begat with Eve, his wofull wyve,
Of men childryng thretty and two,
And of dochteris alyke also.
Be this thow may weill understand
That Adam saw mony ane thowsand
That of his body did discend,
Or he out of the warld did wend.

   Adam leifit in erth, but weir,
Compleit nyne hundreth and thretty yeir ;
And all his dayis war bot sorrow,
Rememberyng, boith evin and morrow,
Of Paradyce the prosperitie,
Syne of his gret miseritie :
His hart mycht never be rejosit,
Remembryng quhow the hevin wes closit
Frome hym and his successioun,
And that, be his transgressioun.
Efter his deith, as I heir tell,
His Saul descendit to the hell,
And thare remanit presoneir,

In that dungeoun, thre thousand yeir
And more, so did boith evyll and gude,
Tyll Christ for thame had sched his blude :
Than, be that most precious ransoun,
Thay wer delyverit of presoun.
 I have declarit now, as I can,
 The miserie of the first man.

HEIR FOLLOWIS QUHOW GOD DISTROYIT ALL
LEVEAND CREATURE IN ERTH, FOR SYN,
AND DROWNIT THAME BE ANE
TERRIBYLL FLUDE, IN THE
TYME OF NOYE.

COURTEOUR.

PRUDENT Father Experience,
Declare to me, or ye go hence,
Quhat wes the cause God did distroye
All Creature, in the tyme of Noye.

EXPERIENCE.

 Quod he, I trymmyll for to tell
That infortune, quhow it befell ;
The cause bene so abhominabyll,
And the mater so miserabyll.
Bot, for to schaw the circumstance,
Manefestlye, of that myschance,
First I mon gar thee understand
Quhow Adam gaif expresse command

That those quhilkis come of Sethis blude,
Because thay wer gratious and gude,
Suld nocht contract with Caynis kyn,
Quhilkis wer inclynit all to syn.
Tyll observe that commandiment,
Cayn past in the Orient,
With his wyfe, callit Calmana,
Quhilk was his awin syster alswa,
Quhare his ofspryng did lang remane,
Besyde the Montane of Tarbane.
And Seth did lang tyme leid his lyfe ;
With Delbora, his prudent wyfe,
Quhilk wes his syster, gude and fair,
In Damascene maid thare repair ;
In that countrie of Sethis clan
Descendit mony holy man.
So lang as Adam was levand,
The peple did observe command ;
Quhen he wes dede, and laid in ground,
And peple greitly did abound,
And Cayn slane, as I have schawin,
And Sethis dayis all ouer blawin,
The sonnis, than, of Sethis blude,
Seand the plesand pulchritude
Of the ladyis of Caynis kyn,
Quhowbeit thay knew weill it wes syn,
Opprest with sensuall lustis rage,
Did tak thame into mariage :
And so corruptit wes that blude,
The gude with evyll, and evyll with gude.
Than as the peple did incres,

Thay did abound in wickitnes,
As Holy Scripture dois rehers :
Quhilk I abhor to put in vers,
Or tell with toung I am nocht abyll ;
The suthe bene so abhominabyll,
Quhow men and women schamefullye
Abusit thameselfis uunaturallye ;
Quhose foull abhominatioun
And uncouthe fornicatioun
I thynk gret schame to put in wryte :
All that Paull Orose doith indyte ;
Quhilk gyf I wald at lenth declair,
It wer yneuch to fyill the air.
Gret Clerkis of Antiquiteis
Hes writtin mony trew storeis,
Quhilkis ar worthy to be commendit,
Quhowbeit thay be nocht comprehendit
At lenth in the Divyne Scripture :
Pot I sall do my besye cure
To tak the best, as I suppose,
That moste pertenis my purpose ;
And, with support of Christ, our Kyng,
I purpose to confirme no thyng
Of the auld Historicience
Contrarious tyll his excellence.
Quhowbeit, sum mennis traditionis,
Contrar Chrystis institutionis,
Of thame thocht sum thyng I declair,
Now latt us proceid forthermair,
And, with ane language lamentabyll,
Declare this mater miserabyll.

COURTEOUR.

Father, the causis wald I knaw
Quhy thay of Nature brak the Law?

EXPERIENCE.

I traist, quod he, that wyckitnes
Generith, throw sleuthfull ydilnes.
The Devyll, with all the craft he can,
Quhen he persavis ane ydill man,
Or women gevin tyll ydilnes,
He gettis eisalye entres;
And so, be this occasioun,
And be the Feindis perswasioun,
The hole warld, universalye,
Corruptit was alluterlye.

COURTEOUR.

Quhat wes the cause thay ydill ware?
That cace, quod I, to me declare.

EXPERIENCE.

Quod he, Be my imaginatioun,
For laik of vertuous occupation:
For of craftis thay had small usage,
Of marchandyce, nor laborage.
The Erth, than, wes so plentuous
Of fruct and spyce delicious;
The herbis wer so comfortabyll,
Delytesum, and medicinabyll;
The fontannis, fresche and redolent;

To laubouryng thay tuke lytill tent.
All maner of beistis, at thare plesour,
Did multyplie, without laubour.
The tyme betuix Adam and Noye,
To se the erth it wes gret joye,
Plantit with precious treis of pryce.
Four famous Fludis of Paradyce
Ran throw the erth, in syndrie partis,
Spreddyng thare branchis in all airtis;
The watter was so strang and fyne,
Thay wald nocht laubour to mak wyne;
The fruct and herbis wer so gude,
Thay maid no cair for uther fude:
And so the peple tuke no cure
Bot past thare tyme at thare plesure,
Ay fyndand new inventiounis
To fulfyll thare intentiounis:
So that the Lord Omnipotent
That he maid Man did Hym repent,
And schew ontyll his servand Noye
That he wald all the Warld destroye,
Except hym self and his meinye.
   Allace! quod Noye, quhen sall that be?
Then said the Lord, Sen thow so speris,
I sall prolong sax score of yeris,
Taryng upon thare repentance,
Or I fulfyll my just sentence,
In the mene tyme, fall thow to warke
Incontinent, and beild ane Arke.
Quhilk Noye began, obedientlye,
And wrocht on it continuallye;

And to the peple daylie precheit ;
To cry for grace he to thame techeit,
And to thame planelye did declair
That God his wand no more wald spair,
Bot on thame he wald wyrk vengence,
To Noye yit gave thay no credence ;
And so they wer incounsolabyll,
Usyng thare luste abominabyll :
And tuke his precheyng in dispyte,
Ay following thare foull delyte,
More and more, tyll that dulefull day
Quhilk all the Warld pat in affray.

COURTEOUR.

Father, ye gart me understand,
Quhen Adam brak the Lordis command,
Tyll augment his afflictioun,
God gave his maledictioun
Onto the Erth, quhilk wes so fair,
That it suld barren be, and bair,
And without laubour beir no corne,
Nor fruct, bot thrissyll, breir, and thorne.
Now, say ye, in the tyme of Noye
To se the erth it wes gret joye,
Plantit with fructis gude and fair ;
The suthe of this to me declair :
Thir sayingis two gar me consydder,
Quhow ye mak thame agree togydder.

EXPERIENCE.

God maid that promys sickerlye,

Quhowbeit, it come nocht instantlye,
Quod he, as Clerkis dois conclude ;
Bot efter, quhen the furious Flude
Distroyit the Erth alluterlye,
Than come that promys sickerlye.
Evin siclyke as God gave command
Adam to twyche nocht with his hand,
Nor eit of the forbidden Tree ;
Geve he did so, that he sulde dee :
Quhowbeit, he deit nocht, but weir,
Efter that day nyne hundreth yeir.
Rycht so, the Propheit Esayas,
Speikand of Christ, the gret Messias,
Sayand, the Bairne is tyll us borne,
To saif mankynd, quhilk is forlorne,
As he had bene borne instantlye ;
Yit wes he nocht borne veralye,
Efter that saying, mony one yeir,
As in the Scripture thow may heir :
Ane thousand yeir, quho reknyth rycht,
Is bot one hour in Goddis sycht.
Exemplis mony I mycht tell,
Wer it nocht tedious for to dwell.
    Tyll our purpose latt us proceid,
Schawand the heycht, and lenth, and breid,
And qualitie of Noyis Arke ;
Quhilk wes ane rycht excellent warke,
Of pyne tre maid, bound weill about ;
Laid ouer with pik, within and out,
Junit full close with nalis strong,
And wes thre hundreth cubittis long,

Fifty in breid, thretty in heycht ;
Thre chalmeris, junit weill and wycht,
And everilk loft above ane uther ;
Withouttin anker, air, or ruther :
Ane rycht cubeit, as I heir tell,
Of mesour now mycht be ane ell.
In the myd syde ane dur thare wes,
For beistis ane easy entres.
This Ark, quhilk was boith lang and lairge,
Maid in the bodum lyke one bairge,
Coverit with burdis weill abufe,
Moste lyke ane house with sett-on rufe,
Quhose riggyng wes ane cubeit braid,
Quharein thare wes ane wyndo maid,
Sum sayis, weill closit with christall cleir,
Quharethrouch the day lycht mycht appeir.
This work the more wes to be prysit,
Because be God it wes devysit.
The makyng of this Ark, but weir,
Indurit weill ane hundreth yeir.

　　Quhen Noye had done compleit this wark,
God did hym close within the Ark ;
With hym his Wyfe, and Sonnis thre,
With thare thre Wyfis, but mo menyé :
And of all foulis of the air
Of everilk kynd enterit ane pair ;
Rycht so, two beistis of everilk kynde ;
For quhy it wes the Lordis mynde
That generatioun suld nocht faill :
Quharefor of fameill and of maill

Of everilk kynd wer keipit two.
Bot to rehers myne hart is wo
The dolent lamentatioun,
That tyme of everilk Natioun,
Sayand Allace! ane thousand syis,
Quhen wynd and rane began to ryis :
The roikis with rerd began to ryve,
Quhen uglie cluddis did onerdryve,
And dirkynnit so the Hevinnis brycht
That Sonne nor Mone mycht schaw no lycht :
The terrabyll trymling of erthquaik
Gart biggyngis bow, and cieteis schaik ;
The thounder raif the cluddis sabyll,
With horrabyll sound appoventabyll ;
The fyreflauchtis flew ouerthorte the fellis ;
Than wes thare nocht bot yowtis and yellis.
   Quhen thay persavit without remede
All Creature to suffer dede :
All fontanis from the Erth up sprang,
And frome the Hevin the rane doun dang
Fourty dayis and fourty nychtis,
Than ran the peple to the heychtis ;
Sum clam in cragis, sum in treis,
And sum to heychast montanis fleis,
With more terrour than I can tell,
Bot all for nocht : the fludis fell,
And wynd did rowt with sic ane reird
That everilk wycht waryit his weird,
Cryand, Allace! that they wer borne,
Into that flude to be forlorne.
Men mycht no help mak to thare wyfis,

Nor yit support thare bairnis lyfis.
The Fludis rose with so gret mychtis
That thay ouer coverit all the heychtis :
Thay mycht no more thare lyvis lenth,
Bot swame so lang as thay had strenth,
And so, with cryis lamentabyll,
Endit thare lyvis miserabyll.

   Above montainis that wer moste hie
Fifty cubeitis rose the See.
Men may imagyne, in thare mynd,
All Creature, in to thare kynd,
Boith beistis and foulis in the air,
In thare maneir maid mekle cair.
The fyschis thocht thame evyll begyld,
Quhen thay swame through the woddis wyld ;
Quhalis tumbland amang the treis,
Wyld beistis swomand in the seis.
Byrdis, with mony pictuous pew,
Affeiritlye in the air thay flew
So lang as thay had strenth to flee,
Syne swatterit doun in to the sea.
No thyng on erth wes left on lyve,
Beistis nor foulis, man nor wyve :
God hailelye did thame distroye,
Except thame in the Ark, with Noye,
The quhilk lay fleittand on the flude :
Welterand amang the stremis wode,
With mony terrabyll affrayis,
Remanit ane hundreth and fyfty dayis,
In gret langour and hevynes,
Or wynd or rane began to ceis ;

Sumtyme effectuouslye prayand,
Sumtyme the beistis vesiand :
For, be the Lordis commandiment,
He maid provisioun sufficient.
    For Noye dwelt in that Ark, but dout,
Ane yeir compleit, or he come out ;
Quhow, at more lenth in Holy wryte
This dulefull storye bene indyte,
And quhow that Noye gan to rejose,
Quhen conductis of the Hevin did close,
So that the rane no more discendit,
Nor the flude no more ascendit.
Quhen he persavit the Hevinnis cleir,
He send furth Corbie messingeir
In to the air for to espy
Geve he saw ony montanis dry.
Sum sayis the Ravin did furth remane,
And come nocht to the Ark agane.
Furth flew the Dow, at Noyis command,
And quhen scho did persave dry land,
Of ane olyve scho brak ane branche,
That Noye mycht know the watter stanche ;
And thare no more scho did sudjorne,
Bot with the branche scho did returne,
That Noye mycht cleirly understand
That felloun Flude was decressand :
And so it did, tyll at the last
The Ark upone the ground stak fast,
On the tope of ane montane hye,
Into the land of Armanye,

And quhen that Noye had done espye
Quhow that the Erth began to drye,
Than dang he doun the durris all,
And lowsit thame the quhilk wes thrall ;
The Foulis flew furth in the air,
And all the beistis, peir and pair,
Past furth to seik thare pasturages :
Thare wes than, but aucht personages,
Noye, his thre Sonnis, and thare Wyvis,
On Erth that left was with thare lyvis ;
Quhoine God did blys and sanctyfie,
Sayand, Incres and multiplie.

   God wait geve Noye wes blyith and glaid,
   Quhen of that presoun he wes fraid.

   Quhen Noye had maid his sacrifyce,
Thankand God of his benefyce,
He standand on Mont Armanye
Quhare he the countrie mycht espye ;
Ye may beleve his hart was sore,
Seying the Erth, quhilk wes affore
The feilde so plesand and perfyte,
Quhilk to behald wes gret delyte,
That now was barren maid, and bair,
Afore quhilk fructuous was and fair ;
The plesand treis beryng fructis
Wer lyand revin up be the rutis ;
The holsum herbis and fragrant flouris
Had tynt boith vertew and cullouris ;
The feildis grene, and fluryst meidis,

Wer spulyeit of thare plesand weidis.
The Erth, quhilk first wes so fair formit,
Wes, be that furious Flude, deformit ;
Quhare umquhyle wer the plesand planis,
Wer holkit glennis, and hie montanis :
Frome clattryng cragis, gret and gray,
The erth wes weschin quyte away.

   Bot Noye had gretast displesouris,
Behauldand the dede creatouris,
Quhilk wes ane sycht rycht lamentabyll ;
Men, women, beistis, innumerabyll
Seying thame ly upone the landis,
And sum wer fleityng on the strandis :
Quhalis and monstouris of the seis
Stickit on stobbis, amang the treis ;
And, quhen the Flude was decressand,
Thay wer left welteryng on the land.
Affore the Flude duryng that space,
The Sey wes all in to ane place ;
Rycht so the Erth, as bene desydit,
In syndrie partis wes nocht devydit,
As bene Europe and Asia
Devydit ar from Africa.
Ye se now, divers famous Ilis,
Stand frome the maine-land mony mylis :
All thir gret Ilis, I understand,
War than equall with the ferme land.
Thare wes none Sey Mediterrane,
Bot onely the gret Occeane,
Quhilk did nocht spred sic bulryng strandis
As it dois now ouirthort the landis.

Than, be the ragyng of that Flude,
Tha Erth of vertew wes denude,
The quhilk affore wes to be prysit,
Quhose bewtie than wes dissagysit.
Than wes the maledictioun knawin
Quhilk wes be God tyll Adam schawin.

   I reid quhow Clerkis dois conclude,
Induryng that moste furious Flude
With quhilk the Erth wes so supprest,
The wynd blew furth of the South-west;
As may be sene, be experience,
Quhow, throw the watteris violence,
The heych montanis, in every Art,
As bair forgane the South-west part:
As the montanis of Pyraneis,
The Alpis, and rochis in the seis;
Rycht so, the rochis, gret and gray,
Quhilk standis into Narroway.
The heychast hyllis, in every art,
And in Scotland, for the moste part,
Throuch weltryng of that furious flude,
The cragis of erth war maid denude:
Travellyng men may consydder best
The montanis bair nyxt the South-west.

COURTEOUR.

Declare, quod I, or ye conclude,
Quhow lang levit Noye efter the flude.

EXPERIENCE.

Quod he, In Genesis thow may heir

Quhow that Noye wes sax hundreth yeir,
The tyme of this gret punysment,
And aye to God obedient ;
And wes the best of Sethis blude ;
And als, he levit efter the Flude
Thre hundreth and fyfty yeris,
As the same Scripture wytnes beris,
And wes, or he randerit the spreit,
Nyne hundreth and fyfty yeris compleit.
 To schaw this storie miserabyll
At lenth my wyttis ar nocht abyll :
And als, my Sonne, as I suppose,
It langis nocht tyll our purpose
To schaw quhow Noyis sonnis thre
Gan to incres and multyplie ;
Nor quhow that Noye plantit the wyne,
And drank tyll he wes dronkin syne,
And slepit with his membris bair ;
And quhow Cham maid for hym no cair,
Bot leuch to se his Father so,
Quhowbeit his Brether wer rycht wo ;
Nor quhow Noye, but restrictioun,
Gave Cham his maledictioun,
And put hym under servytude
To Sem and Japhet, that war gude ;
Nor quhow God maid ane covenent
With Noye, to mak no punysment,
Nor be no Flude the peple droun :
In signe of that conditioun,
His rane-bow sett in to the air,
Of divers hevinlye colouris fair,

For to be ane perpetuall sing
Be Flude to mak no punyssing.

This Story geve thow lyste to knaw,
At lenth the Bibyll sall thee schaw.

HEIR ENDIS THE FIRST PART.

THE SECUND BUKE.

IN THE FIRST, THE BEILDYNG OF BABILONE
BE NEMROD; AND QUHOW KYNG NYNUS
BEGAN THE FIRST MONARCHIE; AND
OF THARE IDOLATRYE; AND
QUHOW SEMIRAMIS GOVERNIT
THE IMPYRE, EFTER HIR
HUSBANDE KYNG
NYNUS.

COURTEOUR.

FATHER, I pray yow to me tell
The first infortune that befell,
Immediatlye efter the Flude;
And quho did first sched saikles blude?
And quho Idolatrye began?

EXPERIENCE.

Quod he, I sall do as I can:
Efter the Flude I fynde no storye
Worthy to putt in memorye,
Tyll Nemrod began to ryng
Above the Peple as ane Kyng,
Quhilk wes the principall man of one,
That beildar was of Babilone.

COURTEOUR.

That story, Maister, wald I knaw,
Quod I, geve ye the suthe wald schaw,
Quhy and for quhat occasioun
Thay beildit sic ane strang dungeoun.

EXPERIENCE.

Than said to me Experience,
I sall declare, with diligence,
Those questiounis at thy command.
Bot first, Sone, thow mon understand
Of Nemrod the Genealogie,
His strenth, curage, and quantitie;
Quhowbeit Moyses, in his first Buke,
That storye lychtlye did ouer luke:
Of him no more he doith declare,
Except he was ane strang huntare.
Bot utheris Clerkis curious,
As Orose doith, and Josephus,
Discryvis Nemrod at more lenth,
Boith of his stature and his strenth.
This Nemrod was the fourt persoun
Frome Noye be lyne discendyng doun:
Noye generit Cham, Cham generit Chus,
And Chus, Nemrod: the suthe bene thus.

This Nemrod grew ane man of mycht;
That tyme in erth wes none so wycht:
He wes ane gyand stout and strang;
Perforce wyld beistis he doun thrang.

The peple of that hole Regioun
Come under his dominioun ;
No man thare wes, in all that land,
His stalwartnes that durst ganestand.
No marvell wes thocht he wes wycht,
Ten cubitis large he wes of hycht,
Proportionat, in lenth and breid,
Afferand to his hycht, we reid.
He grew so gret and glorious,
So prydefull and presumptuous,
That he come inobedient
To the gret God Omnipotent.
   This Nemrod was the principall man
That first Idolatrye began.
Than gart he all the peple call
To his presens, boith gret and small,
And, in that gret conventioun,
Did propone his intentioun.
My Freindis, said he, I mak it knawin
The gret vengeance that God hes schawin,
In tyme of our fore father Noye,
Quhen he did all the Warld distroye,
And dround thame in ane furious flude :
Quharefor I thynk we sulde conclude
Quhow we maye make one strang defence
Aganis sic watteris violence,
For to resyste his furious ire,
Contrare boith to flude and fyre.
Lat us go spye sum plesand feilde,
Quhare one strang biggyng we may beilde,
One Citie, with ane strang dungeoun,

That none ingine may ding it doun ;
So heych, so thyke, so large, and lang,
That God tyll us sall do no wrang ;
It sall surmonte the Planetis sevin,
That we frome God may wyn the hevin.
Those peple, with one ferme intent,
All tyll his counsell did consent,
And did espy one plesand' place
Hard on the flude of Euphratace.
The peple thare did thame repair,
In to the plane feilde of Synear,
Quhilk now of Caldie beryth the name,
Quhilk did lang tyme flureis in fame.

    Thare gret Fortres than did thay founde,
And kaiste tyll thay gat souer grounde :
All fell to warke, boith man and chylde,
Sum holkit clay, sum brynt the tylde.
Nembroth that curious campioun,
Devysar wes of that dungeoun.
No thyng thay sparit thare laubouris,
Lyke besy beis upone the flouris,
Or emottis travelling in to June :
Sum under wrocht, and sum abone :
With strong ingenious masonrye,
Upwarte thare werk did fortifye.
With brynt tylde, stonis large and wycht,
That Towre thay rasit to sic hycht
Abufe the airis regioun,
And junit of so strong fassioun,
With syment maid of pyk and tar,

Thay usit none uther mortar,
Thocht fyre or watter it assalit,
Contrare that dungeoun nocht avalit.
The land aboute wes fair and plane ;
And it rose lyke one heych montane.
Those fuliche peple did intende
That to the Hevin it sulde ascende.
So gret one strenth wes nevir sene,
In to the warld, with mennis eine.
The wallis of that wark thay maid
Two and fyftye faldome braid.
One faldome than, as sum men sayis,
Mycht bene two faldome in our dayis :
One man wes than, of more stature
Nor two be now : thareof be sure.

   Josephus haldis opinioun,
Sayand the heycht of this dungeoun
Of large pasis of measure bene
Fyve thousande, aucht score and fourtene.
Be this raknyng, it is full rycht
Fyve mylis and ane half in hycht :
Ane thousande pais tak for ane myle,
And thow sall fynd it neir that style.
This towre, in compass round aboute,
Wer mylis ten, withouttin doute :
Aboute the cietie of stagis
Foure houndreth and four score, I wys ;
And, be this nommer, in conapas,
Aboute three score of mylis it was :
And, as Orosius reportis,
Thare wes fyve score of brasin portis.

The translatour of Orosius
In tyll his Croniele wryttis thus :
That, quhen the Sonne is at the hycht,
Att none quhen it doith schyne most brycht,
The schaddow of that hydduous strenth
Sax myle and more it is of lenth.
   Thus maye ye juge, in to your thocht,
   Gyfe Babilone be heych, or nocht.

QUHOW GOD MAID THE DYVERSITIE OF LANGUAGIS AND MAID IMPEDIMENT TO THE BEILDARIS OF BABILONE.

EXPERIENCE.

THAN the gret God Omnipotent,
To quhom al thingis bene present ;
That wer, and is, and evir salbe,
At present tyll his Majestie ;
The hid secretis of mannis hart
From his presens may not depart ;
He, seand the ambitioun,
And the prydefull presumptioun,
Quhow thir proude peple did pretende
Up throuch the hevinnis tyll ascende,
Quhilk wes gret folye tyll devyse
Sick one presumptuous interpryse :
For, quhen thay wer moste delygent,
God maid thame sick impediment,
Thay wer constranit, with hartis sore,

Frome thyne depart, and beild no more.
Sick languagis on thame he laid,
That none wyste quhat ane uthir said :
Quhare wes bot ane language affore,
God send thame languagis three score.
　　Affore that tyme all spak Ebrew ;
Than sum began for to speik Grew,
Sum Dutche, sum language Sarazyne,
And sum began to speik Latyne.
The Maister men gan to go wylde :
Cryand for treis, thay brocht thame tylde :
Sum said, Bryng mortar heir atonis
Than brocht thay to thame stokis and stonis.
And Nembroth, thare gret campioun,
Ran rageand lyke one wylde lyoun,
Manassyng thame with wordis rude :
Bot nevir one worde thay understude.
Affore thay fand hym gude and kynde ;
Bot than thay thocht hym by his mynde,
Quhen he so furiouslie did flyte.
Than turnit his pryde in to dispyte,
So dirk eclipsit wes his glore,
Quhen thay wald wyrk for him no more.
　　Beholde quhow God wes so gratious
To thame, quhilk wer so outragious :
He nother braik thare leggis nor armis,
Nor yit did thame none uther harmis,
Except of toungis divysioun.
And, for fynall conclusioun,
Constranit thay wer for tyll depart,
Ilke cumpanye in one syndrie arte :

Sum past in to the Orient,
And sum in to the Occident,
Sum South, sum North, as thay thocht best,
And so thare poleysie left wast.
Bot quhow that cietie wes reparit
Heir efter it salbe declarit.

OF THE FIRST INVENTIOUN OF YDOLATRIE; QUHOW NEMBROTH COMPELD THE PEPLE TYLL ADORE THE FYRE IN CALDEA.

COURTEOUR.

Now, Schir, said I, schaw me the man
Quhilk first Ydolatrie began.

EXPERIENCE.

That sall I do, with all my hart,
My Sonne, said he, or we depart.
Quhen Nembroth saw his purpose failit,
And his gret laubour nocht availit,
In maner of contemptioun
Departit furth of that regioun,
And, as Orosius doith rehers,
He past in to the land of Pers,
And mony one yeir did thare remane,
And syne to Babylone come agane,
And fand huge peple of Caldie
Remanand in that gret cietie,
That wer glaid of his returnyng,

And did obey hym as thare kyng.
Nembroth, his name for tyll avance,
Amang tham maid new ordinance,
Sayand, I thynk ye ar nocht wyce,
That to none God makis sacrifyce.
    Than, to fulfyll his fals desyre,
He gart be maid ane flammand fyre,
And maid it of sic breid and hycht,
He gart it byrn boith day and nycht.
Than all the peple of that land
Adorit the fyre, at his command,
Prosternit on thare kneis and facis,
Beseikand thare new God of gracis.
To gyf thame more occasioun,
He maid thame gret perswasioun :
This God, said he, is moist of mycht,
Schawand his bemys on the nycht :
Quhen Sonne and Mone ar baith obscure,
His hewinlie brychtnes doith indure :
Quhen mennis memberis sufferit calde,
Fyre warmyth thame, evin as thay walde.
Than cryit the Peple, at his desyre,
Thare is no God except the Fyre.
    Or thare was ony imagerie,
Began this first Idolatrie.
At that tyme thare wes none usage
To carve, nor for to paynt Image.
Than maid he proclamatioun,
Quho maid nocht adoratioun
To that new God, without remede
In to that fyre sulde suffer dede.

I fynd no man, in to that lande,
His tyrannie that durste ganestande,
Bot Habraham, and Aram his brother,
That disobeyit, I fynd none uther;
Quhilk dwelland war in that countre,
With thare Father, callit Tharie.
Thir brether Nembroth did repreve;
Sayand tyll hym, Lord, with your leve,
This fyre is bot ane Element,
Praye ye to God Omnipotent,
Quhilk maid the Hevinnis be his mycht,
Sonne, Mone, and Sterris, to gyf lycht:
He maid the fyschis in the Seis,
The Erth, with beistis, herbis, and treis:
And, last of all, for to conclude,
He maid Man, to his similitude:
To that gret God gyfe pryse and glore,
Quhose ring induris evermore.
　　Than Nembroth, in his furious ire,
Thir brether boith keste in the fyre:
Habraham be God he wes preservit,
Bot Aram in the fyre he stervit.
Quhen Thara harde his sonne wes dede,
He did depart out of that stede,
With Habraham, Nachor, and thare wyffis,
As the Scripture at lynthe discryffis,
And left the land of Caldea,
And past to Mesopotamia,
And dwelt in Tharan all his dayis,
And deit thare, as the story sayis.
The lyfe of Habraham, I suppose,

No thyng langith tyll our purpose :
In to the Bibyll thou may reid
His verteous lyfe in worde and deid.
    Now to thee I have schawin the man
    That firste Idolatrie began.

OF THE GREIT MISERIE AND SKAYTHIS THAT CUMMIS OF WEIRIS, AND QUHOW KING NYNUS BEGAN THE FIRST WEIRIS, AND STRAIK THE FIRST BATTELL.

COURTEOUR.

FATHER, I pray you, with my hart,
Declair to me, or we depart,
Quho first began thir mortall weiris,
Quhilk everilk faithfull hart effeiris,
And everie polesye doun thrawis,
Express agane the Lordis lawis ;
Sen Christe, our Kyng omnipotent,
Left peace in tyll his Testament.
Quhow doith proceid this crueltie
Aganis Justice and Equitie ?
In lande quhare ony weiris bene,
Gret miserie thare may be sene :
All thyng on erth that God hes wrocht
Weir doith distroye, and puttis at nocht :
Cieteis, with mony strang dungeoun,
Ar brynte, and to the erth doung doun ;
Virginis and matronis ar deflorit ;

Templis that rychelie bene decorit
Ar brynt, and all thare Preistis spulyeit ;
Pure orphelenis under feit ar fulyeit,
Mony auld men maid childerles,
And mony childer fatherles ;
Of famous Seulis the doctryne,
Boith natural science and divyne,
And everilk vertew, trampit doun
No reverence done to relegioun ;
Strenthis distroyit alluterlie ;
Fair ladyis foreit schamefullie,
Young wedowis spulyeit of thare spousis,
Pure laborars houndit frome thare housis.
Thare dar no merchand tak on hand
To travel nother be sea nor land,
For boucheouris, quhilk dois thame confounde :
Sum murdrist bene, and sum ar drounde :
Craftis men of curious ingyne
Alluterlie put to rewyne :
The bestiall reft, the commounis slane,
The land but lauboring doith remane.
Of pollesye the perfyte warkis,
Beildingis, gardyngis, and plesand parkis,
Alluterlie distroyit bene :
Gret graingis brynt thare may be sene :
Ryches bene turnit to povertie,
Plentie in tyll penuritie.
Deith, hounger, darth, it is weill kende,
Of weir this is the fatell ende :
Justice turnit in tyrranye,
All plesour in adversitye.

The weir alluterlie doun thrawis
Boith the civill and cannoun lawis :
Weir generit murthour and myschief,
Sore lamentyng without releif.
Weir dóith distroye realmes and kyngis ;
Gret princis weir to presoun bryngis ;
Weir scheddis mekle saikles blude.
Sen I can saye of weir no gude,
Declare to me, Schir, gyf ye can,
Quho first this miserie began.

HEIR FOLLOWITH ANE SCHORTE DISCRIPTIOUN
OF THE FOUR MONARCHEIS : AND QUHOW KYNG
NYNUS BEGAN THE FIRST MONARCHIE.

EXPERIENCE.

OF Weiris, said he, the gret outtrage
Began into the secunde aige,
Be creuell, prydefull, covetous kyngis,
Revaris, but rycht, of utheris ryngis.
Quhowbeit Cayan, afore the Flude,
Wes first schedder of saikles blude,
Nynus was first and principall man
Quhilk wrangus conquessing began,
And was the man, withouttin faill,
In erth that straik the first bataill.
And first inventit imagerye,
Quhare throw cam gret Idolatrye.

We most knaw, or we forther wend,
Of quhome king Nynus did discend.
Nynus, gyf I can rycht defyne,
He was frome Noye the fyft, be lyne :
Noye generit Cham, Cham generit Chus.
And Chus, Nembroth, Nembroth, Belus,
And Belus, Nynus, but lesing.
Of Assyria the secund king,
And beildar of that gret Citie,
The quhilk was callit Nynevie,
And wes the first and principall man
Quhilk the First Monarchie began.

COURTEOUR.

Father, said I, declaire to me
Quhat signifyis one Monarchie.

EXPERIENCE.

The suith, said he, Sonne, gyf thou knew,
Monarchie bene one terme of Grew :
As, quhen one Province principall
Had hole power imperiall,
During thare dominationis,
Abufe all Kyngis, and Nationis,
One Monarchie, that men doith call ;
Of quhome I fynd Four principall
Quhilk heth rong sen the Warld began.

COURTEOUR.

Than said I, Father, gyf ye can,
Quhilk Four bene thay, schaw me, I pray yow.

EXPERIENCE.

My Sone, said he, that sall I say yow :
First rang the Kings of Assyrianis ;
Secundlye, rang the Persianis ;
The Greikis, thridlye, with swerd and fyre
Perfors obtenit the Thrid impyre ;
The Fourte Monarchie, as I heir,
The Romanis bruikit mony one yeir.

Latt us first speik of Nynus King,
Quhow he began his conquessing.
The auld Greik historiciane
Diodorus he wryttis plane
At rycht gret lenth of Nynus king,
Of his impyre and conquessing ;
And of Semiramis, his wyfe,
That tyme the lustyest on lyfe.
It wer too lang to putt in wryte
Quhilk Diodore had done indyte ;
Bot I sall schaw, as I suppose,
Quhilk maist belangith thy purpose.
Quhen Nembroth, Prince of Babylone,
Oute of this wrechit warld wes gone,
And his sonne, Belus, deid alswa,
The first Kyng of Assyria,
This Nynus, quhilk wes secunde Kyng,
Tryumphandlie began tyll ryng,
And wes nocht satifyit nor content
Of his awin Regione, nor his rent :
Thynkand his glory for tyll avance

By his gret peple and pussiance,
Throuch pryde, covatyce, and vaine glore,
Did hym prepare to conques more,
And gatherit furth ane gret armie
Contrare Babilone, and Caldie,
Quhareof he had ardent desyre
Tyll june that land tyll his Impyre,
Quhowbeit he had thareto no rycht :
Bot, by his tyranny and mycht,
Withouttin feir of God or man,
His conquessing thus he began.

   His peple beand in arraye,
To Caldia tuke the reddy waye ;
Quhen that the Babilonianis,
Togither with the Caldianis,
Hard tell Kyng Nynus wes cummand,
Maid proclamationis through the land,
That ilka man, efter thare degrie,
Sulde cum, and saif thair awin countrie.
Quhowbeit thay had no use of weir,
Thay past fordwart withouttin feir,
And pat thame selfis in gude order,
To meit kyng Nynus on the border.
In that tyme, ye sall understande,
Thare wes no harnes in the land,
For tyll defende nor tyll invaid,
Quharethrow more slauchter thare wes maid :
Thay faucht, throw strenth of thare bodeis.
With gaddis of irne, with stonis, and treis.
With sound of horne, and hyddeous cry,
Thay ruschit togither rycht rudely,

With hardy hart and strenth of handis,
Tyll thousandis deid lay on the landis.
Quhare men in battell naikit bene,
Gret slauchter sone, thare may be sene.
Thay faucht so lang and creuellie,
And with uncertane victorie,
No man mycht juge, that stude on far,
Quho gat the better nor the war :
Bot, quhen it did approche the nycht,
The Caldianis thay tuke the flycht.
Than the Kyng and his cumpanye
Wer rycht glaid of that victorye.
Because he wan the first battell
That strykken wes in erth, but faill ;
And peceably of that regioun
Did tak the hole dominioun.
Than wes he king of Caldia,
Alsweill as of Assyria.

    As for the king of Arabie,
In his conquest, maid hym supplie.
Of this yit wes he nocht content,
Bot to the realme of Mede he went,
Quhare Farnus, king of that cuntrie,
Did meit hym, with one gret armie.
Bot king Nynus the battell wan,
Quhare slane were mony nobyll man ;
And to that Kyng wald gyf no grace,
Bot planelie in one publict place,
With his sevin sonnis and his ladye,
Creuellie did thame crucifie.
Of that tryumphe he did rejoise ;

Syne fordwart to the feilde he gois :
Than conquest he Armenia,
Perse, Egypt, and Pamphilia,
Capadoce, Leid, and Mauritane,
Caspia, Phrigia, and Hyrcane ;
All Affrica, and Asia,
Except gret Ynde ane Bactria,
Quhilk he did conques eftèrwart,
As ye sall heir, or we depart.

    Now wald I, or we further wend,
That his Ydolatrye wer kend ;
Syne, efter that, withoute sudjorne,
Tyll our purpose we sall returne.

QUHOW KING NYNUS INVENTIT THE FIRST
IDOLATRIE OF IMAGIS.

    NYNUS one Image he gart mak
For King Belus his fatheris saik,
Moist lyke his father of figoure,
Of quantitie, and portratoure :
Of fyne golde wes that figoure maid ;
Ane crafty croun apone his haid,
With precious stonis, in toknyng
His father Belus wes ane Kyng.
In Babilone he ane tempyll maid,
Of crafty work, boith heych and braid,
Quharein that image glor[i]ouslie
Wes thronit up triumphandlie.
    That Nynus gaif ane strait command

Tyll all the peple of that land,
Alsweill in tyll Assyria
As in Synear and Caldia,
Under his dominatioun,
Thay suld make adoratioun,
Apone thare kneis, to that figour,
Under the pane of forfaltour.
Thare wes no Lorde, in all that land,
His summonding that durst ganestand:
Than young and auld, boith gret and small,
Tyll that Image thay prayit, all,
And cheangit his name, as I heir tell,
Frome Belus to thare greit god Bell.

   In that tempyll he did devyse
Preistis, for tyll mak sacrifyse.
Be consuetude than come one law,
None uther God that thay wald knaw;
And als, he gaif to that Image
Of Sanctuarie the privilege;
For, quhatsumever transgressour,
Ane homicede, or oppressour,
Scand that Image in the face,
Of thare gylt gat the Kyngis grace.

COURTEOUR.

   Declare to me, sweit Schir, said I,
Wes thare no more Idolatry,
Efter that this fals idole Bell
Wes thronit up, as ye me tell?

EXPERIENCE.

   My Sonne, said he, incontinent.

VOL. I.   U

The novellis throuch the warld thay went,
Quhow king Nynus, as I haif said,
One curious Image he had maid,
To the quhilk all his natioun
Maid devote adoratioun.
Than everye cuntrie tuke consait,
Thay wald king Nynus contrafait :
Quhen ony famous man wes deid,
Sett up one Image in his steid,
Quhilk thay did honour frome the splene,
As it Immortall God had bene.
Imagis sum maid, for the nonis,
Of fyne gold, sum of stockis and stonis,
Of sylver sum, and evyr bone,
With divers namis tyll every one :
For sum thay callit Saturnus,
Sum Jupiter, sum Neptunus ;
And sum thay callit Cupido,
Thare god of lufe, and sum Pluto :
Thay callit sum Mercurius,
And sum the wyndie Eolus ;
Sum Mars, maid lyke ane man of weir,
Inarmit weill with sword and speir ;
Sum Bacchus, and sum Appollo,
Of namis, thay had ane houndreth mo.
   And quhen one Lady of gret fame
Wes dede, for tyll exalt hir name,
One Image of hir portratour
Wald set upe in one oratour,
The quhilk thay callit thare goddess :
As Venus, Juno, and Palles,

Sum Cleo, sum Proserpina,
Sum Ceres, Vesta, and Diana ;
And sum the greit goddess Minarve
With curious collouris thay wald carve.
Amang the Poetis thow may see
Of fals Goddis the genalogee.
  So thir abhominationis,
Did spred ouerthort all nationis,
Except gude Habraham, as we reid,
Quhilk honourit God in word and deid ;
For Habraham had his beginnyng
In to the tyme of Nynus king.
Nynus began with tyrranie,
And Habraham with humylitie :
Nynus began the first Impyre ;
Habraham of weir had no desyre :
Nynus began Idolatrye,
Habraham, in spreit and veritye,
He prayit to the Lorde allone,
Fals imagery he wald have none.
Of hym discendit, I heir tell,
The twelf gret Trybis of Israell.
Those peple maid adoratioun,
With humyll supplicatioun,
Tyll hym quhilk wes of kyngis King,
That hewin and erth maid of no thyng :
Dede Imagis thay held at nocht,
That wer with mennis handis wrocht,
Bot the Almychtie God of lyve.

  My Sonne, now haif I done discryve
Thir questionis, at thy command,

The quhilkis thow did at me demand.

COURTEOUR.

Quhat wes the cause, Schir, mak me sure,
Idolatrye did so lang indure
Out throuch the warld so generalie,
And with the Gentilis, specialie ?

EXPERIENCE.

Quod he, Sum causis principall
I fynd in my memoriall.
First, wes throuch princis commandiment,
Quhilk did Idolatrie invent :
Syne, singulaire proffeit of the preistis,
Payntours, goldsmythis, maisonis, wrychtis :
Those men of craft full curiouslie
Maid imagis so pleasandlie,
And sauld thame for ane sumptuous pryce,
So, be thare crafty merchandyce,
Thay wer maid ryche abone mesure.
As for the Preistis, I thee assure,
Large proffeit gat, ouerthort all landis,
Throuch sacrifyce and offerandis,
And be thair fayned sanctitude,
Abusit mony one man of gude ;
As, in the tyme of Daniell,
The preistis of this idoll Bell.
Quhen Nabuchodonosor king
In Babilone royallie did ring,
Those priestis the kyng gart understand,
That Image, maid be mennis hand,

He wes one glorious God of lyfe
And had sic ane prerogatyfe,
That, by his gret power devyne,
Wald eait beif, muttone, breid and wyne :
And so the King gart, every daye,
Affore Bell, on his aulter laye,
Fourty fresche wedderris, fatt and fyne,
And sax gret rowbourris of wycht wyne,
Twelf gret loavis of bowtit floure,
Quhilk wes all eaitin in one houre,
Nocht be that Image, deif and dum,
Bot be the preistis all and sum,
As in the Bibill thow may ken,
Quhose nummer wer thre score and ten :
Thay and thare wyfis, everilk day,
Eait all that on the aulter lay.
Than Daniell, in conclusioun,
Schew the King thare abusioun,
And of thare subtlety maid hym sure,
Quhow onderneth the tempyll flure,
Throuch ane passage thay cam, be nycht,
And eait that meit with candell lycht.
The Kyng, quhen he the mater knew,
Those preistis, with all thare wyffis, he slew :
Thus subtellie the Kyng was sylit,
And all the peple wer begylit.

My Sonne, said he, now may thow ken
Quhow, by the Preistis and craftismen,
And by thare craftines and cure,
Idolatrye did so lang indure.
    Behauld quhow Johne Boccatious

Hes wryttin workis wonderous
Of Gentilis superstitioun,
And of thare great abusioun,
As in his gret Buke thow may see,
Of fals Goddis the Geneologie,
Of Demagorgon, in speciall,
Fore-grandschir tyll the Goddis all,
Honourit amang Archadience,
And of the fals Philistience,
With thare gret devilische god Dagone,
With utheris idollis mony one.
  Bot I abhor the treuth to tell
Of the Princis of Israell,
Chosin be God Omnipotent,
Quhow thay brak his commandiment:
Kyng Salomone, as the Scripture sayis,
He doitit in his latter dayis;
His wanton wyffis to compleis,
He curit nocht God tyll displeis,
And did committ idolatrye,
Wyrschipyng carvit imagerye,
As Moloch, god of Ammonitis,
And Chamos, god of Moabitis,
Astroth, god of Sydonianis.
So, for his inobediens
And fowle abhominatioun,
Wer puneist his successioun:
His sonne Roboam, I heir tell,
Tynt the Ten Trybis of Israell,
For his Fatheris idolatrye:
As in the Scripture thow may see.

OF IMAGEIS USIT AMANG CHRISTIN MEN.

COURTEOUR.

FATHER, yit ane thyng wald I speir.
Behald, in every kirk, and queir,
Throch Christindome, in burgh and land,
Imageis maid with mennis hand,
To quhome bene gyffin divers names :
Sum Peter, and Paull, sum Jhone, and James ;
Sanct Peter, carvit with his keyis ;
Sanct Mychaell, with his wyngis and weyis ;
Sanct Katherine, with hir swerd and quheill ;
Ane hynde set up besyde Sanct Geill,
It war too lang for tyll discryve
Sanct Francis, with his woundis fyve ;
Sanct Tredwall als, thare may be sene,
Quhilk on ane prik heth boith hir eine ;
Sanct Paull, weill payntit with ane sworde,
As he wald feycht at the first worde ;
Sanct Apolline on altare standis,
With all hir teithe in tyll hir handis ;
Sanct Roche, weill seisit, men may se,
Ane byill new brokin on his thye ;
Sanct Eloye he doith staitly stand,
Ane new hors schoo in tyll his hand ;
Sanct Ringane, of ane rottin stoke ;
Sanct Duthow boird out of ane bloke ;
Sanct Androw, with his croce in hand ;
Sanct George, upone ane hors rydand ;
Sanct Anthone, sett up with ane sow ;

Sanct Bryde, weill carvit with ane kow ;
With coistlye collouris fyne and fair,
Ane thousand mo I mycht declair,
As Sanct Cosma, and Damiane,
The sowtars Sanct Crispiniane :
All thir on altare staitly standis,
Preistis cryand, for thare offerandis,
To quhome, we Commounis, on our kneis ;
Doith wyrschip all thir Imagereis ;
In kirk, in queir, and in the closter,
Prayand to thame our Pater Noster ;
In pylgramage frome town to toun,
With offerand, and with orisoun,
To thame aye babland on our beidis,
That thay wald keip us in our neidis.
 Quhat differis this, declare to me,
 From the Gentilis Idolatrye ?

EXPERIENCE.

 Gyff that be trew that thow reportis.
It goith rycht neir thir samyn sortis :
Bot we, be counsall of Clergye,
Hes lycence to mak Imagerye,
Quhilk of unlernit bene the buikis ;
For, quhen lawit folk upone thame luikis,
It bryngith to rememberance
Of Sanctis lyvis the circumstance ;
Quhow, the faith for to fortifye,
Thay sufferit pane rycht pacientlye ;
Seand the Image of the Rude,
Men suld remember on the blude.

Quhilk Christ, in tyll his passioun,
Did sched for our salvatioun ;
Or, quhen thow seis ane protrature
Of blyssit Marie, Virgen pure,
One bony Babe upone hir kné,
Than, in thy mynde, remember thé
The wordis quhilk the Propheit said,
Quhow sche suld be boith mother and maid.

   Bot quho that sittis doun on thare kneis,
Prayand tyll ony imagereis,
With orisoun, or offerand,
Kneland with cap in to thare hand,
No difference bene, I say to thé,
Frome the Gentilis idolatrye.

   Rycht so, of divers Nationis
I reid abominationis,
Quhow Grekis maid thare devotioun haill
To Mars, to saif thame in battaill ;
Tyll Jupiter sum tuke thare voyage,
To saif thame frome the stormys rage ;
Sum prayit to Venus frome the splene,
That thay thair luffis mycht obtene ;
And sum to Juno, for ryches,
Thare pylgramage thay wald addres.

   So doith our commoun populare,
Quhilk war too lang for tyll declare
Thare superstitious pylgramageis
To mony divers Imageis ;
Sum to Sanct Roche, with deligence,
To saif thame frome the pestilence ;
For thare teith, to Sanct Apolleine ;

To Sanct Tredwell, to mend thare eine :
Sum makis offrande to Sanct Eloye,
That he thare hors may weill convoye :
Thay ryn, quhen thay haif jowellis tynte,
To seik Sanct Syith, or ever thay stynte ;
And be Sanct Germane, to get remeid
For maladeis in to thare heid ;
Thay bryng mad men, on fuit and horsse,
And byndis thame to Sanct Mongose crosse :
To Sanct Barbara thay cry full faste,
To saif thame frome the thonder blaste :
For gude novellis, as I heir tell,
Sum takis thare gait to Gabriell ;
Sum wyffis Sanct Margaret doith exhort
In to thare byrth thame to support :
To Sanct Anthony, to saif the sow ;
To Sanct Bryde, to keip calf and kow :
To Sanct Bastien thay ryn and ryde,
That frome the schote he saif thare syde ;
And sum, in hope to get thare haill,
Rynnis to the auld rude of Kerrail.
  Quhowbeit thir simpyll peple rude
Think thare intentioun be bot gude,
Wo be to Preistis, I say for me,
Quhilk suld schaw thame the veritie,
Prelatis, quhilk hes of thame the cure,
Sall mak answeir thareof, be sure,
On the gret day of Jugement,
Quhen no tyme beis for to repent,
Quhare manyfest Idolatrye
Sall puneist be perpetuallye.

HEIR FOLLOWIS ANE EXCLAMATIOUN
AGANIS IDOLATRYE.

EXPERIENCE.

IMPRUDENT Peple, ignorant and blynd,
  By quhat reasone, law, or authoritie,
Or quhat autentyck scripture, can ye fynd
  Leifsum for tyll commyt Idolatrie ?
  Quhilk bene to bow your body, or your kne,
With devote humyll adoratioun,
  Tyll ony idoll maid of stone or tre,
Geveand thame offerand, or oblatioun.

Quhy did ye gyf the honour, laude, and glore,
  Pertenyng God, quhilk maid all thyng of nocht,
Quhiik wes, and is, and sall be evirmore,
  Tyll imagis by mennis handis wrocht ?
  Of follysche folke, quhy haif ye succour socht
Of thame quhilk can nocht help yow in distres ?
  Yit reasonably revolve, into your thocht,
In stok nor stone can be none holynes.

In the desert, the peple of Israell,
  Moyses remanyng in the Mont Synaye,
Thay maid one moltin calf of fyne mettell,
  Quhilk thay did honour as thare God verraye :
  Bot, quhen Moyses descendit, I heir saye,
And did consydder thare Idolatrye,

Of that peple thre thousand gart he slaye,
As the Scripture, at lenth, doith testifye.

Because the holye propheit Daniell
   In Babilone Idolatrie reprevit,
And wald nocht worschip thare fals idoll Bell,
   The hole peple at hym wer so aggrevit,
   To that effect that he suld be myschevit,
Delyverand hym tyll rampand lyonis sevin:
   Bot, of that dangerous den, he wes relevit
Throuch myrakle of the gret God of Hevin.

Behald quhow Nabuchodonosor, king,
   In to the vaill of Duran did prepare
One Image of fyne gold, one mervallous thing,
   Thre score of cubyts heych, and sax in square,
As more cleirlye the Scripture doith declare,
To quhome all peple, by proclamatioun,
   With bodeis bowit, and on thare kneis bare,
Rycht humelye maid adoratioun.

Ane gret wounder, that day, wes sene also,
   Quhow Nabuchodonosor, in his ire,
Tuke Sydrach, Misach, and Abednago,
   Quhilkis wald nocht bow thare kne, at his desyre,
   Tyll that Idoll, gart kast thame in the fyre,
For to be brynt, or he sterit of that steid:
   Quhen he belevit thay wer brynt, bone and lyre,
Wes nocht consumit one small hair of thair heid.

The Angell of the Lord wes with thame sene,
   In that hait furneis passing upe and doun,

In tyll ane rosye garth, as thay had bene;
   None spott of fyre distenyng cote nor goun,
   Of victorie thay did obtene the croun ;
And wer, to thame that maid adoratioun
   To that idoll, or bowit thare body doun,
One wytnessing of thare dampnatioun.

Quhat wes the cause, at me thow may demande,
   That Salomone usit none imagerye
In his tryumphand Tempyll for tyll stande,
   Of Abraham, Isaac, Jacobe, nor Jesse,
   Nor of Moyses thare savegarde throuch the see,
Nor Josue, thare valyeant campioun :
   Because God did command the contrarye
That thay sulde use sic superstitioun.

Behald quhow the gret God Omnipotent,
   To preserve Israell frome Idolatrye,
Derectit thame one strait commandiment,
   Thay suld nocht mak none carvit imagrye,
   . Nother of gold, of sylver, stone, nor tre,
Nor gyf worschip tyll ony similytude
   Beand in hevin, in erth, nor in the see,
Bot onelye tyll his Soverane Celsitude.

The Propheit David planely did repreve
   Idolatrye, to thare confusioun
In gravit stok or stone that did beleve,
   Declaryng thame thare gret abusioun ;
   Speakand, in maner of dirysioun,
Quhow dede idolis, be mennis handis wrocht,

Quham thay honourit with humyll orisioun,
Wer in the markat daylie sauld and bocht.

The Devyllis, seand the evyll conditioun
　　Of the Gentylis, and thare unfaithfulnes,
For tyll agment thare superstitioun,
　　In those idolis thay maid thare entres,
　　And in thame spak, as storyis doith expres :
Than men belevit of thame to gett releif,
　　Askand thame help in all thair besynes ;
Bot finallye, that turnit to thare mischeif.

Traist weill, in thame is none Divinitie,
　　Quhen reik and rowst thare fair colour doith faid :
Thocht thay have feit, one foot thay can not flee,
　　Quhowbeit the tempyll byrn abone thair heid :
　　In thame is nother freindschip nor remeid.
In sic fyguris quhat favour can ye fynd ?
　　With mouth, and eris, and eine, thocht thay be maid,
All men may se thay are dum, deif, and blynd.

Quhowbeit thay fall doun flatlyngis on the flure,
　　Thay haif none strenth thare self to rais agane :
Thocht rattonis ouir thame ryn, thay tak no cure :
　　Quhowbeit thai breik thare neck, thay feill no pane.
　　Quhy sulde men psalmes to thame sing or sane ?
Sen growand treis that yeirly berith frute
　　Ar more to pryse, I mak it to thé plane,
Nor cuttit stockis wanting boith crope and rute.

Of Edinburgh the gret idolatrye
　　And manifest abominatioun,

On thare feist day, all creature may se :
   Thay beir ane auld stock Image throuch the toun,
   With talbrone, troumpet, schalme, and clarioun,
Quhilk hes bene usit mony one yeir bigone ;
   With preistis and freris in to processioun,
Siclyke as Bell wes borne throuch Babilone.

Aschame ye nocht, ye seculare prestis and freris,
   Tyll so gret superstitioun to consent ?
Idolateris ye have bene mony yeris,
   Expresse agane the Lordis commandement :
   Quharefor, brether, I counsall yow, repent :
Gyff no honour to carvit stock nor stone ;
   Geve laude and glore to God Omnipotent
Allanerlie, as wyselie wryttis Jhone.

Fy on yow, Freris ! that usis for to preche,
   And dois assist to sic idolatrye,
Quhy do ye nocht the ignorant peple teche
   Quhow ane dede image, carvit of one tre,
   As it were holy sulde nocht honourit be,
Nor borne on Burges backis up and doun ?
   Bot ye schaw planely your ipocrasie,
Quhen ye passe formest in processioun.

Fy on yow, fosteraris of idolatrye !
   That tyll ane dede stock dois sic reverence,
In presens of the peple, publykelie !
   Feir ye nocht God, to commit sic offence ?
   I counsall yow, do yit your diligence
To gar suppresse sic gret abusioun.

Do ye nocht so, I dreid your recompence
Salbe nocht ellis but clene confusioun.

Had Sanct Frances bene borne out throuch the toun,
  Or Sanct Dominick, thocht ye had nocht refusit
With thame tyll haif past in processioun,
  In tyll that cais sum wald haif yow excusit.
  Now men may see quhow that ye have abusit
That nobyll Town, throuch your ipocrasye :
  Those peple trowis that thay may rycht weill use it,
Quhen ye pas with thame into cumpanye.

Sum of yow hes bene quyet counsallouris
  Provocand princis to sched saikles blude,
Quhilk nevir did your prudent predecessouris :
  Bot ye lyke furious Phariceis, denude
  Of charitie, quhilk rent Christ on the rude :
For Christis floke, without malyce or ire,
  Convertit fragyll faltouris, I conclude,
Be Goddis worde, withouttin sweird or fyre.

Reid ye nocht quhow that Christ hes gyffin command,
  Gyff thy brother doith oucht thé tyll offend ;
Than secretlye correct hym, hand for hand,
  In freindly maner, or thow forther wend :
  Gyff he wyll nocht heir thé, than mak it kend
Tyll one, or two, be trew narratioun ;
  Gyf he, for thame, wyll nocht his mys amend,
Declare hym to the congregatioun :

And, gyf he yit remanith obstinat,
  And to the holy Kirk incounsolable,

Than lyke ane Turke hald hym excomminicat,
  And with all faithfull folk abhominabyll;
  Banysing hym, that he be no more able
To dwell amang the faithfull cumpanye :
  Quhen he repentis, be nocht unmerciable,
Bot hym resave agane rycht tenderlye.

Bot our dum Doctoris of Divinitie,
  And ye of the last fonde religioun,
Of pure transgressouris ye have no petie,
  Bot cryis to put thame to confusioun :
  As cryit the Jowis, for the effusioun
Of Christis blude, in to thare byrnand ire,
  Crucifige, so ye, with one unioun,
Cryis, Fy ! gar cast that faltour in the fyre.

Unmercifull memberis of the Antichrist,
  Extolland your humane traditione
Contrar the Institutione of Christ,
  Effeir ye nocht Divyne punytione ?
  Thocht sum of yow be gude of conditione,
Reddy for to ressave new recent wyne ;
  I speik to yow auld boisis of perditione,
Returne in tyme, or ye ryn to rewyne ;

As ran the perverst Prophetis of Baall,
  Quhilkis did consent to the idolatrye
Of wickit Achab, king of Israell,
  Quhose nommer wer four hundreth and fyftie,
  Quhilkis honourit that Idoll opinlye :
Bot, quhen Elias did preve thare abusioun,

VOL. I.   X

He gart the peple sla thame cruellye ;
So at one hour came thare confusioun.

I pray yow, prent in your remembrance
    Quhow the reid Freris, for thare Idolatrye,
In Scotland, Ingland, Spane, Italy and France,
    Upone one day wer puncissit pictuouslye ;
    Behald quhow your awin brother, now laitlye,
In Ducheland, Ingland, Denmark, and Norowaye,
    Ar trampit doun, with thare ipocrasye,
And, as the snaw, ar meltit clene awaye.

I marvell that our Byschoppis thynkis no schame
    To gyf yow freris sic preheminens,
Tyll use thare office, to thare gret diffame,
    Precheing for thame in opin audiens :
    Bot, mycht a Byschope eik tyll his awin expens,
For ilk Sermone, ten Ducatis in his hand,
    He wald, or he did want that recompens,
Go preche hym selfe, boith into burgh and land.

I traist to se gude reformatione
    Frome tyme we gett ane faithfull prudent King
Quhilk knawis the treuth and his vocatione :
    All Publicanis, I traist, he wyll doun thring,
    And wyll nocht suffer in his realme to ring
Corruppit Scrybis nor fals Pharisiens.
    Agane the treuth quhilk plainlye doith maling :
Tyll that kyng come, we mon tak paciens !

Now Fairweill, Freindis ! because I can nocht flyte
    Quhowbeit I culde ye mon hald me excusit,

Thocht I agane Idolatrye indyte,
   Or thame dispyte that wyl nocht yit refuse it.
   I pray to God that it be no more usit
Amang the rewlaris of this Regioun.
   That commoun peple be no more abusit,
Bot gyf Hym glore that bair the creuell croun;

Quhilk techeit us, be his Devine Scripture,
   Tyll rycht prayer the perfyte reddy way;
As wrytith Matthew, in his sext chepture,
   In quhat maner and to quhome we suld pray
   One schort compendious orisone, everilk day,
Most proffitabyll for boith body and saull;
   The quhilk is nocht derectit, I heir say,
To Jhone nor James, to Peter nor to Paull,

Nor none uther of the Apostlis twelf,
   Nor to no Sanct, nor Angell in the Hevin,
Bot orely tyll our Father, God hym self;
   Quhilk orisioune it doith contene, full evin,
   Most proffitabyll for us, petitionis sevin;
Quhilk we lawid folk the Pater Noster call.
   Thocht we say Psalmis nyne, ten, or alevin,
Of all prayer this bene the principall;

Be reasoun of the makkar quhilk it maid,
   Quhilk wes the Sonne of God, our Salviour;
Be reasoun, als, to quhome it suld be said,
   Tyll the Father of Hevin, our Creatour,
   Quhilk dwellis nocht in tempyll nor in tour.
He cleirlye seis our thocht, wyll, and intent:

Quhat nedith us at utheris seik succour,
Quhen in all place his power bene present?

Ye princis of the preistis, that suld preche,
    Quhy suffer ye so gret abusioun?
Quhy do ye nocht the sempyll peple teche
    Quhow and to quhome to dresse thare orisoun?
    Quhy thole ye thame to ryn frome toun to toun,
In pylgramage, tyll ony imagereis,
    Hopand to gett thare sum saluatioun,
Prayand to thame devotlye on thare kneis!

This wes the prettike of sum pylgramage:
    Quhen fillokis, in to Fyfe, began to fon,
With Joke and Thom than tuke thay thare vayage
    In Angusse, tyll the feild chappel of Dron:
    Than Kyttoke thare, als cadye as ane con,
Without regarde other to syn or schame,
    Gaiff Lowrie leif at layser to loupe on:
Far better had bene tyll haif biddin at hame.

I have sene pass one mervellous multytude,
    Yong men and wemen, flyngand on thare feit,
Under the forme of feynit sanctytude,
    For tyll adore one image in Loreit.
    Mony came with thare marrowis for to meit,
Committand thare fowll fornicatioun:
    Sum kyst the claggit taill of the Armeit:
Quhy thole ye this abominatioun?

Of Fornicatioun and Idolatrye
    Apperandlye ye tak bot lytill cure,

Seand the marvellous infelicitye
   Quhilk heth so lang done in this land indure,
   In your defalt quhilk heth the charge and cure.
This bene of treuth, my Lordis, with your leve,
   Sic pylgramage heth maid mony one hure,
Quhilk, gyf I plesit, planelye I mycht preve.

Quhy mak ye nocht the Scripture manifest
   To pure peple, twyching Idolatrye ?
In your precheing quhy haif ye nocht exprest
   Quhow mony kyngis of Israell creuellye
   Wer puncissit, be God, so rigorouslye ?
As Jeroboam, and mony mo, but doute,
   For wyrschippyng of carvit Imagerye,
War frome thare realmes rudlye rutit oute.

Quhy thole ye, under your dominioun,
   Ane craftye preist, or fenyeit fals armeit,
Abufe the peple of this regioun,
   Onely for thare perticular profeit,
   And, speciallye, that Heremeit of Lawreit ?
He pat the comoun peple in beleve
   That blynd gat seycht, and crukit gat thare feit,
The quhilk that palyard no way can appreve.

Ye maryit men, that hes trym wantoun wyffis,
   And lustie dochteris of young tender aige,
Quhose honestie ye suld lufe as your lyffis,
   Permyt thame nocht to passe in pylgramage,
   To seik support at ony stok Image :
For I have wyttin gud wemen passe fra hame,

Quhilk hes bene trappit with sic lustis rage,
Hes done returne boith with gret syn and schame.

Gett up ! thow slepist all too lang, O Lord ;
  And mak one haistie reformatioun
On thame quhilk doith tramp doun thy gratious
      Worde,
  And hes ane deidly indignatioun
  At thame quhilk makith trew narratioun
Of thy Gospell, schawing the Verytie.
  O Lord ! I mak thé supplicatioun,
Supporte our Faith, our Hope, and Charytie.

HEIR FOLLOWIS QUHOW KYNG NYNUS BEILDIT
   THE GRET CITIE OF NYNIVE' ; AND QUHOW
      HE VINCUSTE ZOROASTES, THE KYNG
            OF BACTRIA.

[EXPERIENCE.]

  THIS Nynus, of Assyria king,
  Quhen he had maid his conquessing,
  To beild one Citie he hym drest,
  Chosing the place quhare he thocht best,
  Quhare he had first dominioun,
  In Assyria, his awin regioun.
  Thocht Assur, as the Scriptur says,
  Quhilk come affore Kyng Nynus dayis,
  And foundit that famous Citie,
  The quhilk was callit Nynivé.

Bot, as rehersis Diodore,
Nynus that Citie did decore
So mervellous tryumphantlye
As ye sall heir immedeatlye,
Upone the flude of Euphrates,
Quhilk to behald gret wounder wes.
One hundreth and fyftye stageis
That Citie wes of lenth, I wys :
The wallis, one hundreth fute of heycht,
No wounder was, thocht thay wer wycht :
Sick breid, abufe the wallis thare was,
Thré cartis mycht sydlinglis on thame pas :
Four hundreth stageis and four score
In circuit, but myn or more.
Of towris, aboute those wallis, I wene,
Ane thousand and fyve hundreth bene,
Of heycht two hundreth fute and more,
As wryttis famous Diodore.

  The scripture makis mentioun,
Quhen God send Jonas to that toun,
To schaw thame of his puneisment,
Out throuch the Citie quhen he went,
Thre dayis jornay tyll hym it wes :
The Bybill sayis it wes no les.

  My Sonne, now haif I schawin to thé
Of the beildyng of Nynivé :
For the agmentyng of his fame,
Nynus gart call it efter his name.

  Quhen he that gret Citie had endit,
To conques more yit he intendit,
And did depart from Nynivé,

And rasit up one gret armie
Of the most stalwarte men and stoute
Of all his Regionis round aboute :
In gret ordour tuke thare jornay
Towarte the realme of Bactria.
Of wycht fute-men, I understande,
He had sevintene hundreth thousande,
Without hors-men and weirlyke cairtis,
Quhome he ordourit in sindry partis ;
Quhilk tyll discryve I am nocht abyll,
Quhose nummer bene so untrowabyll,
   Zeroastes, that nobyll kyng,
Quhilk Bactria had in governyng,
That prudent Prince, as I heir tell,
Did in Astronomye precell,
And fand the Art of Magica,
With naturall science mony ma ;
Seand king Nynus on the feilde,
Fordwart he cam, with speir and scheilde,
Foure hundreth thousand men he wes,
In his Armie thare wes no les ;
And mett king Nynus, on the bordoure,
Rycht vailyantlie, and in gude ordoure,
On the vangarde of his Armie.
On thame he ruscheit rycht rudelie,
And of thame slew, as I heir saye,
One hundreth thousand men, that day :
The reste that chaipit war unslane
To Nynus gret oiste fled agane.
   Of that king Nynus wes so noyit,
He restit nevir tyll he distroyit

All hoill that Regioun, upe and doun,
And frome the King did reif the croun,
And maid the realme of Bactria
Subjectit tyll Assyria.
And in that samyn land, I wys,
He tuk to wyfe Semiramis;
Quha, as myne Author dois discryve,
Was, than, the lustiest on lyve.
That beand done, without sudgeorne,
Tyll Nynivé he did returne,
With gret tryumphe of victorie.
As myne Author dois specifie,
Boith Occident and Orient
War all tyll hym obedient.
It wald abhore thé tyll heir red
The saikles blude that he did sched.
Quhen he had roung, as thow may heir,
The space of thre and fourtye yeir,
Beand in his excelland glore,
The dolent deith did hym devore,
In quhat sorte, I am nocht certane:
Sum Author sayis that he wes slane,
And left, tyll bruke his heretage,
Ane lytill Babe of tender aige:
Young Nynus wes the chyldis name,
Quhilk efter fluryste in gret fame.
Sum sayis that, be his Wyflis treasoun,
Kyng Nynus deit in presoun;
As I sall schaw, or I hyne fair,
Quhow Diodore hath done declair.

HEIR FOLLOWIS SUM OF THE WOUNDERFULL DEDIS OF THE LUSTIE QUENE SEMIRAMIS.

[EXPERIENCE.]

Nynus huiffit so ardentlye
Semiramis, his fair ladye.
Thare wes no thyng scho wald command
Bot al obeyit wes fra hand.
Scho, seand hym so amorous,
Scho grew proude and presumptuous,
And at the King scho did desyre
Fyve dayis to governe his Impyre;
And he, of his benevolence,
Did grant hir that preheminence,
With sceptour, crown, and rob royall,
And hole power Imperiall,
Tyll fyve dayis wer come and gone,
That scho, as King, sulde ring allone.
Than all the Princis of the land
Duryng that tyme maid hir ane band :
With bankat royall myrrellie
Scho treatit thame tryumphantlie.
So, the first day, the peple all
Came tyll hir servyce, bound and thrall ;
Bot, or the secunde day wes gone,
Scho tuke sic glore to ryng allone,
Be one deceit, maid thame amang,
The King scho patt in presone strang.
I reid weill of his presoning,

Bot nocht of his delyvering :
Quhow evir, it wes in tyll his flowris
He did of deith suffer the schowris,
And mycht nocht leuth his lyfe one houre,
Thocht he wes the first conqueroure :
Quhose conquessing, for to conclude,
Wes nocht bot gret schedding of blude.
 Now have ye hard of Nynus king,
Quhow he began, and his ending ;
Quhowbeid myne author, Diodore,
Of him haith wryttin mekle more.
Princis, for wrangeous conquessing,
Doith mak, oft tymes, ane evyll ending :
Thocht he had lang prosperitie,
He endit with miseritie.

OF KYNG NYNUS' SEPULTURE.

[EXPERIENCE.]

 THE Quene a sepultur scho maid,
Quhar sche King Nynus body laid,
Of curius crafty wark, and wycht,
The quhilk had stagis nine, of hycht,
And ten stagis of breid it wes :
Diodore saith it wes no les.
For aucht stagis one myle thow tak,
And thairefter thy nummer mak ;
So, be this compt, it wes, full rycht,
One myle and als one stage of hycht,

Except the Towre of Babilone,
So heych one wark I reid of none.
  Semiramis, this lustye Quene,
Consyddring quhat dainger bene
To haif one King of tender aige,
Quhilk mycht nocht use no vassalage,
Scho tuke one curagious consait,
Thinkand that scho wald mak debait,
Geve ony maid rebellioun
Contrar hir Sonne, or his regioun,
Quhome sche did foster tenderly,
And kepit hym full quyetly.
Scho laid apart hir awin cleithyng,
And tuke the rayment of ane king :
Quhen scho wes in tyll armour dycht,
Mycht no man knaw hir be one knycht.
Scho vailyeantlye went to the weir,
And to gyf battell tuke na feir,
Dantyng all realmes rounde aboute,
That all the warld of hir had doute ;
More fortunat, in hir conquessing,
Nor wes hir husband, Nynus King.
  Babilone scho did fortyfie,
Templis and towris, tryumphandlie,
So plesandlye did thame prepair,
Quhilk in the erth had no compair,
Quhowbeid Nemrod, of quhome I spake,
The hydduous dungeoun he gart make,
And of the Ceitie the fundiment,
To quhome God maid impediment :
Quhare Nemrod left, thare scho began,

And pat to wark mony one man
Of all the Realmes round aboute,
Of most ingyne scho socht thame oute.
Scho had, wyrkand with tre and stonis,
Twelf hundreth thousand men at onis ;
Go reid the buke of Diodore,
And thow sall fynd the nummer more.
On everilk syde of Euphrates
That nobyll Cietie beildit wes ;
And so that ryver of renown
Ran throuch the mydpart of the town.
Ouerthort that flude scho bryggis maid
Of marvellous strenth, boith lang and braid :
Thay wer fyve stagis large of lenth,
On everilk bryg scho maid ane strenth.
The circuit, as I said affore,
Foure hundreth stagis and foure score ;
The wallis hycht, quho wald discryve,
Thre hundreth fute, thre score and fyve.
Sax cairtis mycht pas, rycht easalie,
Abufe the wallis of that Cietie,
Sydlingis, without impediment.
Consydder, be youre jugement,
Geve those wallis wer hie, or nocht,
And also curiouslye wer wrocht,
As Diodore hes done defyne,
Quhilk doith transcend my rude ingyne,
Of Babilone the magnificens ;
To quhome ye wald gyf no credens,
Geve I at lenth wald put in wryte,
Quhilk Diodore hes done indyte.

Compare of cieties fynd I none
Tyll Nynivé and Babilone.
Frome Nynivé, in Assyria,
Tyll Babilone, in Caldia,
By bryggis plesandlye ye may pas
Upone the flude of Euphratas.
Amang the fludis of Paradyce
This Euphratas maye beir the pryce.
All warkis quhilkis the Quene began
Transcendit the ingyne of man.
The proud Quene Pantasilia,
The Princes of Amasona,
With hir ladyis tryumphandlye,
At Troy quhilk faucht so vailyeantlye,
Nor yit the fair Madin of France,
Danter of Inglis ordinance,
To Semiramis, in hir dayis,
Wer no compare, as bukis sayis ;
Except tryumphand Julyus,
Strong Hanniball, or Pompeyus,
Or Alexander the Conqueroure,
I fynd no gretter werioure.
    Wald I rehers, as wryttis Clerkis,
Hir wonderfull and vailyeand werkis,
It wer to me one gret laubour,
And teddious to the auditour :
Quhat scho did in Ethopia,
And in the lande of Medea :
Beildand citeis, castellis, and towris,
Parkis, and gardyngis of plesouris,
For the exaltyng of hir name,

And immortall to mak hir fame.
Of Jarcieus the heych montanis
Scho gart ryve down and mak thame planis :
Gret Orontes, that montane wycht,
Twenty and fyve stagis of hycht,
Tyll hir Palyce to draw ane louche,
By fors of men scho raif it throche.

Had scho kepit hir chastitie,
Scho mycht have bene one A per se.
Quhen scho had ordourit hir impyre,
Of Venus wark scho tuke desyre ;
One secreit mansioun scho gart mak,
Quhare scho maist plesandlye mycht tak
Young gentyll men, for hir plesour ;
The quhilk scho usit abufe mesour :
One man allone mycht nocht be abyll
To stanche hir luste insaciabyll :
Quhen scho wes satifyit of one,
Scho gart ane uther cum anone :
The lustiest of all the land
Cum quyetlye, at hir command :
Quhen thay, at lenth, had lyin hir by,
Scho slew thame all, rycht creuellye.
Quhen hir Sone come tyll aige perfyte,
Of hym scho tuke so gret delyte,
Scho causit hym with hir to lye,
Amang the rest, rycht quyetlye.
Sum sayis, throuch sensuall lustis rage,
Scho band hym into mariage,
And held hym under tutorye,
To uphald hir auctoritye.

QUHOW THE QUENE SEMIRAMIS, WITH ONE GRET ARMIE, PAST TO YNDE, AND FAUCHT WITH THE KYNG STAUROBATES, AND OF HIR MISERABYLL END.

EXPERIENCE.

QUHEN scho had lang tyme levit in rest,
To conques more scho hir addrest ;
Because of divers scho hard tell
Quhow that the Ynde Orientell
Preceid in gret commoditeis,
As bestiall, cornis, and fructfull treis,
Al kynde of spyce delicious,
Gold, sylver, stonis precious ;
And quhow that plentuous land did beir
Corne, frute, and wyne twyse in the yeir ;
With oliphantis innumerabyll,
In battell wounder terrabyll.
Scho, herand this, and mekle more,
Belevand tyll agment hir glore,
Gart mak strait Proclamationis
In all and syndrie Nationis,
Schawand quhow it wes hir desyre,
All Princis under hir impyre,
In Egypt, and Arabia,
In Perce, and Mede, and Caldia,
In Grece, in Caspia, and Hyrcane,
In Capadoce, Leid and Maritane,

In Arminie, and Phrigia,
In Pamphilie, and Assyria,
That ilke Land, efter thare degre,
Sulde bryng tyll hir ane gret armie,
In all the gudlye haist thay may,
And meit hir in tyll Bactria ;
Declaryng thame that hir intent
Was tyll pas to the Orient,
And mak weir on the King of Ynde.
Frome tyme thay knew quhat wes hir mynde,
Than, be thare selfis, ilke regioun
Come fordwart, with thare garnisoun,
Tryumphantlye, in gude array,
Tyll Bactria tuke the reddy way,
And maid thare mostouris to the Quene.
Bot sic ane sycht wes never sene,
In battell ray so mony one man
At onis, sen God the warld began.
Bot Spanye, France, Scotland, Ingland,
Ducheland, Denmark, nor yit Yrland
War nocht inhabit in those dayis,
Nor lang efter, myne Author sayis.

Ethesias he dois specifie
The noumber of the great Armie,
Sayand, thare come, at hir command,
Fute men threttye hundreth thousand,
Of hors men, mountit galyeardlye,
Fyve hundreth thousand, veralye,
One hundreth thousand cameilis wycht,
On everilk cameill raid ane knycht,
Preparit tyll passe in to all partis.

Thare wes ane hundreth thousand cairtis :
Two thousand boittis with hir scho careis,
On hors, cameilis, and dromodareis,
Bryggis for to mak scho did conclude
Ouerthort Yndus, that furious flude,
Quhilk bene of Ynde the utmoist bordoure ;
On the quhilk flude, with rycht gude ordoure,
Of hir bairgis scho bryggis maid,
Quharcon hir gret oiste saifly raid.

COURTEOUR.

Father, I wald men understude
Quhow sic ane marvellous multytude
Mycht be att onis brocht to the feild,
Reddy to feycht with speir and schield.
Sum men wyll juge this be ane fabyll,
The mater bene so untrowabyll.

EXPERIENCE.

It may weill ye, my Sonne, said he,
As, be exempyll, we may se
Quhow David, king of Israell,
His peple gart nummer and tell
Be Joab, his cheif capitane,
As Holy Scripture schawis plane :
Of feychtand men, in to that land,
He fand threttyne hundreth thousand.
Sen David, in that small countre,
Mycht have rasit sic ane armie,
To this Lady it wes na wounder,
The quhilk had greter realmes ane hunder

Nor Davidis lytill regioun,
Thocht scho had mony a legioun
Of men mo nor I tauld affore :
Tharefor, my Sonne, marvell no more.
   Staurobates, the king of Ynde,
Gretlie perturbit in his mynd,
Heryng of sic ane multytude,
To mak defens he did conclude,
And send one message to the Quene,
Prayand hir Majestie serene
That scho wald, of hir speciall grace,
Gyf hym licence to leif in peace ;
Failand of that, thocht he suld dee,
That he suld gar hir fecht or flee :
And tyll his god ane vowe he maid,
Gyf no peace mycht of hir be had,
And gyf he wan the victorye,
That he the Quene suld crucifye.
At this bostyng the Quene maid bourdis,
Sayand, it sall nocht be, no wourdis
Sall gar me passe frome my purpose,
Bot mychtie straikis, as I suppose.
The messingeir schew to the Kyng
Of hir presumptuous answeryng,
Than Staurobates, wyse and wycht,
Come fordwart, lyke ane nobyll knycht,
With mony one thousand speir and scheild,
Arrayit royallie on the feild ;
Thynkand he wald his land defend,
Or in the battell mak ane end.
   The Quene, apone the uther syde,

Full of presumptioun and of pryde,
Hir banaris plesandly displayit,
With hardy hart and uneffrayit.
Apone Yndus, that famous flude,
Thay met, quhare sched wes mekle blude.
In bote, in balingar, and bargis,
The twa Armyis on utheris chargis.
Semiramis the battaill wan,
Quhare drownit and slane wer mony one man,
So that the walter of the flude
Ran reid, myxit with mannis blude.
The King of Ynde, with all his mycht,
Frome Yndus flude he tuke the flycht :
Tyll his cheif cietie he reteirit,
Quhare in his presens thare appeirit
In battell raye ane new armye,
Of rycht invincibyll chevalrye,
With elephantis ane hydduous nummer,
Quhilk efterwart maid mekle cummer.
   Semiramis and hir cumpanye,
In the mene tyme, full cruellie
Distroyit the bordouris of that land,
Tuke presonaris mo than ten thousand.
Sche tuke one couragious consait,
Gret elephantis to contrafait :
Sche had ten thousand oxin hydis,
Weill sewit togydder, bak and sydis,
With mouth, and nois, teith, eris, and eine,
Quyke elephantis as thay had bene,
Rycht weill stuft full of stray and hay,
Quhareof the Yndianis tuke affray.

Apone cameilis and dromodareis
Those fals figouris with hir scho careis.
Sere Yndianis, quhen thay saw that sycht,
Afferitlye thay tuke the flycht ;
For sic one sycht wes never sene,
Gyff naturall beistis thay had bene.
The Kyng hym self wes rycht affeirit,
Tyll he the veritie had speirit,
And knew, be his exploratouris,
Thay wer bot fenyeit fals figouris.
Than, manfullye, lyke men of weir,
Fordwart thay came withouttin feir ;
Rycht so Semiramis the Quene.
Quhilk for ony man wes aye fyftene.
Thir two armeis full creuellye
Thay ruscheit togydder so rudlie,
With hyddous cry and trumpettis sound,
Tyll thousandis dede laye on the ground.
Semiramis had sic one nummer,
Tyll order thame it was gret cummer.
Than the gret elephantis of Ynde,
Rycht strang and hardy of thare kynde,
Fordwart thay came, and wald nocht ceis,
Tyll throuch the myddis of the preis
Of the gret oist thay rudlye ruscheit,
That men and horsse tyll erth thay duscheit.
Those fenyeit beistis, withouttin spreit,
Wer fruschit and fulyeit under feit.
The King of Ynde, with curage kene,
Met with Semiramis the quene,
He rydand on ane eliphand :

Bot scho with hym faucht hand for hand,
And gaif the King so gret assaye
That he wes nevir in sic affraye.
To stryke at hym scho tuke no feir,
So weill scho usit wes in weir.
His straikis scho had bot lytill comptit,
Wer nocht the King wes so weill mountit.
Athir at uther straik so faste
Tyll thay wer tyrit at the laste.
The King he thocht himself eschamit
With one woman to be diffamit,
And wes determit nocht to flee,
Thocht in that battell he suld dee.
As man the quhilk disparit bene,
He rudely ran upone the Quene,
And through the arme gaif hir ane wound
Quhilk tyll hir hart gaif sic one stound
That sche constrainit wes to fle.
Than all the rest of hir armie,
Quhen thay persavit that scho wes gone,
Tyll Yndus flude thay fled, ilke one.
The Quene ouerthort the flude sche raid
On bryggis quhilk is wer of botis maid ;
With hir, one sobir cumpanye,
Quhilk with hir fled affraytlie.
The Yndianis followit on the chace :
Than on the bryggis come sic one praice
Of fleand folkis quhilk wes gret wounder,
So that the bargis krake in schonder.
Sum sank, sum doun the revar ran :
Than drownit thare mony one nobyll man ;

Quhilk wer gret pietie tyll deplore,
As wryttis famous Diodore ;
And, fynallie, for to conclude,
Wes never sched so mekle blude
At one tyme sen the Warld began,
Nor slane so mony one saikles man ;
And all throw the occasioun
And the prydefull perswasioun
Of this ambitious wyckit Quene ;
Sic one wes nevir hard nor sene,
   Staurobates, the kyng of Yude,
Gretlye rejoysit, in his mynde,
Of this tryumphe and victorye :
Semiramis, with hart full sorye,
Seand sa mony tane and slane,
Tyll hir countré returnit agane,
Lamentand fortunis variance
Quhilk brocht hir to so gret myschance,
Affore quhilk wes so fortunat,
And than of confort desolat.
   Hir Sonne, one man of perfectioun,
Consyderand his subjectioun,
His lybertie he did desyre,
That he mycht goverane his impyre :
Seand his Mother vicious,
And, with that, so ambitious,
As myne Author doith specifye,
He slew his Mother creuellye :
Quhat uther cause, or intentioun,
I fynd no speciall mentioun :
Sum sayis, to be at libertie ;

Sum sayis, for hir adulterie ;
None uther cause I can defyne,
Except punissioun devyne.

　Of this fair Lady coragious
Behald the endyng dolorous ;
Quhilk wes bot twenty yeir of aige,
Quhen sche began hir vassalage,
And rang triumphandlye, but weir,
The space of two and fourtye yeir :
Quhen scho was slane, scho wes thre score,
With yeiris two, scho wes no more ;
As Diodore wryttis in his buke,
His Cronikle quho lyste to luke.

　　Of this Lady I mak ane end,
Thynkand no way I can commend
Wemen for tyll be too manlye,
Nor men for tyll be womanlye,
For quhy it bene the Lordis mynde
All creature tyll use thare kynde ;
Men for tyll have preheminens,
And wemen under obediens ;
Thocht all wemen inclynit be
Tyll have the soveranitie,
As this lady, quhilk wald nocht rest
Tyll scho hir husband had supprest,
Tyll that intent that scho micht ryng,
Allone to haif the governyng.

　Ladyis no way I can commend
Presumptuouslye quhilk doith pretend
Tyll use the office of ane Kyng,

Or Realmes tak in governyng,
Quhowbeit thay vailyeant be and wycht,
Going in battell lyke one knycht,
As did proude Pantasilia,
The Princes of Amasona,
In mennis habyte, aganis reassoun :
Siclyke I think derisioun,
One prince to be effaminate,
Of knychtlye corage desolate,
Neglectand his auctoritie,
Throuch beistlie sensualitie,
Accompanyit, boith day and nychtis ;
With wemen, more than vailyeant knychtis ;
Sic kyngis I discommend at all,
Exempyll of Sardanapall.

COURTEOUR.

Father, said I, schaw me quhow lang
The successioun of Nynus rang.

EXPERIENCE.

That sall I do, with diligens,
My Sonne, said he, or I go hens.
Sen I haif schawin, at thy desyre,
Quhat man began the First Impyre,
Now wald I it wer to thee kend
Of that Impyre the fatell end.

QUHOW KING SARDANAPALUS FOR HIS VITIOUS LIFE MAID ANE MISERABILL END.

[EXPERIENCE.]

Betuix this Conquerour Nynus
And sensuall Sardanapalus
I can nocht fynd no speciall storye
Worthy to put in memorye,
Except quhilk I haif done discryfe
Of Semirame, king Nynus wyfe :
Bot I can fynde no gude at all
To wrytt of kyng Sardanapall,
Quhilk wes the saxt and threttye kyng
Be lyne from Nynus discendyng.
At lenth his lyfe for to declare
I thynk it is nocht necessare ;
Because that mony cunnyng clerkis
Hes hym discryvit in thare werkis :
Quhow he wes last of Assyrians
Quhilk had the hole preemynens,
That tyme of the First Monarchie,
In Cronicles, as thow may se,
The last and the most vitious kyng
Quhilk in that Monarchie did ryng.
That Prince wes so effeminate,
With sensuall luste intoxicate,
He did abhor the cumpanye
Of his most nobyll chevalrye :
That he mycht have the more delyte

Tyll use his beistlye appetyte,
Conversit with wemen nycht and daye,
And clothit hym in thare arraye,
So that na man that hym hed sene
Could juge ane man that he had bene :
So, in huredome and harlotrye
Did keip hym self so quyetlye,
The Princis of Assyrience
Of hym thay could get no presence,
Thus levit he contynuallye,
Agane nature inordinatiye.

    Quhen to the Persis and the Medis
Reportit wer his vitious dedis,
With the rewlaris of Babilone,
Thay did conclude, all in tyll one,
Thay wald nocht suffer for tyll ryng
Abufe thame sic ane vitious kyng :
Bot Arbaces, ane Duke of Mede,
He darflye tuke on hand that dede.

    Bot first he come to Nynivé,
.To see the kyngis Majestie,
And tyll one of the kyngis gaird
He gaif one secreit ryche rewaird,
Tyll put hym in ane quyet place,
Quhare he mycht se the Kyngis grace,
And be onsene with ony wycht.
Bot he saw nother king nor knycht
In tyll his maisteris cumpanye,
Except Wemen, allanerlye :
And as ane woman he was cled,
With wemen counsalit and led ;

And schamfullye he wes syttand,
With spindle and with rock spinnand.
Quhen Arbaces that sycht had sene,
His corage raisit from the splene,
And thocht it small difficultie
For tyll depryve his Majestie.
    Than raisit he the Persianis,
With Medis and Babilonianis :
Inarmit weill with speir and scheildis,
Tryumphantlye thay tuke the feildis.
    The Kyng raisit Assyrianis,
Togither with the Caldianis,
And thame resystit as he mycht ;
Bot, fynallie, he tuke the flycht,
To saif hym self, in Nynivé.
Than seigit thay that gret Cietie,
Contynuallie, two yeir and more,
As wryttis famous Diodore ;
Tyll that the flude of Euphrates
Arose with sic one furiousnes,
Quhare throuch ane gret part of the Toun
By violence was doungin doun.
Than, quhen the Kyng saw no remeid
Bot to be takin, or to be deid,
As man disparit full of yre,
Gart mak ane furious flammand fyre,
And tuke his gold and jowellis all,
With sceptur, croun, and robe royall,
With all his tender servitouris
That of his corps hap gretest curis,
Togydder with his lustye Quenis,

And all his wantoun concubenis,
And in that fyre he did thame cast,
Syne lappe hym self in, at the last,
Quhare all wer brynt in poulder small.
    Thus endit Kyng Sardanapall
Withouttin ony repentence,
As may be sene be this sentence,
Heir followyng, quhilk he did indyte
Affore his deith in gret dispyte :
Quhilk is ane rycht ungodly thing,
As ye may se be his dyting.—

EPITAPHIUM SARDANAPALI.

Cum te mortalem noris, præsentibus exple
Delitiis animum, post mortem nulla voluptas.
Et Venere, et cœnis, et plumis Sardanapali.

Now haif I schawin, with deligence,
The Monarchie of Assyrience,
The quhilk at Kyng Nynus began,
And endit at this myscheant man,
And did indure, withouttin weir,
Ane thowsand, twa hundreth, and fourty yeir,
As dois indyte Eusebius :
Reid hym, and thow sall fynd it thus.

HEIR ENDIS THE SECUND PART.

NOTES.

NOTES.

THE DREME.—*Page* 13.

"This is plainly Lyndsay's first production, of which we
know anything. The principal note of time is the obvious
intimation that *his youth-hood was now nearly overblown.*
The domination of the Douglases separated the King from
'the companions of his youth' in 1524, when Lyndsay, 'the
chemist, fiddler, statesman, and buffoon,' was reformed on a
pension. During the payment of this pension, and the ex-
istence of that domination, Lyndsay would not dare to *dream*
what was disagreeable to the dominating powers. It was the
King's happy escape from the odious power of the Douglases
in July 1528 which unbent the writer's genius, and unbound
our poet's pen, to 'tell ane mervellous vision.' He intimates
indeed, that he had been long idle ; and that idleness, the
ground of iniquitie, had so dulled his spreits, he wist not at
what end to begin. While investigating the cause of Scotland's poverty, under the sage direction of experience, he
attributes that evil to the want of justice, policy, and peace ;
and that want he assigns to the 'infatuate heads insolent,'
who had small eye to the commonweal, and only looked 'to
their singular profit.' This, then, is a pretty plain description of the sad misrule of the Douglases, which ended with
the King's acquirement of power, in July 1528. The *Dreme,*
of course, must have been written after the terror of their
domination had disappeared. The poet makes *Jhone the
Commonweill* describe the state of the southern borders,
where nothing could be seen but *reif, theft,* and *mischief.*
This description was true, before the King caused severe
justice to be inflicted on the principal thieves, and reclaimed
the borderers, in 1529, after the expulsion of the Douglasses.

The whole context of *The Dreme* evinces, then, that it was written towards the end of the year 1528 ; But it was not printed for many years."—CHALMERS.

THE DREME first appears in a printed form in the two foreign editions of Lyndsay's poems, simultaneously printed with the name of Samuel Jascuy, at Paris, in 1558. The present text is from the volume printed in Scotland, evidently in the year following, by John Scot. Chalmers gave the preference to the smaller edition by Jascuy ; and some of the various readings may perhaps come nearer the original text, but these variations are not of much importance. The Dreme is included in every subsequent edition of Lyndsay's poems. Mere variations of orthography do not require special notice.

Line 31.—*Didis marciall.* The youthful King being ignorant of Latin, the Chronicles of Scotland, by Hector Boethius or Boyce, printed at Paris 1527, along with the first five Books of Livy, were translated for his use in 1536, by John Bellenden, Archdeacon of Murray. This translation of The History and Croniklis of Scotland, was printed at Edinburgh by Thomas Davidson without date, about the year 1540. A metrical version of the same Chronicles was completed at that time and at the King's expense, by a contemporary poet, William Stewart. This metrical Chronicle, preserved in a single MS. at Cambridge, extending to 61,282 lines, was carefully edited by the late Mr. Turnbull, and published at London by authority of the Master of the Rolls. 3 vols., 1858, royal 8vo.

Line 70 — *Ouer all the land.* It will be observed in old Scottish poetry that such words as *ower* (*over*) are usually pronounced as monosyllables.

Line 196—*More for deneiris.* "*Deneiris*, money : so afterwards Lyndsay (see p. 356, note on line 985) has *telling thair deneiris*, counting their money."—CHALMERS.

The same phrase, *denneir*, also occurs in Lyndsay's "Satyre of the Three Estatis." See vol. ii., p. 191.

> Bot I gat never ane denneir
> Yit, for my recompence.

Line 233—*O Empriour Constantyne.* It is by no means improbable that Lyndsay, (who reverts to this subject in his Papyngo, line 803), might here have had in view the well-known lines in Dante's *Inferno* (xix. 115).

> Ahi Constantin, di quanto mal fu
> Non la tua Conversion, ma quella dote
> Che da te finse il primo ricco Patri !

Which Milton thus rendered into English blank verse,

> Ah ! Constantine, of how much ill was cause
> Not thy Conversion, but those rich domaines
> That the first wealthy Pope receiv'd of thee !

Milton also quotes allusions by Petrarch (Sonnet 108) and Ariosto (Orlando Furioso, canto 34) to Constantine's gift to the Roman Pontiff, "whereby it may be concluded for a receiv'd opinion, even among men professing the Romish faith, that Constantine marr'd all in the church : as it was at this time Antichrist began first to put forth his horne." (Of Reformation, &c., p. 30, Lond., 1641, 4to.)

Line 385—*The Speris of the Planetis Sevin.* "The Planetary system was thus divided : I. The Primum Mobile, or first motion. II. The Crystalline Heaven, in which were placed the fixed stars. III. The twelve signs of the Zodiac. IV. The spheres or circles of the planets in this order, viz., Saturn. Jupiter, Mars, Sol, Venus, Mercury, and lastly the Moon, which they placed in the centre of universal Nature. Again, they supposed the Earth to be surrounded by three elementary Spheres, Fire, Air, and Water. Milton, in his Elegy on the Death of a fair Infant, makes a very poetical use of the notion of a *primum mobile*, where he supposes that the soul of the child hovers

> Above that high First Moving Sphere,
> Or in th' Elysian fields, &c.

—WARTON, (Hist. Engl. Poetry, Sect. xxxii.) See also Paradise Lost, Book iii., line 483.

Line 413—*Dryer than the tounder*, or "t'other, the other ; a perversion for the rhyme."—CHALMERS. This is a very unsatisfactory explanation, the obvious meaning is, *drier than any tinder*. Thus in Douglas's translation of Virgil's Æneis,

> The sonnys mid cirkill remanis under
> Hait Torrida Zona, *dry as ony tunder.*

Line 510 —*Rycht melodious Harmony.* This alludes to what was called the Harmony of the Spheres. See Henryson's Orpheus and Eurydice, a poem which might have suggested some of the finest descriptive passages in Lyndsay's Dream. The author flourished in the reign of James the Third, and his poem, originally printed at Edinburgh in 1508, was included in the first collected edition of his Poems and Fables. Edin. 1865. Post 8vo.

Line 513.—*The Hevin callit Christallyne.* Milton, (Par. Lost, Book iii., line 481), has,

> They pass the Planets seven, and pass the Fixet,
> And that Crystalline sphere, whose balance weighs
> The trepidation talkt, and that first mov'd.

Line 748—

> *Of Plinius, and worthie Ptholomie,*
> *Quhilkis war expert in to Cosmographie.*

The "Historia Naturalis" of Pliny and the "Geographia" of Ptolemy of Alexandria : both works might furnish, were it required, abundant illustrations of this portion of Lyndsay's Dream.

Line 955—*Betuix the Merse and Lowmabane.* "Between Berwickshire and Lochmabane, a town in Dumfriesshire, the ancient seat of the Bruces, Lords of Annandale."—CHALMERS. The Merse is the name given to a district in Berwickshire, on the northern bank of the Tweed, throughout the whole space where the river serves to divide the two kingdoms. Lochmaben is one of the royal boroughs.

Line 964—*In the Oute Ylis*, that is, in the Western Isles or the Hebrides.

Line 985—*In tellyng thair deneris*, in counting their money, as in line 196. The word *deneir* is evidently derived from the Latin *Denarius*, the name of a Roman silver coin.

Line 1092—*Frome lychorie*. The temptations held forth to the young Prince by designing and worthless persons at Court, as described in next poem, the Complaynt to the King, (lines 233-252) had unfortunately a much greater influence than all Lyndsay's admonitions in this Exhortation.

THE COMPLAYNT TO THE KING.—*Page* 46.

"THE COMPLAYNT of Lyndsay arose from the situation in which he found himself at the age of thirty-nine. Early in life, he had been appointed, as we have seen, principal page to James V., at the epoch of his birth. In this office our poet had been everything during a dozen years to the young prince : He had been his sewer, his carver, his cupbearer, his pursemaster, his chief cubiculare : But, while Lyndsay was everything to the prince, and the prince was everything to Lyndsay, a revolution happened in the state during the year 1524 ; owing to the intrigues of the Queen-mother, which put an end to so endearing a connection : for her own gratification, the King *was taken from school* at the age of twelve, and put at the head of the government, in order that others might misgovern his kingdom. Lyndsay was reformed on a pension, which he admits was punctually paid ; arising from the King's continued kindness. James V., who very soon began to think and feel like a king, made several efforts to free himself from this thraldom. And he became king indeed, by throwing off the domination of the Douglases in 1528. Immediately after, our poet addressed to the *Kingis grace* his *Complaynt*, which is composed in eight-syllable verse of very easy flow, and which lays before the King his services, in familiar terms, and speaks of his want of reward with freedom and manliness. Of the *Complaynt*, Warton remarks, that it is written generally with elegance, sometimes with tenderness, and always with vigour. It is now chiefly valuable for its picture of the manners of the age, for showing the intrigues of the court, and for telling, in an agreeable style, his own personal story. The *Complaynt* was written in 1529."—CHALMERS.

Mr Chalmers elsewhere says, "As the preceding Dreme is quoted in the Complaynt, this must necessarily have been written subsequent to the Dreme, the first of his labours." "The whole context of the Complaynt" (he adds) "thus fixes the writing of it to the last six months of 1529."—This conclusion seems to be incontrovertible, from some of the subsequent allusions contained in the Complaynt. It apparently was first printed among his Minor Poems, by John Scot in the year 1559.

Line 16—*The day of thy Natyvitie.* King James the Fifth was born in the palace of Linlithgow in April 1512.

Line 82—*My Lord Chancelare.* This was Gawin Dunbar of the family of Cumnock, and nephew of Gawin Dunbar, Bishop of Aberdeen (1518-1532). The education of the young prince had been entrusted to him, at the same time that Lyndsay became "his daily servitour." Dunbar, the King's tutor, succeeded Archbishop Beaton in the See of Glasgow in 1524, and was appointed Lord Chancellor on the 21st of August 1528, which office he held during the rest of the King's reign. He was turned out towards the end of 1543, to make room for Cardinal Beaton. Archbishop Dunbar died on the 30th of April 1547.

Line 92—*Pa, Da, Lyn.* The first syllables that thou did mute (articulate) were, PA-[pa] DA-[vid] LYN-[dsay.]

Line 93—*Than playit twenty sprynyis, perqueir.* Then, upon the lute, I played twenty tunes, off-hand.

Line 99—*In to my Dreme.* The preceding poem by Lyndsay : the earliest of his compositions known to exist.

Line 120—*Ane clips fell in the mone.* "Clips, eclipse, as Chaucer has *clipsy,* for eclipsed. The allusion is to the revolution in the Scottish government during the year 1524,

when the king was twelve years of age, and the Douglases
gained the ascendancy. The king's old servants were dismissed."—CHALMERS.

Line 195—*And geve the Thesaurair be our freind.* "This
potent Treasurer was Archibald Douglas, the uncle of the
Earl of Angus, who seized the government in 1524."—
CHALMERS. The accounts of Archibald Douglas of Kilspindie,
as Treasurer, extend from 15th Oct. 1526 to the 29th August
1527: the intermediate accounts till October 1530 are not
preserved. Douglas, as Treasurer, was succeeded in 1528 by
Robert Bertoun of Over-Bertoun.

Line 223—*Bot be his Bowis war weill cumit hame:* the Papal
Bulls, or letters from the Court of Rome, granting or confirming Presentation to Benefices in Scotland, a right claimed and
exercised by the Pope.

Line 311—*That tyme, so failyet wes thair sycht.* "The
allusion here is to the flight of Archbishop Beaton from the
violence of the Earl of Angus."—CHALMERS.

Line 317—*Baith gyding Court and Sessioun.* "The Bishops
were the most active, because the most able men, both in the
Court and in the committees of Parliament, for administering
justice, before the establishment of the Court of Session."—
CHALMERS.

On the establishment of the College of Justice, in May
1532, the Senators consisted of a President, and twelve
Judges, one half occupying the Spiritual side of the Bench,
and the other the Temporal, this continued till 1640, when
the former class was suppressed, and the judges ordained to
be wholly Temporal.

Line 356—*At Lythgow, Melros, and Edinburgh.* "Linlithgow—On the 13th September 1526, where the Douglases defeated the Earl of Lennox. *Melros*—24th July 1526, when the
Douglases defeated the Scots. *Edinburgh*—30th April 1520,
when the Douglases defeated the Hamiltons in a conflict on

the streets of Edinburgh, which was called *Cleanse the causey.*
For the Lords who were slain, see Pitscottie, 215."—CHALMERS.

Line 366—*Bot tyll new Regentis maid thair bandis.* "The
allusion is to the bonds of man-rent, which arose from the
feebleness of government and the turbulence of the times."—
CHALMERS.

Line 368—*The quhilk gart all thair bandis bryste.* "The
King made his escape in 1528 from the Douglases, which circumstance *burst* many *bonds.*"—CHALMERS.

Line 372—*That thay war faine tyll trott ouer Tweid.* "The
Douglases were attainted in September 1528; and obliged to
flee over the Tweed into England."—CHALMERS.

Line 450—*Now am I sure to get rewaird.* "Lyndsay was
soon after made Lion-King; so that he had the reward which
distinguished him ever after."—CHALMERS.

Line 476—*Efter the daye of Jugement.* This jocular way of
assigning the repayment to an impossible date, occurs also in
his Satyre of the Three Estaitis, p. 191, line 13.

> I will get riches throu that rent
> Efter the day of Dome.

THE TESTAMENT AND COMPLAYNT OF THE
PAPYNGO.—*Page* 63.

"LYNDSAY'S own *Complaynt* had succeeded so well, that he
soon resolved to write a fresh Complaynt of a very different
personage. When our poet closed his *Complaynt,* in 1529,
every thing and every body seem to have been reformed;
there was nocht,

> Without gude ordour, in this land,
> Except the *Spiritualitie.*

He now brings out the king's *parrot* to laugh at the *ecclesiastical persons* and proceedings, approaching, in his ambition of
satire and ardour of reform, to the very border of scurrility

and profaneness. It must, however, be allowed that, if his
satire be sharp, it is, at the same time, sly ; if his reprehen-
sions be vehement, they are often just ; and if his design be
generous, his views are narrow, and his means are bad. He
divides this satirical poem, that is written in seven-line
stanzas, with alternate rhymes, and in ten-syllable verse, into
several sections, which are judiciously applied to different
topics. *The Prolog* he begins by apologizing, according to
the practice of the poets, for his want of *ingyne*, and for his
deficience of *mater* ; the *poets auld* having exhausted, in
termes rethorical, everilk matter, both *tragedie* and *storie*,
and that *sa ornatlie*, that nothing remained for his *dull intelligence* either of subject or embellishment. He now breaks
out into a just celebration of *Chaucer*, *Gower*, and *Lidgate*,
who were conceived to be beyond compare, and said to be
inimitable ; ' Whose sweet sentence through Albion ben sung.'
From celebrating thus the fathers of English poesy, Lyndsay
proceeds to speak, in *termes aureait*, of Dunbar, Douglas, the
bishop of Dunkell, and other poets of his country, both the
dead and the living, with whose writings and merits he seems
to have been perfectly acquainted : our author, shows, indeed,
throughout his various poems, that he had read much, and
remembered what he had read, as we might infer from his
retrospections and adaptations. Lyndsay goes on, in his
second division, to illustrate an axiom, which is of great
importance to mankind, that ' Wha climmis too high, perforce
his feet must fall.' To establish this position, he perches the
parrot on the topmost branch of the highest tree, whence she
is thrown down, when Boreas blew a *fretting blast*, and when
he gives her not only power of speech, but endows her with
the faculty of reflection. Our poet, in his third section, by
an easy fiction, makes this unfortunate bird 'give her counsall
to the King,' by spreading out before him the Scottish
Chronikillis, ' Whilk might be *mirrour* to his majestie.'
Lyndsay makes the Papingo, in his fourth division, address
her *brether of the court*, on whom she tries to impress this
lesson of experience, ' Wha sittes maist hie sall find the sait
maist slidder.' Our poet, in his last section, introduces ' the
commoning betwix the papingo and her haly executoris ; the

pye, a canon regular ; the raven, a black monk ; and the gled,
a holy freir. In the conversation of the Papingo with such
executors, the reader will find what might easily be expected
in such a place, from such parties, much retrospective history,
many elegant fictions, and some useful satire. The *Complaynt
of the Papingo*, which is one of the most finished of Lyndsay's
pieces, was written by him at the age of forty, in the year
1530." CHALMERS.

The first edition of this poem, and indeed of any one of
Lyndsay's poems, is that printed at London by John Byddell
in the year 1538. That this or some others of his earlier
pieces had passed through the press in Scotland during the
author's life is highly probable, but no vestiges of any such
impressions have been discovered, the original edition of
"The Dialog," in 1554, of course excepted. The 1538 edition
of the Papyngo and the two in 1558, are much alike, but the
orthography of the former is somewhat Anglicised. The
Papyngo was again reprinted by John Scot, when he subjoined
Lyndsay's minor poems to his second impression of "The
Dialog," in 1559. It is likewise contained in all the subsequent editions of Lyndsay's Poems.

Line 20—*Thair libellis bene lerand.* "Recounting the
names of several of the early Scottish Poets, Lyndsay uses
this phrase, that though dead, their writings survive. *Libel*,
from the Latin, literally a little book, is now almost always
used for Satire, or defamatory writing, called *famosus libellus*;
but in the Civil Law paper it signifies a declaration or charge
in writing against a person exhibited in Court."—CHALMERS.

Line 80—*One Papyngo.* "*Papingo* was merely the Scottish
mode of spelling the English *popingay*; as indeed Lyndsay
himself spells the same word, *papingay*, in his *Monarchies*.
This is the old English name of the *parrot*; as in Chaucer,
"Singeth wel merier than the *popingay*;" also in Shakspeare,
"To be so pestered with a *popingay*;" and Coles explains the
popingay to be a *greenish* parrot. CHALMERS.

Papejay, papingay, papingoe. See Jamieson's Dictionary,
a parrot or parroquet, O.E., *popingay.* He quotes the King's

Quair, also Gawin Douglas, who, in reference to Caxton's translation of Virgil, says,—

> Quhilk is na mair lyke Virgill dar I lay,
> Than the nycht Owle resembleis the Papyngay.

Line 159—*Thou art rycht fat, and nocht well usit to flie.* Without some such explanatory words the tumbling of the Papyngo or parrot from the top of the tree, and its fatal effects, might seem to be very absurd.

Line 494.— *The Savage Iles, trymblit for terrour of his justice,* explained by Chalmers "as the Western Isles." James IV, displayed unwonted energy and decision in personally crushing their rebellious spirit, and bringing the inhabitants of the Western Highlands into a state of subjection.

Line 495.— *Eskdale, Euisdale, &c., durst nocht rebell.* Chalmers remarks that "those Border districts were not so famous for rebellion, as for theft and robbery."

Line 507.— *Of Floddoun Feilde.* James the Fourth was slain on the 9th September 1513: from the calamitous and irreparable results, it might well be called *That moste dolent daye.*

Lines 553-540.—Lyndsay in these lines refers to and deplores the manner in which public affairs had been managed during the King's minority; the great power of the Queen Dowager, and her fall after her quarrell with the Earl of Angus her second husband.

Line 626.— *Adew Edinburgh.* "Edwynsburgh is the original name; the other appellations are only derivatives. I mean to give a dissertation on this name in a more proper place."—CHALMERS. This intention he performed in his *Caledonia,* vol. ii., p. 555.

Line 633— *Adew fair Snawdoun.* "*Snawdoun* means Stirling Castle. We here see that Lyndsay transmits a tradition which was known to William of Worcester, in the preceding

364 NOTES.

age, about *Arthur* and his *round table;* about Stirling being called *Snowdon,* or West Castle. It was called West Castle, I believe, in contradistinction to the Castle of Blackness."— CHALMERS.

Line 634—*Thy Chapell Royall.* "The Chapel Royal of Stirling Castle was founded by James IV., and richly endowed by him with the dilapidations of several monasteries.— Spottiswood 327 ; Keith 288."—CHALMERS.

Line 538—*Adew Lythquo.* "The Palace of Linlithgow was no doubt a pleasant residence in the age of Lyndsay ; and might possibly have been a *patrone,* which is the old word, or *patron,* which is the reading of the ed. 1592 and Sibbald, for *pattern.* The old word is nearest the Fr. *patron,* and still nearer to the Dutch *patroon."*—CHALMERS.

The Palace of Linlithgow was a favourite royal residence in the reign of James the Fourth. It was enlarged or completed by his son and successor ; and here Mary Queen of Scots was born, a few days before the death of her father, James the Fifth, in December 1546. The greater part of the palace was destroyed by a wilful fire in 1746. In connexion with the old church and lake, it is still a picturesque and beautiful object.

Line 640—*Farewell Falkland, &c.* "Lyndsay, we see, speaks feelingly of the palaces and places where he had *led a lustye lyfe* with James V. The Palace of Falkland had certainly once a tower or keep, wherein the Duke of Rothesay was starved to death ; and so might well be called a fortress or strength by Lyndsay, who knew it in its ancient state."— CHALMERS.

THE ANSWER TO THE KINGIS FLYTING.—*Page* 107.

Among the remains of Early Scottish Poetry, the most remarkable specimens of FLYTING, a term equivalent to scolding, are those of Dunbar and Kennedy, about the close of the fifteenth century. See Dunbar's Poems, vol. ii. 1834. We cannot but regret that, since Lyndsay's coarse and indelicate Answer has been preserved, the King's verses should not also have accompanied it. In the edition published by Henry Charteris, in 1568, where it first appears, it is said to have been "never befoir imprentit." It has retained its place in all the subsequent editions of Lyndsay's Poems.

"The grossness of manners in ancient times allowed and encouraged the familiarity of fools and the satyre of poets; hence the establishment of a jester, or the *king's fool*, and the allowance to a poet-laureat. Henry VIII. had shown his nephew, James V., an example of *flyting*, and of the practice of familiarity with buffoons. It was, of course, natural for the fool and for the buffoons to be insolent to those who would bear it, and slavish to others who could chastise their audacity :

> The bold *buffoon*, whene'er they tread the green,
> Their motion mimics but with jest obscene.

The practice of *flyting* became very familiar in Scotland during the reign of James IV., when the greatest poets, Dunbar and Kennedy, scolded one another unmercifully in *jests obscene.*"—CHALMERS.

Line 21- *The Prince of Poetry.* This courtly compliment to the young King leaves no doubt as to the claim of KING JAMES THE FIFTH to be reckoned among the Scottish Makers or Poets.

Line 69—*Ane buckler furth of France.* The allusion here to the King's intended marriage with a French princess, led Chalmers to fix 1536 as the date of this poem.

THE COMPLAYNT OF BAGSHE.—*Page* 110.

"It was much the fashion with Lyndsay, as we have seen, to throw his matter into the form of a *Complaynt* for the purpose of satyre. It was equally his custom, as it had been the practice of the poets in every age, to adopt the easy fiction of making his birds and beasts to think and speak

for the moral effect. The King's Papingo, in her dying
moments, uttered many a *saw*: 'His weapons holy *saws* of
sacred writ.' Lyndsay now brings out 'the Kingis auld
hound *Bagsche*,' at the royal command, to ridicule favourit-
ism and to inculcate the practice of beneficence amid the
gales of prosperity. The maxim is proved throughout :—
Highest in court, next the gallows. This *Complaynt* of
Bagsche is composed in eight-line stanzas, with alternate
rhymes, and in eight syllable verse, which glides in very
flowing eloquence. This satyre was written immediately
before the King's first marriage, and during the year 1536.
George, Earl of Huntly, succeeded his father in 1523 ; and
from the king's kindness he obtained many grants of land in
the period from 1530 to 1540. When the King went to
France in 1536, the Earl was made one of the regency. While
Bagsche, the gift of this great Earl, was a favourite,

> He of na creature tuke care ;
> Bot, lap upon the Kingis bed,
> With claith of gold, thoeh it was spred.

"Had the King been a married man such a freedom could
not have been used, even by a favourite, without chastise-
ment. The demerits of Bagsche drove him into banishment,
and he was succeeded by Bawtie, 'the king's best beloved
dog ; '———

> Who now lyis on *the Kingis night gown*.

"If the King had been married it is impossible that
Bawtie could have been thus indulged to sleep upon the
king's night gown. The whole context seems to evince that
the Complaynt of Bagsche was written by Lyndsay for the
King's amusement before he sailed for France in 1536."—
CHALMERS.

This poem is not printed in either of Jascuy's editions,
but is included in the various editions printed in Scotland in
and after 1568.

Line 50. - *The capitane of Badzeno.* "Probably the captain
of Badzenoch, a country and castle of the Earl of Huntly."
—CHALMERS.

Badenoch a mountainous district in Inverness-shire, was in early times a lordship of the Cummins. On their forfeiture in the reign of Robert the Bruce, the lands of Badenoch came into the possession of the Huntly family.

Line 103—*Betuix Ashwednisday and Paice.* That is *Paice* or *Pasch* for Easter. Ash Wednesday, of course, was the first day of Lent, when eating meat was prohibited by the Romish Church, unless by special licence.

THE DEPLORATIOUN OF THE DEITH OF QUENE MAGDALENE.—*Page* 119,

"As a court poet, Lyndsay was often summoned by the circumstances of the times, which were eventful, either to celebrate a wedding, or to deplore a death. James V. seems to have early determined to match himself with some of the daughters of France. His personal Voyage to that kingdom, after various embassies had failed, appears to have fixed his final choice on Magdalene, the eldest daughter of Francis I. But, though they were betrothed on the 26th of November 1536, the marriage was not solemnized till the 1st of January 1537 ; the physicians having advised Magdalene against a measure which might embitter her days and hazard her life. The King and Queen arrived in Scotland on the 27th of May, and on the 7th of July 1537, Magdalene died, amidst the preparations for the celebration of her nuptials and arrival by an affectionate people. This sad event gave occasion to our poet's *Deploratioun of the Deith of Quene Magdalene*, which is composed in seven-line stanzas of alternate rhymes, except the two last, and in ten-syllable verse. Like much of Lyndsay's poetry, this *Deploratioun* is a mixture of fact and fiction, of religion and mythology, of fitness and impropriety. It was written by him, as we know from the event, during the year 1537."— CHALMERS.

"The events thus evince that the *Deploratioun* was written in 1537. And it was printed in the French edition of 1558, and reprinted in the English edition of 1566, as well as in the subsequent editions."—CHALMERS.

This interesting poem first appears, as mentioned in the above note, subjoined to THE DREME, in the foreign edition of Lyndsay's poems, "Imprinted at the command and expenses of Maister Samuel Jascuy in Paris," 1558. It was included in the English edition by Purfoote of 1566, by Charteris in 1568, and in all subsequent editions. In the London reprints by Purfoote, in 1575 and 1581, the title is altered to "The Bewayling of the Death of Queen Magdalen."

Line 77—*Our richt redoutit Roy.* "Our poet, who saw the splendid spectacle of the marriage of James V. with Magdalene, probably gave to Pitscottie his minute account, in p. 288-9."—CHALMERS.

Line 99—*Thief! saw thow nocht, &c.* WARTON quotes part of this expostulation with Death, describing the whole order of the procession as a striking and lively prosopopeia, and points out as deserving of attention "this artificial and very poetical mode of introducing a description of these splendid spectacles, instead of saying playnly that the Queen's death prevented the superb ceremonies which would have attended her coronation." (Hist. Engl. Poetry.)

Line 201—*Thocht rute be pullit, &c.* "Though the root of the *flower-de-lys* be pulled, yet shall the smell of it keep always two realms in amity. Lyndsay thus concludes his Deploratioun with a very elegant thought." -CHALMERS.

This may remind some readers of a conceit, by Moore in his Irish Melodies :

" Like the vase, in which roses have once been distill'd,
  You may break, you may ruin the vase if you will,
  But the scent of the roses will hang round it still."

THE JUSTING BETWIX JAMES WATSOUN AND JHONE BARBOUR.—*Page* 127.

" The mourning for Magdalene did not prevent James V. from sending ambassadors to France to demand in marriage Mary of Loraine. The King and the Widow of Longville were married by proxy, on the 23th of May 1538. She arrived at Crail, in Fife, on the 10th of the subsequent June, and the marriage was immediately solemnized at St Andrews, which is said to have been then a beautiful city. On that joyous occasion was exhibited the celebrated *justing* 'betuix James Watsoun and Jhone Barbour.'

"Lyndsay, we have seen, acted a conspicuous part at the solemnization of the royal espousals. And he now compylit this ludicrous account of the *romantic* justing of the king's *twa medicinars* for the entertainment of the Kingis grace and Quene. This compilation was originally printed in the edition 1568, and has kept its ground in the subsequent editions."—CHALMERS.

This burlesque poem first made its appearance in the edition of Henry Charteris, 1568.

Some entries in the Treasurer's Accounts confirm not only the supposed date of this poem, but the identity of the two champions. In December 1538, James Watsone was appointed "in John Murray's place (quhom God assolzie), yemen in the King's chamber," while John Barbour is styled "grume in the wardrop," thus both being in Lyndsay's words, the King's familiar seruitors,

And of his chalmer baith cubicularis.

In August 1539 there was given "ane caiss of silver, to James Watsone, barbour."

The following entry in the Treasurer's Accounts, May 1539, may have had some reference to this mock tournament of Watsoun and Barbour at St Andrews "Item, deliuerit to Williame Smebeird for carriage of the Kingis harnes, speris, and uther justing geir fra Edinburgh to Striueling, and fra

Striueling to Sanctandrois in Aprile and Maij, as his parti-
cular compt beris, £4 16s. 8d."

SUPPLICATION AGAINST SYDE TAILLIS.—*Page* 128.

"There are few notes of time in this *Supplication* which
Lyndsay made to the King *in contempt of syde taillis*, and
which had often been made before, and continued to be
made in after times. The Poet speaks, however, of the
propriety of dress and politeness of behaviour which distinguished the French ladies. This praise seems to intimate
that Lyndsay had now returned from France, where he had
been to witness the King's marriage. The Poet speaks in
several places of *the Queen*, and of the *Queen's Majesty*. This
intimation points to the presence of the Queen ; and both
those circumstances, which are not contradicted by any op-
posing fact, are sufficient to fix the writing of the supplication to the year 1538. It was first published in the edition
of Lyndsay's works 1568, though it was, no doubt, handed
about before. It was comprehended in the subsequent
editions, and, strange to tell, it was printed singly on two
folio pages in 1690."—CHALMERS.

This line has been quoted to confirm rather a vague con-
jecture of Lyndsay in early life having visited Italy. See
Memoir.

KITTIE'S CONFESSION.—*Page* 136.

"In this ridicule of Auricular confession there is scarcely
any note of time. By making captious inquiries about *Inglis
bukis*, the confessor plainly alludes to the English translation
of the Scriptures. By adverting to the dates of that translation, and the circumstances of the times, it seems to be
apparent that *Kitteis Confession* must have been written in
the intermediate period from 1536 to 1543. There would
have been no fitness in those questions after it was made
lawful by Lord Maxwell's act, to have the holy writ in the

vulgar tongue without offence, and after the Regent Arran
had caused that Act to be published on the 19th of March
1541-2. It is to be recollected also, that our Sir David Lyndsay sat in that Parliament. This Confession was, therefore
written, we may suppose, in 1541. It was printed in the
edition of 1568, being "compylit (as is belevit) by Schir David
Lyndsay of the Mount.' Such is the intimation of Henry
Charteris, the publisher of that edition, who appears to have
been well acquainted with Lyndsay and his labours.—
CHALMERS.

This poem, which first occurs in Charteris' edition of 1568,
has this title, "KITTIE'S CONFESSION, compylit (as is beleuit,)
BE SCHIR DAUID LYNDESAY OF THE MONT, &c."

THE TRAGEDIE OF THE CARDINALL.—*Page* 141.

"The odious assassination of this great but obnoxious
Prelate was achieved by a band of ruffians, who were in
the pay of Henry VIII., on the 28th of May 1546. Lyndsay
immediately sat down to gratify his prejudice, by satirizing
the memory of Beaton, and incidentally protecting the lives
of the assassins. This *Tragedie* was printed at London in
1546 [1546-7]. It was reprinted in the French editions of
1558; and it was again printed by Johne Skott at St.
Andrews in the subsequent year. This *Tragedie* has been
retained in the subsequent editions of Lyndsay's works."—
CHALMERS.

"Lyndsay's *Answer to the King's Flyting*, his *Supplication
against Syde Tails*, and his *Kitteis Confession*, show the
grossness of the times; his *Tragedy of Cardinal Beaton*
evinces the atrocity of the age and the men. This great and
ambitious prelate was the third of the seven sons of John
Beaton of Pitfour, in Fifeshire, by his wife Isabel, the
daughter of Monypenny of Pitmilly. He was born in 1494,

four years after Lyndsay. He studied the civil and canon laws in France, where he became the King's resident in 1519. He was nominated Commendator of Arbroath in 1523, and abbot of that opulent house in 1525. He was made keeper of the Privy seal on the fall of the Douglases in 1528. He was sent envoy, in 1533, to France, where he was consecrated Bishop of Mirapoix, an event which evinces the notions that were entertained of his influence; and the Cardinal's hat was sent him in 1538. He succeeded his uncle, as Archbishop of St. Andrews, in 1539. He became Chancellor and prime minister on the 13th of December 1543; and he was assassinated in his own castle at St. Andrews on the 29th of May 1546, at a moment of ferment in the state and feebleness in the government. Such was the person, and such the fortune, which our poet, who was perfectly acquainted with both, converted into a rhyming narrative, or *tragedie*, for reviling the dead and reforming the living. It is written in seven-line stanzas of ten syllable verse, which rhyme alternately, except the two last. And Lyndsay, who was perfectly acquainted with Johne Boccace, and John Lydgate, the monk of Burye, sat down, immediately after that dismal event, to write the Tragedie of Cardinal Beaton in 1546."—CHALMERS.

Chalmers, in these remarks, makes no reference to the martyrdom of George Wishart. This was three months before the castle of St. Andrews (from the windows of which this tragedy had been witnessed) was surprised, and Cardinal Beaton murdered, on the morning of Saturday the 29th of May 1546. Chalmers asserts that this assassination was achieved by a band of ruffians who were in the pay of Henry VIII.; and that Lyndsay "immediately sat down to gratify his prejudice by satirizing the memory of Beaton," &c. It is quite clear that its composition was not *immediately after* "that dismal event," as Lyndsay himself, at line 428, says that the Cardinal's body had lain unburied "for seven months or more" in a leaden coffin, (according to Knox) at the bottom of the Sea Tower, nor in fact was it till after

the Castle had surrendered about the end of January following, 1549-50. See Knox's Works, vol, i., pp. 176-182.

Lyndsay's poem was soon after this annexed to an account
of Wishart's martyrdom, "Imprinted at London by John
Daye and William Seres," without date, but evidently in
1547.

Line 5—*Jhone Bochas.* "Johne Boccace died at the age
of 62, in 1375. It was the book of Johan Bochas, of the
Fall of Princes, which was translated by Lydgate, and
printed in 1494 and in 1527, and which was probably alluded
to by Lyndsay."—CHALMERS.

The original work of Bochas, or Boccaccio "De Casibus
Virorum Illustrium," in Latin, was translated into different
languages. In Lyndsay's time, at least two editions, in
English verse, had been printed of "The Book called John
de Bochas descriuinge the Falle of Princis, Princessis, and
other Nobles, translated into English by John Lydgate,"
at London by Richard Pynson, first in 1494 and again in
1527, both in folio.

Line 81—*At cartis and dyce.* "In a MS. account of the
receipts and expenditures of the Cardinal Archbishop of St.
Andrews, in the Advocate's Library, there are the two following payments to the Cardinal: 21st Mar. 1540-1, paid my most
reverend Lord at Edinburgh, L.20, 18s. for *playing* with the
King's majesty. 18th May 1541, paid to my most reverend
Lord at St. Andrews, L.22, for *playing* with the King's
majesty. The bishops of England were in the same age
equally satirized for playing cards and dice. Roy, in his
Briefe Dialogue, satirizing the clergy, says,

> To play at the *cards* and *dice*,
> Some of them are nothing nice,
> Both at hazard, and mumchance."—CHALMERS.

Line 116—*Tuke sic melancolie.* "The allusion here is
to the battle of Solway, where the greatest number of the

Scottish nobles, being corrupted by the artifices of Henry VIII., chose to surrender rather than to fight."- CHALMERS.

Line 119—*He did depart.* The King died on the 14th December 1542.

Line 233 *I made one strenth.* The ruins of the Castle of St. Andrews are too well known to require any description. It was founded about the year 1200 by Roger, Bishop of St. Andrews ; but being frequently destroyed, it was at various periods restored or enlarged. Cardinal Beaton was occupied in strengthening the fortifications when it was surprised and seized by Norman Lesley, Kirkaldy of Grange, and others, to the number of fifteen persons, who engaged in the bold enterprise of assassinating the Cardinal. Soon after their success, during the time that the Castle was besieged, it was resorted to as a place of safety by Knox, Lyndsay, and various persons who had not in any way been concerned in the slaughter, but were under suspicion of favouring the Reformers.

Line 260—*Ane spectakle.* This refers to the conspirators suspending by a sheet the dead body of the Cardinal over the Castle wall, to satisfy the Provost and citizens in confused crowds who demanded admittance, that they might speak " with my Lord Cardinall." (Spottiswood's History).

Line 262—*Ane manifest myracle.* " In the margin of the first edit. of Knox's Hist. of the Reformation, thanks were offered to God, for the *godly* act of slaying the Cardinal, as Hume has remarked after Keith. There is the same thanksgiving on the margin of Dr Anderson's MS. Hist. of Scotland." —CHALMERS.

Chalmers has here misrepresented the marginal note on p. 145 of the suppressed edition of Knox's History, printed at London about 1586. It *does not give* thanks to God on account of the murder, but refers to " *the godly admonition* " given by Melvin to the Cardinal to repent of his wicked life, " but especiallie of the schedding of the blood of that notable instrument of God, Maister George Wisharte, which albeit the flame of fyre consumed befoir men ; yitt cryes it, a

vengeance upon thee, and we from God ar sent to revenge
it." These are Melvin's, not Knox's words; and Dr P.
Anderson merely copies from Knox.

The marginal note reads, "The most godly facte and
wordes of James Melvin."—In reference to this, I may quote
my own note on the passage, in the edition of the Reformer's
Works, vol. i. p. 177. Edin. 1846.

"Knox must certainly be held responsible for this marginal
note, which has given rise to so much abuse. But after all,
this phrase, '*the godly fact and words*,' applies to the *manner*
of putting Beaton to death, as a just punishment inflicted on
a persecutor of God's saints, rather than an express com-
mendation of the act itself."

Line 266—*Thay sallit me.* See Knox's Works, vol. i. p.
179, note 2.

DESCRIPTION OF PEDDER COFFEIS.—*Page* 158.

This poem which has not hitherto found a place in any
edition of Lyndsay's Poems, is here given on the somewhat
doubtful or suspicious name—LINDSAY—to whom it is
attributed in George Bannatyne's MS. 1568; yet some of
the phrases may be found in nearly similar words in his
Satyre of the Three Estaites. It was originally published by
Lord Hailes in 1770, and republished by Sibbald, in his
Chronicle of Scottish Poetry, vol. iii., 1804, and by myself
in "Select Remains of the Ancient Popular Poetry of Scotland," Edin. 1822, 4to.

THE HISTORIE OF SQUYER MELDRUM.—*Page* 161.

"Sir David Lyndsay and Squire Meldrum of Cleish, as
they were both freeholders of Fifeshire, were acquainted
with each other. They often met at *Struther*, the residence

within the same shire of Lord Lyndsay, where our Poet was
a frequent visitor and our Squire a constant resident. The
more retired part of the character and adventure of Meldrum,
Lyndsay acquired from his information. The poet, indeed,
informs us—

> And secreitis, that I did not knaw
> That nobill Squyer did me schaw.

" We thus perceive how well informed Lyndsay must have
been with the whole adventures of Meldrum, which were
rather singular in themselves, and which he deemed worthy
of remembrance, ' as a due recordation of his virtues.'

> Quhilkis poetis puts in memorie,
> For the exalting of thair glorie :
> Quharefor, I think, sa God me saif !
> He suld have place amangis the laif.

"The *Testament* of Squyer Meldrum was *compylit* by
Lyndsay, who delighted to change his measures in seven-line
stanzas with alternate rhymes, except the two concluding
verses, which rhyme together. This legend of Meldrum is
declared by very competent authority, the judicious compiler
of the *Specimens of English Poetry*, to be the best of Lyndsay's
poetry, and to rank with the most polished pieces of Drayton,
who flourished a century after him. The storie of Meldrum
was first published probably in 1592, and was composed about
the year 1550."—CHALMERS.

" This Historie was founded on the extraordinary adventures of a well known person in Fifeshire, William Meldrum,
the laird of Cleish and Binns. He was born probably about
the year 1493, at the house of Cleish, in the parish of
Cleish, which lies within Kinross-shire rather then in Fife,
By his poetical biographer, are we told :

> He was bot twentie yeiris of age,
> Quhen he began his vassalage.

" His first service, or *vassalage*, or adventure, was on
board the Scottish fleet, which, under the command of the
Earl of Arran, burnt Carrickfergus, on the *Ireland coist* in

1513.   From Carrickfergus Arran sailed to Calais, where,
as the poet tells,

> Hary the aucht, King of England,
> That tyme at Caleis was lyand.

"From history we know that Henry VIII. lay at Calais
in July 1513.   Meldrum remained in France during the
war. Peace between England and France, which included
Scotland, was made on the 13th of September 1514.
"The *Squyer* at length returned to Scotland in 1515, at the
age of twenty-two. Such was his fame ·that wherever he
went, he was well received by the men for his spirit, and
by the women for his gallantry. Scotland, existing under
an anarchical minority, furnished such a *squyer* many a
field, both for the conflicts of war, and the dalliances of
love.   His concluding adventure in both happened on the
road from Edinburgh to Leith, in August 1517, when
jealousy and hatred, in the person of Stirling of Keir,
marched out with fifty men, to cut off his retreat to Fife.
On that occasion Meldrum defended himself with uncon-
querable bravery, till he was nearly cut to pieces.   De la
Bastie, a French knight, who then ruled Scotland, as *locum
tenens* for the Duke of Albany, did himself immortal honour
by the spirit and enterprise with which he pursued and took
the assassins. Yet by the skill and care of the surgeons of
Edinburgh, the Squyer was enabled to survive many years,
though he must have existed in a very crippled state. After
a while he was invited by the aged Patrick Lord Lyndsay
of Byres to act both as deputy sheriff of Fife, and as
marschal of his household. The same connection continued
with John Lord Lyndsay. That he lived many years, and
died in his old age at the Struther, Lord Lyndsay's seat in
Fife, is certain. Yet he first made his *Testament*, and appointed his executors :

> First, David, Erle of Crawfuird, wise and wicht;
> And, Johne, Lord Lyndsay, my maister special ;
>
> The third sall be Sir Walter Lyndsay, ane noble knight,

" From all those intimations it is probable that the *Historie* and *Testament* of Meldrum were some of the last of our poet's labours and were perhaps written about the year 1550. —CHALMERS.

Although somewhat doubtful when Squyer Meldrum was first published it had appeared in a printed form if not in 1582, certainly before the year 1585. In the collected editions of Lyndsay's poems in 1582, in 1592, and again in 1597, its title is included in the list of contents, but the only editions of Squire Meldrum of an early date known are those at Edinburgh in 1594 and in 1610.

Mr Chalmers, I imagine, in supposing that this poem was composed about the year 1550, has placed it six or eight years too late. The allusion in line 1497, proves indeed that it was subsequent to the death of Sir John Stirling of Keir, in 1539.

> Line 29.—*Ane nobill Squyer . . . during his lyfe,*
> *I knaw my self, thairof I wryte,*
> *And all his deidis I dar indyte.*

As Lyndsay survived the Squyer for several years, the statement of Pitscottie that the latter lived for fifty years after escaping the murderous attack on his life in 1517, is manifestly erroneous. If *fifteen* years were substituted for *fifty*, a near approach would be made to the probable date of Squyer Meldrum's death.

> Line 71.—*Gude Williame Meldrum . . .*
> *And borne within the Schyre of Fyfe*
> *To Cleische and Bynnis richt heritour.*

Cleish is a small parish in Kinrosshire, extending six and a half miles in length, by about one in breadth. It is surrounded by a range of low hills. The stream or river Gairney, which divides the parish from Kinross, falls into Lochleven. The old house called the Place of Cleisch, is a large massive building, surrounded with fine old trees. The original building is about 85 feet high, the walls still almost entire.

Binnis is in the neighbourhood of Cleisch, and lies near the foot of Benarty, not far from Lochleven.

Line 93.— *And as thay passit be Ireland coast.*
  The Admirall gart land the oist ;
  And set Craigfergus in to fyre.

Pitscottie, following Sir David Lyndsay, asserts that the
Earl of Arran (but assigns no ostensible reason), instead of
conducting the fleet direct to its destination, passed up the
west sea on the coast of Ireland, and "thair landit and brunt
Craigfergus with all uther villages, and then came fornent the
town of Air, and thair landit and playit thameselves, and
reposed be the space of forty days," and only set out for
France on learning the King's extreme displeasure at such
delay. Such a statement, if the dates and other circumstances
are duly considered, is quite incredible. As the fleet sailed
from the Frith of Forth on the 27th of July, if forty days
afterwards elapsed, as here alleged, the voyage to France
could have been made a very short while before the death
of James at Flodden.

We need therefore have little hesitation in asserting that
this narrative by Pitscottie shows his usual want of minute
historical accuracy; and that the account given by Sir David
Lyndsay of the Squyer's adventures at Carrickfergus, and his
amours with the Irish lady, is a poetical fiction.

Line 343—*Monseour de Obenie.* Robert Stewart, Lord
D'Aubigny, was created a Mareschal of France, when, says
Chalmers, "there were only four Mareschals in that kingdom."
Robert, Lord of Aubigny, was descended from the Darnley
and Lennox family. He was Captain of the King of France's
Guards. In November 1520, he arrived in Scotland on an
embassy from the French King, for preserving peace during
the minority of James the Fifth ; and was instructed to
recommend that the Duke of Albany should be allowed to
remain in France.

Line 590—*Efter the weir, quhill peice wes tane.* "The peace
between Henry VIII. and Louis XII., was concluded on the
16th [15th] September, 1514."—CHALMERS.

Line 611.—*Louis the King of France.*   Louis XII. died on the 1st of January 1514-15.

Line 856.—*Out throw Stratherne.*   That is, the vale of the river Earn, Perthshire.   But it has a wider interpretation, as applied to a large district adjacent to this beautiful river and its tributaries, extending from about Comrie on the west to Abernethy on the east (Chambers's Gazetteer of Scotland.)   See also the little volume, entitled the Beauties of Upper Strathearn, by Charles Rogers, LL.D.   Edinburgh, 1854, 12mo.

In noticing Gleneagles, Dr. Rogers says, "the oldest part of the building has an inscription with the date 1624, but the remains of an older mansion or castle are situated on a height north of the present house, and a small edifice, surrounded by a cemetery, stands in the immediate vicinity."

Line 864.—*Ane lustie Ladie.*   In the privately printed volume, "The Stirlings of Keir," p. 34, we have the following information :—" Marion Lawson, relict of John Haldane of Gleneagles, who was killed at Flodden, survived him for the long period of forty years, her death having occurred in July 1553.   [Register of Acts and Decreets by the Lords of Session, 13th December 1555, vol. xii.]   Marion must have been a young woman as well as a young widow, when first visited by Squire Meldrum in 1515.   From the Gleneagles Papers it appears that she and her husband were infeft in the barony of Haldane on 23d April 1513, about which time their marriage had probably taken place."   ("The Stirlings of Keir," p. 34, note.)

This note requires some correction.   What the Gleneagles Papers are I cannot say ; but we have in the public records authentic information on some points connected with the Haldanes of Gleneagles at this period, which may correct the statements of our peerage writers.

John Haldane of Gleneagles, obtained the honour of knighthood, and in 1508 married Marjory Lawson, daughter of Mr. Richard Lawson of Humbie and Hieriggs (near Edinburgh), a

person of wealth and distinction, who was Provost of Edinburgh in 1492, and again in 1504 and 1505 ; and also Justice-
Clerk during the previous part of the reign of King James
the Fourth (from 1491 to 1506). In Douglas's Baronage, (p.
581,) is an account of the Lawsons of Cairnmuir, descended
from a younger son of the Justice-Clerk. It might indeed be
supposed from the above note in "The Stirlings of Keir"
that his daughter was married only a few months before her
husband's death at Flodden. She undoubtedly was married
in the year 1508, as will be shewn conclusively in the note to
line 1496 at Page 383.

Line 1178.—*Taryand upon dispensationn.* That is, the
Squyer intended to complete their marriage as soon as the
Pope's licence was obtained.

Line. 1211.—*Sa it fell anis upon ane day.* Pitscottie
is the only early writer who gives a detailed account
of the assault on Squyer Meldrum by Stirling of Keir.
The following extract from his well-known Chronicle is
collated with an old MS. in the University Library, Edinburgh,
and other copies in my own possession.

"The King of France sent letters in Scotland to the Duke
of Albanie, to come and speak with him in all goodlie haste
for such affaires as he had adoe at that time. The Duke of
Albanie, obedient unto the King of France desyre, patt the
Realme in order, and left Monsieur Delabatie Regent in his
place, to his returning out of France, and gave him command
to use all men equallie, and, in the meanetime, went to his
ships and past to France. [7th June 1516]

"In this meanetime, Delabatie beand Regent, as we have
showen, remained in the Abbey of Holyrood hous, and ane
guard of Frenchmen about him to the number of fourscoir
of Highbitters, to be readie at his command when he charged.
And so it happeneth at this time, on the moneth of (*blank*)
and in the yeir of God one thousand five hundred and (*blank*)
yeeres. At this time, there was ane Gentlemen in Edinburgh
named WILLIAM MELDRUM, Laird of Binnes, who had, in
companie with him, ane fair Ladie, called the Ladie Glen-

aigles, who was daughter to Mr Richard Lawson of Humbie,
provest of Edinburgh.   The which Ladie had borne to
this Laird too bairnes, and intended to marrie her, if he
might have had the Pope's Licence, because her husband
before and he was sib : yet, notwithstanding, ane gentleman,
called Luke Stirling, invyed this love and marriage betwixt
thir two persons, thinkand to have the Gentlewoman to
himselfe in marriage ; because he knew the Laird might not
have the Pope's licence be the Lawes ; therefore he solisited
his Brother sone, the Laird of Keir, with ane certaine companie of armed men, to set upon the Laird of Binnes to take
this Ladie from him be way of deed ; and, to that effect,
followed him betwixt Leith and Edinburgh, and set on him
beneath the Ruid Chapell, with fiftie armed men ; and he
again defended him with five in number, and fought cruellie
with them, and slew the Laird of Keir's principall servant
before his face, defendand himselfe, and hurt the Laird that
he was in perrell of his life, and sex and twentie of his men
hurt and slaine ; yet, through multiplication of his enemies,
he was oversett and driven to the Earth, and left lying for
dead, hought of his legges and strucken thorow the bodie,
and the knoppis of his elbowes stricken fra him.   Yet, be the
mightie power of God, he escaped the death, and all his men
that were with him, and lived fiftie yeere thereafter."

Line 1463.—*Bot thir luifars met never agane.*

.   .   .   .

For scho aganis hir will mariit.

Of this second marriage, which is not at all improbable,
there is no record.   That Lyndsay should say, it was contrary
to her own inclination is somewhat strange, if he was aware
that she remained her own mistress in retaining Gleneagles
in fee, during the long period that intervened between the
death of her husband in September 1513, and her own death
in July 1553.

Line 1483.—*To the Regent.*   The Regent or Governor John,
Duke of Albany, during his absence in France, had appointed

Sir Anthony D'Arcie de la Bastie (commonly written or pronounced La Bastie or Bawtye) to act as his deputy. On the death of Lord Hume he became Lieutenant and Warden of the Borders, which, from his being a foreigner, gave great offence, and led to his slaughter by David Hume of Wedderburn, as mentioned in the following note.

Line 1484.—*Bot he, allace! wes richt sone slane,*
            Be David Hume of Wedderburne.

This took place on the 17th of September 1517. The event is fully described by Pitscottie, by David Hume of Godscroft (in his Latin History of the Wedderburn Family), and other writers. Bishop Lesley notices the fact that La Bastie's head was cut off "and affixed on the town of Dunse, 19th September 1517." (History, Bannatyne Club, p. 110.)

Line 1496.—*Bot afterward, as I hard say,*
            On Striviling brig upon a day
            This Knicht wes slane with crueltie.

Sir John Striveling, or Stirling of Keir, knight, succeeded to his father, Sir William, in 1503, and survived till 1539. In the work, "The Stirlings of Keir and their family papers, by William Fraser," Edinburgh, privately printed, 1859, 4to, Luke Stirling, who is spoken of as uncle at p. 21, appears to have been the fourth son of Sir William Striveling of Keir, who died between 1468 and 1471. He must have therefore been a very unlikely suitor to a "young widow" in 1517; but Mr Fraser, in narrating this treacherous assault, says, " In justification, so far, of Sir John Stirling's conduct to Squire Meldrum, *it is not too much to suppose* that the lady of Gleneagles and Luke Stirling may have been engaged to be married at the time that the Squire made his fatal appearance at Gleneagles Castle, and overcame the heart and virtue of the lady by his fame and superior address." It undoubtedly is a great deal *too much to suppose* any such prior engagement, when we consider the interval that had elapsed after her husband's death at Flodden, and also the age of Luke Stirling, whose father is said to have died half a century before. The

lady in question, however, not only had legitimate issue by her
husband, but also two children by the Squyer previously to
this cowardly and murderous assault, which took place
beneath the Rood Chapel, between Edinburgh and Leith.

Sir John Stirling himself was slain previous to 5th November 1539. On the 4th of November 1542, David Schaw and
George Dreghorn had a respite, under the Privy Seal, "for
the slauchter of umquhile John Strivilling of Keir, knycht."
—(Stirlings of Keir, p. 35, Reg. Secr. Sig., vol. xviii.) Mr
Riddell states that Sir John Stirling was murdered by Schaw
of Cambusmore, near Stirling, in a fit of compunction for
having been the unworthy instrument of Keir in assassinating
Buchanan of Leny, whose daughters, co-heiresses, he had
stript of a great part of their estate.—(Comments on the
Keir Performance, with Drumpellier's Exposition, by John
Riddell p. 227, &c. Edin. 1860, 4to.)

In a previous note (p. 316) I mentioned that Marjory
Lawsoun was married in the year 1508, and had legitimate
issue before her husband's death. In a charter dated 28th
of May 1508, he is styled "Joannes Haldane de Glennegas
miles, filius et haeres quondam Jacobi Haldane de Glennegas
militis." Eight months later, Sir John had another charter
under the Great Seal, by which certain lands in Perthshire
(which are specified), were erected into the free Barony of
Haldane, in favour of himself, and of Marjory Lawsoun his
spouse in conjunct-fee. Dat. apud Edinb. 20 die Januarii
1508." (Reg. Magni Sigilli, Lib. xv. No. 74).

They had another conjunct charter of the lands of Culze-
more, dated 23d of April 1513. (Ib., Lib. xviii. No. 174). In
the Privy Seal Register, we find the Precept of this conjunct
charter in favour "Johannis Haldane de Glennegas militis et
Marjorie Lawsoun ejus sponsae super terris de Calzemore le
Ros, &c. jacentibus infra barronias de Haldane et Glennegas.
Apud Edinburgh, 30 Aprilis Anno Mo. vo. xiij. et regno
Regis xxvto." (vol. iv. fol. 233.)

By virtue of this infeftment, the widow remained in possession of the property until her death in July 1553. It seems
very strange that Mr Fraser, in referring to the Register which

records the time of this Lady's decease, should have overlooked or concealed the fact that the person at whose instance this action was raised against the sheriff of Perth and other officials, *was the legitimate grandson* of Sir John Haldane, by his wife the LADY OF GLENEAGLES.

Mr Riddell in one of his works on the controversy respecting the succession to the title of the Earldom of Lennox, gave a short extract from the curious deed of 1555, above mentioned, which proves that the Lady Gleneagles by her first husband had a legitimate son, who carried on the succession of the family. Mr Fraser was probably indebted to Mr Riddell's extract for his reference, although withholding the information it contains, as I think he could scarcely have misunderstood its import.

Line 1519. — *Thair dwelt in Fyfe ane agit Lord.* This refers to Patrick, fourth Lyndsay of Byres, who had a ratification of the gift of the office of Sheriff of Fife to himself, his son, and grandson, in 1519. He died at an advanced age in 1526. —(Wood's Peerage of Scotland, vol. i. p. 334.)

Line 1617.—*And John, Lord Lyndsay, my Maister special.* Mr Chalmers in the course of his investigations was enabled to refer to two deeds which confirm this statement in regard to WILLIAM MELDRUM OF BYNNIS. "William Meldrum (he says) was a witness to a charter from John, Lord Lyndsay of Byres to William Lyndsay, dated the 31st of March 1529. William Meldrum of Binns was a witness to another charter of Lord Lyndsay, dated the 15th of May 1532.—(Pub. Rec.) This is the latest authentic notice of William Meldrum." This vague reference to "Pub. Rec." should rather have been, "Reg. Magni Sigilli," (Lib. xxiv., No. 208, and Lib. xxvii., No. 90), being two charters of confirmation under the Great Seal.

Line 1617.—"John, the sixth Lord Lyndsay of Byres, who succeeded his grandfather in 1526, and died in 1563, leaving by Lady Helen Stuart, the daughter of John, Earl of Athol, three sons and six daughters." Douglas's Peerage, 161.

Line 1620.—"Sir Walter Lyndsay, Lord of St. John. In Monteith's Theatre of Mortality 1711, mention is made of the monument in the parish church of Torphichen of 'Walterus Lindesay, Justiciarius Generalis de Scotland, et Principalis Praeceptor Torphichensis, 1538. The same inscription is in Sibbald's Hist. Linlithgowshire, p. 25. This, then, was of Squyer Meldrum the third executor, who died in 1538, if we may believe his tombstone.'"—CHALMERS.

Line 1589.—*Thus at the Struthers into Fyfe,*
This nobill Squyer loist his lyfe.

The time of Squyer Meldrum's death is not ascertained. It probably was about 1533 or 1534.

Struther or the Struthers is again mentioned at line 1801. It is in the parish of Ceres, about two miles to the south-west of the village of Ceres. The building, now in ruin, was formerly the seat of the Earls of Crawford, surrounded with a noble park, and stately beech trees.

Line 1824.—*Sterne of Stratherne :* The Star of Strathern, or the Lady of Gleneagles.—See previous note on the Haldanes, line 864. The property of Gleneagles, in the parish of Blackford, Perthshire, so long in the family of Haldane, now belongs to the Earl of Camperdown.

ANE DIALOG BETUIX EXPERIENCE AND ANE COURTEOUR.—Page 225.

Although Parts First and Second of the DIALOG are contained in the present volume, the NOTES on this portion (lines 1 to 3378), will be given in the next volume, (page 331, &c.,) along with those on the latter portions of the Poem.

www.ingramcontent.com/pod-product-compliance
Lightning Source LLC
Chambersburg PA
CBHW031059110726
47900CB00003B/987